# The Poisoned Crown

## By: Kelsey L. Robinson

# REVIEWS

"The Glass Dagger by Kelsey L. Robinson was a masterfully crafted adventure novel. I had a fantastic time following Ella's story, and I was on the edge of my seat as she uncovered the truth behind her training and as she struggled to find her purpose within the world. ... This book is for the people who wish they could escape reality and live a life similar to Ella's, with the power to do whatever you choose. I definitely look forward to following Ella's story unfold in her future adventures and quests. This book is not one to snooze on and I recommend it to everyone within the genre."
~ Madds, Goodreads

"I just reviewed The Glass Dagger by Kelsey Robinson. #TheGlassDagger #NetGalley So so good!! It's diving into another world that leaves you wanting more. It's such a cool premise and the world building is entrancing. I cannot recommend this book more and wait to see what is coming next!"
~ Janie, Goodreads

I could not put this book down, Cinderella turned to a badass spy is amazing!!! Definitely my fave read so far.. cant wait for more!!!
~ Kayle, Goodreads

For My Southlands A302 Family

I hope everyone else finds a family like mine.

One where you instantly belong and know you're home.

# ALSO BY

## THE KINGDOMS OF ASSASSINS CHRONICLES

The Glass Dagger

The Kingdoms of Assassins Anthology

The Poisoned Crown

Rairene
Grècia

N
S
Trudel
Vicuria
Evrotia

# FOREWARNED

The Poisoned Crown is an adventure fantasy set in a dark fairytale adaptation world with teenage assassins. It includes elements regarding torture, war, combat, poisoning, blood, intense situations, death, and mental manipulation through poison that are shown on the page. Readers who may be sensitive to these elements, please be aware that you're entering into the dark fantasy world of the Kingdom of Assassins...

# CONTENTS

# PROLOGUE

ELLA

Ella guided her horse in silence as the dark of night engulfed them. Or...she thought it did. The shadows continued to ripple towards her and it took every instinct she had to not jump off her horse each time one got too close.

'It wasn't real' was her mantra now.

However, the blood dripping down her back and side was very real.

But the shadows in the dark that congealed and moved weren't real. Ella shook her head. She had to focus and get them to safety. Their lives depended on it. But the enchanted poisons running through her body, courtesy of Lucifer, were at war in her body. She remained silent in her torment.

David didn't seem to mind it.

He hadn't said a word to her. Though Ella suspected it was more from a lack of not knowing what to say. Here he was, riding next to the person he thought killed his mother, an assassin he had vowed to capture, an assassin who was his friend. An assassin who had saved his life multiple times and killed others to do so.

Lucifer's face, frozen in surprise, flashed in her eyes.

He had deserved to die.

After all that had done to her growing up and everything from yesterday...gods had it been only yesterday? Ella shook herself. He had deserved it. Her current tormentors, Leech and Blaze, vied for her attention, running her body through a cycle of freezing to burning temperatures. She wasn't sure which one would kill her first. The constant change in body temperature, or Mire and Malice as they blurred her lines of reality.

Ella blinked rapidly against their blurred torchlight.

That was *not* a leopard preparing to pounce from the forest.

Ella cleared her mind as exhaustion took its toll and won the battle with her body. But they *had* to keep moving. The more distance between them and Aumont tonight, the safer they would be. The safer *David* would be.

Ella's head lolled forward, her eyelids weighing heavily.

"What's wrong with you?" David questioned.

It was the first thing had said to her since leaving Aumont.

"I'm just tired." Ella looked at him, hoping to get a glimmer of the David she had gotten to know, who, before the ball, had liked her.

"There's something wrong. You're whiter than your hair and my magic—" David brought his horse beside hers, grabbing the reins.

She breathed in his earthy, dusty book magic smell.

"Stop the horses. Now."

"I'm fine—ow."

David lightly touched her shoulder, the one she'd taken an arrow through.

"You were in such a hurry that you didn't let him properly bandage it." David glared at her through the firelight. She wasn't sure if his anger was for overlooking the wound, or for simply giving him more trouble.

She turned away and focused on the forest. There was barely an animal path to follow. They had entered the deepest depths of the forest that separated Riset from the neighboring villages. It was late enough that no one would see them. But they would be stuck in the dark. Again. Darkness flooded her eyes as the saddle seemed to tilt off her horse.

Her mind went dark.

She didn't faint. That much she could discern.

She floated from her body, light yet heavy.

Ella heard her horse stomp its hooves, and the owls in the nearby trees, yet she couldn't see. Her heart lurched as she twisted around, trying to find the firelight, but not even her body would move.

"David, make it stop." Ella's voice shook as their surroundings continued to vanish.

"Ella, what's wrong?" His voice was so far away. Was he leaving her?

"I can't see. I can't see. Gods, what's happening, make it stop." Ella tried to breathe.

"Where's the damn healing kit?" David spoke…from somewhere. He was…somewhere…right?

She gasped as she was thrown back into her body as something soft was pressed into her shoulder. The pain ran like fire through her back and chest as David leaned her forward to rest against the horse.

"You've lost too much blood. Why didn't you say anything? We could have stopped an hour ago..."

Ella faded out, closing her eyes.

"... dammit Ella, there's one on your side. You didn't even bother with—"

Ella did her best to stifle her groans. To keep him from seeing how much it hurt to clean her wounds. She squeezed her eyes until white stars burst into the darkness. Mire rose to strike, and she could have sworn it was Lucifer beside her and not David. But he was dead. She had killed him. Lucifer could never hurt her again.

"I uh..." Ella tried to remember how she had been stabbed in the side. "Tremaine...she..." Her stepmother had stabbed her when they had fought.

"I have to get you off the horse."

She found the strength to turn her head and look at him. Even in the shadows, he was beautiful. His brown eyes appeared black and angry as he gazed at her. Before she could drift off again, Ella dismounted without an ounce of grace.

David helped her lie down on her side, a lantern near her. She split her attention between him and the light. She could do that and the shadows wouldn't get her. They would leave her alone. Ella watched him work in silence, his golden brown eyes locked on her injuries. His brow furrowed in anger. But his hands were gentle.

Ella closed her eyes as she drifted.

"All done."

She opened them in time to see David cross his arms and look her over.

"Let's get you back on that horse." He held out a hand.

"I can do it." Ella swiped his hand away and stumbled to her feet, swaying as the blood rushed to her head.

The ground shifted beneath her feet as she rested against the side of her steed. If she ever drank too much wine, she imagined it would feel like this. She lifted her left leg towards the stirrup, clutching the pommel with white-knuckled hands. Ella swayed, letting her body adjust, taking deep breaths.

David reached for her.

She fell against her horse as spiders crawled out of him.

Her legs gave out, and she landed hard on the unforgiving forest floor. The spiders continued to come as the flames' shadows slithered over the wet forest floor, reaching for her.

Ella held in her scream.

"What's happening? Ella, please let me—"

"You were in the room, David. You heard what Lucifer said." Ella sat up slowly, willing her body to work. Leech froze her feet, crawling up her toes and ankles.

"I thought he said that to taunt you—"

"Doesn't mean he wasn't telling the truth."

"How many poisons are you processing right now?" David crouched in front of her, blocking the light and its spiders.

Ella ticked them off. "Leech, Mire, Blaze, and Malice."

David sat back on his feet. "How are you still conscious? How long have they been running through you? Do you know how strong they are?"

"Um…" Ella closed her eyes as she did a rough estimate. "Snow made them, so they don't get any stronger than that. And probably…twelve hours." She had to lie down. Fire raged against the ice, breaking her body into a sweat as it shook. "David…" She opened her eyes to look out at complete darkness. "I don't know how much more I can handle."

"Henry told me to get to Oakwell Hold as a stopping point."

"That's a little sentimental, don't you think?"

"It's the best we have right now. Let's see if we can get a little farther." David hoisted Ella onto his horse as her world dimmed and a different battle warred within her.

Ella woke up on the hard dirt of the forest with no memory of *how* she had gotten on the ground. She blinked, rolling over in her cloak to gaze up at the towering redwoods guarding them. Fog rolled through their branches, coating the land in silence. A small fire gently died beside her, and the horses were tied up to the trees.

No one was around. Their only companions were the birds waking up with them.

"What happened?" She rubbed her pounding head, easing up to a seated position, and testing her balance.

"You fell off your horse when your body convulsed," David whispered as he prodded the fire. His eyes remained on the flames, dark circles underneath.

"Did you get any sleep?"

He gave her a look that dared her to ask that question again.

"Thank you…for standing guard." Ella pulled her cloak tighter, looking for her daggers, looking to see if David was armed as well.

The world tilted and Ella found herself once again sprawled out on the ground as Malice gripped her mind.

She opened her eyes, or…thought she did…only to find shadows crawling for her.

"David," she said his name, unable to form another coherent thought as fear gripped her and squeezed.

"We need to get to Oakwell. I need a better look at those wounds and you need to rest. Seeing as how you know Snow White, I'm going to guess you'll have a better idea for how long this will last."

"Days," Ella moaned. "It'll take days."

"Well, it looks like we need to get going then." David got up and quickly saddled the horses.

By the time Ella found the will and ability to get to her feet, the fire was out and David had cleared the camp of any trace. She gingerly touched her side, wincing at the sting left by Lady Tremaine, her last parting gift. Ella got onto her horse with moderate difficulty, catching up to David.

He rode them hard, pressing to get to Oakwell Hold that night instead of in the morning. They barely spoke, not that she could have managed. It took all of her concentration to stay awake and on the horse. After she fell off for the second time, David rode behind her, keeping her stable. His musty book scent swirled around her, reassuring her.

"What do I need to prepare myself for David?" Ella leaned into him, comforted by his strong, warm arms. She had helped Raven so many times. But that had only been one poison at a time. Not four.

"None of the poisons in you are fatal. You have to remember that. Your mind will try to play tricks on you. I've never heard of anyone ingesting this many, so I'm not sure what will happen. The key will be to not panic. If you panic, your body will try to work harder, which could kill you," David whispered in her ear.

He was so close to her. So painfully close, yet so far away.

"Right...so don't panic when I think I'm going to die." Ella's arms hung uselessly by her side as Leech crawled up them, removing all sense of feeling.

"The fevers, chills, hallucinations...as your body loses the fight, they'll become worse. But the poison will also wear off, so it's a matter of keeping your will to survive stronger than the poison."

"Sounds...wonder..."

Ella lost track of her thoughts, her vision darkening. It continued to darken even as the sun remained high in the sky.

"You'll be okay Ella. I'm here with you."

"Thank you..." Ella crumbled up inside at his words.

He hated her, yet he was willing to care for her. She wondered when that hatred and disgust would win over the healer inside of him.

The first sign she had that they drew closer to the stronghold was the smell of the ocean's briny salt water licking the air. They had skirted the downs, not realizing how close they had come to some of them. Too close for Ella's liking. If anyone traveling had seen them...seen her...she shoved the thought aside. They were safe.

Seabirds circled above the trees, their caws echoing over the water that crashed in the distance. The redwoods went right up to the beach's edge, giving them a chance to sneak up to the stronghold. A white powder-fine sand led from the forest edge to the stronghold and the ocean beyond. Most would consider its looming gray stones ugly. Not Ella. To her, they were safe and happy. So many memories lingered in her mind of the summers spent within those walls.

The rest of the stronghold comprised four towers, multiple bedrooms, and a couple of entertaining rooms. There was even a small throne room, though no king had ruled from Oakwell in over a hundred years.

Ella gazed up at the stones that stood watch over the sea and its horizon. Should war come to Rairene, it would be one of the first locations to be utilized. It was in the perfect spot on the coast from Rairene to Evrotia. If anyone wanted to reach Riset from the south, they would have to sail past Oakwell first.

David paused their horses at the edge, looking for any signs of life. Ella's heart hammered, and it wasn't from nerves or her proximity to David. Her vision blackened on the edges, fading in and out. Ice charged through her body in an attack she hadn't felt building.

"David…" Ella slipped out of his arms, their warmth and safety gone as she tumbled off the horse. Everything went black, and an all-consuming freeze gripped her body.

# CHAPTER ONE

ELLA: EIGHT MONTHS BEFORE LADY TREMAINE'S
DEATH

Ella counted the steps she took, her fingers tapping against her thumb with each beat as she paced around her deep plush carpeted room. It was more immaculate than usual. She hadn't been able to stop herself from cleaning. She'd had to organize it, otherwise, she would have gone mad waiting for Raven to walk through her door. Raven, her sister, had once again decided it was better to get herself into trouble than face her inner battles. Hadn't she gone through enough in that fighting ring? Though who was she kidding? She and Luca had been apart for a while and she still felt the pang of emptiness in her heart where there had once been laughter and love. So much love. And they had ended on *good* terms.

Raven hadn't had that luxury.

Ella fisted her hands as she thought about *him* and what his actions had done. Raven got herself so wound up in work and the dark markets that she no longer knew who she was. Ella sometimes couldn't tell who she was. Her sister had not been in those sapphire eyes the last time Ella had looked.

Snow White had gazed back at her with cold, calculating, assessing eyes. Eyes that kept the doors to her emotions securely locked.

Ella walked around the circumference of her room again. Raven had *promised*. She had promised she would be back in two hours. Two. Hours. Which was...Ella glanced at her small ornate clock...four hours ago. Ella bit her lip one last time before changing into her sneak suit and braiding her white hair back to hide it under a brown wig. She strapped three of her glass daggers into their sheaths, draped a black cloak over her shoulders, and left.

Before she could go on the hunt, there was one thing she had to do. She needed to bring backup, and there was only one person she could take.

Ella walked down the plush carpeted hallway two doors and softly knocked. The last thing she needed was for all of Aumont's other assassins to wake up. The door opened slowly.

"Ella? Do you have any idea what time it is?" Drea whispered.

"I do. Can I come in?" Ella looked down the hallway, making sure no one else lurked in the shadows. Drea nodded, stepping aside slowly.

"I need your help," Ella said before Drea could talk. "Raven needs your help," she clarified.

"Why are you coming to me? Why not Mira or Calla?" Drea crossed her arms as she shifted all of her weight to her right leg.

"Raven is going through something...and I've done all that I can, but I need someone who's an enchanter who has also...gone through her pain," Ella replied. It wasn't a direct answer. She didn't want to tell Drea that Raven had been spiraling, barely keeping herself from losing control. But if that was about to happen, she needed another enchanter there to help...or to lessen the damage.

"Raven is experiencing pain like I've experienced pain?" Drea adjusted her arms to tighten around her waist.

Ella wondered if she did that to avoid touching the scar on her face.

"It's not the same. It will never be the same. But the heartbreak...is similar."

"I see." Drea was quiet for a minute as she looked toward her window. "Why not bring Calla then? She's more talented than—"

"Calla can't fight—"

"Neither can I. Not anymore." As if to make her point, Drea pointed to her cane and then her left leg.

"But it's still there. You can still wield your sword should you need to...and...I might need you to."

"Just what exactly has Raven gone and done?"

"Can I tell you on the way? She was supposed to be back hours ago." Ella motioned towards the door, shifting back and forth on her feet. She couldn't let Drea know exactly how desperate she was for her help. How bad it might be when they found Raven. The last time...Ella shook off the thought.

Drea nodded, limping over to her wardrobe to change into her long-for-gotten sneak suit. Ella watched as Drea's movements slowed. Her hands stopped moving altogether when she reached for her long, curly brown hair. Hair that she used as a shield every day.

"Nightshade." Ella waited for Drea to meet her eyes in the mirror. "You should leave it down."

Drea nodded. She turned away from the mirror, grabbed her cloak, cane, and short sword. The two of them moved quietly down the halls they had sprinted down as children.

Ella saddled their horses, Dream and Night. They mounted and began running through the night towards Riset. The two assassins rode in silence, racing their horses towards the city of their beloved kingdom. Most days, it was a twenty-minute ride. Ella pushed them faster. Raven might be many things, but a liar she was not.

They slowed abruptly when they got to the gates of Riset and saw the glow of a fire. A lot of fires. Smoke mixed in with the low-hanging clouds that crept over the city.

"Oh, no."

Ella glanced at Drea, an eyebrow raised.

"It's All Hallows Eve, Ella." She motioned towards the fire. "We won't be able to sneak around anymore."

Ella guided Dream toward the city bustling with life in the middle of the night. Heat fluctuated around them, dismissing the cool breeze that had accompanied them to the city. She led their horses over the partially cobbled streets and around the masses of people in the lower fifth circle. Their road quickly dwindled into mud as they got farther into the circle and closer to the underbelly of the city. Ella scrunched her nose as beer and body odor drifted over her.

They stopped in front of a dilapidated pub with a wooden door that had once been beautifully carved and was now so damaged the original design was no longer discernible. The pub, known as The Rotting Pumpkin House, was empty. Well, emptier than Ella had expected. A couple of resident drunks lay on some tables, either passed out or halfway there. A barmaid wiped down the tables, and a serving boy was sweeping away the hay that had been laid out in the center of the pub. The spot where an illegal fighting ring had been tossed together.

Ella pinched the bridge of her nose. She was never letting Raven come to one of these again without her. If her sister wanted to run from herself, so be it, but she wouldn't be running alone.

"What exactly has Raven gotten herself into?" Drea muttered under her breath.

"A fighting ring," Ella replied as she examined the occupants once more.

"We're closed." A gruff, middle-aged man sauntered over. His blond hair was tied back, his green eyes cold as he looked them over. "You don't belong in here."

"We won't be staying long. We're looking for someone." Ella tilted her head just slightly. He was enormous, and the scar on his neck told Ella he didn't let others mess around with him.

"As you can see, we're closed. No one is here."

"And I am certain she was." Ella stepped closer to him. "Tall, well built, black hair, and she can kill anyone faster than they can blink. Sound familiar?"

The man stepped away as he blinked, buying himself time. "I've never heard of any man like that, let alone a woman."

Ella crossed her arms and stared him down. "I don't believe you."

"I don't care." The man positioned himself in front of Ella, once again blocking her from entering. "Leave."

"Let's go." Drea rested a hand on Ella's shoulder, pulling her attention from him.

She glanced around the bar once more. The barmaid locked eyes with her for a moment before tilting her head towards the side of the pub.

"Fine." Ella yanked her shoulder and turned on her heel.

"Ella, I'm sorry for suggesting we leave—"

"I'm not." Ella walked farther down the alley beside the pub. An enormous bonfire burned at the end as revelers mingled around it. She stopped halfway down and faced Drea.

Drea gripped her cane as she caught up to her, leaning heavily.

"Why? That man knew who Raven was." Drea stopped and massaged her hands.

"He did. But hopefully, his barmaid will help us." Ella leaned against the wall and smiled when the barmaid opened the door, carrying a sack of trash.

"Your friend was here tonight. She won many of the fights."

"Then where is she?" Ella stepped closer as the barmaid stepped back, closing the door.

"She was boastful and thought she could win the last fight." The woman paused as she tightened the wrap around her black hair.

"What do you mean, *thought* she could win?" Ella put her hand on the door, keeping it open. Raven had to be okay. She would be okay. Ella calmed her breathing.

"She lost."

Ella's heart thundered in her ears at those two simple words. These rings didn't have any rules. Losing usually meant you were dead or close to it.

"What...do you—"

"Is she alive?" Drea interrupted, stepping up behind Ella.

"Yes, oh, sorry, I didn't realize how that sounded. She's alive. They captured her. I heard they shackled her and hid her."

"Shackled her?" Ella's pulse pummeled her nerves as she thought of Raven in enchanter's shackles, cut off from her power.

"Do you know who took her or where she might be?" Drea murmured.

Ella faced her stepsister. How could she be so calm? Raven was in danger, shackled, and had lost more than just a fight.

"I'm not sure. But I know that a merchant who sells in the dark markets left later than usual."

"And who would that be?"

"Lord Grosvenor." The woman closed the door.

Ella rubbed her face as she leaned against the door. Why couldn't Raven have stayed safe?

"Ella?"

She looked up at Drea as she gripped Ella's hand and pulled her away from the door.

"Do you know who Lord Grosvenor is?"

"No. Do you?"

"I do. He's not a powerful man in court, but in the dark markets, he has a lot. I'm surprised you don't know who he is."

"Me too. Surely this man is a threat. Why aren't we watching him?" Ella questioned as Drea walked them back to their horses. Someone had started another bonfire nearby, and Dream and Night shifted.

"Mother probably doesn't think he's worth it right now. We only have so many people at our disposal."

Drea stumbled, falling against the wall.

"Drea." Ella jumped to her side.

"I'm...fine." She pushed off the wall. "It's just my leg. Let's go." She left without looking back at Ella. Her left hand roughly massaged her thigh. Drea limped back to Night and got on with shaky confidence.

"Drea—"

"We don't have time. Whatever deal he's brokering, it'll be done before the sun is up. Wherever he's keeping Raven won't be for much longer. And I don't know about you, but I would like to get *some* sleep," Drea snapped.

"Then let's go." Ella sidled Dream beside Drea.

Drea never mentioned her pain. Ella couldn't recall a time she had seen Drea show any sign of physical weakness. She always had her cane with her, but it was always an extension of her.

As Drea led them through crowded streets of celebrating citizens and around multiple bonfires, Ella thought about the fact that she had never spoken to Drea about her injury. Not that they had a relationship where she would be open about it. But Ella was curious and wondered if one day, maybe, they could.

Ella looked up at the unassuming gate.

She and Drea had made it to the third circle and now stood before a perfectly average home. It was well-built and had a stone fence surrounding it, just like the other homes of merchants in the third circle. No one had stopped them or asked them where they were going as Riset continued to celebrate All Hallows Eve. Ella glanced at Drea for confirmation that they were in the correct place. She nodded before clicking her tongue to walk Night over to an alleyway.

"There are no guards and no people around. Are you sure this is correct?" Ella muttered.

"Yes. He keeps a low profile for a reason." Drea dismounted. "Let's go before the residents of this street return. Even though you hate this celebration, it's helping us for now."

Ella followed her, watching Drea take deliberative steps toward the fence. Ella took out her lock picks and inserted the tension rod. She pursued it with the pick, feeling the release of each pin. As the gate swung open, Ella withdrew one of her glass daggers and snuck in. The home was two stories with yellowing stones and a well-organized garden of hedges, grass, and a few maple trees that had begun to turn orange.

Ella crept to the front door and inserted her picks again. No carriages were outside, and the stables sounded empty. Hopefully, no one was home and no one would have to die. The front door swung open before Ella finished picking the lock.

She tilted her head.

No one was on the other side waiting to attack, yet the door had opened without her unlocking it. Ella slowly took a step inside, careful of how she set her foot down to avoid any squeaky steps. If Drea hadn't been confident about the owner of this home, Ella would have walked right back out. Cobwebs decorated more furniture than anything else in the home. The smell of dust and rot swirled as Ella disturbed the floor.

She withdrew another glass dagger.

Drea reached the threshold, stepping inside with the telltale tap of her cane. Ella flicked a glance at her. Drea had withdrawn her sword as well. Ella's muscles tensed as she walked farther into the house, all of her senses paying attention to the smallest thing. Wind whispered through the house from upstairs, signaling open windows. Ella's breath misted in front of her, indicating that a fire had not been lit in a long time.

A small creak sounded behind her.

Ella twisted on her feet to face the front door as it closed.

Darkness descended as it cut the moonlight off.

But she still saw the shadow in the dark.

A guard had taken an enchantment. Wonderful.

The sound of metal on metal broke throughout the room as Drea engaged with their assailant. Ella ran over, all sense of secrecy gone as she worked on protecting Drea. Ella barrelled into the person, launching herself at them to roll them away from Drea and engage with them herself. The body was light as they flew through the air. The attacker gasped for air as they collided with the wall. Ella didn't give them time to think or find a new way to hide as she thrust her dagger into their chest, twisting to make sure their death was swift. She pulled her blade free, cleaning it on the attacker's clothes before moving away from them.

"Are you okay?" Ella whispered.

"Yes. I was fine." Drea's voice was bitter.

"I need us to save our strength for whatever we're about to face. Being in this house alone is a task enough." Ella commented as she surveyed their surroundings. Her eyes adjusted to the darkness and the vacant home around them.

"Let's just find her and leave. No more killing unless we're attacked. I just—"

"I know. I want to get out of here too," Ella said as she rested a hand on Drea's shoulder. "Hopefully, there's just the one spooky guard."

Ella listened for the smallest sound as she walked through the home. Her ears strained with the effort as she got to the kitchen and then the dining room. Raven was going to owe her so many sticky cinnamon rolls after this stunt.

The wind continued to blow from upstairs, yet the first floor remained empty. At least to her knowledge. There could be another assailant waiting in the shadows. She just hoped they were as clumsy as the first one.

"Let's go upstairs," Drea murmured when Ella got back from her second sweep.

She nodded, stepping on the wooden step. Its creak seemed to shout in the house as she applied her weight to it. Ella hung her head. Well, if there was someone upstairs, they knew the house had guests now. She sprinted up the stairs and stood ready at the top of them, listening. Waiting.

Nothing.

Ella didn't move until Drea got to the top before searching the rooms. At least with her there an attacker would have nowhere to go. If Ella thought the conditions below were bad, they were nothing compared to the second floor. A thick layer of dust coated everything, with the spiders making up the chief residents living on this floor.

Ella shuddered.

She avoided their webs as much as possible as she searched, and came up empty.

"Drea, are you sure—"

"I'm positive. He must be—"

Both girls dropped to the floor at the sound of hooves on stones clopping closer. Ella crawled on her stomach to the nearest window and looked outside. A carriage rolled up to the stables in the back. Two well-dressed men cloaked in black got out. Two more guards accompanied them. Ella watched as they went farther back into the hedge behind the stables.

"We have to get down there. I think they're keeping Raven somewhere in the garden outback." Ella stood up and moved quickly, getting halfway down the stairs before she stopped.

Drea began her descent, deliberately placing her cane and then foot.

"Go without me. I'm sure you're more than capable of handling some shady grunt workers. I'll be right behind you." Drea reassured Ella.

"But the house is creepy." Ella looked around again.

"It is, but it's more important that you get to Raven."

Ella didn't need to be told twice as she darted down the steps and out the back door. Fog and smoke swirled together in a thick gray haze, covering the garden and all of Riset in a blanket of muted sounds. Both daggers rested comfortably in Ella's hands as she sprinted in the direction the men had gone. When she neared the hedge's edge, she slowed down, listening for their footsteps. They were faint, barely crunching the leaves beneath them. Ella was careful to step around the leaves as best as she could to avoid detection. She just hoped she wasn't too late.

# CHAPTER TWO

## Raven

Raven violently came to her senses, her body thrashing in response to the ambush. They had ambushed her.

"Shit." Raven squeezed her eyes as she determined what had gone wrong.

She's been at The Rotting Pumpkin House fighting. She'd been winning. Raven's power surged with joy at the rush of emotions she'd had while beating her opponent. She had been...brilliant. She knew it. All of them knew it.

And now...she was chained...somewhere.

Raven reeled her power back when it continued to race through her. She had to focus. She had to get back. Ella was probably losing her mind.

Raven blinked against the prickle of pain in the corner of her eyes. She'd *had* to go out. She had to know that she was back to her normal self. That she could fight again and not lose control of herself. She had proved it to herself, and now she was captured.

Raven thought back to that last fight. It was a blur with vague images of her opponent. A scrawny man who had no business fighting her. She would easily beat him. His stance was all wrong, and he wasn't confident holding a blade. But he had defeated her.

Raven tried to piece together more, but every time she did, the memory fractured. Raven swallowed and the telltale flavors of mint ran down her throat. The only poison she knew that had a mint taste was one that inhibited the host's ability to move. Which would also explain the blurry vision and pounding head. Luckily, it wasn't an enchanted poison. Everything else she could deal with later. Right now, her primary concern was getting out. She hoped Ella was out there looking for her. But if she didn't even know where she was, Ella would also have a hard time.

Though she had been awake for a few minutes, her eyes continued to adjust to the pitch-black darkness. They had chained her arms above her head, and her feet dangled free. Raven looked up and saw the top of the hole she was in. Rough stones surrounded her in a circle. She kicked out a leg across from her and hit the other side. Was she in a dried-up wishing well? So much for granted wishes.

Raven's power whispered along her veins, singing softly to be used. How it craved to be used. She bit her lip. Raven had indulged her power a bit too much lately. If she hadn't, she probably could have realized the man she was fighting was about to poison her. Instead, she'd been power drunk and too confident. Maybe she wasn't ready to be back in the field protecting the kingdom.

Raven shook her head.

She was ready. It had been *months* since...Raven choked on his name, unable to say it. Unable to voice anything as her heart clenched tightly, and her throat choked her with anguish. Her magic once again rose to defend her, to heal her fractured soul. Her hands began to light up as her power grew, readying to strike out at anything. But she would not let herself be overcome with her power. Never. She would *never* lose control.

Raven kneaded her power back into place, coiling it back up into a ball.

She shook herself.

She could wallow later. Right now, she had to get out. Raven shoved all of her emotions down and focused on the task at hand. Step one: get out of the shackles.

Raven began to enchant, delicately summoning her power to her. She called it, coyly requesting its help. It was eager to do something, but cautious after she had reprimanded it. Once it realized she was being genuine, some of it came to her, running around her with glee. Raven soothed it and formed her intention that the chains holding her no longer needed to keep their prisoner.

*"Thesauru quem tenetis, non amplius contineri debet,"* Raven spoke the enchantment over and over, solidifying her intentions. As her enchantment grew, Raven gripped the shackles on her wrists and flooded the metal with her intentions. Her power flowed around her fingers like white iridescent starlight and onto the shackles until it encased the metal and formed the enchantment in the locks.

Raven tried the lock.

Nothing.

She groaned.

Raven tried again, switching the meaning of the enchantment from one of protection to one of release.

*"Non es amplius ut seram tuam teneas, captivam possis dimittere."* Raven repeated the enchantment, letting it build until her full intention was formed. Power swirled around her again, binding with the metal.

A clink reached her ears.

She was free.

Raven released her wrists from the shackles and stepped away from the wall.

She was...sort of free. Raven turned her head up to look up at the distance between her and the top of the well. It was...far. Night still held the sky captive, and all she could distinguish was a black wall. She knew it was made of stone, but when her fingers ran over it, the grooves weren't uneven enough to allow for much purchase. Climbing out would not be easy.

She had *really* messed this up.

All she could hope was that Ella was on her way. Raven knew her sister would burn all of Riset to find her. Just as she would if the roles were reversed. Not that Ella would ever find herself in this predicament. She would never do anything so rebellious to end up like this.

Raven grabbed the shackles and yanked on them. The anchor held. She smiled. Raven gripped the chains and pulled herself up. Her bare feet...bare feet? Raven looked down. This would be fun. They had taken her boots. Shrugging her shoulders, she set one foot up on the rough stone and began to climb. Her feet scraped along the rough stones as she walked up the side of the wall. Each step brought her closer to getting home. But with each step, the muscles in her hands and arms shook just a bit more.

Raven continued to climb, the metal digging into her hands.

Though her arms made the shackles clatter, she moved on.

Though her feet had gotten slick on the rough stones, she moved on.

And even though her legs quivered and her shoulders tightened, she moved on.

Raven saw the lip of the well getting closer. She could do this. She would get out, find a mirror, and let Ella know she was okay. Everything would be okay. It had to be. The smell of misty fog and fires drifted over her, enveloping her in a blanket of comfort. Raven closed her eyes for a moment and breathed it in.

She was okay.

She took a step as she neared the anchor holding her chains, hoping she would be close enough to grab the ledge, otherwise all of this was for nothing. Her foot held its grip despite the blood she could feel running free. Raven had accounted for several things when she began this climb. She had gauged that she was twenty feet down and that all of her strength would be put to the test. Had this been a normal test, she would have been fine. But she had to make adjustments for the bruises from her fights in the night, and the aching muscles that had already been worked.

So she made sure to use her whole body while climbing. Every muscle would protest, but she would survive.

Raven re-gripped the chains, her muscles relaxing for one precious moment.

She fell.

Raven landed hard on the ground below.

She twisted in pain. Her ankle and wrist had taken the brunt of her fall. She sat up and leaned against her prison with closed eyes. Nothing was broken, but she couldn't climb out. Raven let out a whimper as she clutched her wrist to her chest. Her power rose to soothe her, spinning out of the ball of power she had loosely kept it contained in.

Raven froze.

The sound of men whispering reached her. She gripped her wrist as her magic continued to pummel her. It was pleading to be used, and she was close to losing her precious control. At least if she held on just a little longer, she could also kill the men who had captured her by fully losing control of her power. Her ankle throbbed as she moved, flaring red in her vision.

She wasn't getting out of this. The great Snow White was undone by a simple fighter. A fighter who had poisoned her. But a scrawny fighter nonetheless. She'd taken out so many worthy opponents that to be destroyed by this…Raven couldn't stomach it. She would not let this be her last fight. She would not go softly in the night. She would die in a burning fire as her enemies burned around her. Raven stood up and got back to the chains, gripping them. Raven put her full weight on them, holding on in case they shook them to see if she was still chained.

Though she could tell they were close, they whispered quietly enough that she couldn't hear a word they said.

"Wake up." The chains shook in her hands as the man's gravely voice scraped over her.

Raven tugged back.

"Not so tough now, are you?" The other man called down.

She remained silent, knowing that would only upset them more than any snarky response that came to mind. The men spoke in hushed tones again. Raven kept her eyes trained on the opening, watching for any sign of what might happen. What she didn't expect was a rope dropping down.

"Step into that and my men will pull you out."

Raven eyed the rope. Why would she do that? What incentive did she have to get hauled out of the well, other than it was currently her only way out.

"Get in now or we're leaving you down there." The men pulled on the rope.

"How do you expect me to get it on while chained?"

"I'm sure you can get creative." The gravely man spoke back.

Raven recognized his voice. He had been cheering for her during the fight. She hadn't been sure at first, but now she was, and she would make him pay. Her power sang a sweet song of revenge. She clamped down on it. The last thing she needed right now was for them to see that she was an enchanter. They clearly thought they could sell her and if they knew she was an enchanter as well…Raven shuddered. She stepped into the loop they had tied and pulled it up under her breasts. This was going to hurt. But at least she would get out. Taking them all on while injured was something she would face in a few minutes. For now, she held onto the chins, letting them jangle against the stone wall as they pulled her up one yank at a time.

# CHAPTER THREE

## ELLA

Ella watched them from the shadows. The two men had shaken hands and then tossed a rope down, calling down to their captive. It had to be Raven. The person hadn't answered, so she couldn't be sure. It if was Raven, she would not stop them until she was out of the wishing well and safely on solid ground. Drea reached for her sword and gripped it in her left hand. Ella loosened her third dagger, palming the other two as she stretched her muscles. She was ready for this night of annoying horrors to be finished.

"Drea," Ella spoke loud enough to be heard. "Horses."

Drea opened her mouth to protest, anger flashing in her green eyes. But she said nothing. Instead, she lightly turned on her heel and walked away, her limp not as pronounced as it had been earlier. She must have massaged it out, Ella thought. But Ella and Drea both knew this was the right play. They would have to be ready to run, and Drea would need to be on Night before anyone else.

Ella shifted her attention back to the four men. The two merchants wouldn't be a concern for her. Ella would be impressed if they could even use a sword properly. The guards would be exhausted from lifting Raven out of the well. As soon as she saw it was Raven, she would attack. The men pulled, and a head full of curly black hair appeared. It was quickly followed by a body in a black leather sneak suit. The woman looked up and the moment Ella saw her deep sapphire eyes, she sprinted out from the hedges, daggers raised.

Ella watched as Raven moved quickly, hitting the merchants over the head with her chains. They were too stunned to react. Idiots. They did not know who they had captured. Ella launched herself at one guard, jabbing him in multiple soft tissue areas until he was on the ground and knocked out. Then she turned her attention to the second one. He came at her with his sword raised. Ella deflected it, the iron of his blade screeching along the thick glass of her daggers. He punched her in the jaw.

Ella flipped away from him, regaining the advantage as she adjusted her jaw, wiping away blood.

Before she engaged him, Raven pounced, wrapping her arms around his neck and holding on until he passed out. She let go before he could take both of them down to the ground, collapsing at her feet.

And then Raven fell to the ground.

"Ra-Noble Lady." Ella leaped to her side as she looked for the injury. Why had she fallen? Where was she hurt? Ella could barely see in the dark as she tried to help her sister. She had almost blown Raven's cover. Not that anyone was conscious to hear it. But she could never be too careful with their real names.

"I'm okay," Raven muttered as she sat up. "I hurt my wrist and ankle."

"If you ever—" Ella's voice hitched.

"I know. I'm sorry. I won't do it again." Raven slowly got to her feet. "Can we go home?"

Ella hugged her tightly. Her friend shook in her grip before returning the hug.

"Let's go home," Ella whispered as she stepped back and wrapped a supportive arm around Raven's waist.

Horses galloped towards them. Raven tensed, grabbing Ella's third dagger from her back as she prepared to fight more men. Ella waited, adjusting her grip as well, just in case it wasn't Drea.

"Drizella?"

"Shocking, I know. Let's go," Drea commanded. "Are they dead?" She looked past them to the four bodies.

"The merchants are." Raven shrugged. "I wasn't about to let them get away with what they were about to do to me and have probably done to others."

"Good." Drea nodded as she turned Night back around.

Ella mounted Dream, holding out a hand for Raven as she launched herself up behind Ella. The three of them rode out swiftly, avoiding the center of Riset as much as possible. The city had quieted; the bonfires burning low as the fog hung low in the air. Anyone they rode past was too tired to pay attention to three women on two horses, cloaked in darkness.

"Raven, the next time you need to—"

"There won't be a next time, Ella. I promise," Raven whispered, squeezing her friend tight.

"Well…if you do, you're taking me with you," Ella replied. "I know you think you're okay and maybe you are, but I don't think you're okay here at Aumont."

"Ella—"

"I know you don't want to leave, but it could be good for you. You'll be in a new place with no memories of him. It won't be forever, just a little bit, right? Didn't Lady Tremaine say it was a two-month assignment as an interim assistant to a queen's spymaster?"

Raven rested her head on Ella's shoulder. "It is. I'll talk to her. She'd already mentioned the assignment to me."

"You know I love you. I only want you to be okay, even if that means not being here with us right now."

"I know," Raven mumbled as sleep dragged at her.

"We're almost home. Get some rest. I'll guide us there."

"Thank you, Ella."

"I would burn all of Rairene for you."

"I would do the same for you," Raven said.

Ella nodded her head as Raven fell asleep against her. She guided them home, knowing that she would miss her sister more than anything. Saying goodbye to her, even for a little while, was going to hurt her more than anything else ever had. It hurt more than losing her mom or leaving the palace. But if Raven needed to heal her heart, then it was what needed to be done.

# CHAPTER FOUR

## Raven: Two Weeks Later

Raven examined the impressive mahogany doors before her, a delicate design framing them in a pattern of ivy and flowers. She pulled on the collar of her uniform, the black fabric seeming to choke her with the high neckline. Raven adjusted the stiff breastplate, moving it one more time into a comfortable position. The breastplate, back, and graves were all black and stone hard, with a red trim that gave the appearance of blood dripping down her side. The shoulder plates weighed heavily, and she questioned how any of the spies in this kingdom fought stealthily.

Her magic grumbled at not being able to enchant her armor. If they caught her with anything enchanted...Raven shuddered, and her magic quieted. She'd seen the body of a discovered enchanter hanging from the gallows on her ride up to the city of Aslar last night.

A hand gently rested on her shoulder.

Raven glanced to her right to look at the small woman who was her maid, Susan. She had been the one to bring her to these impressive doors that only seemed to loom larger the longer Raven looked up at them.

Susan's nimble fingers had gotten Raven into her uniform faster than she could drink her coffee. Somehow, Raven had found the time to do her hair herself. She had twisted and pinned up her short, curly black hair, ensuring it couldn't hinder her during a fight.

"I need a few more seconds to wake up," Raven said, her velvet voice echoing down the empty hall.

Everyone, it seemed, was either avoiding this hall or was inside the throne room on the other side.

After all of her years of training as an assassin and enchanter, after all of her kills, she had been sent on a quick mission to assist the queen's spymaster. Hopefully, it meant Tremaine wanted her to do more upon her return to Aumont. She shifted on her feet, moving her toes and ankles, the weight of the shin guards pressed against her calves.

"How do I look?" Raven looked down at herself once more, adjusting the breastplate. She twisted the graves into position before flexing her hands in the fingerless black gloves she wore.

"You look like a warrior. You terrify me more than the others," Susan whispered before she sneezed.

She let out a deep breath. Her lips lightly twitched into some type of thanks to Susan before she straightened her back and fell into Snow White. She let the cold sweep over her, strengthening her as she became one of the most renowned assassins in Rairene. Not that anyone in this courtroom or the Kingdom of Evrotia would know who she truly was. Raven's magic settled deep within her, ready to protect or be summoned, though she could never let it be seen here.

She grunted as she pushed the large wooden doors open; the hall fell silent. While she may have heard nothing, the room was full of people milling around, sitting, or standing guard. The room was massive; dozens of columns jutted up to the cavernous ceiling. At the end of the long room, sitting on one of the most elaborate thrones Raven had ever seen, was Queen Lyanna.

Raven strode forward, confident in herself as all eyes shifted to observe her. She noted the hall was old and worn from use, much like the rest of the five-story castle. Its stones had yellowed over the years, yet they were bright enough to show the bloodstains on the ground and walls.

There had been little information about Queen Lyanna for Raven to learn during her ship's journey. The palace hadn't thought it necessary for her. Raven clenched her fists at coming into this assignment unprepared. All she knew was that the queen was more feared than loved and killed her people first and asked questions later. It was how she killed people that left others sick to their stomachs. Queen Lyanna had a black gauntlet made of the hardest metal with six-inch-long blades in place of fingers. She would put it on her right hand and plunge it into the heart of her victim, twisting until they bled out beneath her. Raven knew the gauntlet had to be enchanted, though the queen claimed it wasn't.

The woman in front of Raven looked very capable of fulfilling those rumors.

Her golden hair was piled halfway on top of her head, the rest tumbling down in perfect curls to her waist. Her crown stood out from her curls, pointing up to the sky with seven sharp points, each one representing the seven districts of her kingdom. A black cloak rested on her shoulders, spreading out behind her and highlighting the emerald dress she wore tightly fitted to her. An intricate metal design wrapped around her to portray armor. Layers upon layers of fabric tumbled away from her waist, making her seem more imposing compared to the medium height she was. Raven knew that if the queen stood, she would tower over the monarch, yet she could never be as fearsome as this queen.

Raven kept her lips from parting as she stood straighter, her attention focused. A similar movement rippled throughout the crowd as they watched Raven stop before the queen. Observing the Royal Guards, she realized there were only three currently on duty. All were very handsome men. Their scars and stances informed her that each of them had at least earned their spots. All of them stepped slightly closer to the queen, waiting to see what Raven did. She went down to one knee, bowing her head, making sure she kept her eyes open and aware.

"So, you're my new guard?" Queen Lyanna's voice was light and whispered around the room as she spoke in perfect Rairenian. The room remained silent as everyone remained stiff and straight-backed.

"Your guard?" Raven flicked her eyes to the side, sensing two men moving towards her, flanking her side. "It was my understanding that I was here in a...different capacity." She couldn't very well say she was here to assist her spymaster.

"Yes. I had a vacancy open up and I was told you would fill it."

Raven stayed still as the men got closer, not daring to move as she processed this information. Maybe it was her cover for the queen.

"How old are you?" Queen Lyanna spoke in Rairenian, her accent thick, hinting that she was not originally from Evrotia, but another kingdom entirely.

"Eighteen—"

"And you're a woman."

"I assure you, my skills—" Raven stopped when the two men moved. They each crossed a spear over her neck, pressing her chest into her bent knee. She could easily break away, but she had to endure this.

Another man stepped up behind her, pulling down the collar of her uniform. He was looking for an enchanter's mark. Though they were banned, the rumor was Queen Lyanna had a secret force of enchanters working for her. One more reason Raven wondered why Lady Tremaine had sent her, an enchanter. Originally, she had thought she was sent to be in charge of the same secret force...now...Raven frowned. While she knew they wouldn't find her mark, she hadn't been worried until now. Since she could remember, she'd always had a black raven imprinted on her. The bird's head and neck obstructed the star resting at the base of her neck. Its wings stretched out across her back. No one would ever think to look for a mark under her imprint because it wasn't something anyone thought was possible. She and Calla were the only enchanters who bore them.

"There's nothing there, Your Majesty, only an imprint of a bird." The man stepped away. The other two removed their spears.

"You could have asked." Raven stood up, her legs slightly wider as she got into a minimal defensive position.

"I need to make certain none of them get into my court." Queen Lyanna smiled.

"I think I would be quite fearsome if I were to master combat and be an enchanter." Raven kept her face blank. She could not glower at this queen. Could not show any sign of weakness. "If you would like a demonstration of my skills—"

"I don't give a flying fuck about your skills. I wasn't expecting a woman. My sister knew that when she reached out to your mistress," Queen Lyanna muttered, assessing Raven with a jealous, critical eye.

She did her best not to fidget under the scrutiny. Her black hair was perfect, her uniform immaculate.

"What's your name?"

"Raven." She did her best to not comment on the queen's statement about her being a woman.

"You will report to the courtroom every morning at ten. Anything later will be a reason for dismissal. Rowan will be your partner, the rest of your unit will comprise Charles and Bastien."

A guard stepped forward, his eyes black as they stared down at her. A scar trailed down his face from the edge of his hairline to just under his jaw. So, a rainbow of sunshine then, Raven sighed. She inclined her head to him in acknowledgment.

"Rowan." Queen Lyanna waited for him to stand beside her. "Take Raven on a tour of the palace. Get her familiar with how we operate."

"Your Highness—" Rowan's deep, husky voice protested.

"I think Bastien and Charles can protect me for the day. Unless you think you're the only one capable of it?" Her voice rose.

"Not at all." He bowed again and stormed past Raven.

Everyone went to work as Raven jogged to catch up. Now that the show was over, no one needed to keep their eyes trained on the queen. They left the throne room and marched down the hall.

"Try to keep up." Rowan's voice was gruff as he glanced at her. "The queen won't tolerate—"

Raven rammed him against a stone wall. He pushed back, but she only pushed him harder. "Look, I understand you don't want me here or that you think I'm not capable enough for some stupid male reason, but I assure you—"

Several courtiers and servants stopped. A guard rushed over to them.

"I'm fine. Everyone can go about their day," Rowan grumbled. He locked eyes with her.

"I am qualified for this position...whatever it is. Am I really a guard to the queen?" Raven asked as she stepped away from him.

"Of course. What did you think you were supposed to do wearing that uniform?"

Raven looked down at her attire. She would have to talk to Lady Tremaine about her assignment. She had not agreed to being a glorified babysitter. "I assumed it was fit for my role."

"Which it is. Now let's go. We don't have all day." Rowan grumbled.

"Fine with me." Raven opened her arms for him to lead the way. The corner of her lip twitched as he rubbed his neck.

"So, how do rotations work with guarding the queen?" Raven asked as they began their third lap of the palace. Rowan was determined she memorized the layout.

"There are five units, who each take six hours a day actively guarding the queen. They spend the rest of the hours either following up on various assignments, patrolling and inspecting the other guards, or training. We work in pairs, which is why you're mine—"

"Do contain your enthusiasm over it. You're oozing with joy." Raven loosely crossed her arms.

"The fifth unit is there to ensure we get a day off now and then," Rowan finished.

"Where are we going now?" She noted they were going down a different hall.

"Why don't you tell me?"

"Well, I would say the dining hall, but you have yet to show me the entire palace. What about the west wing? We haven't gone near it."

"No one does, it's forbidden," Rowan replied.

"Why?"

"Because our queen demands it," Rowan snapped. "Now, where are we?"

"We're near the dining, but don't we need to relieve Bastien and Charles?"

"They're probably already in the hall. Five units, remember?" Rowan shrugged.

He pushed an old, large wooden door that let out the most horrific noise as it scraped across the floor. Servants swarmed around the room that was more akin to a dungeon than Raven liked. The ceiling was low and held up by wooden pillars that looked ready to fold in with decay at any minute. Raven gently squeezed the bread, wincing as it held strong in her fingers. She set it down and put a spoonful of stew in her mouth. Somehow, she didn't spit it back out. At least the meat was tender.

As soon as Rowan walked down the aisle towards the serving line, everyone parted before him. She paused, assessing as he confidently walked past all the workers in line. Raven grimaced. None of the servants needed to move out of their way. They weren't any more important. She clenched her teeth when they got to the front of the line.

Food in hand, they sat down next to Bastien and Charles. None of them said a word to her. Bastien's red hair darkened in the dim lighting, his tan skin contrasting with his blue eyes. Raven would bet her magic he was from Grecia. Charles, she had no doubt, was from Evrotia with his short, curly black hair, brown eyes, and pale skin.

"I don't think we've been properly introduced. I'm Raven." She stared them down, lightly tapping her fingers on the old wooden table. It surprised her it had held up under their weight.

"See, this is why we don't have women guards. They always want to chat while eating, and I don't," Charles commented, looking between Rowan and Bastien.

"So, that's how it'll be? You're all a bunch of misogynists." Raven gripped her spoon. Her magic gently stirred, wanting to play. Raven tapped it down into a small roll.

"No, men are better at protecting the queen than women," Charles asserted.

Rowan rubbed a hand over his face, his eyes closed.

"That is the definition of someone who is a misogynist." Raven looked at the three of them. "No? Nothing? I guess only time will tell."

"I'm sure you'll think of something to gain our trust," Bastien said, going back to his meal.

Raven ate what little she could stomach, ignoring the slight tweak of a smile pulling on Rowan's lips.

# CHAPTER FIVE

## RAVEN

Raven stayed up late into the night, waiting for her time to scry Lady Tremaine. She pulled out a small mirror and opened it before softly summoning a trickle of the black power that writhed within. It sat in her heart, flowed through her veins, and coated her bones. Sometimes Raven felt she was made entirely of magic, and her skin was holding all of it at bay. She pictured her domineering mistress. Blond hair that was always perfectly placed, the green eyes that held a world of secrets, and the way she held herself as though all others were beneath her.

*"Revelare mihi de te hominem quaerere,"* Raven muttered. She pulled enough power to begin the scry, making sure the flash of her magic wouldn't draw the attention of any late-night wanderers below her window.

*Snow White.* Lady Tremaine looked as stern as ever.

*Good evening.* Raven was quiet, stifling a yawn.

*I trust you got settled in and integrated into the Royal Guards smoothly.* She lifted a brow.

*So you knew my assignment was changing.* Raven said.

*Yes, I didn't find out until you had already left. She killed the guard, by the way. He was too annoying, as she put it.* Lady Tremaine replied.

*Too...* Raven paused, at a loss for words. *Lady Tremaine,* Raven hesitated, biting the inside of her cheek. *What exactly is my objective now? I've never been sent out like this. Normally I observe, infiltrate, kill, and get out.*

*You know more than that, though. Jason was your lover for over a year. He taught you some things about being a spy.*

Raven flicked her eyes to her feet, fisting her hands. She did not want to discuss him.

*The king doesn't want to waste this opportunity to gather information about the queen and everything she does. It's not every day that we get this chance for the crown to provide insider information about a kingdom that has isolated itself. The king will be very grateful for this knowledge, so if she meets with someone important, I want to know about it. Observe her and tell me if anything seems out of the ordinary for a queen. Your expertise in the Evrotian language and others will be your greatest asset.*

*But I wouldn't know what that looks like. Surely, Anastasia—* Raven stopped when Lady Tremaine's eyes flashed.

*I sent you, Snow. I expect you to be excellent and get the job you're being paid for done.*

*When will I know it's done?* She already longed for Ella and Mira, not to mention Calla.

*When I tell you to come home.* Lady Tremaine closed her mirror.

Raven wasted no time getting out of her stiff uniform and crawling into bed with nothing but her undergarment and a knife.

Raven bolted up, chest heaving. She clutched her knife, ready to be thrown. It was a dream. A weird dream. She had never experienced something so real, yet so detached. She tangled her fingers in her hair and pressed them to her head. It wasn't real. She was alive. She was alive, and no one was going to kill her.

Raven ran her fingers the rest of the way through her chin-length hair, her hands interlocking behind her neck.

"Fuck." She noted the dark sky through the slight parting of her thick, dark red curtains. Raven kicked off her blankets and rolled out of bed, her sheets soaked in sweat.

Raven began the morning routine she had established in her early training days. She was the first one Lady Tremaine had recruited to be her little assassin. Because of that, she had been mostly alone. Lady Tremaine used to come in and see how she was progressing with her instructor, but then she left Raven on her own. To cope, Raven established a ritual for getting ready. She exercised for an hour, doing different routines each day. Then she brewed her coffee before bathing. Throwing on a robe, she drank a cup before sitting down with her second by the window to read for a few minutes.

Over the years, she had modified her routine. Her new mentor had completely switched her routine, which meant she had no routine anymore. He didn't give her a rigorous morning to live by. Instead, he disrupted her and forced her to think outside of the box and get comfortable with not being comfortable. But it had worked. He had helped her become even better than before.

Raven's magic coiled, ready to strike at the very thought of him.

She shook herself, strengthening her hold over her magic.

It pushed against her, testing her limits of control.

Though it never bothered her to be at full power, Raven felt the pull to siphon some off. Her emotions were at the perfect point for a good poison, one that would shatter bones the way her heart had been shattered.

She went to her wardrobe and reached into its dark depths, where she had hidden several empty bottles filled with water. She had always wondered why their power worked the way it did. Having never been trained at the academy, she had been given base answers. The glass of the bottles had to be clear for transferring power. The glass would carry her magic through and bind it with the water inside, changing its color and making the liquid inside denser. There was something about the glass that ensured the enchanted materials inside stayed that way. Once a bottle was used for an enchantment, it could never be used for a different enchantment again. If an enchantment wasn't fully formed, the water would look as though some milk had been stirred into it.

Raven focused her intention on pain. The ache that had become a dull thump in the back of her heart expanded, feeding on her, gaining new life as she thought about everything she had gone through over the last year. The thump became a fresh, gaping wound that she gathered up and kneaded into her magic as she stared at the bottle in her hands.

*"et ossa dolo fractionis,"* Raven said. Her magic purred in excitement as it built and expanded outside of her body. It writhed around her fingers, looking for the object it would bond with. Raven repeated her enchantment again, watching her power latch onto the glass and build with her focus. The wound in her soul grew, too. It wove itself into her power, flowing through it down to her hands. What would have been a potion to heal a broken bone was now morphed into one that made the person think every bone in their body was breaking.

Raven watched her power bond with the bottle and flash as it reached capacity. All of her pain subsided. She breathed deeply as the gap wound in her heart lessened back to a dull ache. It was bigger than before, but it would go back to living in a small corner of her heart, eventually. Raven looked at the bottle in her hands and the blue liquid with streaks of black swirling throughout. Fenith.

A brief knock was the only signal Raven got as Susan barged her way into the room. Raven fumbled the bottle, catching it quickly and hiding it behind her back.

"Has anyone told you it's rude to come into someone's room without being invited?" Raven snapped. Her heart raced as her maid hustled in.

Susan sneezed. "Yes, but I find it's faster to just come in."

Raven tightened her grip on the bottle as she slowly slipped it into a pocket in her trousers. She shook out her hands, pulling any lingering magic back in. That had been too close...if Susan had seen...Raven shook her head as Susan bustled around her.

Raven sat down and worked on braiding her hair in order to calm her shaking hands. She looked at herself, wondering, not for the first time, why

Lady Tremaine had chosen her. Raven wasn't a great beauty that could get a man to reveal his darkest secrets. She wasn't a court gossip either. Raven stood taller than most women and was confident in her abilities as a fighter. But how was she supposed to use any of that to earn the trust of the queen? It's not as though she could conjure a physical assassination attempt in front of the queen to demonstrate her worth. Raven shook her head as she watched Susan finish with the rest of her armor.

Raven ate breakfast alone. Rowan and the others had walked in, noticed her, and sat at a different table. None of the servants eating ventured near her, so she sat up straight and ate while watching everyone. Most would have been hurt and uncomfortable eating alone, but not her. Plus, she hadn't been able to get rid of the poison before leaving her room. Susan had to clean and Raven hadn't found a way to hide it without her noticing.

Raven saw a maid sitting by herself, holding perfectly still. When the maid moved, it was with care, her body stiff. She flinched whenever something was dropped. A man sat in the far corner of the hall, trying to go unseen. His eyes constantly shifted, his arms open and resting on his seat. As Raven observed everyone, she formed a better picture of those she would need to monitor and those she could use to her advantage. Raven picked up her plate and walked over to the maid.

"Can I sit here?"

The young woman practically jumped out of her skin, wincing as she pulled on her arm.

"Uh, sure." Her eyes widened before staring at her food.

"I'm Raven." She stuck out her hand, waiting for the maid to grasp it.

"Betsy." Her green eyes remained glued to her food, hands in her lap.

Raven slowly closed her hand before drawing it back. She looked up at a light bell going off, signaling the beginning of the morning shift. Betsy moved slowly out of her seat.

"If you don't want to keep pulling the arm he hurts, splint it. You could pin your sleeve to your dress even," Raven remarked. Betsy glanced at her, her green eyes wide.

Raven picked up her tray and walked away, pausing when she saw the boys waiting for her. All of them had their arms crossed with their heads slightly tilted. They looked like a group of crows examining a new curiosity.

"Can I help you?" Raven mimicked their stance.

"What did you want from Betsy?" Bastien's brow furrowed.

"I was giving her advice on her arm."

All of them frowned.

"Don't we have somewhere to be?" She walked between them, gazing up at the ceiling.

"The queen is sleeping in today, so we're going to go train together," Rowan replied when the silence got too loud.

"Good, I've been wanting to get used to fighting in this getup." Raven stretched her arms as they left the dining hall.

"This getup?" Charles looked at her with his piercing blue eyes. "This is a Royal Guards uniform. You should be so lucky to be chosen to wear it."

"I meant no offense, but don't you find it a little constricting?" she questioned. "It's so stiff and doesn't allow for a lot of flexibility."

"It's never been a problem for the men," Charles retorted.

"Probably because you've never known what it's like to not have a stick up your ass."

Charles straightened slightly as Rowan and Bastien attempted to hide their grins.

As they stretched, Raven took in her surroundings. Large groups of men and some women covered the training grounds. The grounds were made up of several training areas in the back of the palace. One was for archery, another for sword fighting. Each section had varying degrees of mastery. Some of them, Raven spotted, were novices, while others were highly skilled. Most of them, she was glad to see, would easily lose to her. The others... would be more of a fun challenge to demolish. Tucking that piece of information away, Raven turned to her unit.

"So, how does this work? I assume the three of you have mastered your specialty?"

"Two of us spar until one person yields, or there's a kill strike. The other two—"

Raven unsheathed her short swords in unison and attacked Bastien. He swung his sword up in time to block.

Bastien flipped the tables on her, not holding back as he got her on the defensive. They didn't pause when they broke into another class filled with novices. The novices scattered before they could get caught in the fray. Raven jumped far away from him, giving herself a few seconds to regroup and take the offensive. She pushed him toward Rowan and Charles. Sweat trickled down her face as some of her hair fell out of its braid. Her magic tickled her fingers, whispering sweet encouragement. *Not now!* She gently pulled it back. When Bastien made his next move, Raven got in close and kneed him in the gut. He dropped his sword and fell over. She crossed her blades over his neck, stilling him.

"I win." She stepped away from him, swords relaxed at her side.

"You can't fight dirty," Bastien argued.

"Why? It's how real fighting is resolved. I don't need to throw you in a fighting arena, do I?" Raven asked. She walked to Rowan and Charles.

"We fight by the Code of Conduct here, Raven," Rowan commented softly.

She chuckled. "Those rules will not help you. It will give anyone you're fighting the upper hand. If you're so used to fighting by moral standards and rules of combat, then you will always lose."

She looked at all three of them. Each one crossed their arms and glared at her.

"Guess I'm going to have to find another underground fight club," Raven muttered.

"An underground fight club? Those don't exist. At least not in Evrotia, we would know—"

"No, you wouldn't. It's underground," Raven snapped.

"Let's not discuss this right now. Charles and I still need to practice." Rowan withdrew his two daggers, Charles following him and pulling out his ax and mace.

The two of them entered into a dance they knew well. Raven hated to admit that she was impressed at how well Rowan did against Charles despite his obvious disadvantages. She slowly made her way over to Bastien, hoping he'd speak.

"So, what happened to the guard before me?"

"We're supposed to be watching them for flaws," he replied, his eyes locked forward, red hair ruffled from the fight.

"So that means you can't talk at the same time?" Raven kept her eyes trained on Rowan and Charles. "I guess what they say about men from here is true then," her voice lilted, letting it carry enough that someone nearby would hear.

"I will not take your bait, little bird. Just because you have this position doesn't mean I have to like you, and it especially means I don't have to trust you."

"I wasn't asking for that."

"Good. Trust is earned, and despite your little move earlier, I have yet to see that you're skilled enough to beat the novices." Bastien shrugged before moving away.

"I guess I'll have to prove to you otherwise." Raven turned to Charles, watching the way he moved. Even though he held an ax and mace in his hands, he was graceful. It was an interesting combination to watch. Usually, large muscled men chose those weapons, not someone who is lithe and better built for a sword. Eventually, Rowan broke through his defenses and won.

All three turned to her at once, raising their eyebrows.

"You expect me to tell you what you did wrong after seeing you fight once?"

"You're an expert, right?" Charles questioned. "Then give us your opinion. I'm sure that you must be able to form one." He shoved his mace into the belt at his hip as Raven opened her mouth.

"Fine." Raven crossed her arms and cocked a hip. "Rowan, you could have beaten Charles several times during that fight. You needed to bring your feet in a little closer and be a more graceful fighter like Charles. If you had, you would have easily been able to get through his gaping arms."

Raven turned to Charles. "You need to be stronger with your weapons. They aren't frilly little toys for boys to play with. They were forged to be wielded by a powerful person, so act like one." Raven pinned her hair up and straightened her uniform. "Now, I think we all have somewhere to be."

She waited for them to lead. After that speech, she was not about to make it obvious that she didn't know where they needed to go. Charles and Bastien went towards the queen's chambers while Rowan stayed, holding Raven with him.

"Remember what I said about our schedules?" Rowan stepped into a defensive position. "Now, let's see what you can do."

Walking into the throne room an hour later was different this time. No one paid her any overt attention. They went about their own business preparing the room. Everything had to be in its exact place before the queen entered, and that included her and Rowan. They got to the top of the stairs right as the doors swung open. They stood on either side of the queen's throne, observing everything. It was a suitable spot to try to kill the queen. Many people roamed the hall, creating blind spots. At least the windows were closed this time of year. With winter less than two months away, the temperature continued to drop. No one could kill her by shooting an arrow through the glass. Well, only as a last resort would any decent assassin contemplate that.

By the time Queen Lyanna got to her throne, and Bastien and Charles took their positions, the room had quieted. The queen's hour of 'community support' began. Raven used that term, loosely, in her head as the court began. It was hardly supportive. The queen had passed them along to advisors who might deal with the situation.

As the hour dragged, Queen Lyanna slouched in her chair, tapping her nails on the black stone throne. All any of the commoners could talk about was that the crop supply hadn't been as good, and it wouldn't feed everyone. A serious problem. Though not to the queen.

"Your majesty, I was wondering if-if we co-could keep some of what we sent to the palace this year?" The bone-thin woman paled before the throne. She twisted her pale hands, keeping her eyes on the yellowed floor.

Raven flicked her eyes to the queen. One glance was enough for Raven as Queen Lyanna smiled. Raven looked on as the woman continued to shake.

"You want me to allow my people in the palace to starve because you weren't capable of doing your job?"

"Not starve, my queen, never starve. We request that instead of sending seventy percent of the crops, we send sixty. Everyone in the village will survive the winter with their rations, and then we'll turn out a bigger harvest the following year."

It was a solid trade. Raven was in disbelief that they had to give away so much. Surely the queen would—

"Denied."

Raven remained on her feet, though her magic rose, chittering to be used, demanding to be used. The woman before her did nothing. The guards that had flanked her now held her up off the floor.

"Because of your idiocy, you'll spend two nights in the dungeon. Hopefully, that will show you the errors in your request."

"Please, Your Highness…"

One guard grabbed her biceps and pulled. Another joined him when she didn't move.

"Please help us," she whispered.

The guards dragged her out by her arms as she pleaded.

Queen Lyanna groaned, straightening. "Can you believe the nerve of that peasant? We need to eat as well." She looked up at Raven. "What do you think, Guard Raven?"

Raven formulated her response as she ripped her magic into a tiny writhing black mass that screamed to be unleashed on the queen. "I think that…" Raven wanted to tell her she thought the servants and guards would do fine with the shortage. Then she remembered that they already ate the worst food in the dining hall. The shortage wouldn't affect those of noble ranking. "I think you made the best choice, given the circumstances."

"Oh?" Queen Lyanna's voice rose an octave.

Rowan flinched in Raven's peripherals.

"Well, the shortage must already be affecting the palace, given how poorly the staff members and guards eat. If you had given that woman, that peasant," Raven held in the bile, "what she wanted, it would have affected the palace. Who knows if everyone working here could perform their duties? That would mean a palace not as well protected. It was the right choice." Raven rushed her words, hoping the queen's ego got in the way enough to miss the insults.

"Exactly, good observation," Queen Lyanna spoke loud enough for everyone to hear, though it wasn't hard given the silence that had befallen the hall. "Next!"

Sweat trickled down Raven's neck as the afternoon passed.

She had been brazen, outspoken, and rude.

It was something she rarely did, especially if she was intent on keeping her position. Which she was. Yet she had stepped out of place in a court that operated differently. Being in a new kingdom was good for her. Ella had said as much when she was first assigned. It would give her a new place to explore memory-free. She wouldn't remember him here. It had been a year now, and the ghosts of him still lingered around every corner of Aumont.

A bell tolled, breaking Raven out of her thoughts. Queen Lyanna stood and walked down the hall, flanked by Raven and the boys. She kept her eyes open, and her ears tuned into the crowd. No one had tried to kill the queen for years, but one never knew when that might change. When they got to the end of the hall, Charles and Bastien walked past to escort her.

Queen Lyanna's nails dug into Raven's wrist, stopping her.

Raven's eyes widened, but she kept her face passive as she looked at the queen, silencing the swell of her magic. *Shhh.* She hummed, refusing to let it show. Queen Lyanna examined her, head tilted to the side. The queen's eyes quickly flicked to the left as she thought.

Then they hardened into ice.

"If you ever embarrass me like that again, it won't be my nails digging into your wrist." Queen Lyanna spoke low, her voice feather light as she released her grip.

Raven tucked her arm behind her, watching them walk away, Charles and Bastien grinning at her. She gestured rudely at them, turning toward Rowan. He stood a few paces away, arms crossed. She walked past him, refusing to feel like a scolded child. They went through the first three checkpoints without a single word passing between them.

"I have to give you credit for trying to die in such a short amount of time," Rowan remarked.

"Does she not allow for any opinion other than her own? What ruler thinks they're always correct? Or that—"

Rowan clapped a hand over her mouth and dragged into a side passage.

"You do have a death wish."

Raven glared at him over his hand.

"If you think that just because she isn't here means she won't hear what you think about her, then you're crazy."

Raven narrowed her eyes, waiting for him to remove his hand from her mouth.

"Fine, I won't say anything anymore," Raven amended.

Raven walked alone through the palace, clearing her mind before checking in with Lady Tremaine. It was late enough that few people wandered the halls and those who did avoided her.

"Want to have some fun?"

Raven turned to find a man staggering over to her, the pungent smell of ale washing over her before he was leaning toward her.

"I'm good." Raven pushed him away from her.

"Aw, come on, everyone doin' it. You look like you could use some loosenin' up. Has it been long?" He blocked Raven, his breath worse than his body odor. "I have some potions," he whispered wetly in her ear.

"I said no." Raven pushed him harder.

The man stumbled into the opposite wall. She did her best to not hurt him. She didn't know if he was important to the queen, and after this afternoon, she couldn't take the chance.

The man walked until he had her against the wall.

"No one tells me no," he spoke with care as if making sure he said the right threat.

"I. Am."

"I won't tell anyone you slept with someone above your rank," he crooned.

"Why would that matter?" Raven challenged, "I said no."

The man moved his hand, wrapping it around her throat.

Raven narrowed her eyes. She would teach him a lesson quickly about the meaning of consent. *If he threatens a guard, what must he do to the maids?* Raven's magic rose in delight, spinning at the thought of ending this man for his vile behavior. Magic laws be damned.

"Hey!" Rowan's voice reached her from down the hall.

She quieted her magic, pulling back before any sign could show.

Rowan ripped the man away. "What are you doing? Do you know who she is, Lord Roger?"

Lord Roger stumbled several steps, ogling her.

"A filthy lower guard," he sneered, running his hands through his greasy black hair.

Raven crossed her arms.

"She's a Royal Guard, you idiot, and if I recall correctly, you currently aren't in favor with her Majesty. What would she do if she found out you forced yourself on her guard?"

"Thank me for getting rid of someone who couldn't defend themselves—"

Raven scoffed. "Come, try me."

Lord Roger shifted, his dark eyes darting between the two.

"Walk away, Lord Roger, and I won't tell the queen about this." Rowan pushed him again.

The two remained where they stood for a minute as they watched the lord stumble away.

"I had it under control," Raven growled.

"I'm sure you did. But until you learn who you can boss around and who you can't, it's better if I step in."

"What was his problem, anyway?" she whispered through clenched teeth. "Why did it matter that I'm ranked beneath him? It's not illegal to sleep with someone below your station, is it?" Raven nervously chuckled.

"Not illegal, but frowned upon. Queen Lyanna could dismiss you or any other lady from her court. Isn't it like that in Rairene?"

"Not at all. I mean, it's never looked upon well, but you wouldn't be banished from court." Raven tilted her head.

"Well, here you have to hide it."

"And if you don't, you're banished—"

"Or killed by the queen," Rowan stated.

Raven said nothing, hoping Rowan took her silence as coming to grips with the facts, when she was focused on taming her magic. It swirled in anger at the laws and the audacity of Lord Roger. She wanted to lash out and throw all of her anger at the spineless worm. As she focused, kind blue eyes flashed before her, pulling her in, trying to swamp her mind with memories of a person she wished would stay forgotten.

*"We can't do this, Raven," Jason whispered.*

*His fingers played with her hair, his breath whispering at the nape of her neck.*

*"Why not?" She stepped closer to her mentor, her lover. She sighed, the smell of his sweat and soap relaxing her muscles. It was rich and spicy, which she liked.*

*"There are rules...laws...."*

*Raven chuckled. "I don't recall signing something that said I couldn't sleep with my mentor. Our oath says nothing about it." Raven kissed him, pulling his body closer to her.*

"Raven?"

She snapped to attention, tripping over her feet as she ripped herself from the memory.

"Are you okay? Look, this rule...it's important here. Don't bring it up, and you'll be okay. You'll adjust to the idea of it. Everyone else did."

"It wasn't always this way?"

Rowan quirked a brow. "Well, it's been around as long as I can remember. They've only enforced it since King Stewart died." Rowan yawned.

"You need as much sleep as I do." She turned to leave. Lady Tremaine would be waiting for her. She paused when Rowan lightly touched her wrist.

"You sure you're okay?"

"Yes, it just brought up a memory." Raven shrugged, keeping her face void of emotion.

Raven got to her room on tired feet with enough time to take out her mirror and answer it before sitting on her bed.

*Snow White.*

*Good evening, Lady Tremaine.* Raven projected the perfect picture of ease and peace. Her hands rested by her side, though they twitched to release some of her magic.

*Everything alright?* Lady Tremaine asked.

*Yes, Guard Rowan and I ended our patrols a few moments ago.*

*Tell me if we need to adjust our communication.*

Raven nodded, making sure she didn't show a single sign of surprise. Lady Tremaine wasn't usually accommodating.

*What's your report?*

*She operates differently as a ruler. She asked for my opinion, and I gave her my most diplomatic answer, but then she threatened me. Doesn't she have advisors?*

*That is something you'll learn. Before his death, King Stewart had seven trusted advisors, one from each domain. They were the highest authority, right below the king in power. Queen Lyanna banished them for conspiring against her after she killed the princess. They haven't been seen since.*

*Is that what you want me to do? Find those advisors to create an alliance between them and Rairene.* Raven grasped for something tangible.

*When the time comes, but for now, continue what you're doing. Tell me if anyone new arrives, if she behaves differently. Anything that is not normal for her.* Lady Tremaine closed her mirror.

The rest of the week went smoothly. Raven went on all of her patrols and trained. She showed them enough to not question her skills and kept in contact with Lady Tremaine. Each conversation ended with Raven having more questions than answers.

The week that they switched guard duties with Bastien and Charles seemed the same as any other week. They followed the queen everywhere and did nothing. Raven quickly understood why the boys cherished their mornings together so much. It was the only thing she looked forward to as well.

Aside from sitting with Betsy.

The girl was so bashful Raven could barely get her to look her in the eye. She could tell she was making progress when Betsy meekly smiled at her. Every time Raven walked in and saw her with bruises, flinching at every sound, her magic champed at the bit, screaming to be set free. Every time, Raven had to yank its chain, keeping it stuffed inside. No matter what Raven did, or how she phrased her questions, Betsy wouldn't tell her the name of the coward that hurt her. If it was Lord Roger, she couldn't do anything without Betsy confirming it.

During her last patrol for the night, Raven walked down the dimly lit stone halls alone, listening for anything out of place. It was unusually quiet. She relished being able to be by herself for the first time that day. It enabled her to go into hunting mode and be herself, not some uppity personal guard that was more of an ornament than a tool.

Raven rounded a corner and halted. Luckily, the faded carpet runner had done a good job at hiding the sound of her boots to not draw attention to her as a guard and a noblewoman kissed in front of her. Both of them were breathless as they hid in the shadows. Raven swirled around, pressing against the wall.

Charles…Charles was the guard, his black hair shining in the candlelight.

Raven closed her eyes and ground her teeth as she processed the information.

"What are you doing?" A voice from behind her asked.

Raven jumped to attention, hearing the two lovers freeze.

"I'm finishing my evening patrol." Raven turned and stood in front of the darkened hall to face the girl whose hands were on her hips as she stared down Raven.

"How can I help you?" Raven noticed the small tiara on the girl's curly blond hair.

"I have my guards, who are the only ones who do any actual work."

Raven seethed as the princess spoke to her. She placed her hands behind her, itching for her blades. She could pull them out and show the princess how much she could do.

"I'm sorry you feel that way." Raven locked eyes with her. She didn't like Charles, probably liked him the least. But if this princess was anything like her mother, and her body language said she was, she would kill Charles and banish the woman in a heartbeat.

The princess gave an exasperated eye roll to Raven. "Mother isn't forgiving to those who slack off. Don't let me see you doing it again." She walked past Raven in a huff, her nose turned up.

Raven made a face at her back before walking away, heading straight to Rowan, the rest of her patrols forgotten.

"You're early." He stepped away from the wall to watch her approach.

"It was a quiet night, outside of meeting the princess."

"You met Princess Arianna?" Rowan looked her up and down. "How did that go?" A small twitch of his lips gave away his feelings.

"Well, she insulted us by saying we don't do any work, which I would be inclined to agree with if I wasn't offended."

"Yes...well she is difficult to please. She's fifteen, so she thinks she owns the kingdom and can do what she wants. Nothing has been done to make her think otherwise."

"Bold words," Raven said.

Rowan shrugged, not looking at her.

The hairs on Raven's neck stood at attention throughout all of breakfast and into training as Charles eyed her. She ignored him, sparing with Rowan until she heard Bastien growl. She turned in time to see him knock Charles to the ground.

"What's the matter with you?" Bastien demanded, running a hand through his curling red hair.

"Nothing," Charles muttered, his eyes flicking to Raven again.

She shook her head, turning to Rowan.

"I can't fight if he's being weird. Fix whatever the fuck you did to throw him off." Bastien growled, storming over to Raven.

She rolled her eyes and meandered over to Charles as he got to his feet. The grassy fighting ring had a film of dew on each blade of grass as the morning fog rolled away. The short wooden ring that created their fighting ring was slick as well as Raven took care to step over the knee high fence.

She defeated him easily. Twice without even having to try.

"Okay, even I'm annoyed at having to fight you like this—"

She didn't get to finish her sentence as Charles launched himself at her. He forced her into a defensive stance, pushing her backward. He stayed quiet as he herded her around. And she let him. Better for him to get it out now than in an actual fight, since she already could have disarmed him twice.

Charles punched Raven in the jaw, throwing her to the ground.

"Are you done now?" she snarled, wiping dirt off her hands.

"Not even close."

"Well, I am."

Raven took the offensive, not holding back as much. She had been careful to show them enough for them to understand that she belonged, that she could hold her own. That they could trust her to not be a liability. But not now. Now she wanted to show him she was better. So. Much.

Better. She disarmed and gave Charles the killing blow in under fifteen seconds, making sure she still hid some of her skills.

Charles gazed up at her, mouth open.

Raven pulled him up by his tunic, making sure he was close enough to hear.

"I don't care about who you love or sleep with. It doesn't matter to me, and I will tell no one or use it against you. Now get over yourself."

She released him, walking away as he stumbled. Raven breathed in, pulling everything back, pulling her magic in. She did not lose control. Not over something or someone as trivial as Charles being an idiot.

Bastien and Rowan ogled her, their jaws open.

"What?" She frowned. Was she glowing? Was her magic more out of control than she thought?

"My turn!" Bastien yelled, picking up his sword. "Now, give me what you just gave Charles."

Raven let a small twinge of a smile escape her lips.

# CHAPTER SIX

## RAVEN

*This time, Raven was prepared for the nightmare to strike. The encompassing darkness wasn't as scary.*

*Not at first.*

*Then it moved.*

*Raven cowered in a corner as shadows played with her, pulling on her clothing and tearing it away from her. Her hands were tied together, and she wasn't sure if she was blindfolded or if it was truly so dark that she couldn't see.*

*"Take her into the forest and kill her. I never want to see her again."*

*Rough hands dragged her.*

*Raven kicked and tried to scream through the rag in her mouth. She didn't want to die. She was only a child. She wanted to run through the forest and have fun with her friend.*

*The ground dropped out from beneath her, sending her tumbling into nothingness.*

*She screamed.*

Raven woke up on impact, the sensation of slamming into her bed vibrating throughout her. Her pulse pounded as she sat up, trying to collect herself. She had always had nightmares, usually the same one. But it was never this bad. She rubbed her eyes, knowing it was pointless to seek sleep again. Raven climbed out of bed, threw on a cloak, and hoped that a light stroll would clear her mind.

She found her way to the kitchen, a small light shining from within. Inside, she found the chef, a middle-aged man who could've been as old as her father. Graying hair stuck out in every direction, and his apron was covered in more stains than she had ever seen.

"Is it okay if I come in?" Raven knocked lightly to draw his attention.

He glanced over at her, his brown eyes calculating.

"You're the new Royal Guard."

It was not a question.

"All of my staff are terrified of you. Who am I to deny you?"

"Well, hopefully, I'm less terrifying in my nightclothes," she sighed. "And the kitchen is your kingdom, so I defer to you."

She waited, arms relaxed.

"A little less terrifying." He smiled before going to work.

Raven took the invitation and sat, gazing around. Everything was clean and organized, and not a single item was out of place. Three ovens burned on the far wall, heating the room to an almost unbearable heat. She loved it, her magic purring.

"Do you mind if I bake something?" Raven whispered, not daring to let herself hope.

"A Royal Guard that bakes? Never thought I'd live to see the day." He chuckled, motioning for her to get what she needed.

Raven leaped at the chance, not giving him time to change his mind. She raced to the pantry and pulled out all the ingredients she would need to make some hot cinnamon rolls. She warmed the milk, and added in yeast, followed shortly by eggs, butter, sugar, salt, and flour. Once it was all mixed, she took it out and kneaded it.

"Baking has always calmed me. Every chance I got during training, which wasn't a lot, I would sneak away to the kitchen to learn. It's the only thing I've truly loved," Raven confessed, her heart and mind calm as she fell into her ritual.

"How long have you been training?" he whispered.

Raven was painfully aware of the pity lacing his question.

"Since I was seven." She shrugged.

She didn't let it bother her when the chef dropped his spoon in the batter. Instead, she focused on her cinnamon rolls. The rest of her time passed quietly, and if anyone else found it strange, Raven didn't. It had been the one thing Lady Tremaine had allowed outside of her training and mastering her abilities as an enchanter. Not an easy task, but one she had been eager for. Baking re-centered her. Whenever she got overwhelmed by the demands of her training, she wound up in the kitchen, where she could slow down and let her mind slowly work out her problem in the background. As she kneaded the dough, she kneaded her magic, shaping it into a tight ball that was once again securely in place.

The kitchen was full of the smell of cinnamon and sugar when she was done. Taking them out of the fire, she frosted them and served one to the chef.

He scooted forward in his chair.

"These are a delicacy here. How did you learn to make them?" He took another bite.

"The chef where I trained taught me her secret recipe. I think she was from here."

"Can I have the recipe?" He finished the roll.

"Then what excuse would I have to come down here?" Raven smiled.

"If you bake like that all the time, I may have to steal you away from Her Majesty. You can bake down here any time you please."

"Thank you," Raven said. "I'm Raven." She extended her hand.

"Louis." He shook hers, smiling as she dashed to the real world.

"Next!"

Raven shuddered, her eyes closed for a second. Queen Lyanna was in a particularly foul mood. She had been since the four of them entered the courtroom. In the three weeks Raven had been there, she could already tell the difference between a good mood and a bad one. It all came down to the simple inflections in the queen's voice. Raven pitied whatever villager, nobleman, or messenger came before her today.

"What do you need?"

A man covered in dirt and ragged clothing kneeled before her. He grasped his flimsy hat between his fingers, his knuckles white as he searched for words.

"Speak."

"I was-was, I was hoping…" he gazed around, seeking strength, "my children are starving, your Majesty—"

"Why is that my problem?" Queen Lyanna leaned on her throne.

For anyone else, this would portray relaxation and ease, possibly even someone open to talking. It was the exact opposite for the queen. If she slouched, that meant she was annoyed. If she smiled, she was angry. Raven had yet to see what it meant when the queen pursed her lips as she did now. She knew it did not bode well for the man.

"If we could be allowed to not pay taxes for a month—"

Rowan shifted beside Raven. Charles and Bastien did the same. They knew what was coming.

Raven straightened her spine, preparing.

"You expect me to allow you to not pay the money you owe me for living on my land?" Her voice was slow and calculated. Meant to frighten him enough as he thought about what he was suggesting.

"There is no money left to feed my children. If I must pay, can I borrow from the crown? Just enough to make sure—"

Rowan gripped Raven's wrist hard enough to bruise.

She whipped her head to look at him, raising an eyebrow. He ignored her, continuing to stare straight ahead, tightening his grip when she tried to get free without drawing attention.

"My Queen, please, I am begging for help. My children go to sleep crying every night. Their stomachs are so hungry." His hands clutched his hat before him.

Queen Lyanna analyzed her nails before rising and sauntering over to her gauntlet. She grasped it, and turned it in the light, admiring the blood-stained daggers in place of nails.

"Well, we'll have to fix that then, won't we?" Queen Lyanna had never sounded sweeter, kindness dripping from her voice.

She moved quickly. One moment, the gauntlet was before Raven's eyes. The next it was in the man's chest. Rowan's hand kept Raven grounded. Not that she would have done anything, her magic barely stirring in her shock and...horror. That was horror trickling down her spine. Still, Raven was grateful that Rowan held her there. Just in case.

Queen Lyanna twisted her hand in the man's chest before pulling it out. The sound as it left his body was quieter than Raven expected, unceremonious as his body fell to the floor.

"Now you have one less mouth to feed." The queen smiled, her eyes crinkling.

She turned around and strode to her throne, hips swishing, the gauntlet dripping a trail of blood behind her. Queen Lyanna sat down and admired the dark red rivers that crawled down the edges, falling off and onto her dress. Maids rushed in and cleaned the floor, while butlers removed the body.

Raven couldn't move.

She wanted to.

Oh, how she wanted to move.

As her paralysis faded, her magic sang a song of retribution so loud, that she fought to contain it with no one noticing. Raven had always considered herself detached, cold even. She never got involved and felt no emotions. Not after Jason. Right then, though, she wanted to move one foot to her left, remove her blades, whisper an enchantment, and cut off the queen's head. Her magic squealed in delight at the thought. More than anything, it wanted to exact revenge for the poor farmer whose family would now die without him.

Of course, she would be dead afterward.

But it would be worth it.

Only she couldn't move. Years upon years of training and controlling her magic had prepared her for this moment. Rowan still held her, watching her, waiting to see what she would do. She took a breath and stared straight ahead, ignoring her partner and the hand that still kept her ground.

Raven found it was much easier to pretend nothing had happened once the body was gone, and the blood was another light pink stain on the floor. She internally shook herself, gathering her thoughts and emotions quickly, pushing her magic down further into a tight ball. This time, when she pulled against Rowan's grip, he let her, stepping away as the next person came forward.

She tuned out all of it. Couldn't hear anymore. Instead, she observed the crowd, making sure her magic stayed quiet. She looked at the advisors, noting which ones watched the queen, which ones worked, and which ones lazed around without a care in the world.

The sound of pounding dragged Raven from her nightmare.

"Raven." Rowan knocked again.

"Do you realize what bloody awful time it is?" She opened her door enough to stick her head out. He blurred before her as she rubbed her eyes, wiping the memory from her mind.

"We're going out for the day."

Her vision cleared enough to see a slight smile on his face.

"I'm not. I'm staying here. All day. It's my day off, and I want to ponder the decisions I've made that have led me here." Raven leaned heavily on her door, crossing her arms. "Sounds fun, doesn't it?"

"Not in the slightest." Rowan gently turned her around and walked her into her room. "Which is why you're going to get dressed into something comfy, and let me take you on a tour of our wonderful city, Aslar."

Grudgingly, Raven changed into her most comfortable clothing, a loose pair of trousers and a tunic, opting to leave her hair down. She left her swords behind, hiding two small daggers up her sleeves. Raven motioned for Rowan to lead the way.

"Have you gotten to see Aslar yet?"

"Not really. The night I arrived, I rode through it in a carriage." Raven wrinkled her nose. "You'll have to ignore my bitchy mood for a minute. I am looking forward to this, just not before the roosters have crowed."

Raven took in her surroundings beyond the palace gates. The streets closer to the palace were clean and well-kept, the cobblestones in perfect formation. The only people in the streets were maids and butlers getting ready for the day, heading to homes constructed of stone and wood on solid foundations. She pulled her cloak tighter around her shoulders, stuffing her hands in her pockets as they got further into the city.

The disorganized, twisting, cobbled streets turned to dirt and mud. Of course, she had seen Riset, but it was nowhere near this bad. At least in her home, most of the streets were cobbled together. The homes here were a worse story. Raven could tell that at one point the wooden homes used to be nice. Probably as nice as the thatched-roofed homes closer to the palace. Now, the years had taken their toll, and Raven wondered how some remained standing. A few had roofs sagging with rot, while others had so many nails and crossbeams to support it almost as though another home had been built on top of the other.

"Where are we going?"

"Well, if you want the true Aslar, its heart, then you have to go to the market near the middle of the city."

"The heart, huh? Do you know a lot about it?"

"As a Royal Guard, it's my job to know everything about the city," Rowan said.

"When I first got here, it didn't look this bad, even at night. I would have noticed the difference between the feel of the cobblestones," Raven commented, watching more villagers come out of their homes or shops and join them in the street.

"You came from the harbor. There wouldn't be a difference that way. We're on the back side of the palace right now. The queen likes to put up a pleasant face for those visiting, but all it takes is a visit over here to see that it's not real."

Raven studied the people of Aslar as they walked through the marketplace. She saw flashes of a smile, a kind gesture, or a lover's glance. There was still hope for this kingdom. The evidence was there, and even though it wasn't her job, she wanted to help them. Wanted to make their lives good again, her heart and magic demanding it. If only she knew where to start. Raven understood now what Rowan meant by the heart of Aslar. Though it lacked wealth, the people seemed more willing to smile and more willing to let their guard down, barely. The children ran through the streets wearing patchwork clothing that seemed ready to tear at the delicate seams. They chased each other with toys made from straw and fabric scraps. Teenagers worked the stalls under the watchful eyes of their parents, and now and then, a parent looked at their child with pride as they haggled, or made a sale that would let them eat for another day. And throughout the air wafted the most amazing scents of spices as kitchens roared to life.

"Rowan. Stop." Raven held her hand to his chest, freezing both of them.

"What? What is it?" Rowan remained still, eyes darting around.

"There's a fluffy puppy...right...over...there..." she whispered as she bounced on her toes.

"So there is." He looked at the small black husky that trotted past with its owners.

"It's so adorable." Raven gripped Rowan's arm as she followed the puppy's every movement. "Do you think they'll let me pet it?"

"I'm sure if you ask—"

Before Rowan could finish his sentence, she left his side, running over to the couple.

"Who would have guessed that our intimidating...friend...would be undone by puppies," Rowan remarked as he stood over her.

"All dogs." Raven smiled as the puppy licked her face.

Rowan made a face at her, which she promptly returned to him before they let the couple go about their business. They continued, Rowan guiding them through the streets.

"Really? The Black Assassin? This is where you're taking me to eat?" She wasn't sure if it was where he liked to eat, or a subtle indication that he knew what she was. If that was the case...she would handle it when the time came and see just how much he suspected before dealing with him. She really didn't want to kill him. Rowan was starting to grow on her.

"It's always been a favorite of mine." Rowan walked through what someone could barely consider a door.

The rotten door let Raven into a room that was only slightly capable of being called a pub. A few tables rocked back and forth, with some chairs looking as though they would collapse if one more speck of dust landed on them. The people didn't look much better, either. Someone slouched over a table, a pint of beer clutched in his hands. While the others seemed to only be held up by the wall they rested against.

"Charming." Raven walked around as Rowan went to the bartender and ordered for them.

"It's a little worse for wear but still has its charms."

Raven noted Rowan headed directly to a specific table, not once stopping to look at the other options. His shoulders were relaxed, and he was at ease enough to lean in the chair and fold his arms behind his head.

"You grew up here," Raven stated.

No one in their right mind would come here unless it was familiar and calming. It was probably some place Rowan would go to feel safe. Or it was where his father had taken him. The way Rowan tensed while putting both feet on the ground confirmed her thoughts. He looked at her through narrowed eyes, as though her discovering this secret would undo him.

"Raven—"

"If you think I care about that, then you have learned nothing about me. I'm not in the business of judging people for where they're from. Not that this is something you should be ashamed of. I think it's amazing you grew up to become a Royal Guard."

"You don't know what this place represents to others. Everyone would see me as the son of a pauper. They would stop respecting me and force me out."

"Then why would you bring me here if it's so important people don't find out?" Raven furrowed her brow.

"I wanted to see if I could trust you."

"And if I had reacted differently?"

"I would have killed you." He leaned back, his piercing brown eyes never leaving hers.

Raven shrugged. "I can respect that." She nodded. "So, what's the verdict? Can you trust me?"

"Still undecided. We'll see how the rest of the day goes." Rowan leaned forward. "Do you trust me?"

"I don't trust anyone." She spoke softly, breaking eye contact. "Trusting someone gives them power. People like me should distrust everyone."

"Must've been one hell of a breakup."

She looked at him, keeping all emotion from displaying on her face.

"Please, if you don't trust anyone, it has to have been one disastrous ending."

"I only trust three people," Raven conceded, turning away. It wasn't to show that he was right, but to hide the slight twinge of pain that had welled in her eye.

*"Raven."*

*She rolled over to look at Jason. His hand lightly brushed her face, moving her messy hair out of the way. She scooted closer and kissed him, closing her eyes.*

*"I have to go."*

*"You start your new assignment today?"*

*Jason murmured a confirmation, "I shouldn't be gone long. I don't know how often I'll be back until it's done."*

*"Who is it this time?" She didn't want to know. Didn't want the name of the woman Jason would seduce for information for the king. She didn't understand why Luca couldn't do it. Jason was only supposed to teach now.*

*"Some woman that's part of the queen's ladies."*

*Ah, so that was why. She would be closer to Jason's age and never go for someone Luca's age.*

*"I love you." Jason tilted her head up to look at him. She kissed him in response, pulling him closer.*

Raven turned to Rowan when the bartender came over with two plates of food. Rowan tilted his head towards her, which she promptly ignored, focusing on the food instead. Despite the pub's interior design, the food looked edible. Raven feigned a yawn as she rubbed her eyes, trying to hide the tear that had escaped. Rowan remained silent.

"So, how did you get that scar?" she asked, needing a distraction.

Rowan rubbed the crescent scar near his right eye. "I'm not sure. I was eight and woke up with it. My father never told me."

"You never wanted to know?" She further prodded.

"I used to ask him, but he refused, so I gave up." Rowan shrugged. "We should head back. We don't want to arrive past curfew," Rowan commented as the afternoon sun began its descent.

They were halfway to the palace when a scream ricocheted through the alley beside them.

"Get off me."

Raven didn't wait for Rowan as she sprinted down the alley.

The girl screamed again, fueling Raven to move faster. She chastised herself for coming to the city with only two daggers. She would never make that mistake again, no matter where she was headed. Rowan's footsteps pounded behind her as she took a second to survey the scene and take in the five men surrounding a single girl. She cowered against the wall, her clothing ripped and falling off her too-skinny frame.

"Hey, assholes." Raven leaped in, not giving them enough time to process.

She heard Rowan jump in behind her, not letting them get away. She took the second needed to note their rusty knives, not flinching when she had to get close. They didn't stand a chance against her and Rowan. The men quickly found themselves disarmed and knocked out on the ground.

Raven gasped for breath as she spun around, making sure all of them were down. The girl had run off, smart thing. Now all they needed to do was wait for the city guard to arrive.

"Good job Raven. I didn't realize you were trained in hand-to-hand combat as well." Rowan stepped over a man.

"Well, stick around. I have a couple more tricks up my sleeve," Raven panted, her hand clenched tightly to her side. "I need to work out more. I'm never this winded." Raven attempted to steady her breathing, a stitch forming in her side as she moved her hand. A sharp pain radiated out through her stomach.

"You're not out of shape—"

"Clearly, I am." Raven closed her eyes as the ground swayed, dots bursting before her.

"You're bleeding."

Raven saw the alley shift and turn sideways as she lost feeling in her legs. Rowan caught her before she hit the ground.

"Huh, I had forgotten what that's like." Raven slurred as Rowan supported her. "What are you doing?" Raven's eyes dragged themselves closed, her magic unraveling before her. She ripped it back, kneading it until it was a small roll.

"I need to get you somewhere safe to patch you up." Rowan moved quickly. At least it felt quick as her mind spun.

"The palace is the other way."

That, at least she knew.

"You may not make it in time if we go that way." Rowan grunted as he carried her.

Raven drifted in and out, making sure she kept a handle on her magic. She had been pressing a hand to her wound, but now it dangled in the air, limp.

"Raven, I need you to knock." Rowan shook her. "Raven."

"I'm awake. No need to shout." She rolled out of his arms, landing hard on her feet before stumbling into the wall. The dark world swayed as she caught herself. Her magic pulsed in her ears and eyes, deafening her with its pleas to help. She gritted her teeth, clamping it down as she pounded twice on the door before leaning against it.

Raven closed her eyes, bursts of white swirling around her. If she hadn't been bleeding, she would have thought she was drunk.

Raven didn't have time to analyze the man who opened the door she leaned on, falling on top of him.

"What the hell?"

"Sorry Father, I tried to catch her." Rowan picked her up.

"What are you doing here, Rowan? Did the queen order you to do something with her?"

"She was stabbed. I had nowhere else to bring her." Rowan's voice was tight.

*This was his father, right?* Raven thought.

"Great, just what I need, a foolish—"

The sounds of Rowan's father faded away. That or she stopped hearing him when a large black husky walked out from behind him to sit before her. Raven was on her knees, swaying as she beheld the dog. She held the dog's face in her hands, smiling. Raven flicked a glance up to see Rowan's father move about, lighting candles before running a hand through his thick graying hair.

"Hello my friend, you're as black as raven wings," she muttered in Rairenian. Raven rested heavily against the door frame. When had she sat down? Her mind swirled, but there was at least one thing she knew. "Rowan, we can go somewhere else. I think I have enough of my wits to see when we aren't welcome." She forced herself to her feet, looking at the rest of the modest home.

It was small, clean, and orderly, speaking to life in the military or guard. The man himself, though, was not quite put together. His clothing was old and fraying, hanging off his frame.

Rowan's father's eyes met hers and glanced away.

"It's fine, you can stay. I'll grab my supplies. Rowan, get her on the table. My Lady, I'm sorry but we'll need to cut off the middle section of your tunic," Rowan's father ordered, standing up taller as he moved around his home with purpose.

Raven laughed.

"My lady? Sir, I suspect if you knew me, you would think you were more of a lady than I could ever be." Raven stumbled, finding Rowan's strong shoulders supporting her.

Rowan picked her up again and carried her to the table. He quickly cut off the bottom of her tunic. Raven observed him. His eyes flared at the exposed skin. If she hadn't lost so much blood, she probably would have cared that he was seeing the story that was written on her stomach. Raven wondered if he had thought it would be untouched skin, only to find a patchwork of scars. She hoped he wouldn't ask her how she received them.

As it was, she was delirious enough to tell him if asked, especially as all of her focus was on controlling her magic.

"Where did you say she was from?" Rowan's father asked.

"I didn't. Raven's my new partner. She came from Rairene a few weeks ago."

Raven turned her head to see Rowan's father shake himself, color returning to his face.

"I'm sorry about this."

"Sorry about what? It was my—" Raven screamed as his father poured a burning fireball of liquid onto her wound. She knew it was probably warm water and salt, followed by some type of alcohol, but a burning ball of fire was a more accurate depiction to her.

Rowan grabbed a rag and shoved it in her mouth.

"Feather!" Rowan grunted as the dog growled at them before whimpering. He was under the table, Raven realized.

Her chest pumped up and down as she locked eyes with Rowan. She zeroed in all of her focus on him, her magic exploding inside like over-proofed bread, bursting along where the wound was, screaming in her veins to be set free, to protect her from the pain. Raven was certain her magic was pouring out over the wound. She squeezed Rowan's hand and wrapped up her magic, pulling it in like dough until it was the size of her fist.

"I warned you," Rowan's father whispered as he took a wet cloth and wiped away the remaining blood.

The wound wasn't deep, but its lack of depth was made up for in length. Blood slowly ran over, soaking her cloak. They pressed rags against it, staunching the flow and sending fire racing up her spine.

"Rowan, go grab me a needle and thread from my kit."

Raven latched onto him, refusing to let go. If she let go, her control might go with it. Her heart spasmed, unable to steady itself. Rowan returned the squeeze before slowly detaching his hand from hers, one finger at a time.

"It'll be okay."

She kept her eyes locked on him, her anchor and control. Rowan grabbed some rags and an assortment of other items. Raven kept her hands balled against her side and breathed slowly through her mouth.

Feather whimpered from below, pressing his nose against her hand.

"Damn, we need it to stop bleeding before we can stitch it closed. Rowan, apply more pressure. We'll give it a few more minutes before we have to cauterize it."

Raven swallowed, shutting her eyes. Blood rushed through her ears.

"Cauterize it?" Rowan kept his voice calm. "Dad, you can't be serious."

"We need it to stop bleeding, which is why you're going to keep applying pressure before we resort to that."

All of them were silent, Raven unable to think of anything past the pain. If she opened her mouth, she didn't know what would come out, a sob or a scream. She didn't want to find out. Either would be embarrassing.

Raven opened her eyes, pulling her mind together. Her magic was relentless in its need to help, to be set free. It pounded against the barriers she had set up around it. She would keep it contained. She would not lose control.

She would not cause harm to these two men.

Raven prepared herself for the fight of her life. She knew what they were going to have to do. They would have to burn it. She had been through a lot. Had a lot of scars to speak of her trials, but she had never been burned. That was a punishment for Ella alone. Lady Tremaine had kept the burning away from the rest of them. It could get out of control and she didn't want to mar their perfect faces. Most of Raven's scars had faded to light white lines. She did not know how painful it was going to be. Ella had always refused to describe it.

She didn't have to wait long to find out.

Rowan's father brought a knife and candle over to the table. He held the knife over the flame, waiting for it to heat enough without turning red or white.

Rowan stuffed a gag in her mouth right before his father pressed the burning blade against her wound.

Raven screamed, her body contorting on the table.

Her magic flooded her mind and body.

Raven squeezed her eyes shut, gripping her power. The whiplash from pulling the magic was almost as painful as the burn. Rowan held her down, making sure she wouldn't get burned anywhere else. It took a few quick seconds to get the bleeding to stop, but they were the longest seconds of her life. Sweat broke out on her body, soaking her hair and clothes.

She kept her eyes shut as she envisioned spinning her power into a small ball. She prayed the pain would go away. When it finally dulled, she opened her eyes and found Rowan beside her, his father cleaning everything. The dog, Feather, was by her hand, whining.

"Is it done?" her voice scratched.

"Yes, we stitched it closed as well." Rowan sighed as he stood up. "Now we have to go. We're going to have to sneak into the palace."

# CHAPTER SEVEN

## RAVEN

The journey to the palace proved to be more difficult than either of them had expected. Raven stopped every few minutes as wave after wave of dizziness, nausea, and exhaustion swept over her. The burn was unbearable, crawling up her side and trying to swallow her whole. It took all of her training to not sit down in whatever side alley they were in and lie down. Now she knew why Ella had never told her what being burnt felt like. Raven's heart raced at the thought of Ella going through this pain.

"Come on Raven, we're almost there."

"How do you plan on sneaking past the guards? I don't recall seeing a gate that was unmanned." Raven leaned against him, eyes closed, for just a minute.

"There's a hidden door in the wall. No one knows about it, and I mean no one."

"Then how do you?" Raven tilted her head to get a small peek at him.

"My father showed me in case I ever needed to use it. I would say this qualifies," Rowan grumbled as he adjusted her weight.

They walked slowly, their eyes constantly shifting. Though they were close, both knew it was only the beginning of their struggle. Once they were through the gate, they had to get across a lot of open ground unseen, into the palace, and to her room while encountering as few people as possible. If anyone noticed she was hurt...Raven didn't want to think about what Queen Lyanna might do.

Raven didn't see the other door Rowan pulled open, its hinges soundless as they rolled over the ivy trailing down the wall. When they got through, Raven straightened, relieved. She knew exactly where they were, and how they could get in safely.

"Let's go through the kitchen," she whispered when she saw Rowan looking down the wall, at the other, much longer way back.

"How much blood did you lose? The chef is probably there. Raven, I need—"

"I know Louis. He won't say anything."

Rowan paused, doubt and weariness warring in his eyes. She watched him weigh their options before shrugging and heading towards the kitchen. As they moved, Raven shook the fog from her head. Or at least tried to. It was a constant presence, making everything a little blurrier.

"Raven, what..." Chef Louis looked her over as they surprised him.

If she had been more conscious, she would have laughed at his expression. As it was, she rested heavily on Rowan again. Louis came over to her, taking her off Rowan.

"What happened?"

"Something stupid, don't tell anyone...I'll give you the recipe for the cinnamon rolls," Raven whispered as she sat on the hard, cold stone floor.

Louis went into the back of the kitchen as her eyes fluttered while Rowan paced. When Louis came back, he had two glass jars in his hands.

"Take these. They'll help with the pain of whatever stupid thing happened to you."

"What are they?" Rowan snatched them before Raven could examine them.

"Are they enchanted?" she questioned. The thought of taking something enchanted chilled her, sobering Raven for a moment as her magic quivered.

"Of course not. One is for pain. An herbalist made it. The other is a stimulant to help with the foggy brain. She should take one of each in the morning. Only the pain pill tonight. It'll make her sleepier," Louis explained.

Rowan didn't let them go. "We aren't supposed to take medication at all. Queen Lyanna views it as a weakness. She'll have to power through it."

"Maybe in a week she could, but we both know the queen won't let her have that time. Especially since it's a wound she didn't sustain protecting the queen. There's enough in there for a week. After that, hopefully, she's fine to go without them."

"I'm right here. I can make my own choices," Raven snapped.

Rowan curtly nodded, his eyes hooded. He pocketed the pills.

"Okay Raven, we got you inside, which means we can move easily throughout the palace without being questioned. You have to walk on your own and behave normally."

Raven tried to retain everything Rowan had said. She had to move...and walk...on her own. A simple task that the shaking in her legs thoroughly questioned as being feasible. Raven dove into herself, dredging up the last reaches of Snow White that she could find. Her magic responded, strengthening her, a black swirling mass that cooled the wound internally and gave her some wherewithal. Once she stood up, she was as close to her normal assassin self as she could be. Cold, calm, and collected.

"Let's go."

They walked quickly over the thinly carpeted halls, only coming across a couple of courtiers who skidded away from them. None of them wanted to be identified by the queen's Royal Guard. Once they got to her room, Raven stumbled over to her dresser, landing heavily against the drawers. She rested her head on top of the dresser, breathing slowly as she pulled open the top drawer and grabbed a nightshirt. Rowan walked over and helped get her blood-soaked cloak off, tossing it into a cloth sack with her trousers, tunic, and anything else covered in her blood. She collapsed onto her bed, lying on her back as Rowan came up beside her with a wet cloth. Raven squeezed her eyes, clamping her jaw when he removed her bandages and pressed the gauze against it. She opened her eyes when the pain faded and Rowan finished re-wrapping her stomach.

She sat up, quickly falling backward as the edges of her vision blackened. Raven got farther onto her bed and did her best to thank Rowan as he handed her one more pill before leaving the jars on her nightstand.

Raven was dragged from her deep sleep by hands that shook her, the pain instantly reminding her of why she was exhausted. Susan helped her rush through the room to get ready before Raven raced out for breakfast, ignoring the black sack tied up by her door, and grabbing some pills.

Betsy was by herself again when Raven got her food, a fresh bruise on her cheek. She didn't even glance up as Raven sat down. She remained bashful, keeping her eyes on her food.

"I wish you would tell me who he is. That way I could set him straight," Raven commented, her muscles relaxing as the medication worked its own kind of magic.

Raven sat taller, more confident, and less concerned about pushing Betsy.

Betsy's cheeks flushed. "Nothing's wrong." She looked Raven in the eye, her brown eyes solid, daring Raven to say more.

Raven shrugged before turning her attention elsewhere. She left before the boys were done eating, needing to do something other than sit still. By the time they got to the practice field, the fire on her side roared. Raven grimaced as burning heat seared across her skin. She wanted to scream as a single tear formed in the corner of her eye.

But she couldn't.

She couldn't do anything because if anyone knew she was injured, she was dead. That had been the one thing she had gotten from Rowan last night. Raven reached into her pocket and swallowed two pills, hoping no one saw. Would her magic burn through medication faster than was normal? Not that she could mention it to anyone.

The effects were not instantaneous. The entire time they trained, the pain built. Her magic growled in its presence. She called for a water break to gather her composure, and to stop seeing two of Bastien as they sparred.

She observed Rowan approach her through eyes filled to the brim with unshed tears, creating a wall of water to see through. Her fingers itched to hold her injury, to apply pressure, anything to make the pain ease.

"Are you doing okay?" Rowan's lips barely moved as he drank.

"Just peachy," she snapped. "There's nothing I would love more right now than to claw out my insides."

"Did you take the medication?" Rowan took another sip.

"Of course, they barely help…" She turned away from the boys and wiped her eyes, sucking in a breath as the world darkened around the edge of her vision.

"Hey you two, come on, we need to finish up. Queen Lyanna wants to hold court early today," Charles called, jogging over to them.

"Raven and I will spar for the remaining time," Rowan said.

Charles instantly slouched. Ever since they had learned Raven could not only hold her own against them but beat them. They had been jumping at every chance they could get to fight her. At least it seemed she had finally earned their trust. Raven nodded her thanks to Rowan as they got into position and walked through the motions of fighting each other, moving slowly, more precise in their actions, perfecting an already perfect dance.

Raven's pain dwindled to an irritating itch as they got to court. She sighed into it, relaxing. She sensed Rowan gazing at her as they stepped up to their positions. Raven wondered what he saw. Did he notice the shift? Did he see she was more alert, and that her shoulders were relaxed? She stood tall, no longer slouching.

She was finally...herself.

Queen Lyanna drew Raven's attention as she walked up to her throne. She was resplendent in a dark green gown with silver metal coiling around the bodice to form a corset. Her blond hair was piled on top of her head, weaving around her crown. The queen's fourteen advisors turned to watch before turning to their aides to review their own agendas for the day. The gallery fell silent as they looked up at their ruler. Not one of them looked at her with awe or love.

Only hate.

As the day wore on, Raven's mind faded. All thoughts began to blur and fog up, but her body wouldn't let her forget the sharp pain she had in her abdomen. The two pills had worked more than the one meant to keep her awake, and Raven's vision blurred as sleep whispered in her ear.

"Prince Aleksander, Your Majesty," the herald's voice rang over the arches, bouncing off around the room.

Raven straightened, ready for anything.

A lone man strode into the room. He wasn't much older than her. Probably the prince's guard, Raven surmised. His clothing was worn and slightly ragged from his travels. The cloak held no insignia, and though he walked with the grace of an experienced, well-trained fighter, she could tell he was tired. His white hair, while well kept, with two thick braids on the left side of his head, was dusty. His ice-blue eyes kept flicking around the silent room, one hand behind his back, resting on a weapon.

He bowed before Queen Lyanna.

"Nephew, where are your guards?" her voice dropped low enough to warrant concern as she spoke in Trudelian.

"I ride better and faster on my own," the man responded in Trudelian, smiling as he stood. His smile enraptured Raven, hypnotized her with its kindness and warmth. "Besides, I didn't want to miss your ball." He easily switched to Evrotian, his accent light.

Queen Lyanna smiled a true, loving smile.

Raven balked.

The queen opened her arms and hugged the guard... Prince Aleksander. Raven shook the cobwebs from her head. She had to clear her mind.

"You, dear nephew, need to get cleaned up before dinner tonight. Two of my guards will escort you—"

"Aunt, I don't—"

"Two of my guards will escort you."

Charles and Bastien moved.

"Rowan and Raven will take you. Charles and Bastien, you're staying here."

Both men slouched before Charles moved to the other side of the throne. Raven scrunched her lips. What could be so exciting about escorting a prince to his room? She and Rowan followed the prince out. Prince Aleksander took a few minutes, stopping to talk to some noblemen and even some commoners. The moment they got outside of the throne room, and the massive double doors resoundingly closed behind them, a shift instantly happened. Rowan relaxed.

For only the second time since knowing him, he truly relaxed.

"How long are you staying this time?" Rowan was downright cheerful.

Raven tilted her head to the side.

"No idea. Mother told me to go. Said she'd send for me." He shrugged.

His voice sent shivers through the core of her magic with his husky tones. Raven's magic begged to tangle around him.

Rowan broke formation and walked beside the prince. Raven remained silent, watching them talk as old friends.

"So, does she speak?" His voice lightened as he looked over his shoulder at her, his ice-blue eyes igniting more than her magic.

Raven narrowed her eyes at the prince, pulling her magic in as she locked eyes with him. Eyes that looked so much like Ella's. The need to see her friend rose quickly. Both of the men had slowed down until they were next to her.

"Does she speak?" Raven spoke in Trudelian, too consumed with controlling her magic, the pain of her wound, and Ella's eyes, to remember to speak in Evrotian. "She speaks. Sorry if I was too busy doing my job to make conversation," she snapped. Her magic quieted by her anger and aggressive reshaping as she controlled it.

Instantly, she wanted to take all of it back. Who was she? She should not speak to any member of the queen's family that way.

"Feisty, I like her," Prince Aleksander commented to Rowan in Evrotian. He switched to Trudelian as he whispered. "My aunt would have you killed for talking to me that way."

Raven fumed.

He laughed.

"I'm kidding, lighten up."

They continued on their walk down through the palace. Servants and courtiers smiled or nodded at the prince. None of them stopped to chat when they saw the guards with him.

"Raven doesn't lighten up. She has one mode: serious." Rowan smiled, winking at her.

"And you don't?" she smirked, glad that he was keeping her love of dogs safe.

"Okay, clearly the two of you need to have a good rumble in the sheets and work out all of this tension."

Rowan and Raven froze.

"Or I could show you a good romp in the sheets," Prince Aleksander joked, looking over Raven. "You're not too bad. I've definitely slept with worse."

"You're a real Prince Charming. I bet all the girls swoon at the thought of sleeping with you." Raven stepped closer to him, close enough to smell him. Instantly, she found her body relaxing into him, the scent of snow and pine invading her senses. She paused, letting herself adjust and pull herself together. His ice-blue eyes held hers long enough for her to notice the light flecks of green in their depths.

"Maybe not though." She stepped away, looking him over.

Raven smirked and walked down the hall. She told herself it was to make a point, that she couldn't stand there after saying that. But really, it was to hide the blush creeping up her cheeks. It didn't matter that he was covered in dirt, sweat, and long travels. It took everything to keep her magic under control.

Opening his door, Prince Aleksander turned around and leaned against the door frame. His black tunic hung off his sculpted shoulders perfectly. His blue eyes looked at Raven with an intensity she wouldn't have expected from a prince. "If you ever want to know what it's like to sleep with royalty, let me know and we can work on lightening you up."

Raven's eyes widened as he closed the door. Rowan chuckled.

"So that's—"

"Prince Aleksander."

"You and I...there's no...there's no tension?"

"Nope." Rowan turned pink. "He only said that to see if we were. Especially since he wants you."

Raven snorted, looking at the stones beneath her boot.

"He's a good friend, Raven. He's tricky and cunning, especially with women. Be careful. And don't sleep with him for as long as possible."

Raven opened her mouth to protest.

"After that exchange, you're the only woman he's going to pursue."

Raven crossed her arms. "It's strongly frowned upon, remember?"

"So long as you don't get caught, and this is a prince we're talking about. It doesn't exactly apply to him."

"It should. No one is above any law in Rairene. Besides, he's going to wait a very long time. I'm never doing that to myself again," Raven replied, looking towards the ceiling.

"Never doing what?"

"Getting entangled with another person," she spoke loud enough for him to hear.

*"Jason," Raven hesitated. They'd been together for several months, but only sleeping together for two. She bit her lip, wanting him to face her.*

*"What's wrong?" His hand rested gently on her cheek.*

*She closed her eyes and held his hand there. It was a gesture that brought her more peace than he could ever grasp. With her eyes closed, she found the courage to say the most frightening thing she'd ever uttered.*

*"I love you." It came out in a sigh as she opened her dark blue eyes. "I know we're barely...and we're only messing around, and I understand if you don't—" Jason's lips cut her rambling off.*

*His hand left her cheek and wrapped around her waist, pressing her closer to him.*

*"I love you too," he whispered, touching his forehead against hers as they came up for air.*

*Raven closed her eyes and breathed in, pressing his hand to her cheek once more.*

"You speak Trudelian?"

"What?" Raven snapped out of her memory. "Oh...yes...don't you speak it?"

Rowan shook his head. "I know a few words, but you spoke it with hardly an accent." He looked at her, waiting, wearing his tell-me-what's-going-on-face.

"I guess languages come naturally to me." She grimaced. She hadn't meant to slip up, but Prince Aleksander was so infuriating...she'd messed up. Hopefully, Rowan wouldn't say anything.

"All set," Prince Aleksander interrupted them.

Raven straightened and cracked her neck.

"Where would you like to go, Prince Aleksander? To the courtroom?" Raven kept her arms crossed behind her. Her fingers gently pressed against the tips of her short swords. She continued to press them there instead of pressing them against her side. Pain flared in her vision as she blinked rapidly. She didn't want Rowan to think she was weak.

"Definitely not. Why don't we tour the palace? That way I can comment on the changes my aunt has made to the detriment of the palace," he laughed as he walked down the hall.

Raven followed behind, keeping her distance. She would never admit it, especially to herself, but the prince unsettled her, more than anyone had in a very long time. He was unlike any other royal member she had ever met. Some were uptight, others arrogant and narcissistic, and some were kind. Prince David was kind, despite his history with Ella. But Prince Aleksander was nonchalant and carefree. He was either confident enough that he didn't need to be on constant alert, or he was stupid enough to think he didn't have to be. Raven wasn't sure which one she hoped he turned out to be.

Raven's magic writhed against the pain. It longed to be unleashed as sweat broke out in her attempt to contain it. She'd been unable to take any medication. Prince Aleksander was too observant and would ask all the wrong questions. Rowan would wonder why she needed more. She noticed the way he continuously glanced at her as the day wore on.

"Raven, would you mind going to the kitchens to see if Chef Louis has any of his signature crab today?" Rowan asked.

Raven opened her mouth to say something obtuse to him.

"Make sure he knows it's for the prince. I don't care if you take some time to convince him."

She wasn't sure if she loved or hated Rowan right then.

"It really isn't necessary, Rowan. She's clearly tired. Don't make her run around any more than she needs to."

Raven narrowed her eyes, her hands curling into fists.

Normally, she would have said something offensive and walked away rather than viewed as someone who tired easily. But right then, she knew Louis had the pills she needed, and ice. Ice sounded dreamy. Without saying another word, Raven turned on her heel and walked to the kitchen, doing her best to not run.

She shook with pain as she got down the stairs, leaning heavily on the banister, her legs jelly.

"Raven, how are you—"

Raven collapsed. "Ice...and..." she trailed off, unable to remember the names of the pills he had given to her.

Louis jumped into action, not giving her any judgment. He simply walked to the back of his kitchen and got what he needed, yelling for a kitchen servant to get some ice. Raven shoved the pills down, not bothering to count them before swallowing.

"Have you eaten anything today?"

Raven winced against the ice pressed to her side.

"Uh, I think I had some toast and ham?"

Louis sighed as he walked away. She crawled her way onto the stool beside the kitchen counter before laying her head down and closing her eyes. Louis slammed down a plate of food, jolting her awake.

"Eat."

"Won't some high-up snob miss this?"

Louis snorted. "I make so much food for them, and half of it is thrown out."

Raven ate slowly, savoring the flavors and ensuring her stomach didn't revolt. She hadn't had such fine food in a long time. Not even Aumont served food this well.

"I miss my friends," Raven mumbled through bites of sausage and eggs.

"Oh? You were allowed friends from where you come from? Isn't that a bad idea in your...line of work?"

"It is. But when you grow up together and go through the same thing, it's hard to not form bonds."

"And you formed a few?"

"Only three. Ella is the closest. She's almost as messed up as me. Though she went through a lot worse than I did. Came out stronger because of it. Then there's Mira, the definition of gorgeous. If you looked up that word in the dictionary, you'd find her portrait. She's so smart and misunderstood, but great at her job." Raven sighed, pushing the remaining food around on her plate.

"Who's the third?"

"Hmmm?" Raven slowly turned her eyes up to him, pressing the ice firmer against her side.

"You said you have three friends," Louis prompted.

"Right, Calla, my flower. She's a bookworm. Shy, brilliant. Calla means beauty. Did you know that?"

"Okay, you need something to focus you. You're talking like a sad drunk, and I don't think that will help you keep your position."

"Probably not, especially with his majesty, Prince Charming, watching everything I do."

"Prince Charming?" Louis chuckled.

"Prince Aleksander," Raven clarified.

"He's watching everything you do?" Louis crossed his arms and gave her his best fatherly stare. If she'd ever known what that used to look like, she imagined it was pretty close to this.

"Not in an overtly creepy way, but in an, I want to sleep with you sort of way. Only it's never going to work. I've sworn off men for life," Raven proclaimed as she took the other pill Louis handed her.

Raven shook herself.

"You were right about the pain drug, makes you loopy, but pain free." She swallowed it whole.

Raven waited for the pills to kick in some more before leaving the sanctuary of the kitchen and facing Prince Charming. She definitely felt more like herself with them in her system. What could she do under its influence when not in pain? Good thing it wasn't enchanted, she mused. Raven didn't get more time to think as Rowan and Prince Aleksander walked up to her in the dining hall.

"Sorry, he didn't have any crab right now. Hopefully, you still ate some of his delicious food?"

"We did. Now, I think I've deprived my aunt of her guards long enough. I know how to take care of myself in this palace," Prince Aleksander dismissed them, winking at Raven.

She turned around quickly and walked away.

*You're late.*

*It won't happen again.* Raven knew there was no room for excuses when serving the crown.

*Good. Status report.*

*Queen Lyanna's nephew arrived today—*

*Which one?* Lady Tremaine's face didn't display a single ounce of emotion.

*Which one? Prince Aleksander. How many are there?* Raven hoped they would not be coming soon.

*I see. Thank you, and the number does not concern you.*

*That's all I have.* Raven chewed her lip. *How are Ella and Mira? And Calla?*

*They're fine. Any other troubles?*

*I've been unable to gain the queen's trust. She asks for my advice, but doesn't respect my answers. She's always looking at me with quizzical eyes, as though she's trying to place me, or figure me out.*

*She's a very smart woman. There's a reason she's held her power so long despite how she gained the throne.*

Raven zeroed in on that comment, storing it away for further research.

*Gain her trust. That will be the only way for you to truly be successful in your assignment.*

*If you could tell me what I'm trying to learn for the crown, I would know what I need to pay attention to.*

*Everything. Pay attention to everything.* Lady Tremaine ended the scry.

Raven groaned as she flopped onto her bed. She wanted to go home. She looked at herself in the small mirror. Her black hair stood out in contrast to her pale skin, highlighting her chapped red lips. She ran her hands through her hair, taking the time to brush it out before bed. It used to soothe her as a child, or she thought it did. She didn't know where that memory came from, only that she was comforted when she closed her eyes and ran a brush through her short locks.

# CHAPTER EIGHT

## RAVEN

Weeks went by with nothing of importance and Raven was lulled into her routine. Training, guarding, taking a pill, gathering pointless information, and avoiding Prince Aleksander. Then she would go to bed, wake up, and repeat. Raven got nowhere with the queen. Every time she thought she was close, the queen would shut her out. She knew Charles, Bastien, and Rowan attended some meetings with her and the other units, and they did not invite her.

Prince Aleksander joined them now and then in the courtroom to watch his aunt and her subjects. This assignment was getting more and more boring by the day.

"Next!" Queen Lyanna was in a horrible mood. When was she not?

Raven was as well. Her injury had finally healed, but some movements still caused her discomfort. If she was honest, a lot of movements caused her discomfort.

The next person to step forward was a quiet man draped in robes. They were worn and covered in filth. Raven could tell, though, that they weren't old. Nothing was frayed and patches didn't cling to the fabric to keep it together like most commoners wore here. His outfit more resembled Prince Aleksander's travel garb. She had mistaken him for a guard because of it.

Raven stopped listening to his sob story as he moved closer. He had yet to reveal his hands. His eyes darted around the room instead of remaining focused on the queen. Everyone always kept their eyes on the queen, hoping that with her looking into theirs, she would feel more obligated to help them.

Most monarchs would.

Raven flicked her eyes to Rowan and the others. None of them had noticed. None of them saw the danger. There had probably never been a valid threat against the queen before. Of course, people wanted to kill her, all the time, hence having the best fighters as personal guards. However, no one was brazen enough to do so.

Until now.

Out of the corner of her eye, Raven caught Prince Aleksander. He was just as focused on the man before them. Analyzing everything. He was no fool either, apparently.

Raven stepped forward.

The man began to move his arms, his feet moving into an offensive stance.

"What do you think you're doing?" Queen Lyanna questioned.

Raven froze.

Queen Lyanna held her with glinting blue eyes, their fire burning through Raven.

The man froze as well, shifting into a defensive position. She wasn't naïve. She knew he was willing to die for his cause. He probably had some family at home who would benefit from his death and the successful assassination of the queen.

"Guard Raven, I asked you a—"

The assassin moved, and so did Raven.

She jumped in the way as soon as she saw the dagger. It flew straight at her, fast and true. But Raven was faster, and in that moment clarity replaced her pain as she was able to do what she did best. She blocked the knife with her armored arm, picked it up, and threw it directly at him.

She made sure not to kill him.

Her aim was excellent, impaling his foot.

It all happened in the space of a few seconds, and she longed for it to last forever.

No one moved.

Everyone looked at Raven, and she kept her eyes on the assassin. The only person to move was Prince Aleksander, going to the man and tying restraints around him.

"Why didn't you kill him?" Queen Lyanna demanded.

A groan rose to Raven's lips. She held it in, took a deep breath and kept her eyes on the man, refusing to look at the queen, whom she also wished was dead.

"I didn't want to kill him without interrogating him first, your majesty," Raven spoke through gritted teeth.

Queen Lyanna gave a mild sound of approval. "And how did you conclude he was going to kill me?"

Raven glanced around, unsure if the queen really wanted an answer in front of everyone. Queen Lyanna quirked a brow at her delay.

"Well, when he first walked in, it reminded me of when I mistook Prince Aleksander for a guard. Most importantly, what he's wearing would conceal weapons from guards, and his clothing only looks worn, but it isn't frayed or patched. Plus, he never showed us his hands," Raven trailed off.

"Sounds very logical to me. Yet everyone but you and my nephew didn't notice those things."

Raven stared at her feet. She hoped she hadn't gotten the boys into trouble. Queen Lyanna stood up and grabbed her gauntlet. She slid it on and prowled towards the man her nephew held captive.

"Your majesty, don't you want to know who sent him? I can get that information—" Raven stopped when Queen Lyanna drove her fist through his heart and twisted.

Prince Aleksander didn't flinch as the man dropped dead at his feet.

"I already know who my enemies are. Why let this one live?" She tossed her gauntlet at Raven. "Now, I'm going to retire. Guard Raven, you and Guard Rowan are going to do a sweep of all our guards and question the ones who let him through. Bastien and Charles, you're with me."

All of them snapped to attention, hurrying. Queen Lyanna ascended the stairs to her throne, stopping when she was level with Raven. Even though Raven towered over her, she still seemed small.

"And Raven," Queen Lyanna looked her up and down, her voice low, "thank you."

Raven bowed her head, not daring to look up until she knew the queen was no longer there. In fact, the only people left were Rowan, Prince Aleksander, and the dead assassin.

"I don't think I've ever heard my aunt thank anyone before." Prince Aleksander walked over to her and Rowan, avoiding the dead body. "Good job Raven. You really are more than a pretty face."

Raven frowned at him.

"You should see her at training," Rowan remarked, his eyes narrowed at her.

"What's on your mind, Rowan?" Raven walked over to him. The sooner he got it out of his system, the better.

"What he did wasn't as obvious as you implied. We would have noticed."

Raven cocked a hip and crossed her arms. "How many assassination attempts have you thwarted?" Rowan opened his mouth to respond, quickly closing it. "And how many people have you attempted to assassinate?"

Rowan shook his head, his brown eyes dark with storms.

"This is not a reflection of you, Bastien, or Charles. The three of you have trained your entire lives, but honestly until you get experience, you're never going to be ready. Even then, you're still not ready. It's a completely distinct thing to train for it, to *know* that the person you're fighting is a would-be-killer. It's not until you have no idea who the killer is that you truly have to be on the lookout."

Raven motioned to the room, taking all of it in. "That's why what he was doing was obvious to me. Too obvious, actually."

Raven turned away from them and walked to where the assassin lay.

"I understand the location. She's not heavily guarded, not that she ever is. Here it's only the four of us. If I were to try to take her out there," Raven motioned towards the throne, "I would have been the distraction. While someone else moved into position in a different location. He was screaming for us to catch him, even though there was no one else helping him." Raven paced the room, looking at all angles.

"Well, while you think about it, we need to go talk to some guards and let the maids clean up the body." Rowan pushed past Raven and Prince Aleksander, walking towards the main doors.

All the guards swore they hadn't seen him. He must have snuck in through a back door. They would never put her majesty's life in danger. They always checked everyone. Raven had to admit that it was a possibility. A small one, but a viable one. It was a better option for her than one of them missing the dagger and losing their life because of it. She had zero doubt about what their punishment would be. Queen Lyanna never showed mercy or forgiveness. She would not look at this situation lightly, nor should she. It was an enormous breach of their defenses. One they would have to remedy quickly.

By the end of the day, Raven was exhausted and in more pain than she could manage. She hadn't been able to sneak away for some medication. She knew she could probably get by without it, but she enjoyed how it made her steadier and.... invincible.

She relaxed the second she got to her room, her feet dragging on the floor. She stumbled for her nightstand and the glass jars it held. Raven grabbed a cup of water and held one in her hand.

"What a day." A candle was lit by her bed.

Raven jumped, spilling the water down the front of her uniform. "What the fuck? Why would you do that? What are you doing in my room?" Raven glared at Prince Aleksander.

"I thought I would stop by and see how you're holding up. Today was interesting."

"Maybe for you, I've had worse." She turned around and tossed the pill in her mouth, swallowing quickly.

"I'll bet you have." Prince Aleksander stood up and assessed her. For the first time, it wasn't as someone admiring her figure, but as someone who was trying to figure out who she was. "What did you swallow?"

"Nothing." She turned away from him as she walked over to her wardrobe.

"Right, just like whatever injury you have on your side is nothing." Prince Aleksander kept his face void of emotion. "You should be careful. Pills to help with pain can be addictive."

"Someone's observant." Raven didn't bother denying it. To do so would be foolish. "Really observant, actually. You should have missed those signs as well this morning. Yet, you saw all of them. How does a prince know what an assassin looks like?" Raven glanced over her shoulder at him.

"I'm a very observant prince." He shrugged.

"Rowan is observant. You spotted him from experience." Raven pulled out her nightclothes and began taking off her armor. She didn't care that he was in her room, or that he was watching. She wanted answers, and she would get them this way. Raven turned her back to him as she stretched, loosening stiff muscles.

"I have the same training you do," he offered.

Raven snorted. "I doubt you had the same training."

It was then that Raven pulled off her tunic, showing Prince Aleksander all of her scars. The criss-crossed ones that had silenced Rowan, and the same scars that Jason had kissed in the night. Her tattoo contrasted against her pale skin, looking alive in the candlelight while hiding her enchanter's mark.

"You're right, I don't think I had the same training," he whispered.

Raven snapped her head sideways. His eyes were downcast enough to give her privacy. "Please spare me the pity. Believe me when I say that I've been given enough." She made the mistake of turning her body to face him. All she wore were her pants and breast band, her stomach, and her recently healed injury, on full display.

"When was the last time that was properly examined?" Prince Aleksander demanded, striding over to examine her. She'd never seen him upset before, his ice-blue eyes clouded with storms the closer he got.

"Well, I've done the best I can from my angle. Susan usually examines it for infection, but she's been ill, and I can't have anyone see me in the infirmary, so it's been a few days." Raven acknowledged. Though she hadn't had Susan help her at all, Raven didn't want to put her in a position to lie, plus...Raven liked to do things on her own.

"May I take a look? Why haven't you properly treated it?" He led Raven into her washroom, unceremoniously peeling away the sweaty gauze.

"I didn't receive this lovely thing in the line of duty. Well, it was, but not while I was guarding your aunt. I don't need to give her any reason to dismiss me."

"How did you get it?" Prince Aleksander was gentle as he assessed her wound, his fingers sending shocks of heat through her body. Her nerves and magic melted like butter at his touch.

"Rowan was showing me around Aslar when a girl screamed. I was foolish and only brought small daggers with me to fight the men. One of them was lucky." Raven shrugged, not seeing the point of lying to the prince. He already had enough information to bury her. What was one more?

"And the men?" he growled.

"Dead or in jail. Rowan and I didn't wait around. I almost passed out from blood loss." Raven flinched against the wet cloth. "You could get both of us dismissed if you said anything."

"I like Rowan. He's a talented guard, and a good friend. I've known him since I was two. Even though I'm her nephew doesn't mean I'm obligated to tell her anything. Especially when I don't agree. Plus, I'm still trying to woo you," he joked halfheartedly.

Raven went scarlet as he smiled. "Right, well, thank you for cleaning my healed stab wound." She walked away quickly, her arms crossed over her chest.

"Now look who's all shy. A minute ago you had no problem stripping in front of me, so long as it suited your needs."

Raven cast a glance his way.

"I know when I'm being played," he laughed. She'd never heard him genuinely laugh. It was light, and sent a whole new rush of sensations spinning through her magic, heating her up.

"Well then," Raven walked over to where he leaned against her door. She got close to him, stopping just inches away. She raised up on her toes and rested a hand on his chest, angling her head until her lips were just a breath away from his. She looked into his eyes and down to his lips. Her magic sang in her ears, pleading to touch him. "You should also know when someone isn't interested," Raven whispered. She slowly moved him off her door and opened it for him.

Prince Aleksander grinned as he leaned against it. "Oh, I do, and you are clearly attracted to me. It's only a matter of time before you're the one going after me," he whispered in Trudelian. He rested a hand on her shoulder, lighting more of her body on fire. Raven reined in the urge to set her hand on his and press it against her cheek.

"Good night, Prince Aleksander," she responded in Trudelian, stepping away from him.

"What? No more Prince Charming?" He walked backwards, spreading his arms wide in question. A small smile played on his face as Raven closed the door.

She fell asleep the moment she laid down, the covers still pulled down.

*She was running through the palace again, always trying to outrun whatever chased her. Raven was dead if it reached her. This time, the dream morphed, and it was no longer a nightmare. A boy was chasing her, his laughter echoing down the hall as they played. She was just as small as her nightmares.*

*"Wait up," she hollered.*

*She kept tripping over her dress. Why did she have to wear a dress while her friends got to wear pants and tunics? She could never keep them clean, and everyone always got mad at her. She didn't want everyone to get mad. Everyone was already scary enough, mad enough, without her getting her nice dress dirty.*

*"Wait up, Rowan." She ran around a corner and there he was.*

*Well, not the Rowan she knew now, but Rowan as a child. Or what he may have looked like as a child.*

Raven sat up quickly, her mind ripping her from the dream. What was that? Her head pounded as she tried to convince herself that it was, in fact, a dream.

Raven skipped breakfast, opting for the first time in a long time to relax in bed. Her waist was a dull ache since it had been properly cleaned. She rolled over and took some pills, noticing she was getting low.

Raven frowned.

She had already asked Louis for some five days ago. He wouldn't want to give her more any time soon. Especially since this should have lasted for ten days. She could always steal from him...no...she wouldn't do that.

Susan bustled in, not waiting for Raven to open the door. "Late morning?"

"I thought I would skip breakfast," Raven commented. She got out of bed and sat next to her window to gaze outside. A light drizzle of rain fell as autumn slowly gave way to winter. She hoped it would snow soon. She loved the cold and the weather it brought.

"At least have your coffee." Susan handed her another cup.

"Always." Raven sipped more as they started their daily routine.

Raven let her mind rest and drift away. Susan moved around her, putting her armor on and making sure she was set for the day. Raven lifted her arms to her hair, flinching at the movement.

"Let me." Susan brought over a chair.

Raven sat down, twisting her hands together. No one touched her hair. Ever.

"Prince Aleksander was seen leaving your room late last night," she commented, her fingers swift.

"Nothing happened. We were discussing the events from earlier in the day at court," Raven replied, her eyes trained on the mirror, watching Susan's nimble hands walk through her hair.

Susan replied, but Raven had tuned her out. Instead, she thought about what having Prince Aleksander's hand on her shoulder had done to her. She wasn't sure if it was only yesterday, or if his annoying confidence was breaking through her wall, but what she was sure of was that her wall wasn't going anywhere.

*"Jason...have you ever thought...ever thought about—" Raven stopped, biting her lower lip as she changed her mind. She wouldn't ask.*

*"Thought about what?" Jason moved closer to her in bed, his hand lightly trailing up and down her arm before holding her hand.*

*"Thought of having a life outside of this house? What it might be like...I guess? It's silly."* Raven laughed nervously, trying to pretend it wasn't important.

*"I have. Not seriously...at least not until recently."* Jason gently pulled her chin up to look at him. *"I would want you there with me. Living out in a forest, or near one. Someplace completely separated from the world, a place where we could be us and not have to worry about anything."*

*"That sounds like a fairytale."* Raven curled into him, closing her eyes.

"Raven? Hello? Anyone there?"

Raven looked up in the mirror, locking eyes with Susan.

"Sorry Susan, I got lost. What were you saying?"

"Never you mind, it wasn't important, only gossip. Now, your hair is done and you have to go." Susan moved away quickly, her brown eyes downcast.

Raven flushed. "I'm sorry for not listening to you. I promise I will next time."

The boys arrived at the training field right as she did, all of them laughing. They broke off into their normal pairs, starting off with stretching in the dewy grass.

"We missed you at breakfast," Rowan spoke as they spared.

"Did you?" Raven kept her face still. "I slept in."

"Of course we missed you."

Raven and Rowan navigated each other easily, their breath fogging in the air.

"Rowan, did you play here as a child?"

"My dad used to be a Royal Guard for King Stewart, so I would visit. Why?"

"Just wondering." Raven didn't pry any further, fixating on her dream and not paying any attention to her form as they fought.

"I thought you said she was good."

Raven snapped out of her thoughts as Prince Aleksander walked over, fog from the coast curled around the training grounds fighting rings. The grass was covered in a thick layer of dew, making the floor of their rings slick.

"She looks like a flailing novice." His hair was pulled out of his face, his two braids still perfectly intact.

"I didn't sleep well," Raven muttered. "I'll be better soon. I need the caffeine to kick in."

"Tell me it was the thought of me keeping you restless," Prince Aleksander smiled.

"And you expect me to call you Prince Charming?" Raven snickered, walking away from him.

"Come on, if you're the best, prove it. Right now. No more of this caffeine deprivation excuse."

"Okay, who do you want to see me fight?"

All three men stepped away.

"Me, of course."

Raven eyed him. He was serious. He smiled at her, resting his hands lightly by his side, his eyes looking over every inch of her. This time he was analyzing his opponent, looking for weaknesses.

"Fine, what form?"

"The best kind," Prince Aleksander stretched, "hand to hand."

Raven pulled out her swords and tossed them to Rowan. She took off her armor. Prince Aleksander only wore loose fitting clothing, and she would let nothing hinder her. As she got everything off, all of them looked at her with wide eyes.

"You boys are looking at me like I've grown an extra limb," Raven snarled.

"I better understand why the prince is so taken with you," Charles heckled as Prince Aleksander met her on the wet training field.

"The thing is Charles, I appreciated her for having all of her armor on. You need to see her without her armor to feel safe admiring her." Prince Aleksander spoke softly, his brow furrowed.

Raven flipped Charles off as she looked at the prince. She hadn't expected him to defend her. Raven remained silent as they faced each other, finding her focus for the first time all morning.

Everything fell away from her mind as she sunk into herself. One second, she was Raven and the next; she was Snow White. Almost Snow. She didn't want to fully show everything.

Raven got into her fighting stance, waiting for the prince to make his move. He was no longer Prince Aleksander. He was her opponent, the person she was going to bring down. Prince Aleksander moved after a minute, going for her face.

They were evenly matched. For now.

It was evident in the way he moved.

Prince Aleksander may be arrogant and annoying, but at least he could back up his words with actions. Both of them fought viciously against each other, working hard to get in blows through the other's defenses. Sometimes one of them would break through. Quickly followed by the other, finding a way in.

Raven wondered how long it would continue. Neither one of them would willingly give up a win.

Charles was cheering them on from the side. Bastien and Rowan remained silent. Raven knew Rowan was silent out of concern. Her injury took the moment to pinch her side, reminding her of its presence.

Her mind lost track of everything but her heart beating and the power in her muscles.

Eventually, she noticed the shift.

Prince Aleksander moved a little slower, and Raven pressed her advantage. He was good, but she was better. She couldn't show them how much better, especially not her magic, but she could give them a taste more. Maybe then Prince Charming would respect her. Her heart raced at the thought.

Prince Aleksander froze for one second to catch his breath, and Raven pounced.

She may have been tired or distracted earlier, but she certainly wasn't anymore. Her magic rushed through her veins, coating her bones and fueling her. She twisted him around to his knees and wrapped an arm around his neck, while the other rested on the opposite side of his head.

If she pulled hard both ways, she would snap his neck.

Prince Aleksander held his hands up in defeat, only putting them down once Raven stepped away from him.

"Most women I've fought would have lost on purpose to not embarrass their prince." Prince Aleksander rubbed his neck.

"I'm not most women, and you're not my prince," Raven replied. "And if they lost on purpose, then they did you and themselves a disservice." She picked up her armor and began strapping it on.

"How so?" He followed her, picking up some of the armor to help her.

Raven paused, studying him. He really wanted to be told.

"By letting you win, they didn't show you where you were flawed in your training, which slowed your abilities. It also ruined their self-confidence and probably made them look weaker to the men they worked with." Raven lightly flinched when Rowan walked up behind her and helped her strap on her breastplate and back guard.

She lowered her head in thanks before sliding in her blades.

"You really think that because they let me win a couple of fights that all of that happened?"

He wasn't being sarcastic or rude, as expected. Most men would have been offended by her judgment. Instead, she found curiosity and concern.

"I do. Imagine how much better you could have been if you had learned from every fight you lost, not just those lost to men. Imagine how much more respect those women would have gotten for not being afraid to beat their prince rather than kowtowing to him."

Raven adjusted her armor, making sure it sat correctly.

Bastien pulled out his mace and swung.

He forced Raven into a defensive position. She got her short swords out in time to block his sword. Raven held them for a second, pausing long enough to see Rowan move toward them. She shook her head. Raven moved tactfully, avoiding Bastien and tiring him out. After a minute, she broke through and pinned him to the ground, her blade at his neck.

"Better, but still dead." Raven spoke through labored lungs. She sat on his chest as the others walked over. "Now, do you mind telling me what that was about? I thought we had gained trust in each other."

"I would if I knew you were showing us everything. Someone your age shouldn't be this good, or this cold. You should have had an emotional reaction to being attacked like that. Any of us would have." Bastien spat.

"You think if I lost control of my emotions that you would trust me more? Don't you think it would make you trust me less if you thought I was hysterical every time something surprising happened? What good does that do except make you question if I'm fit for this position?" Raven leaned closer to him. "You will never see me lose control." It was a truth she held close to her heart. She could never allow herself to lose control, not of her emotions, not of her magic. She would never do that again.

"You're eighteen—"

"I'm a trained assassin, Bastien."

His green eyes widened, mouth dropping open. The others remained silent.

"I said nothing for a reason. Now you're clearly freaked out." Raven got off of him.

"Freaked out? I'm not...freaked out." Bastien's face turned scarlet.

Raven turned to the others. "As if you didn't know. Come on, what woman my age is as skilled as me without going through the type of training it takes to be an assassin?"

"None. It's nothing to fear, either. If she was going to kill any of you, she would have already." Prince Aleksander helped Bastien stand. "I think the three of you should take this chance to learn from her. It's not every day you get to learn from an assassin." He looked over at Raven, slumping his shoulders when she didn't thank him for defending her.

Raven wondered how far she could push it with them. Shrugging, she looked each one of them in the eye. "If you really want to learn how to fight like me, then we need to find an underground fighting ring. It's how I learned to fight dirty."

*Raven smiled at the guard, candlelight touching his shoulder as he let her inside the warehouse. It didn't surprise her that an underground fighting tournament was hosted in the dump of a warehouse on the docks. She was, however, surprised by its condition inside. Plush seats circled the makeshift stadium, surrounding a giant caged arena. Vendors selling enchanted potions and weapons, as well as exquisite jewelry and clothes, lined the walls. The rich and noble mingled with potion dealers and courtesans. A crime lord chatted up an earl's daughter. The earl's daughter laughed, lightly touching his shoulder, her black gown sparkling in the candlelight.*

*Raven had never understood why people loved to watch others beat each other up. It disgusted her that someone would willingly sell their body to be a spectacle for someone else's profit. Sometimes even die for it. This group had a 'no rule' policy during some matches. If she hadn't been on an assignment to kill one of the fighters, she would have been tempted to shut the whole place down by alerting one of the king's advisors.*

*Announcers came out to inform everyone that the fighting was about to commence. Raven took her seat three rows from the front. She wanted to see exactly how her target fought. She leaned back, her muscles tense as the fighting began. Raven wasn't comfortable in her dress. It fit too tightly around her waist, constricting her lungs. The floor-length gown would be a hindrance for her, but Lady Tremaine had insisted. She needed to blend in as a member of the noble class, not as an assassin, and certainly not as a criminal.*

*Fighter after fighter went into the arena and got the shit beat out of them. And the audience cheered. They stood up and yelled at the fighters who didn't do enough, didn't injure their opponent enough.*

*It was deafening.*

*Raven crossed her arms. They were halfway through the night and her target would come up soon. She wondered what her target had done to warrant the crown ordering their death. Whatever it was, it was bad.*

*The fighters took a break, and the audience was entertained by jesters. Raven took the time to survey the arena and review the fighting. It had been very sloppy. She could tell that most were acting in the fights. Some of them she knew were very real, and involved real fighters. She saw their scars, their broken noses, and their burns. They were the gladiators everyone was there for. Everyone else in between was purely for show, keeping the blood boiling and the money flowing.*

*Someone gripped her shoulder, a head with a clown face painted on it growled in her ear.*

*Raven acted on instinct.*

*She grabbed the clown and threw him into the wooden arena's cage. Everyone fell silent as the clown stood up. Raven gathered her composure, kneading her magic in, blood racing in her ears.*

*"What the hell? You want an actual fight, bitch?" the clown screamed in her face.*

*Raven remained silent, staring at his very wide, frightened brown eyes.*

*"You think you can do whatever you want? Well then, come on, bring it on, let's see what you've got," the clown man said.*

*The stage master ran out into the middle of the arena. Raven noted his excitement. He was practically jumping out of his skin. She moved out of her defensive stance, straightening her dress.*

*"Next time, I would recommend you don't grab your patrons." Raven sat down. She would not be baited.*

*The entire room erupted in boos. Everyone wanted to see a 'noble' fight. Even the nobility.*

*"Come up here. I promise my fighter will be gentle. Let's give these people a show. Let's show them that even the nobility can fight in the ring," the stage master's voice echoed.*

*The clown had moved into the arena, staring Raven down. His knuckles clenched white as he paced, chest puffed up. She already knew how she would win the fight.*

*"Come on, let's fight—"*

*Raven sighed. It would only be worse once she beat him.*

*The audience chanted, "Fight! Fight!" Raven didn't know what to do.*

*The choice, however, was decided for her when the crowd shoved her out of her seat.*

*Everyone cheered when she put her hands on the wooden beams and got help from men to lift her up. The stage master opened the door and let her in.*

*"Do I get to change at least?" Raven walked to a corner.*

*"I think this makes it more interesting, don't you?" He smiled, looking her over.*

*She sliced a cutting look at him, wishing she could kill him instead. All the crown had to do was ask.*

*"It looks like we're about to have an impromptu fight for all of you! Get your bets in fast. Who will win? The Clown or The Noble Lady? Each one with their own set of skills. The Clown who has trained to fight or The Noble Lady who has been trained on how to take the perfect sip of tea? I think I know where I would bet."*

*Raven looked at the roof. If only she could have bet on herself. She wasn't about to lose a fight with someone who only pretended they knew how to fight. Those eyes behind the paint had been scared, and if she was close enough, she would bet they still were.*

*After a few minutes, the stage master began their fight. Raven hung back, waiting for the clown to come to her. He moved, instantly giving away his intention at the point of his toes. Raven dodged, moving at the right second so that the clown crashed into the wooden frame. The audience quieted. This was not how someone of the noble class fought. She needed to end it quickly and easily.*

*That was the plan, anyway.*

*Raven was about to end the fight when he withdrew a dagger, and everything changed.*

*The fighter changed. His mannerisms were more threatening. Raven assessed he wasn't a professional fighter, but definitely someone who had fought in the street. A low level man for hire. The crowd felt the shift. Raven sensed all of them leaning forward in their seats.*

*Then the proper fight began.*

*Raven let her instinct kick in and sing in her ear. She disarmed the fighter and held him at knifepoint in under ten seconds.*

*It was as though the entire warehouse was an enchanter's magic waiting to implode.*

*"The Noble Lady wins," the stage master stuttered in disbelief.*

*Raven stood over his clown.*

*The magic burst and the crowd erupted, chanting her name, 'Noble Lady'.*

*Raven gazed out at them, her heart pounding as she soaked in the praise. No one had ever cheered for her before. No one had been happy for her to win a fight. But they were. They relished it. Craved it.*

*Raven craved it.*

*Now she understood. The fighters fought because if they won, they were adored. Praised. Liked, maybe even loved.*

*The clown remained on the ground, curled up in a ball, awaiting their punishment.*

*"If you ever want a job, talk to me." The stage master handed Raven a card. She tucked it into her dress before leaning down to the clown.*

*"Now who's the bitch?"*

*She stood up and walked away, jumping out of the arena and strutting up the stadium and out of the warehouse.*

*She needed to breathe. Oh, how she needed to breathe. Her magic danced along her veins. Her assignment could wait another night. Tonight, she would let herself have this.*

# CHAPTER NINE

## RAVEN

"Raven, come with us," Queen Lyanna summoned her after court ended.

Raven paused. This was when the queen and her Royal Guard units went behind hidden doors with a select few other members of her inner circle. The meetings never lasted long, but they had always forced Raven to sit outside and wait like a lapdog.

The room was incredibly dull. Nothing adorned the long room. A table stretched the length of the room, where each person took a seat and looked at the queen. This had probably been King Stewart's war room, now stripped to nothing.

"Today was better than I had hoped. Not too many complaints, though we still need to work on that. Make sure they divert all complaints about food and taxes to the men I have appointed in overseeing that region. I don't have seven of them for nothing. I put them in charge and pay them well to do more than sit on their asses all day and sleep with every maid that walks past them. Any suggestions on that?"

The boys and everyone else remained silent, looking at their hands.

"Raven?" Queen Lyanna growled.

"Perhaps your seven minions could be given time to meet with those from their regions before seeing you? If the problem can't be resolved by them, then it goes to you. If it's something trivial or not worthy of your time, that lord is punished or loses his region altogether. I think that once that happens to one, the others will not be so lazy with their time."

Queen Lyanna leaned forward, her dark blue eyes narrowing the longer Raven spoke.

"Interesting idea, but what did you call my advisors?" Her hand rested on her chin, her fingers curling up.

"The seven minions...they're known for following their leader's orders and being incredibly loyal to them." Raven paused, looking up at the queen's seven pointed crown instead of her calculating eyes that seemed to see right into her. "I'm sorry if I offended you."

"You didn't. It's entirely accurate. I'm curious about where you thought of the name." Queen Lyanna's gaze held Raven.

"It just came to me." Raven racked her brain trying to think of a better answer, especially since it seemed to be important to the queen that she answer correctly.

"Raven, where did you grow up? I'm realizing that I know very little about you."

"I remember nothing before the age of seven. I was told..." Raven gathered herself. "I was told I had a bad horse accident and hit my head. So I remember nothing."

"I see."

Raven nodded, casting a glance at Rowan. His brow furrowed, his eyes darting back and forth between them.

"I think we're good for today. Rowan and Raven, I have an assignment for the two of you. Princess Arianna is going for a horse ride tomorrow with Prince Aleksander. I want the two of you to be their guards."

Rowan and Raven looked at each other.

"Your majesty, given the recent attempt on your life, is that the—"

"Given the recent attempt on my life, I would like to ensure the safety of my daughter and beloved nephew. That is why I'm asking two of my most capable guards to look over them." Queen Lyanna walked out, not waiting for any response.

Raven and Rowan stretched as they prepared themselves the following afternoon in the stable. "This is a pointless assignment. Prince Aleksander can protect both of them. Why send us away?" Raven questioned.

"Maybe Aleks requested it?"

Raven snorted. "Maybe, but the princess hates us. She thinks we're incompetent. She would never agree to go without her unit."

"Well, I guess we'll find out." Rowan nodded.

Raven followed his motion and found both royals waiting outside the stable. Princess Arianna stood with her arms crossed. Prince Aleksander looked even better in his riding leathers and soft black tunic. His white hair was pulled halfway up, keeping his eyesight clear for the ride.

"Have fun," Bastien muttered before he and Charles left for their rounds.

Princess Arianna stormed off the second they reached them, heading for her horse. The stables were large with a second floor for the boys that worked there to sleep in should anyone need to grab a horse in the night. Rows upon rows of horses lined the stables. Prince Aleksander stayed near Rowan, watching his cousin. Raven wondered if she had always been this way, a perfect replica of her mother.

"Where did you want to go riding, Ari?" Prince Aleksander asked as they took their horses from the stable hands. His black stallion muffled his hair. "I know, I've been gone. A beautiful lady has grabbed my attention." He laughed, swinging up onto his horse.

"Why don't you lead the way, cousin? You'll get your way either way," Princess Arianna replied, her eyes narrowed at Raven.

Raven remained silent as Prince Aleksander led them out.

They trotted over cobblestones through Aslar, weaving their way through the crowd of noblemen and women. Raven and Rowan remained on high alert. If something was going to happen, this was the place to do it. They paired up, Rowan next to the princess, and Raven with Prince Charming. Thankfully, he knew enough to remain silent and continue on their path. Once they got to the outer gates, it was a different story. Sloping hills greeted them, and in the far off distance, the forest that bordered snow-capped mountains loomed before them. It was a sight Raven drank in like a beggar starved of water. Dark clouds rolled high in the sky, holding onto their rain and casting the earth in dark tones of green.

*"What about this place?"*

*Raven looked over at Jason. His brown hair settled on his shoulders, his cheeks flushed from the wind gliding over his face.*

*"What about it?" Raven asked, gazing at the meadows brushing up against an imposing forest with waist high grass.*

*"As a place to live. There's a village not too far away for supplies, but we could build a house over there and spend our lives here. It's perfect, and no one could sneak up on us."*

*Raven moved her horse closer to Jason's. Blood still glistened on his face in the sun's dimming rays. She leaned over and kissed him, ignoring the metallic taste of blood on her lips. Blood that she knew didn't belong to either of them. Hell, she wasn't even sure if it was from his lips or hers.*

*"It's perfect, but let's go before those guards catch up to us, huh?" She smiled, winking, before taking off.*

Raven shook herself as Prince Aleksander broke into a gallop. Joy sparked in Raven's eyes as she got to ride for fun. The four of them raced for the forest, the horses enjoying the open ground. She gave her horse free rein and closed her eyes for the briefest of moments. Her mind emptied, and there was only her horse, the air, and the ground beneath her. If she could have flown, she would have. The magic in her blood sang a pure melody, simply happy to be there with her. It built with her joy, pressing against her skin. She would have to enchant soon, Raven thought. Her fingers itched with the need to release her power. She pulled it back, promising to use it soon. Their horses slowed down too soon, but even she knew that galloping into a forest was a bad idea.

"Aleks, we're switching," Princess Arianna commanded.

"You want to lead?" he asked.

"No, I want to speak with Guard Raven. So we're switching guards."

Raven flicked her eyes over to him, waiting for the protest, for the sly speech that would get him what he wanted. But it never came. Instead, he moved his horse ahead as Rowan trotted to him, Raven waiting for the princess to catch up.

They rode in silence, the princess purposefully keeping their horses slower. Raven watched the men get to an uncomfortable distance.

"Your highness, I respect the need for privacy, but I must insist that we stay close enough for my partner to get to me, or I to him quickly should any danger arise."

"When you say partner, are you speaking about Guard Rowan or my cousin?"

"Guard Rowan, of course, your highness. If I gave you the impression that anything unprofessional is happening between me and your cousin—"

"You didn't," she interrupted. "But I know him, and if he thinks you're getting in trouble because of him, he may slow down and focus on someone else."

Raven opened her mouth to thank her.

"Someone important and of an acceptable standing."

"Of course, your highness."

"You didn't think I was doing it as a kindness, did you?"

"Your highness—" Raven blushed. This was not the conversation she wanted to have with a fifteen-year-old.

"We aren't living in the twelfth century. I wouldn't tell my mother."

"I—" Raven floundered under the young woman's scathing eyes.

"I am ordering you to tell me. Everyone thinks you're a cold, heartless bitch. It's probably why my mother hasn't ripped your heart out yet."

"I have no heart." Those words dropped into her. She wanted to feel something again. But ever since she had poured all of her hatred into that potion...that black twisted potion...she hadn't felt much. Her intention had been so strong while creating it, she wasn't sure how long it would be until she could truly feel emotions again. She had been so exhausted...she'd slept for days afterward.

"If you want to be successful here, you'll need to remain that cold, heartless bitch and stay away from my cousin."

"Of course, Princess Arianna." Raven bent her head forward in a bow.

She looked up to see Prince Aleksander and Rowan riding back to them. The two were laughing as they approached.

"Have a nice girl chat, cousin?" Prince Aleksander asked.

Princess Arianna smiled at him. Relief poured through Raven at the conversation change.

"Right, now that that's over, I have a proposal." He looked between the two women.

He sighed dramatically.

"Raven, I propose a race. After you beat me the other day, I've been looking for a way to pay you back."

"You think a horse race will redeem you?" Raven quirked a brow.

"In Trudel, a horse race is the highest testament of skill and endurance." Prince Aleksander stood up high in his seat.

Raven tilted her head. "Fine. Where are we racing?"

"Through here." Prince Aleksander motioned towards a large animal path that would allow for two horses. "If I win, I get bragging rights—"

"And if I win?"

"I'll leave you alone." He shivered.

"Deal."

Raven walked her horse over to him, lining them up together. Rowan went to the side, looking towards the sky as he sighed.

"All right, whoever gets to the giant oak at the end and back here first wins." Rowan raised his arm up.

The moment he cut his arm down, they were off.

Raven's stallion charged down the path, his golden mane flying. She looked to her right, smiling at Prince Charming. They were evenly matched. Again. Raven spurred her steed on, pushing him. The trees blurred past her as wind whipped her hair.

She faced forward and barely saw the rope fly across their path.

Raven had enough time to shout a warning before her steed sent her flying as he stumbled over the line.

Raven found the ground quickly, watching it as she spun her body through the air to land on her feet. Her heart raced as she grabbed her weapons from their sheaths, skidding on her boots, burning her hands on impact. She looked up to see her horse recover before the men attacked.

Nine shadows descended from the towering trees, their faces covered in black fabric. Her eyes flicked over to Rowan and Princess Arianna. Four men surrounded them as Rowan pulled out his sword and Princess Arianna had, to Raven's shock, her own short blade.

Six of the shadows surrounded her. Her magic surged, singing to enchant her blades, to activate the dormant spells interwoven into them and slice through her opponents like ripe apples. *Shhh...*Raven hushed, shaping it into a small loaf. *Not now.* They were decent enough as fighters, but as soon as Raven took their measure, she knew these assailants were outmatched.

Prince Aleksander joined her moments later. She shook her head as both of them fought their opponents, backs pressed together. They were seamless together. Raven's magic rose, singing as it tried to join in. Raven held it back before focusing on the sound of steel clashing against steel. She broke through each opponent's defenses, less worried about keeping them alive than getting out safely.

Prince Aleksander was as quick to disarm and kill the men as she was. In what felt like minutes, but was probably seconds, they had dispatched them all. Raven hadn't felt such a strong connection with someone while fighting since she had been around Ella. Both of them did a full circle, weapons drawn, ensuring there would be no more surprises before taking off towards Rowan and Princess Arianna.

Only two men remained.

The moment they saw Raven and Prince Aleksander coming toward them, they fled.

"Everyone okay?" Raven spun around, her blood covered blades out and ready.

"Yes, though so much for going for a long ride." Princess Arianna sighed as she put her short blade away. "I guess it's not just my mother they're after."

"Let's get you home." Rowan led her to her horse.

Their ride was swift and silent. The sun had crested the mountain's tips, their shadows racing ahead of them. The storm clouds still held onto the rain, but darkened as they raced against time. Once Aslar was in view, Rowan took out a small black horn.

Its roar echoed over the hills, and Raven was sure up to the palace. It was three long blasts, each one longer than the last. The princess was in danger, clear a path, send guards. As the gates opened, Rowan didn't slow down to wait for them to open all the way. Instead, he got through with enough space for his feet. Princess Arianna followed closely behind, with Prince Aleksander and Raven in the back.

Raven tried to not stare at everyone as they passed. Guards lined the road, holding everyone back until they got by, their horses' hooves the only sound. All the commoners and noblemen alike looked at them with varying degrees of anger, fear, or concern. Though she wanted to avert her eyes and stare at her horse, Raven kept her head turning. She could only imagine the type of chaos that had ensued after Rowan blew the horn's call. All the guards would have rushed to clear a path. By any means necessary. And she was sure she didn't want to know what actions had been taken.

Queen Lyanna was nowhere to be found when they got to the palace, but Princess Arianna's unit waited for her.

"The ones we killed are still in the forest. Bastien, Charles, and I will go with you to retrieve their bodies, Guard Zachary," Rowan ordered when one guard glared at him.

None of them moved, waiting for the princess.

"Did I stutter? I believe I gave you a direct order, Guard Zachary."

"Sir." The head guard bowed his head before going to get his horse. Bastien and Charles mounted theirs. The remaining three shifted their positions, not once taking their eyes off the princess.

"Are you coming, cousin?" Princess Arianna questioned as she reached the stables.

"I'll go in a bit, Ari. I want to make sure I'm not injured before going to my room."

"We'll escort you," she asserted.

"No, you're going to go to your room and find a good way to calm down. I don't know how many times your life has been in danger. But I have been in enough to recognize that all of that adrenaline pumping through you is going to leave your body quickly. When that happens, my dear cousin, you're going to want to be in your room relaxing." Prince Aleksander hugged her.

"Aleks—"

"I'll be fine. I know from personal experience that Guard Raven can watch out for those she's entrusted to protect."

Raven did her best to not roll her eyes.

Prince Aleksander kissed Princess Arianna's forehead and patted her on the head before turning away from her.

"What was that? You're not injured, I would have noticed," Raven spoke before could stop herself.

"You noticed, huh?" He smiled. Prince Aleksander lightly held her arm and steered her towards his room. "You're right though, I'm not injured.

However, you're still recovering, and I want to look at it before you do another half-assed job of cleaning your injury and taking more pills because of it."

Raven glared at him. Even so, she followed, knowing that she had to at least make sure he made it to his room before she went to hers. Adrenaline and magic throbbed in her veins, heating her up. Prince Aleksander's fresh snow scent didn't help matters...

*"You need to calm down." Jason analyzed her as she bounced on the balls of her feet.*

*"Do you realize what I did? What I got away with?" Raven's eyes were wide with triumph, her magic sparking around her hands.*

*At fifteen, she had killed her target, gotten trapped, and then escaped, all with no one figuring out who she was. Jason hadn't been able to get into the room where they had tortured her. Not to say that he hadn't tried. The bruises on his hands and arms proved he had thrown his body over and over against the door.*

*"Yes, I heard everything. Raven, you need to calm down, otherwise, your body is going to crash from the adrenaline loss, and as an enchanter, you can't afford—"*

*"You mean like this?" Raven stood up on her toes and kissed him.*

*It was quick and light, just daring enough for her. She stepped away from him, her face red. Raven hadn't kissed him before. She'd wanted to for weeks, but had never been brazen enough. Until now. She kissed him again, wrapping her arms around his neck as he picked her up and pressed her against him.*

Raven closed her eyes and tried to still her beating heart. Prince Aleksander had her lie down on his bed so that he could examine her wound and clean it. So there she was, lying on his bed, with her tunic off, and pants splattered with blood. Her arms dangled over her eyes. At first, she had tried to admire the wooden ceiling of his room, and then the stone fireplace against the wall. And then she tried to admire the books that lined his bookshelves. But her eyes kept wandering to him, so she'd had to close them.

"I'm an enchanter Raven, if you would like for me to grab one of my potions and help the wound, I can."

Raven looked at him. "You're an enchanter?"

He nodded, white hair falling free.

"And your aunt doesn't care?"

"Not about me being an enchanter. It's not as if she can do anything about it."

"Thank you for the offer, but no thank you." She leaned back, closing her eyes again. He wouldn't have the healing serum Calla had developed. It was the only thing Raven knew of that could heal an enchanter without tainting their magic. Raven couldn't let him see her worry, and his blue eyes were too hypnotizing at the moment. She didn't want to tell him she too, was worried about how long it was taking this wound to heal and that she had liked what the pills did to her.

"Are you sure? I'm very good at healing potions," he reassured her.

"I'm positive. I don't use potions." She took slow, steady breaths. She could do this. She could calm herself down. Her magic slowly settled in her core.

"Suit yourself." Prince Aleksander returned to cleaning her wound. "You can open your eyes, by the way. I'm all done."

"I'm attempting to calm down," Raven replied.

She cracked open an eye to find Prince Aleksander looking down at her, his hair completely free of its binding, fell over his face. His blue eyes looked at hers, and only her eyes. He consistently confused her. He ogled her openly, yet when she was exposed, he respected her and treated her with a reverence she hadn't felt before. His hands were gentle as they ran over her skin, eliciting an excited trill from her magic. Ever since Jason, she hadn't allowed herself to be with anyone. It felt too intimate, but she knew this would be anything but intimate. It would be a chance to have a short fling that would let her release some stress and have some fun.

"Oh, screw it." Raven pulled his tunic, pulling him down to her as she kissed him. Her magic burst in glee, singing in harmony with his heartbeats, wanting to dance with him.

"Raven, what are you doing?" Prince Aleksander broke their kiss and supported himself on his arms, encasing her beneath him. His face was inches from hers, and Raven's magic spun around her veins at the touch of his lips.

"I was kissing you." Raven sighed. "Look, I need to calm down. You need to calm down, and honestly, what better way is there? So—"

Raven didn't get the chance to say anything else as Prince Aleksander kissed her. He pulled her onto his enormous bed, laying down next to her, not once breaking contact as his hand trailed down her side. Her hands twirled through his hair. She ran her nails along his skin, smiling at his shudder.

His smell intoxicated Raven as they lost more clothing, twisting up in the sheets. He played with her, teasing her into submission and a desire she hadn't felt in a very long time. Her senses were overwhelmed as she let her mind unwind and focus on Prince Aleksander's fingers touching her, and coaxing her into a state of bliss. Eventually, exhaustion overtook them and Raven fell asleep in his arms. For the first time in weeks, she didn't dream at all.

# CHAPTER TEN

## RAVEN

The morning came too soon. Raven had enjoyed her night in bed with the prince and all of the distractions he had provided her. The fight from the previous day came crashing back with all of her questions. How had they known they were going to be in the forest? The ride hadn't been officially scheduled and had been a last-minute request from the queen. Yet, the attack had felt targeted towards her, not the princess. The majority of the fighters had been focused on her and Prince Aleksander. She had a hard time believing the attack was targeted towards the prince, though she struggled to think of any reason for it to be directed at her. Before she could continue her internal debate, Rowan walked into the prince's room while she was still tangled in sheets, demanding answers.

"What?" She pulled the sheets up farther as Rowan walked up to the end of the bed.

"Rowan, what the hell?" Aleks walked out of his washroom in nothing but his underwear.

"I'm not going to tell anyone." He sighed. "Now, despite what Princess Arianna believes, that ambush was not meant for her. Who's after you Aleks?"

"Me? They weren't after me," Aleks said. He got his brown pants on before slipping a white tunic over his chest. Raven scrunched her lips in disappointment.

"All of their attention was focused on the two of you," Rowan replied.

"Exactly, the two of us. And of the two of us, who had six men converging on her," Aleks claimed as he motioned toward Raven.

She looked between the two of them, searching for more of an explanation.

"Why would it be for me? I've done nothing here," she asserted. Maybe they would have some creative thoughts.

"Maybe someone from your kingdom found out you're here?" Rowan suggested. The state of his curly brown hair showed he also had got little sleep but for a very different reason.

"The only person with my location is my mistress, and anyone who would want revenge is dead. I'm a stranger here. I don't go by my assassin's name here. I'm a ghost. Why do you think they aimed it at me? Why not at Prince Aleksander?" Raven crossed her arms, shoulders pressed towards her ears. She couldn't tell them she worked for the King of Rairene, and that he also probably knew she was spying for him. She left out Ella and Mira knowing her location. They would never betray her.

"Raven, when I flew from my horse, none of them attacked me as they should have. Whereas when you flew off yours, they descended on you. If they had been going after Ari, they would have kept four men on us, and six on them," Aleks rationalized.

"But why? What did I do?" Raven ignored the fluttering in her magic. She wrapped it up and held it tight, comforting it as she would a delicately formed ball of dough. She was fine.

"I'm not sure." Rowan looked around the room, shoulders slumped. "We can't tell the queen. She'll dismiss you."

"What's your assassin's name?" Aleks asked.

Raven glared at him.

"What, maybe it means something to us here? What if a courtier was talking about trying to kill you and we didn't know?"

Raven laughed. "I will not tell you my codename just because we've slept together. And I will not tell Rowan, either. That name makes me vulnerable."

She got out of bed, wrapped in the sheets, and walked to the washroom.

"I'm going to get dressed, and you two are going to think of a different reason for those men to have attacked us. At least a more plausible one." Raven did her best to not let their theories affect her, because they were right. Someone was after her, and she had no idea why. By the time she left the prince's room, she still had some extra time in the morning to escape into the kitchen. It was still early enough that just a few of the chef's helpers were there, and all of them knew her.

"Raven, I heard about yesterday. Are you okay?" Danita asked as she snatched a freshly baked muffin from the tin before Louis could stop her.

"I'm fine." Raven sighed. "Louis, can I knead anything for you?"

He went over to his proofing shelf and grabbed down a bowl filled with dough. Raven dumped the contents on the well floured surface and began kneading the loaf to develop the gluten and to work out some of her nerves. She glanced to her right to Louis, preparing a couple of quiches brimming with meats and vegetables, all of which she knew would never be served to the palace staff. Raven turned back to her dough, kneading more of it.

"Hey, slow down there. We want to enjoy our bread, not find it over-done," Louis said as he came over and grabbed the loaf from under her hands. "Here, knead this rye. It needs some of that aggression."

Raven quirked a small smile of apology to him before getting to work on the rye. She worked until her mind settled and all thoughts of the previous day vanished. By the time she was done, breakfast had passed, and she had to run to the training field with her unit.

Raven picked up her mirror and poured some magic into it. The white glow of her power convulsed around her hands as she expelled some into the glass, careful to not shatter it. She sighed as the power left in a joyous rush, feeling more comfortable in her skin. Raven's power rarely got this full. At least she had bought herself a few weeks before she would need to release more.

Lady Tremaine's annoyance was written in the single uplift of a brow. *You better have one hell of an excuse for not answering last night.*

*Thank you for your concern. I'm fine. Someone tried to kill the queen a few days ago.*

A slight tug of Lady Tremaine's lips confirmed Raven's suspicions.

*Then yesterday, I think someone sent an ambush to kill me. Has anyone found out I'm here? That Snow White is here?*

That caused concern to flash across her eyes. *Of course not. What makes you think they targeted you?* As Raven relayed the story, Lady Tremaine's brows continued to furrow. At least she knew Lady Tremaine hadn't set it up. *Did anything new happen recently? Outside of the assassination attempts?*

*Queen Lyanna invited me to one of her private meetings. She was finally beginning to trust me, which I owe to you.*

Raven kept her eyes downcast. If he actually had children, Raven knew they would always be fed, but they would grow up without their father, and she didn't think that was a worthy exchange.

*I'll have someone look into the ambush. Don't worry, your location is safe. You've told no one who you are, correct?*

Raven stared her down in answer, resisting the urge to raise her brow.

*Don't forget to pick up the mirror next time.*

Rain poured down for the next two weeks. Several times Raven and Rowan had to wade through basements knee-deep in water to let it all out. She spent her nights rolling in the sheets with Aleks, finding a new way to relieve her stress. That's all it was, a good time. At least that's what she told herself, repeatedly. It didn't matter that every time he smiled at her, her heart lurched. She was wanted by someone who was so clearly above her station in life, but only wanted, for now. It also didn't matter that he let her sleep in his bed almost every night, even if all they did was sleep.

She woke up gasping for air, her hands clutching her neck as she tried to not make a noise. Smoke burned her nose as breathing came back to her. Raven sat up, moving her hands, confirming she was alive. She was okay.

She took a breath, her eyes wide open. She was in Aleks' room. It was nighttime, there was a full moon. The rain continued to fall outside. Raven closed her eyes and took a slow, steadying breath. It was just a dream.

Aleks rolled over and wrapped an arm around her. Serenity overcame her, safety found in the strengths of his arms. She snuggled down as he held her close.

"Another nightmare?" he groggily asked, his eyes shut.

Raven nodded.

"Want to tell me about it?" Aleks whispered, nuzzling close, kissing the space in her neck that she loved the most.

Raven paused. She rarely talked to him about her nightmares. She had only found out that he knew she was having them. Something about her breathing changing, he had claimed.

"It's always the same..." Raven mumbled. "I'm tripping over bodies...dead bodies...people I don't know." Raven paused. "A fire chases me, but the bodies keep building up and up and I can't get out. Ican'tgetoutIcan'tgetoutIcan'tgetout." Raven hyperventilated.

Aleks rubbed her back, mumbling nonsense as she calmed her thrumming heart. Her magic raced, trying to determine the threat.

"I um..." Raven ran her hands through her hair. "I see a guard, but I don't know who he is. He grabs me and keeps me from screaming. I try to get away from him, but I can't and he throws me into the fire."

Aleks remained silent for a moment as he rubbed his hand up and down her arm. "That sounds like the massacre that happened here after my uncle's death."

"Massacre?" Raven kept herself still. Was that how Queen Lyanna got her crown? Surely she would have read about it? No wonder Lady Tremaine said her ascension to the throne was complicated.

"There were no survivors. Did you read about it somewhere?" His hand stilled on her shoulder.

"I guess so." Raven turned to face him, unwilling to admit that she hadn't, and face the questions that piled up in her mind because of it. "I've been meaning to ask you something."

"What's on your mind before the sun has risen?" Aleks smiled, his eyes squinting open.

She knew it was because of her obvious switch in subjects.

"The color of your hair..." she lifted a hand to brush it out of his face, its smooth white strands, strands so similar to Ella's, getting tangled in her fingers. "Is it typical of Trudelian people? And the braids?"

"The braids are typical, though more often found in the military. And my hair color isn't very common. There's a crazy myth that generations ago my ancestor was poisoned. They were an enchanter though and were able to direct the poison to kill the color of their hair instead of them. I'm sure they never thought that it would pass along to their offspring. Now only someone with hair like mine can rule Trudel. Good thing my older brother Kai also has white hair, giving us a 'pure royal' status. For example, my aunt. Her hair is more of a light blonde, not white. There are rumors it's because my grandfather, the king, was unfaithful and that Lyanna is his mistress's daughter," Aleks explained.

Raven furrowed her brow. "I never learned about an enchanter being able to direct poison within themselves."

"Feeding more of the myth, he was an enchanter with a double star mark. I haven't heard of one being alive in decades, but they're supposed to essentially be made of endless, unquenchable magic that allows them to do things other enchanters cannot. Once again, speculation. It makes for a great story though." Aleks laughed. "Though I'm sure there are others out there with hair as white as mine. We can't be the only ones."

Raven let her hand fall out of his hair before she went to sleep with more questions to hunt down.

Queen Lyanna tapped her nails against the stone throne. No one was coming to court with the rain pouring down, and the hillsides flooded.

Raven had thought she would enjoy the break from complaints, but it made her agitated. She didn't think the queen's boredom would be good for anyone. Queen Lyanna stood up quickly, bringing everyone to attention. She walked to her private room, motioning for Raven's unit and Prince Aleksander to follow.

"You four get the night off."

"Your majesty—"

"I will be fine. I'll employ two of Arianna's guards for the evening until the next unit arrives. I'm getting restless, which means that the four of you are as well. Go blow off some steam however you see fit."

All of their jaws dropped.

"Queen Lyanna, I must protest—" Rowan began.

"At the sake of your life?" she questioned.

Rowan closed his mouth.

"Now go. You'll never get this chance again."

All of them left, trying to hide their confusion. Aleks stayed behind.

"Well, that's different." Charles looked backward.

"I know what we can do," Raven remarked, a glimmer of a smile in her eyes.

"I'm going to relax." Bastien walked away.

"Or we could go to an underground fighting ring," Raven teased, pure glee coating her voice.

Bastien slowed, turning around to join them, scratching his curly red hair.

"How did you have time to find one?"

"I have friends, you know." Raven was not going to tell them how she had had to convince Conrad to search for the fighting club. It had taken a lot of cajoling to get him to go along with it. He was not one to break the rules. It was only when she mentioned it was to gain the trust of her unit that he acquiesced.

"Now, go put some plain clothing on, and I'll meet all of you in thirty minutes at the gate," Raven ordered before walking to her room, thankful she had brought some dresses with her. She pulled out a simple brown dress that wouldn't draw any attention to her and brushed out her hair, braiding half of it up. Tucking daggers into her clothing, she took two pills and walked to the gate.

Rowan got there first, pulling her to the side.

"Raven, is this a good idea? You're still on your...medication...should we be going out into Aslar?"

"We'll be fine. Promise me something." She waited for him to nod his head. "When we get there, don't let me get in the ring."

"Then why go? This isn't—"

Bastien and Charles walked over, all conversation ceasing.

"Al-Prince Aleksander told you to take advantage of being around an assassin. This is part of that." Raven covered her face with a hand when she saw what Charles and Bastien wore. "You can't go dressed like that."

"Why? We're in plain clothes." Bastien looked down at himself.

Both of them wore black clothing, their cloaks clean.

"You scream Royal Guard. Mess up your hair, and I apologize in advance, but you can get a new one." Raven pulled out her knife and cut off parts of their cloaks.

"It'll have to do." She sighed.

"It'll have to do?" Charles growled. "These are, they're—"

"A dead giveaway. Now, let's go. We have to walk down there. That should help with the rest of your appearance."

By the time they got down to the harbor, all of them had a thick layer of city grime on them. Raven strode up to the warehouse door and knocked. A large woman opened it, looking them over with a critical eye.

"You lot are new." She crossed her arms.

"Doc sent us. Said that the special apples we wanted were here," Raven stated.

The woman looked at them again, went inside, and closed the door behind her.

"Wait, she has to check," Raven spoke before any of them could comment.

"You aren't really about to go in there, are you?" Aleks stepped out of the alley and walked over. His cloak was pulled up far enough to obscure his face and, most notably, the hair he had tied out of his face.

"Of course we are. When else will we get this chance?"

"If one man in there figures out one of you is a Royal Guard, you're dead."

"They won't say anything. They're not meant to be in here, just like we're not meant to be. So if anyone wants to make any moves or tell the queen, they'll have to explain how they knew we were there."

The woman returned before Aleks could voice more objections. She let them in, and Aleks begrudgingly followed.

Raven glanced around, noting that the setup was like the one she had competed in, but there was a slight difference. Everything was cheap. The stalls and merchants of Rairene were lavish. They sold everything anyone could want from the dark markets at steep prices. In Evrotia, she didn't find the same atmosphere of sophistication she had expected. The stalls were sturdy enough, with merchants selling their wares such as quality clothing, some jewelry, and a few even had some potions. But the sense of superiority and decadence was gone. The floor was covered in hay instead of stones, and the seats were nonexistent save for a few select boxes that had some wooden chairs.

The fighting had already begun, with the house only half full. Evrotia was worse off than Raven had realized.

"It exists." Charles looked at everything, failing to keep his jaw off the floor.

"Of course it exists," Raven retorted.

"Why weren't we informed?" Rowan questioned.

"You may be her most elite guards, but you are not her spies, or in charge of the kingdom's security," Aleks snapped before Raven could reply.

The five of them walked to the front of the ring. It was densely populated and would hide them from any prying eyes. Fighter after fighter stepped into the ring, with the same fighter always winning. He was a large man, made entirely of muscle. He never seemed to tire. Raven analyzed everything he did, noting his weak spots and strengths. What he lacked in wit, she noted, he made up for with brute strength, and a little bit of a Force potion. Though he would be easy to outmaneuver. Why had he been brazen and stupid enough to take the potion at all? It's not like he needed it. After thirty minutes of fighting, there was a break and some novice fighters got to go on stage. Raven kept her eyes open, looking out for any unwelcome guests in the audience. She didn't need a repeat of the jester.

After the break, the stage master, a different one from before, walked out into the arena.

"Shit."

It was *her* stage master. What was he doing here? His blond hair was perfectly placed, pulled back into a tail at the base of his neck. His white skin seemed paler under these flames than in Rairene. His clothing had certainly seen better days as he wore a cloak with a few holes that had been hastily repaired, if the poor stitching was any indication.

Aleks and Rowan turned to her. She wondered how pale she looked as she flipped her hood over her face. Pretty pale based on the concern that flashed in their eyes. Raven slowly turned around, trying not to grab anyone's attention.

"My Noble Lady, you're not leaving so soon, are you?" the stage master called.

Raven froze.

"Ladies and Gents, do I have a treat for you. We have a champion fighter in our midst. Please, join me on stage, Noble Lady."

Raven looked up at him, her eyes narrowed. His brown eyes glinted with barely restrained anger.

*"You good to fight?" the stage master eyed Raven.*

*She was jittery and on edge. She knew it. He knew it.*

*"I'm fine. I'll win your fight and all of that money," Raven replied.*

*Her hands shook as she tightened the wraps around her fingers. She couldn't lose it right now. Not now. Not ever. She would never lose control. Raven grabbed her magic and choked it until it was smaller than her fist.*

*The stage master called her into the ring to a raucous cheer. She rubbed her eyes hard, holding it all back. Her opponent was new. She hadn't even gotten to see him fight yet. Not that she cared. She knew she would win.*

*He was intimidating to anyone but her. Raven jumped in, and the fight began. It started off normal, but her vision continued to blur. Why was it doing that? Raven shook away the tears, and couldn't avoid the cut to her side. Her opponent took charge and broke through Raven's defenses, punching her to the ground and kicking her in the stomach.*

*Raven crawled to her feet to fight.*

*He threw her against the corner.*

*Raven slumped against the wooden pillar, trying to center herself. Her head pounded, her hearing was fuzzy, and her vision blurred.*

*Her opponent paced in front of her, waiting for her to get up.*

*"Raven."*

*Her name flitted through to her. Turning her head, her vision darkening, Raven saw Ella through a swollen eye.*

*"What are you doing here?" Raven hissed.*

*"I knew something was wrong with you. You need to forfeit. He's going to kill you."*

*"Let him. I don't care," Raven whispered, her heart shattering.*

*"Well, I do."*

*Before Raven could even try to move to stop her, Ella jumped into the ring, pulling out her daggers.*

*"I'll fight in her stead." Ella stood up against the stage master.*

*Raven could hear him protesting. He wanted his fight.*

*He got one.*

*Ella fought and beat Raven's opponent. Then a second, and then a third. All the while, Raven remained slumped against the corner, attempting to stay conscious. As she watched her best friend, her soul sister, fight for her, she couldn't stop the tears from coating her face.*

*Ella suddenly appeared before her, sorrow in her wide, ice-blue eyes. Her hands gently held Raven's. Ella helped Raven to her feet, taking most of her weight.*

*"What happened?" Ella whispered.*

*"I saw him..." Another round of tears burst forth as what was left of her heart shattered into fragments of glass. "I saw Jason with...her."*

*Ella pulled Raven close, hiding her from the world.*

*"You ruined everything." The stage master charged at them. Ella positioned herself between them, holding out a dagger.*

*"You got your fight. Three. Your Noble Lady is leaving before I report you to the crown."*

*"Ha. You know nothing of the crown. If I ever see you again, you're as good as dead." He promised.*

*"Come on everyone, let's get our Noble Lady up here."*

The room chanted her name. Even though none of them knew what it meant. All they knew was they were going to get a fight. Raven's hand rested against the scar on her waist.

"Don't do it," Rowan whispered, gripping her biceps. "You remember what you told me?"

"Of course, but I didn't know he would be here. If I don't go...we're all dead." Raven looked around at the grunts who had encircled them. She knew he would try to force them to stay or kill them. He wouldn't be successful, but people would get hurt. And she couldn't let that happen, not when it was her fault. She had truly messed up, and they would never trust her again, but the least she could do was make sure they got out. Raven ripped her arm free and moved up to the ring.

"Looks like we have a show, Ladies and Gents. Our Noble Lady hails from Rairene, though by the looks of it, she's fallen out of grace."

The stage master leaned in close to Raven. "It looks like you'll get to pay me after all for all of that money I lost that night. Don't mess it up."

The stage master called out the undefeated man, a fresh circle of red rimming the iris of his eye. She cast her gaze up to the ceiling. She honestly did not see how no one hadn't beaten him yet.

Raven rolled her shoulders and stretched. She caught a look exchanged between Aleks and Rowan, ignoring them. The man yelled something profane at her in Vicurian. The corner of her mouth twitched, waiting for him to make the first move.

She beat him in two minutes.

He collapsed on the ground, unconscious, when Raven got on his back and held him in a chokehold.

"Enjoy your money, we're done."

Raven walked out of the ring and kept going.

All four quickly followed. No one said a word as they walked up to the palace. Raven stopped right outside the gate, slumping her shoulders as she turned to face them.

"I apologize for putting you in danger. If I had…if I knew it was him…I wouldn't have come. We have a history, and it didn't end well, and I'm sorry." Raven clenched her hands tightly. The shaking had started again. Those memories were ripping through her faster than she could deflect them. Her magic rose to protect her, and she shut it down, promising to let it be used soon. She deserved this pain.

Charles and Bastien nodded. Charles even rested his hand on her shoulder and squeezed before walking away. Aleks and Rowan remained.

"I'll be okay. I just…need to distract myself." Raven sniffled as she walked away from them.

She had thought she would be fine going to the fighting ring. If it had been anyone else…she would have been *fine*. That last fight where Ella had saved her…Raven blinked rapidly as she got to her room, holding her spiraling magic inside. She found an empty glass bottle and filled it with water. It wasn't pure or meant to be enchanted, but it would have to do.

Raven focused on the glass in her hands, letting her magic sing through her veins. Her hands glowed as her magic flared out and around her fingers, her power transferring to the water inside.

"*Et ossa dolor fractionis.*" Raven formed the intent of pain and broken bones. She pictured how it felt to feel a bone shatter, much like her heart. A pain that ripped through your muscles and nerves, like a dagger shredding all of her emotions. As she imagined the agony, she watched the water change from clear to gray, with dim yellow spots inside.

Raven tilted her head. That was new. Though it could be from the water source, she surmised. Raven made two more until her power was under control.

A knock on her door was her only warning before Aleks walked in.

Raven hid the enchantments in her desk.

The moment he reached her, she pulled him to her and kissed him.

They got to her bed and held each other. Aleks didn't ask her questions, and she didn't offer any explanations.

# CHAPTER ELEVEN

## RAVEN

Once the rain was gone, the snow took its place. Winter made it clear it was there to stay as cold and ice settled into the bones of the palace and its occupants. Bringing more commoners to Queen Lyanna's throne room, begging for help.

Help they did not receive.

Not even one of the queen's lords did anything. Raven was beginning to think she should have let that man kill the queen. Or that she should do it herself. Given the coup, Princess Arianna wasn't the true heir to the throne. Whoever would take her place had to be a better ruler than her mother. Of that, Raven was certain.

She shifted on her feet as she looked back and forth along the long table filled with the queen's elite, with Queen Lyanna in the center. All of them spoke in hushed tones, not daring to sound jovial as the wait staff moved around them. Dinner was late. Not so late that everyone got hungry, but late enough that the queen noticed. When it was finally before her, the queen had to wait for her food taster to try everything first. Raven kept her eyes from rolling.

The food taster collapsed, knocking Bastien over.

Queen Lyanna looked at the girl on the floor, her eyes empty, her mouth foaming. No one moved. Everyone who had already eaten vomited their food, and the guards closed the doors.

"Bring. Me. The. Chef." It wasn't loud, yet her voice still echoed through the room.

They had pushed all the food to the center of the table as if distance was the only thing keeping them alive.

"Oh please, your food isn't poisoned. If it were, you'd be dead by now." Queen Lyanna sighed, slumping in her chair. "I was looking forward to dinner tonight."

Raven examined the queen's food and sniffed it, looking for the type of poison. She smelled the slightest hint of flowers. Raven furrowed her eyebrows. At least the girl had died quickly. What was Louis...Raven froze.

He was being dragged up to the room.

It had become known to everyone in the palace that they were friends. Word had spread quickly after he had let Raven bake with him. More than anything though, Raven couldn't believe it, refused to believe he had done this. Someone else must have touched the food between the kitchens and the table. Louis would set everything straight. If he didn't...

Raven looked up as the doors swung open.

Two guards walked in, Louis between them, head hung.

"Chef Louis, what do you have to say?" It was the most diplomatic thing Queen Lyanna had ever uttered.

"There is nothing to say, Your Highness, that would eliminate my guilt."

Not a single person moved.

"I'm disappointed. Your food is always spectacular. You've worked for the palace longer than most. Why the change?"

Raven guessed that this was an attempt the queen had not expected.

"I'm tired of making all of this food for you and still seeing the people of this kingdom starve. You could loosen up on the taxes for a couple of years, yet you refuse to show your people mercy. You refuse to be a good, worthy leader of this kingdom. King Stewart would be ashamed! His daughter should be on the throne!"

Raven couldn't stop her mouth from dropping. She guessed he had been given a script, yet everything still rang true. He would never have done this on his own, but Raven knew that he probably wanted the motivation for a long time.

"I see." Queen Lyanna shifted her gaze to Raven. "Guard Raven, the two of you are close. Do you think Chef Louis is capable of committing treason on his own? Or do you think we should torture him for the information?"

If he was tortured, so much more would come out, and all of it would be about her and her little pill habit. Raven bit her lip.

"I think if asked, Chef Louis would give us the information we seek. Torture is unnecessary. A quick death I think—"

"A quick death? Don't you think that's a little too merciful for someone as heartless as me? A little too soft toward someone who committed treason?" The queen's voice was conversational, as though discussing the snow instead of killing her chef.

Raven's one normal, calm, quiet friend.

"I think that showing your people you're capable of mercy during a difficult time for them would give them hope." Raven stood taller, twisting her hands behind her.

"I think the reason you're suggesting a quick death is out of your friendship with him."

Everyone in the room remained silent during their exchange. Everyone was reading between the lines of the conversation from a guard who knew how to twist her words and a queen who did not take kindly to showing grace.

"If it is my loyalty, that's in question, then let me..." Raven sucked in a breath, "let me be the one to end his life."

Queen Lyanna raised her eyebrows, the biggest sign of surprise Raven had ever seen across her blue eyes.

"Very well." She gestured towards Louis.

He didn't struggle. Not once.

Raven remained silent as she took out her short swords.

A light tap on her shoulder drew her attention. Rowan stood beside her, holding out his sword. He didn't have to say a word.

Hers wouldn't be able to kill him quickly.

Rowan's face was stone as he looked at her, his brown eyes expressing his sorrow for her.

Raven sheathed her blades and clutched his sword, nodding.

As Raven walked towards Louis, she remembered every single time he had helped her. He had been the first real friend to her. Took care of her when she was injured. Supplied her with the medication. Over the last two months, their friendship had grown to one of trust and Raven knew, she *knew*, Lady Tremaine had gotten to him.

This was the ultimate piece.

If the queen didn't trust her implicitly after this, then she never would.

Memories of being in the kitchen swamped her.

Laughing for the first time in a year.

Feeling free and normal, another girl who could bake. That would all be gone now. Raven blinked. She walked slowly, making sure she didn't stumble. The staff would never let her into the kitchen. They had started to like her. They didn't scatter anymore when she walked in early in the morning. They stayed, listened to her talk, and told her their own stories.

It would all be...gone.

Raven's magic thrashed against its cage.

She shoved it down as she approached him. Raven balled it up so small into her core that barely any emotion got through. Louis didn't look up at her. If he had, Raven knew she wouldn't have been able to go through with it. The guards had shoved Louis to his knees, their hands gripping his shoulders. His head hung down, exposing his neck.

Raven hefted Rowan's sword over her head.

She had lifted many swords before.

But no other sword had ever felt so heavy as this one did.

Raven lined herself up and closed her eyes. She tightened her muscles and lifted the sword over her head, but stopped. She took a deep, ragged breath, hoping the queen didn't hear it. Didn't see the tear that had slipped down her cheek.

Raven tensed her muscles again.

"I'm sorry," Louis whispered to her.

"Me too," Raven spoke softly as she swung.

It was harder than she thought it would be to decapitate someone.

Especially with a blade that wasn't enchanted. It's why she always poisoned people. Even going in, she knew it was going to take all of her strength to get the blade through on the first swing, and she only got it through.

Louis's head rolled away from her, blood spraying her when she hit the artery, bathing her and the floor in red.

Raven breathed in again and walked to her position behind the queen, not daring to glance behind her.

Tears burned down her throat as she refused to let them fall down her face.

Raven remained perfectly poised for the rest of the evening. She supposed she looked quite fierce in her current state as the blood dried on her clothes and skin. Drying on her face. But she didn't dare wipe it off or make a move to clean herself.

Instead, she stood resolutely behind the queen, who beamed with joy.

The queen didn't mind that she had to wait an extra thirty minutes for her new meal. She didn't mind because she bounced up and down as they picked up Louis's body and mopped up the blood. Raven didn't look at Rowan who would only show pity, or Aleks who...she didn't want to think about what she would see in his eyes. At least not until it was in the pitch black of her room. Until then, she focused on the things that would fuel her fire.

*"Jason?" Raven stepped out of her doorway to look down the hall. There he was, sneaking in. Why he felt he had to sneak in was beyond her.*

*"Jason."*

*He froze.*

*"I've been wondering when I would see—"*

*"Quiet. Do you want to wake the entire house?" His eyes were dark, his brow furrowed. "You would think for someone your age that you would be smarter."*

*"All I said was hi, but if you're going to talk to me that way, then fuck off." Raven turned around and walked away.*

*He followed her to her room, but she stopped him at the door.*

*"Oh, I'm sorry, I didn't realize this was a room for people who were smarter than me," Raven slammed the door in his face.*

After dinner, the queen dismissed her. Raven left without saying a word to anyone. She walked mindlessly through the palace, wandering until she found somewhere safe.

Raven stood in front of Alek's door, unable to knock.

"Raven?" Aleks walked up behind her.

He slowly opened his door and guided her in.

Blood still covered her.

She stood in his room, unsure of where to go. Aleks led her to the washroom, lighting several candles. He got the warm water in the tub as Raven stood mindlessly in front of him. He turned her, moved around her gently, and pulled off the armor.

Raven looked in the mirror, into dark blue eyes that held no sign of life. What brief glimmer had remained...was gone.

Her clothes…did not want to detach from her. Raven let Aleks lead her into the tub, waiting for the water to soak through the tunic before trying to remove it again. Aleks wiped all the blood off, gently using a cloth on her face. She looked at him, all emotions stuffed down so far that nothing would bring them back. She didn't want to feel anything again. Aleks led her out of the washroom, dressed her in one of his sleeping tunics, and wrapped her up in blankets, holding her close.

# CHAPTER TWELVE

## RAVEN

Raven woke up to the sound of screaming.

She'd never done that before…woken up so terrified that only her screaming could pull her from her nightmare.

Someone had died.

Someone she loved had died. She remembered the pain, the loss so great it still clutched her heart as she woke up. But she couldn't remember the person. Raven wasn't sure which bothered her more, that she used to care for someone that much, or that she had no idea who they were.

Aleks sat up and stroked her shoulder. She shook beneath his hands; her face buried in his pillow. She hoped she hadn't scared him too much.

"What's wrong with me?" It was a whispered plea.

"It's another nightmare. You went through something traumatic last night—"

"No. Not like that. Someone died…"

"Louis—"

"Yes. I remember. This wasn't about him. It was someone from my past...and it hurts Aleks," Raven choked out. "I don't like it." She sat up and leaned over the side of the bed, waiting to see if her stomach's threat of revolting was true. Her body was covered in sweat as she continued to shake.

Raven gathered herself and stood up. She picked up her armor, still covered in blood, and left her wet clothes behind. She had Alek's tunic on, and it covered her enough to make it to her room.

"Raven, come to bed. You still have a few hours before you have to get up...you went through a lot."

She ignored his pleas as she walked over to him, gave him a long passionate kiss, and left his room.

After she dumped her armor in her room and found a plain robe and cloak, Raven wandered around the palace, waiting for the empty pit in her to fade. She would not let it affect her ability to function.

Eventually, she found herself in the kitchens. Her only comfort, now probably stripped away from her. A dim candlelight called to her and she couldn't stop herself. For a moment, she forgot Louis wouldn't be down there.

"Get out of my kitchen." A woman stared at Raven. Her blond hair was twisted in a bun, flour covered her apron. Her green eyes shot straight into Raven's dark, twisted soul that wouldn't stop bleeding.

All Raven could do was look past her. Her stomach twisted from the impact of what she had done. A phantom sting pierced her side. Where was she going to get the pills now? She was going to have to steal his stash before anyone else did.

"Didn't you hear what I said? Get out of my kitchen."

"Can I have some tea?" Raven's mind had shut off. It could only focus on one thing, and one thing only. Surviving.

"Just because you're a Royal Guard doesn't mean I'm at your beck and call. I have other stuff to do, and even though Louis catered to your every whim doesn't mean I will."

Raven didn't let his name break her. It couldn't.

"I didn't ask you to make me breakfast grumpy. I asked for a cup of tea. Normally I would do it myself since no one else can make a proper cup, but I simply don't have the mental capacity right now. So if you wouldn't mind, I would like some tea." Raven sat down, her shoulders slumped.

The new chef harrumphed, but did as Raven requested. She banged it down in front of her, startling Raven out of her void.

Raven took a sip, her eyes closed. They opened slowly to look at the chef with wide eyes.

"Thank you…" Raven waited for her name.

"Gabriella and you're welcome."

Raven cradled the cup in her hands and left, not once looking at the grumpy chef.

Raven took out her mirror, closed her eyes, and looked within for her magic. It was a small whirling mass, unsure of itself. Raven called to it, letting it flow freely through her veins and muscles. She pulled a small amount and thought about Lady Tremaine as she channeled the image into the mirror.

*Snow White, to what do I owe the pleasure?* Lady Tremaine was not pleased as storm clouds gathered in her emerald eyes.

*How much money is his family getting for his death?*

*I didn't think you cared about that sort of thing, Snow. All that matters is your oath.*

*How. Much.* Raven ground out through her teeth. If she could have reached through the mirror and grabbed Lady Tremaine, she would have.

*They will live comfortably for the rest of their lives. Is that to your satisfaction?*

*The king wants me here enough to sign off on innocent people dying? We didn't have to do it. I'm sure his children would have preferred their father to live. I had something building—*

*I'm sure you did. Queen Lyanna barely trusted you. Now she has seen you kill a friend for her. That will take you far. As for the king, it is not your place to question his orders or what he commands to get the best results possible. What's your oath again?*

*I swear, by the blood in my veins and the bones of my ancestors, to protect the kingdom and the crown, or may the gods strike me down.*

*There's nothing in there about questioning your king. Don't let it happen again.*

*Will you tell me what I'm supposed to be doing then? Is it that big that you need me to have her complete trust first?*

Lady Tremaine remained silent for a few moments, her expression giving away nothing. *You are to work on finding the location of King Stewart's former seven advisors.*

*They all died in the coup. I was told there were no survivors.*

*Did they?* Lady Tremaine cut off the conversation.

Raven wasn't Calla. She couldn't touch an object and see a person's entire life. Her magic didn't work that way, at least not that she knew. Calla's training had been more in-depth. She was far out of her comfort zone.

All thoughts or ideas about Lady Tremaine's request drifted to the corners of Raven's mind as the winter ball rapidly approached, and Queen Lyanna's mood created a new definition of the meaning: short-tempered. The commoners seemed to only come in bigger droves, and the advisors did little to filter them out.

"Tell me, which region are you from?" Queen Lyanna's voice whispered over the dim roar of the people behind them. All of them vying for a moment with their queen.

Raven quirked a brow. This was new. Was she going to show some kindness?

"The Northern Region, your majesty...the winters up there..." The man, wearing a cloak that could barely be considered more than a limp tablecloth, trailed off as the queen looked down at him.

Raven looked the man over, his hands twisted in what had once been a well-knit cap and was now coming apart. He was missing one finger. Another had begun to turn purple. Raven's magic and her heart lurched forward, yearning to help him. To bring him out of the cold and give him the care he so greatly needed. She knew that one of her healing potions, or even Aleks, could remove the frostbite and save his finger. But Queen

Lyanna, in her ignorance and scheming, had banished the enchanters, and their potions with them.

"Lord Ulrich, please approach."

Raven snapped herself out of her musings as a large, well-dressed man grunted to his feet. His necklaces clanged together as he waddled over. Raven thought he might pass out with the effort before he reached the queen.

"Your majesty, I—"

"Do you remember what I ordered you and your colleagues to do a while ago?"

"You ordered us to—"

"To filter through the rabble so that I may devote my time to more important needs. That way, I wouldn't have to listen to a hundred poor men come before me in one day and tell me how poor they are. How they can't pay their taxes, and how their children are starving. I couldn't give two fucks about them. I want to make sure that those who are important are being heard, and this," she motioned to everyone who stood before her, "muddles everything up."

The people of Evrotia went quiet as their queen told them they meant nothing to her. Raven braced herself for them to rush the throne. She knew it was pure fear of their monarch, and probably being too malnourished, that kept them at bay.

"Queen Lyanna, the people want to speak to their queen. I and the other advisors mean nothing to them." His hands remained pressed together as he looked up at her.

"And do you remember what I said would happen should you not uphold my order?"

Lord Ulrich blanched, stepping backward.

"I would kill you and replace you." Queen Lyanna was calm, her anger a frozen chill Raven was used to.

"Your majesty, I...I—" Lord Ulrich stuttered for words. He spun to the other advisors, seeking help, a lifeline. "I helped you keep that crown!" He continued to walk farther, as though distance would be the difference between life and death. "I helped you get that crown," he growled.

"Raven."

Raven looked sideways at the queen, feeling useful for once.

"Kill him." She motioned lazily with her hand, sighing as though ordering this man's life forfeit was too much of an inconvenience for her.

Raven didn't hesitate. She wanted to hear more about how Lord Ulrich helped her get the crown, but she was Snow White, and Snow White did not disobey orders. She wanted to kill. Her magic wanted to sing through her veins and finally punish someone responsible for this horrific disaster of a kingdom.

So she did.

Raven smirked as she prowled down the ten-stone steps, swords in hand.

Lord Ulrich kept backing up, but Raven eventually circled him around to the middle of the room, facing his queen. She knew Queen Lyanna would want to see his death, revel in the glory of watching his life leave his pudgy eyes. He stank of sweat and wine as she held him.

He was begging. Crying to be spared. He would do better, he promised. All of it fell away from Raven. His pleas meant nothing to her when the pleas of so many were behind her, screaming to be heard.

Raven glanced up at the queen as she held him, waiting to see if his pleas changed her mind. Queen Lyanna's icy blue eyes met Raven's and for the first time, both women felt the smallest twinge of agreement and satisfaction that judgment was being correctly dealt with.

Raven drove one sword into his heart, while the other sliced his throat. For a split moment, her blade caught on his vocal cords. She remained calm and emotionless as he fell off her sword and blood pooled around her boots.

She shrugged and walked to the queen, her magic simmering with pleasure.

"Now, who wants to talk to the peasants from their region before sending them to me?" Queen Lyanna asked.

The remaining six men jumped up, their skin void of color, eyes wide as they skirted around Lord Ulrich's body.

"Lord Cenric."

A tall, handsome man stood up and glided over to them, hands clasped before him. Everything about him was immaculate. Raven had never seen him before. She would have remembered a man with his warm, intelligent brown eyes that were a little too smart.

"My queen, how may I be of service?" His silky voice rippled against Raven's internal walls, instantly reinforcing them.

"You only traveled here for the winter ball, but you're now in charge of the Northern Region and will need to move some belongings into the palace. It's not the region your father once presided over, but I hope you take it and are smart enough to not end up like your predecessor."

"I'll have everything moved here and take care of my region with pride." He inclined his head as befitting his new station. Lord Cenric gave Raven a soft wink before turning around and bringing those left from the Northern Region with him to his new chambers. He didn't even bother avoiding Lord Ulrich's body, his blood trailing behind, soaking his robes.

"No one knows about us, right?" Raven rolled over and looked at Aleks.

"Correct...well besides Rowan, but I mean he knows everything." Aleks sighed, closing his eyes.

"Good."

He opened a single eye to look at her.

"I mean, it's frowned upon, and all we're doing is messing around, and if the queen found out..."

"She would do nothing. I'm her nephew, and I've seduced many women before you. Should she find out, that's what I'll tell her. I mean, that is all we are to each other, right?"

"Exactly." Raven's heart skipped. "Messing around...that's it..."

"Sounds good to me." Aleks closed his eyes to get some more sleep.

Raven remained wide awake, her mind buzzing with the events from the prior day.

She slowly got out of bed, put on some loose clothing, and went for a jog. No one bothered her this early. No one flinched away. It was her, the ground beneath her feet, and her thoughts. By the time she was done,

Raven's mind was focused and clear. The pill had helped as well. She walked silently through the halls, heading for her room.

"What do you mean, it's missing?"

Raven paused at the corner, leaning against the wall.

"Someone broke into my suite and looked for that map. It was all I had left from King Stewart. He entrusted that piece to me." The woman's voice kept pitching up and down.

"Are you going to tell the queen?"

The woman snorted. "I would rather die than tell her that her late husband was sleeping with me."

"She wouldn't know that's what it meant."

"She would wonder why a piece of a map was so important to a lowly noblewoman. She's smart enough to put the clues together."

The two women always stayed in the back of the throne room, avoiding the queen's gaze. She had never paid them any attention. Maybe she should have. Raven walked away before they could see her. Susan was already in her room, bustling around to get her set for the day.

"Is this what you do when I'm not here?"

Susan grinned before moving over to Raven and taking off her sweaty clothes.

"I'm only tidying. I've never taken care of someone messier than ya."

"It's the only thing that didn't catch during my training." Raven stepped into the shower. She washed all of Aslar's grime off of her.

Susan had everything laid out for her once she was done, her clothes in perfect condition. Her already bare room was spotless.

"Are you looking forward to the ball tomorrow?"

Raven snorted. "I'm on guard duty. There's nothing fun about having to stand on the side and watch a bunch of rich nobles get drunk, flirt, and have fun."

"At least you'll get to wear that gorgeous gown," Susan gushed.

Raven looked over at the red ball gown hanging from her wardrobe. "What was she thinking of having me wear that? What does she think I'm going to do if something happens and I have to do anything that requires more than walking? I'm going to have to cut a giant slit in the dress and ruin it," Raven complained.

"Well, at least you'll look beautiful while fighting dangerous men."

Raven smiled as she put the finishing touches on her braid.

Betsy sat in her usual spot in the dining hall, alone and bruised.

"I swear Betsy, one of these days, I'm going to walk in here and you won't be at this table. Know why? You'll be dead, and it's all because you won't tell me who the bastard is that beats you." Raven kept her voice low.

"Guard Raven."

She rolled her eyes when Bastien walked over to them, his arms crossed. He motioned for her to follow him out to training.

"Did it occur to you that Betsy understands what will happen to her if she tells you who it is that's hurting her?" He navigated down the walkway outside the back of the palace.

"You know who it is," Raven accused. She caught up to him, nearly tripping over a broken stone in the walkway.

"Have you also considered that she's trying to make the best of her situation? Then every morning you walk in, demanding to be told who it is, and telling her she's going to end up dead? If she tells you, she would be dead anyway, Raven—"

"Then why not leave?" Raven challenged. She ignored all the other guards moving around them as they got closer to their training ring.

"I'm sure she wants to. Unfortunately, most people's lives are more complicated than yours."

Raven scoffed.

"She probably has a family depending on her for the meager wages that she earns. Wages that are going to be better than any other place can afford. Most people have a reason to stay in a horrible situation, and if she tells you who it is, she will die, and then what will her family do without her help?"

"My life isn't as...simple as you might think. But I concede your point," Raven acknowledged. "You could still tell me. Nothing says I can't pay him a visit in the dark and make it hard for him to do anything but take a piss."

Bastien walked away as Raven made more remarks on what exactly she would do.

# CHAPTER THIRTEEN

## RAVEN

The courtroom was decorated in swathes of blue and silver fabric cascading from the ceiling to the floor for the winter ball, enhanced by the snow falling outside. All around, everyone danced and laughed. Princess Arianna enjoyed herself as every single eligible bachelor presented himself to her, despite her age. Queen Lyanna even danced with a couple of her advisors. All of them had been scrambling to stay in her good graces. All of them glared at Raven whenever their eyes met hers.

Raven stayed on her side of the throne, resisting the urge to readjust her gown. It was constructed of a well-fitted bodice with delicately designed metal twirling its way up from her waist, and up and over her shoulders to wrap around her neck in mock armor. The skirts swirled around her, though she had demanded fewer layers than was standard given her position. It was beautiful, and she felt like a warrior princess armed for battle. Its red coloring was too close to spilled blood for Raven's taste. She knew she was stunning, but found herself, for the first time, uncomfortable in her skin.

"What are you doing?" Raven frowned at Aleks. He was bowing before her, his arm extended.

"Asking you to dance." He stood up and looked her over. "You look beautiful in that dress. It deserves to be seen."

Raven tilted her head at Rowan.

"The queen won't punish you. She lets all of us dance during the ball. And if anything happens, you're still armed." He smiled, pointedly looking at the spots where she had hidden her seven daggers.

Raven nodded stiffly to him before taking Aleks' hand.

The dance floor parted before them and she hoped it was because the Prince of Trudel was on the floor, not because a Royal Guard had the audacity to join him.

"Stop glancing around and look at me." He laughed when Raven continued to look everywhere around her but at him.

He disarmed her more than she was willing to admit, even to herself. Despite their time together, there was something...extra...about him that made the magic in her veins respond to his very existence, a sensation she'd never experienced before.

"It can't be helped. If anything happens while I'm out here with you—"

"Nothing will. Remember who you're talking to. I'm going to be offended if you don't dance with me, and then you'll have to stay on the floor for another dance." Aleks smiled.

Raven snapped her head to look at him, his eyes laughing as they captured hers and she could not look away as Aleks waltzed them around the room.

"Stop that," Raven mumbled.

"Stop what?" His grin grew as Aleks ran a hand through his white hair. He had taken out his two braids, a simple small one on the left side. The rest of his hair hung freely to his shoulders in loose waves.

"We agreed no one would know about us, and you're looking at me like you've seen me naked."

"You're right." His smile dropped as he attempted to be serious. Ten seconds later, though, his heart-stopping smile returned. "I'm sorry, I tried. It can't be helped. I'm the luckiest man in the room right now."

Raven ducked her head, hiding a smile.

"Was that a smile?" Aleks tilted her head up to look at him. He leaned in close, speaking in Trudelian. "You look beautiful when you smile, Guard Raven."

He stepped back, bowing as their single dance ended. Raven curtsied, grateful that for once her hair was down and covering her blushing cheeks and the smile that wouldn't go away. She wished she had ignored him and earned herself that threatened second dance. She would have done anything at that moment to stay on that floor with him without a care in the world as they danced in each other's arms.

Raven got off the floor quickly, taking her position next to Rowan. He looked sideways at her, his eyes dark. He didn't say a word thankfully as the dancing continued and Prince Aleksander moved to other fawning women, and she told herself that it didn't matter.

Raven and Rowan only had to break up two fights throughout the night. She punched one man when he made her rip her gown. Guards carried him out on a stretcher, unconscious.

Princess Arianna glared at her.

"You didn't have to knock him out, Guard Raven." She stomped her foot.

"He was going to stab someone." Raven narrowed her eyes at the princess.

Princess Arianna walked away as Raven massaged her hand. It was the princess who had started the brawl. She would not show her any kindness. Raven walked over to Rowan as he smiled at her. He had finished escorting the other man out of the room, who was so drunk he could barely walk a straight line. Raven ran her hands through her hair, lightly massaging the small headache away.

"I need to cut my hair." She examined its length.

"I think you should let it grow out," Rowan commented as he looked over her bruised hand.

"Do you know what I'll have to go through every morning if I let it grow out?"

"Run a brush through it?" He laughed.

"Ha ha...I'll have to braid it through a leather strap with metal spikes."

"Why?" He glanced at her.

"Well, if someone grabs my hair, they won't be able to hold on. Without it, you're completely at someone's mercy when they hold your hair. You can't go anywhere, and it's harder to fight."

"Unless the person grabbing it is Prince Aleksander?" Rowan teased, his voice low.

Raven scrunched her lips. "My love life is not important."

"I'm only saying if you two wanted to be discreet, dancing was not a good idea."

"I told him he was being obvious—"

"Actually, it was you."

Raven's jaw dropped.

"I don't think anyone here, including myself, has seen you smile. A genuine smile. They all think you want to sleep with him now."

"Great." Raven stopped talking as Queen Lyanna walked over and sat down on the throne, a small smile on her face.

"Don't you think it's quaint that these boys are throwing themselves at my daughter when they know she's already engaged?"

"Your majesty?" Raven was unsure if she should reply.

"Princess Arianna is engaged to the Prince of Vicuria, our neighbors to the east. A handsome prince. He should arrive any day now. He was supposed to be here before the ball." She pouted.

"Is the wedding soon?" Raven asked. She couldn't see the fifteen-year-old wanting to get married soon.

"Not until she's eighteen, but I wanted them to know each other first, like King Stewart and I did." She smiled.

Raven straightened, her attention shifting to a cautiously approaching guard with snow dripping off of him. Queen Lyanna noticed him a second later, timidly standing before her.

"Yes?" She was in a more pleasant mood than Raven had realized.

"Your majesty, two men and a horse arrived. They claim they're carrying the Prince of Vicuria."

"Claim?" Raven asked.

"They were attacked. The prince is badly wounded."

"And where are they now?" The queen sat straighter.

"I told them to stay outside—"

"In the snow?" Raven questioned. Even she could see how big of a slight that would be to a prince. If he was anything like Princess Arianna, he would be overly offended.

"Bring him in. Now," Queen Lyanna ordered, her cheerful mood gone. "Guards Rowan and Raven with me. We will meet them at the front doors like proper hosts." She stood and walked faster than the frozen guard, forcing him to sprint ahead.

No one noticed their passing other than to briefly step out of the way. Bastien and Charles closed in behind them, their weapons loosened. Raven too had loosened her daggers and palmed them.

Their brisk walk took them to the towering double front wooden doors, where two guards wavered on their feet. Their clothing was shredded, and Raven noticed, tinged with red. Both leaned heavily on their swords. The man they stood in front of was lying across his horse. His blond hair was matted, and his arms lying limply against the shaking horse's hide. If it wasn't for the small puffs of air coming from the rider, Raven would have sworn he was dead.

"We're all that's left of our convoy carrying Prince Adam of Vicuria. He needs medical attention, Your Highness," the guard spoke slowly in Evrotian before falling over.

He landed hard on the stone steps.

Raven broke formation, crouching down by him. She turned him over, her hands covered in blood from the hidden stomach wound.

"He's dead." She set him down gently, ignoring the blood soaking into her dress.

"Get the prince to the infirmary," Queen Lyanna ordered. "Do not let the princess see him."

Raven's eyes widened briefly at the queen's protection.

"She'll never marry him if she sees him looking like this...like a beast," she whispered before heading back in. "Bastien, Charles, you're with me. Raven and Rowan, you two are to make sure he gets the help he needs. Then we'll figure out a place for him to live and recover in."

Raven and Rowan stayed behind with the prince and his remaining guard.

"She seems friendly," the guard spoke, swaying from side to side.

"That was friendly." Raven took the horse's reins and escorted them quickly. "What happened? How big was your convoy?" She asked in stilted Vicurian.

"Wolves, M'Lady. We had crossed the mountains when it went silent...then the wolves attacked. There were ten of us. Most of us had been guarding the prince since he were a lad."

Raven did her best to keep up with the guard's thick Vicurian accent while translating for Rowan.

"The prince, brave soul, wanted to fight, but Garth and I, we got him out. One wolf jumped on the prince's horse. It was a long fight to kill that one." The guard sighed, his steps slowing the more he talked.

Raven caught him before he fell to the ground.

Rowan and Raven got him onto the horse next to the prince. As soon as they walked into the infirmary, the healers jumped into action.

Both of them sat to the side, watching them work. Raven palmed a pill and popped it in her mouth when she felt Rowan's attention turn away. Her stress decreased, along with the headache. Raven couldn't help but feel some awe as the healers worked. She knew basic aid, but since she was the one causing harm, they had never trained her to save a life, not like this. The healers came over to them, explaining that they had to stitch the prince up a lot, and had to take drastic measures to stop the bleeding. Rowan and Raven looked at each other. This news would not please Queen Lyanna.

"Would we be able to see him for ourselves?" Raven asked.

The healer nodded, leading them to a private room. Prince Adam lay on his back, bandages covering most of his body. They had cut his hair to reveal angry red stitches before the nurses could cover them with cloth bandages. Half of his face was concealed, along with his chest where the wolf's claws had dug in. A nurse walked out quickly when she noticed them.

"Give me a mirror," Prince Adam demanded in Vicurian. Though it was hardly above a whisper, his voice still commanded the entire room.

"Prince Adam, I don't think—"

"Give me the mirror." He tried to sit straighter before wincing in pain.

Raven knew he and Princess Arianna would get along fine as she handed a mirror to him.

He threw it against the wall. "No wonder the queen didn't want her daughter to see me. I'm a monster. I won't let that beautiful creature meet me until I'm perfect again." Prince Adam crossed his arms, lying heavily on his bed.

"Prince Adam, you realize that with wounds that deep—"

"They will heal," he stated as he closed his dark brown eyes filled with nothing but anger and determination.

Raven didn't care to argue.

"Guard Raven and I will update the queen on your condition," Rowan commented, leaving as hastily as they could.

"I thought his guard said he was brave. Maybe my Vicurian is rusty. That kind of loyalty didn't match the man we met," Raven remarked as they walked down the hall.

"He's vain, that doesn't mean he doesn't care about the people who serve him. Or have you not noticed that Aleks can be vain as well?"

"At least his vanity is charming...nothing like that."

"Well, maybe Princess Arianna will find him charming."

Raven shuddered.

"You're more relaxed than I would have expected."

Raven remained silent.

"Could it have anything to do with that pill you tried to hide from me?"

"What are you talking about?" Raven kept her attention focused squarely ahead.

"I'm concerned about you, Raven. You shouldn't need them anymore. You need to be careful. I like you and don't want to see the queen do something, so instead please try to stop taking them. You've changed ever since you got them, and I—"

"You don't like this version of me? Someone who's more confident and focused and shows you up?"

"I don't care about that. I care that you're addicted to this pill and can't realize it yourself. I hope you figure it out before it affects your life," Rowan growled as he left her with her thoughts.

# CHAPTER FOURTEEN

## RAVEN

"May I help you?"

Raven spun at the alarm in Susan's voice. She withdrew a blade and walked over to her door. "Lord Cenric." Raven relaxed enough to put Susan at ease. "What can I do for you?"

"May I speak with you? Privately?" he requested, eyeing Susan.

Raven moved to give him access, reassuringly patting Susan's shoulder as she left, her brown eyes filled with concern.

"What can I do for you?" Raven crossed her arms behind her, her fingertips resting on the tips of her short swords.

"That's unnecessary, Guard Raven. I'm not here to threaten you." Lord Cenric walked over to her window and looked at the courtyard below. "Do you wish to protect the queen?"

"It's the job they hired me to do."

"Yes, of course. I would never suggest otherwise. But some would only protect her while on duty, and those who would go out of their way to protect her. Which one are you?"

Raven pondered for a minute, assessing his angle, "I will do what needs to be done to protect the queen."

"Some members of the court have confided in me that their suites have been broken into recently. Only small things have been stolen, nothing of too much importance, not enough at least to bother the queen with. However, I think it should be shared with the Royal Guard."

"What was stolen?"

"It's bits of maps and documents from King Stewart. Treasures they hold dear, treasures they wouldn't want the queen to be aware of." Lord Cenric walked to her door. "I trust you'll not tell the queen about any of this until you think it prudent to do so?"

"What's so important about an old map and documents outside of sentimentality? Is there private information on them?"

"Some of them have sensitive information. As for the map, I couldn't tell you what it's about. None of them will divulge that to me, only that it's vital they get it back." Lord Cenric left before she could ask more questions.

Raven's head spun with the information. As she walked to breakfast, she debated how to tell her boys. Maybe she would tell Rowan and let him decide. He was the unit leader, after all. All thoughts of Lord Cenric vanished the moment she entered the dining hall. The atmosphere reeked of anger and fear.

So much fear.

Shouts reached her ears, and she didn't hesitate. Somehow, Raven knew where to go.

A crowd had gathered around the table she sat at.

Around the table, Betsy ate.

Servants scattered as her blades slid out of her sheaths. Raven could barely control the power within her as it rose to her level of fury. If she hadn't trained for so long on controlling it, she would have burst. But she couldn't let an ounce show…if she did…she was dead. Raven pulled the magic as it growled.

Raven snarled, everyone moving away from her. Everyone but the man.

The man who was beating Betsy in front of them.

Raven didn't take the time to look at Betsy. She didn't want to examine the broken arm hanging out of its sling, or the blood dripping from her broken nose, and the way she had tried to make herself into a smaller object when she couldn't move any further on the uneven rock flooring. Never again would she let this continue. Not again.

Raven zeroed in on the man.

She grabbed him by his silk robes and threw him five feet away from her. Her magic sang, screaming in a blinding rage to be used. It begged to be woven into her swords that could burn and cut through anything with a single swipe. Raven took a breath and held her magic at bay, shaping it into a tightly braided loaf that created a loop of power, allowing it to be manageable until she could find a better way to reshape it. She didn't bother looking at the man as he groaned. All she could focus on was Betsy and the blood dripping off the knife in her already broken arm. Small streams of red ran between Raven's feet as she crouched before her.

"Are you okay?" Raven whispered. Her hands shook as she gripped them together. Raven didn't dare touch her. She didn't know what her magic would do. What *she* would do.

Betsy looked past Raven, her brown eyes wide with terror.

"You bitch, you're going to pay for that," the assailant said.

Raven heard him charge up behind her, grabbing something off a table, a knife, she assumed.

She waited for him to get closer. Right when she felt him behind her, Raven spun around and up, letting her magic break just slightly out of its loop and fuel her veins enough as she knocked his pathetic knife away and grabbed him by the throat.

"Lord Roger, why am I not surprised?" Raven's voice had never dropped so low. She lifted him so that only his toes touched the ground.

"You don't...whom...dealing with..." he rasped, his face turning red.

"So you mean I'm not dealing with a pathetic man who gets his kicks out of beating a maid and trying to force himself onto a Royal Guard? I'm sorry, do you have a twin?" Raven lifted him higher, all pain gone as her magic swirled within her.

But it never broke through. She would never lose control.

Both of his hands gripped her arm, trying to break the hold.

"If I ever see so much as a *scratch* on Betsy again, I will kill you. I don't care if it's not even your fault. If she is anything but in perfect health, I will hold you personally responsible. I will drag you before the queen, and I will be the one to tear your heart from your spineless body," Raven whispered, her eyes glazed over with a fury so sharp, she wasn't sure if she should kill him right then. The longer she looked at him, the more images of a man long forgotten took his place.

Raven's magic twirled in glee and desire to enchant him. For a second, it flared in her. She could do it. She could be the first-ever enchanter to enchant another life and bend them to her will. Her magic rumbled its approval. It had been so long since she had truly unleashed it.

"Guard Raven, let him go." Rowan broke Raven's concentration enough to resist the urge.

Charles and Bastien stood behind him.

Raven noticed the awe in Charles' eyes...and the fear. Rowan was the perfect picture of inscrutability.

Raven dropped Lord Roger unceremoniously to the ground. He scrambled to his feet, gasping for air, a piece of metal glinting in his hand.

Raven leveled a blade at his throat before he could lunge.

"Do it. *I dare you.*"

He dropped the knife and turned around, his robes ruffling around him as he bolted out of the dining hall. As soon as he left, the room breathed, and everyone's pent-up emotions unfurled. Women cried, men moved tables, and healers were summoned.

All the while, Raven sat beside Betsy.

Raven rode a high from that confrontation for the rest of the day. She hadn't been so energized in a long time. For a split second, she had desperately hoped Lord Roger would attack her. Give her a reason to draw blood. But he was a coward. Thankfully, Betsy was okay. Raven found out later he had come in and started yelling at her. Betsy had fought this time. But so had Lord Roger. At least she had fought, Raven conceded. All of it brought up memories of an event that had gone entirely different for her.

She had tried to help a woman years ago, tried to do things correctly, and the girl...she had ended up killed by the man she refused to leave. He was giving her a good life; she had told Raven, who cared if he hit her a couple of times? Raven had pleaded with her, to no avail. But this time, Raven had been there to stop it.

She smiled at the thought of the fear in Lord Roger's eyes as she had held him. Her magic had surged. If she had given it any more reign, she would have glowed with her power. She would never try to enchant someone. The risk was too great, but she came close today. Too close. Thank the gods Rowan had interrupted her.

Raven shook her head and closed the book in her hand after reading the same line ten times. "Aleks, what information do you have about Lord Cenric?"

"A bit, why?" He turned his attention towards her, the candlelight illuminating his hair and eyes.

"He came to my room a few days ago—"

"He did what?" Aleks couldn't keep the contempt from clouding his face.

"He wanted to tell me about some robberies that have been happening in the palace. He thought a Royal Guard should be informed." Raven fiddled with the blanket, uncertainty teasing the edges of her mind about opening up to him.

"Has my aunt been told?"

"No. He said none of them would tell her. Do you think he's telling the truth? I had heard two women discussing something being stolen before he came to see me."

Aleks paused, twisting his lips to the side. He always looked extra handsome when he scrunched them.

"Lord Cenric...is someone to be wary of. How much do you know about how my aunt came to power?"

"Not a lot. It's not written anywhere. Believe me, I've tried," Raven muttered. She'd gone to the palace historian and asked, and gotten nowhere. She had gone to the library and found zero information there as well.

"It's not written anywhere...yet," Aleks amended. "When my aunt came to power ten years ago, Lord Cenric played a significant role. His father was King Stewart's closest and most trusted of the seven advisors. In his need for power, Lord Cenric helped my aunt form a coup that took power from those advisors the same day King Stewart was killed in an apparent hunting accident. A lot of good, powerful men and women died that day, set on fire for the kingdom to see. I love my aunt, but I do not condone how she became queen. I'm not sure what Lord Cenric is trying to stir up with you, especially since you gained my aunt's trust, and he gained a new title. But I would be careful, Raven. He's a master of manipulation."

"Were the King's seven advisors killed that day?"

"No. They disappeared. Well, all but Lord Cenric's father, Lord Garth. They killed him." Aleks murmured.

"I'll be careful," Raven assured him. At least now she had the confirmation she needed for Lady Tremaine's command. Six advisors were alive, and Raven needed to find them.

As the days grew shorter with winter's full grasp, Raven couldn't shake the sense that someone was watching her. There was no definitive proof that would be too easy. No, it was the way the hairs on the base of her neck stood up when she moved around the palace at night. She knew that if she could just turn fast enough, she would see them. But she never could. Lady Tremaine remained unreadable, as always when Raven looked at her through the mirror.

*Snow White, how may I be of assistance?* She was short and abrupt. Something was off.

*Someone's following me. I need someone else here who can help me. Maybe Ella could come?* Raven didn't dare to hope.

*No.*

Raven's shoulders deflated.

*Ella cannot be distracted by you.*

Raven lowered her head. Ella would have been perfect. She could have inserted herself into the palace and found out exactly what had been stolen.

*Mira perhaps?*

*I've already sent Calla.*

Raven's head snapped at attention. *Calla? She's not trained for this.*

*I've already sent her—*

*You're sending her to her death. Calla's an enchanter, one who has not been trained to use her magic to fight. She doesn't know how to hide what she's feeling—*

*Like you are now?* Lady Tremaine admonished.

Raven stood straighter.

*I don't agree with your decision, but if you think it best, then I will concede.*

Raven saw the door behind Lady Tremaine open. Ella and Jaq walked in, smiling. Her heart lurched at seeing her soul sister. Her magic swirled in happiness and longing to hug her friend.

Lady Tremaine's back was to them. Raven was going to say something to Ella, something small, when Lady Tremaine noticed them.

*I don't need you to agree.* She ended the conversation.

Raven had to figure out who was following her before Calla arrived. Lady Tremaine may be willing to risk her safety, but Raven was not.

"Rowan, what would you do if someone was watching you?" Raven looked to her partner over their dinner. They had walked down into Aslar to eat during their day off. Both needed a break from the palace.

"Do you think someone is watching you?" Rowan gulped down a beer, watching her. He rubbed the end of the scar on his face.

"I know I'm not imagining it, despite what Aleks thinks. I swear, even when I'm sleeping in my room, someone is watching me. The only time I feel safe is when I'm in Aleks' room and that's because he's a fucking prince. No one is that stupid."

"If you want, I could stay over and see if anyone comes near your room?"

"You'll be exhausted tomorrow, and we're already working enough—"

"That's why coffee was invented." Rowan smiled.

*Raven stood over two graves. Both were ornately decorated, and both were left blank. Grief pulled her to the ground, sucking her under. It crushed her. She couldn't be an orphan. She was too young. Only people with nothing were orphans. She had everything. She couldn't have...nothing. Fire chased her, its screams yelling at her to leave. The heat licked her feet as she ran through the palace; the graves forgotten. Hand grabbed her legs and pulled her down, dragging her over cobblestones. Her screams echoed through the empty halls, but nobody came.*

*No one cared enough to help the orphan who had nothing.*

Raven woke up to a hand over her mouth. Instantly, she gripped her attacker's hand and twisted his wrist so that it was behind him.

"Raven, it's me...Rowan." He remained calm as Raven held him, the nightmare still dripping free.

"Rowan?" She released him, leaning back into her bed. "What happened?" Raven wiped away the tear staining her cheek before wrapping her arms around herself.

"You started screaming and then crying. Are you okay?" Rowan lightly grasped a shoulder, looking her over in the moonlight.

She removed his hand. "I will be. It was another nightmare. I get them all the time."

"Even around Aleks?"

"Yes, even around Aleks. Why does that matter? It's not as if I can control them," Raven snapped.

"Sorry, you're right, it's...just...surprising for him." Rowan didn't finish his thoughts, a snap outside catching their attention.

Rowan moved to the window. Raven came up behind him in time to see a dark figure run away. Both of them leapt out the window and sprinted through the garden. Raven unsheathed one of her daggers as she gained speed. She will end this tonight. No more dark shadows following her. Raven would unmask them and finally get some answers. The garden hedges loomed before her, their height casting shadows over each other in the moonlight. Raven heard Rowan nearby, just as determined as she was. The man fleeing them dove around a corner, with the two of them splitting up to cut him off.

Raven went left, careening around the corner to catch a glimpse of the masked man running down another path. Damn, he was fast. She sprinted faster, her lungs filled with air as she neared him. She grabbed a smaller dagger and took aim. It missed.

Raven didn't let that failure slow her down as she pursued him.

She launched herself around the next corner and grabbed his dark tunic, using her momentum to slam him against a hedge, her dagger pressed against his neck.

"Rowan?" Raven asked as she quickly stepped back.

Rowan kept his hands visible as he relaxed.

"Did you see which way he went?" Raven gasped for air.

"No, I thought you were him," Rowan said as he scratched his head.

"Well, at least I'm not imagining it," Raven commented as they headed back to the palace.

"Why would anyone be following you?"

Raven bit her lip and looked down. "I've been meaning to tell you—"

"Raven." Rowan crossed his arms, portraying the big brother she adored.

"There was never a good time—"

"What is it?"

As she relayed everything that she had been told, she observed a myriad of emotions cross his face. Anger, suspicion, and concern.

"I didn't want to bother you if it wasn't important," she rushed, locking eyes with him.

Rowan stood there in the middle of the palace gardens, absorbing the information. "Damn. Are you sure those robberies are real? I mean, why this information? Why you? Why not me, Bastien, or another unit?"

"It's because no one trusts him—"

"With good reason. Raven, how could you be so—"

"I was investigating and verifying first. I wanted to make sure he was correct. I'm not someone who blindly follows someone. You know me better than that."

"Have you figured out what was stolen?"

"Only pieces of a map from King Stewart. No one is being very forthcoming. For all I know, these pieces could be of a map showing secret passageways in the palace or of the royal forest."

"Secret passageways?" Rowan laughed.

"The members of the noble class are not telling me, so it left my imagination to wander. Besides, you already know of one. Who's to say there aren't more?"

Rowan stood outside of her door, both of them silent as they thought of what to do.

"Well, since neither of us will have a good idea in the middle of the night, go to your room to get some precious sleep," Raven ordered.

Raven faced Aleks as he stared at the wooden ceiling. He did that more and more, she noticed; staring into nothing. Thinking of something. She wished he would talk to her about whatever bothered him. They might be having fun, but she was someone he could talk to. A fresh breeze swirled around them, caressing Raven with Aleks' snow and pine smell. Raven sighed. She was doing the same thing to him. She turned on her side and placed a hand on his chest.

"Someone is following me, Aleks."

"Raven, we've had this conversation—"

"Rowan saw them as well. He stayed in my room the other night, and someone showed up."

Aleks tensed beneath her hand. "Did Rowan see who it was?"

"No, they ran away," Raven paused, "I think it's because of the robberies Lord Cenric told me about."

"Ah...those. Did Rowan also warn you away from him?"

"He did...he also agrees with me that something must be important to those robberies for someone to follow me."

"Maybe Lord Cenric hired someone to make you paranoid and push you more," he suggested, a smile playing on the corner of his lips.

"I'm being serious Aleks—"

"I'm being serious too. I told you, Lord Cenric is a master manipulator. Be careful when dealing with him." Aleks brushed a hand against her cheek. Raven tried not to flinch at the memories the motion brought. "Are you going to tell my aunt?"

"No." She was entering dangerous territory. Even when she tried to trust others, she knew where they stood. But Aleks was constantly crossing lines she didn't expect.

"They refuse to bring it to her attention. I think they're afraid of what she'll do if she learns they were hiding something from her." Raven said.

"Well, were the items important?"

"They seem to be more sentimental than anything." Raven kept her eyes on him. Aleks remained still, his eyes fixated on the ceiling.

"I think you're overreacting. If they don't want to report it, then it's nothing and they don't want to worry their queen."

"I guess." Raven turned away from him, hiding her disappointment. Why did it matter to her so much what he thought? Her magic shrunk at his dismissal of her thoughts.

She felt Aleks relax beside her.

"I haven't felt this paranoid in a long time—"

"Your previous job didn't make you paranoid?" Aleks snorted.

"Oh, it did, but in a cautious way. I'm usually the one making others paranoid. That's why I wish you would take this seriously."

"We're having fun Raven, nothing about us is serious," Aleks snapped.

*Where had that come from?* Raven thought as she twisted to look at him. But he refused to look at her, opting to keep his eyes locked on the ceiling.

"You're right, nothing about you is worth being serious about." Raven got out of his bed and tossed her clothes on.

She walked out of his room and down the barely lit corridor. How could she be so idiotic? He would never care for her. She should be used to it, Raven scolded.

Jason had been the same.

*"I'm leaving."*

*It was a whisper. Raven shifted on her feet, gazing up at him. Lines creased his perfect face. He had asked her to meet him at their spot next to the lake, which was a thirty-minute walk from Aumont. It was peaceful and secluded, their perfect escape.*

*"When are you coming back?" Raven bit her lip, knowing the answer deep in her magic. It had tried to soothe her the moment she'd laid eyes on him.*

*"I'm not."*

*Raven had never really given credit to the power of words until those two sliced through her magic, cutting her very soul.*

*"I'm in love with my target—"*

*"Jason...please..."*

*A simple plea.*

*To stay.*

*"Please, stop. This isn't funny." Raven wrapped her arms around herself. Her magic rose, cracking in her heart.*

*"I'm not joking. I'm leaving, and I'm never returning."*

*Raven gripped herself tighter. Her magic convulsed around her hands, illuminating the surrounding forest.*

*"But everything we talked about—" Raven gently pulled her magic back. She would maintain control. She could do it. As she looked at the green eyes, she loved oh so much...she could do it.*

*"They were lies. I never wanted that life with you."*

*"I don't believe you," she whispered. Raven saw the glisten in his eyes. The life she had adored seeing in their depths had vanished. "Jason..." A tear rolled down her face.*

*Her magic exploded, demanding to be let go to take away her pain.*

*It flared around her hands.*

*"Raven—" Jason rested his hand on her cheek.*

*"No!" Her magic flared brighter. She stepped away from him, breathing slowly. "You don't get to do this. You don't get to break my heart, Jason."*

*Raven wound up her magic. She would not lose control. She paced on the edge of the lake, pulling and twisting until her magic was manageable again. Her magic flared in her vision, turning everything red. Sparks burst in her eyes as she looked at him.*

*"What about the children you talked about having with me?" she challenged.*

*"Lies."*

*"The house we would build on the grassy slopes far away from here, nestled against the forest?" She would get him to realize he was wrong. Her magic squirmed under her control as she continued to rein it in.*

*"Lies."*

*"That you love me." Raven maintained her control as she walked up to the man who was shredding her essence, took his hand, and rested it on her cheek. "Was that also a lie?"*

*Tears burned down her face as she held him there.*

*"It was all a lie." Jason swallowed.*

*Raven didn't bother to keep her emotions hidden. If she had, her magic would have imploded and she would have drowned in its depths.*

*"You're breaking all that I am."*

*Jason stepped away from her. "Then it's time that you grew up, Raven. You're seventeen now. Be an adult and learn that life isn't fair. It's always a game, and sometimes you only have two bad choices before you. Even if you don't like them, you still have to choose."*

*"And I was the worst choice," Raven said.*

*Raven's magic shuddered at his rejection. Everything shrunk as she stepped farther away from him. Her legs lost all strength as she landed hard on the grass. She didn't bother to look up as he walked away, leaving her in their spot. Their favorite perfect spot.*

*Her heart shattered, and her magic splintered.*

*There, in the shadows of the trees, Raven grieved the loss of her heart. She became lost in the depths of her shattered heart as they cut her into something new. Something that never wanted a broken heart again. As she pulled her magic in, she built it into something new. Something that would never let her heart be broken again.*

Raven walked blindly down the halls to her room, crawled into bed, and slept as her heart cracked.

# CHAPTER FIFTEEN

## CALLA - ONE WEEK AGO

Calla made it to the edge of the ship as her stomach relieved itself of any scrap of food she had managed to swallow. Her hands shook as they tried to keep her from collapsing. She'd already tried to save face and not throw up the first two days. Calla was not about to disgrace herself further in front of the crew. She did, however, allow herself to lean heavily against the wall and close her eyes. More bile rose in her throat. She was able to stand up when it wracked her body again. Hands gently pulled back her dark brown curly hair before it could get caught in the mess. A calloused hand came into view, holding a cup of water.

"Swish and spit."

Calla swirled the water in her mouth, instantly rejecting the taste.

"That was awful." Calla heaved when her stomach twisted again.

"I put some lemon in. That usually helps."

Calla slowly faced the shipmate. "Thank you for helping. I'm sorry for snapping." She wiped away the last bit of vomit.

As the secondhand shipmate looked her over, she assessed him. He was only a few years older than her, his blond hair pulled loosely into a short ponytail. Everything about him intimidated Calla. His green eyes spoke of his youth and free spirit, a life at sea. That, more than anything, threw her off. Calla was used to understanding someone within moments of meeting them, and he confused her. Usually, all she had to do was lightly pull her magic and touch someone, and she could get a clear picture of who they were as a person. But she couldn't do that.

He might sense it, and she was going to a kingdom where enchanting was strictly forbidden. So it left her to her judgments. Everything about his life spoke of a hardened man and criminal, yet the one man before her was uncertain of himself.

Calla stepped back, wavering on legs made of liquid.

He caught her, steadying her against him.

"It'll pass soon enough. Everyone gets sick their first time on a ship," his deep voice soothed her.

"They said only women got sick on a ship."

"They're liars, the lot of 'em. All of them got sick on their first day. It impressed them you held out for two." His eyes twinkled with mischief.

"Well, I'm glad I could impress some sailors," Calla remarked before walking away from him and towards her room. The ship rocked beneath her feet, tripping her at each step.

Calla headed for the door leading below deck when a wave pushed the ship sideways, knocking her against the wall. She winced as each wave sent her stumbling against the opposite wall. Her cabin was at the very end of the short hallway. But to Calla, the ten steps she needed to take loomed before her.

The entire assignment loomed before her.

How was she supposed to get into the palace of one of the worst queens known to enchanters, find Raven, hide her true identity, and search for the king's missing advisors? Calla was not one to be in the trenches. She was one of the most skilled enchanters employed by Lady Tremaine...at least...she thought she was. Mostly due to her rigorous training from her mentor, Lord Conrad. His only complaint about her was that he could never determine how powerful she was.

Her father had had the foresight to put a tattoo of a howling black wolf over the mark at the base of her neck. He had even refused to tell her if she was powerful, or barely passable as an enchanter. Hopefully, she would know one day.

Her cracked creaky wooden door flew open, darkness greeting her.

Calla paused.

She may not have been trained to be in the field, but she knew enough to remember when she had locked her door. Calla didn't enter, sensing another life inside. She turned around slowly.

Then she ran.

She ran until she got to the secondhand shipmate.

"There's someone in my cabin." Calla said nothing else as thoughts of someone in her room spiraled through her magic.

The secondhand shipmate turned to her, a frown on his face. His eyes darkened at her interruption.

"Why would anyone want to hide in your room?" One crewman sneered as he looked at her.

Calla held firm, resisting the urge to hold on to her golden rose necklace, opting instead to twirl her fingers into her extremely curly brown hair. If there was anything her friends had taught her, it was to listen to her gut.

"There is someone in there."

"You better be right." The secondhand shipmate drew his sword. He remained silent the entire time he walked to her room. Calla walked closely behind, more than happy to let him go first. She stayed outside as he walked in and quickly out.

"There's no one in there." He walked past her, not looking at her.

"There was someone in my room."

He turned to face her. "There's not anymore. Let me know if someone bothers you."

Calla watched him leave, standing outside of her cabin for a few more minutes, bracing herself. She had locked the door.

She always did.

Calla sat up, the hairs on her arm raised. Her dark brown eyes darted around, adjusting to the early morning light. No one was there, she repeated to herself, over and over. Calla got up and moved everything that had shifted in the night back to its rightful place. More at ease, she made sure her potions and empty jars were securely and discreetly hidden. Going through her normal routine, Calla began by siphoning off the magic that had built up overnight. It had yet to become uncomfortable, but it was starting to tickle her skin.

Every day, she siphoned off some to keep it at a dull throb in her stomach, and not a roar in every fiber of her soul. She would have to siphon off more the closer she got to Evrotia. She didn't know when she would get a moment to use her magic again, and she hadn't gone through a long period of not using her magic since she was nine. That's when Lady Tremaine had found her. To this day, Calla didn't know *how* Lady Tremaine had found her. It had been shortly after an incident involving her and a horrid lady. She had come with Lord Marcel to assess her and convince her to move to Aumont. She had been so excited she hadn't noticed how anxious her father was. It wasn't until years later that she had remembered the way her father held onto her tighter that morning, and she hadn't seen him since.

Calla held the golden rose necklace her father had given to her that day as she walked up on deck and took in the sun. It was her mother's necklace and her only possession. She closed her golden brown eyes, soaking in the rays. What was her father doing right now? Was he creating a new potion, or enchanting anything to keep up with his skills? Were her sisters happy? They would almost be thirteen now. She wondered if they even remembered her. They had only been six. Was she just a dream to them?

"The crew said there was a woman on board." A man dressed in a red perfectly tailored coat walked over to her. His black hair was tied in a ponytail at the nape of his neck. He didn't stop until he was right before her, towering over her.

Calla clutched the railing of the ship as he got closer than she wanted. He leaned toward her. Calla ducked and stepped out of his way.

"Come here, you—" He raised a hand above her.

"Lord Edouard."

He paused as the secondhand shipmate walked over to them.

"Can I help you?"

"She won't let me near her," Lord Edouard said as he leaned against the wall.

"This lady is a guest on our ship. She's not to be touched by anyone."

"The lady?" Lord Edouard's voice was thick with disgust. "She's not a lady, and she should do as I please, especially dressed like that."

Calla straightened her dress. It was a plain blue dress that fit her okay and was only a little tight around the shoulders and waist.

"I can assure you, she is not for anyone to buy, and unless she says otherwise, you are to leave her alone while on my ship." He crossed his arms, staring Lord Edouard down.

Lord Edouard turned on his heel and walked away, not once looking back.

"Thank you." Calla dusted herself off, needing to fidget. She soothed her magic, pulling it in as it shook with her fear.

"Are you okay?"

She nodded, ignoring the shake in her hands.

"My name's Christopher, but everyone calls me Chip."

"Is it because you're always grumpy and 'have a chip on your shoulder'?" Calla asked.

"Ha ha." Chip deadpanned. "I chipped my tooth as a child." He escorted her up to the deck. "Our destination is five days away." He pointed at the horizon, took out a telescope, and showed her.

"Only five days, huh?" Calla looked through the glass, seeing seagulls flying over a sea of ships. "I think I can hide in my room for two days..."

"You don't have to hide because of Lord Edouard. Stay by me and no one will come near you." Chip assured her.

For four days, Calla stayed by his side. Since Lord Edouard was a guest of the captain and a member of the lower noble class, there wasn't much Chip could do besides stay next to her. The night before they arrived in the port of Aslar, Chip walked into Calla's cabin and locked everything.

"What's your plan when we dock? Where are you supposed to go?"

"Someone's supposed to meet me there. I have to get a job at the palace," Calla divulged.

"If I took you to shore tonight, would you be able to covertly find your people tomorrow?"

Calla tilted her head.

"As soon as we dock tomorrow and you're off this ship, I can't protect you from him. He will pursue you, and I don't know what he'll do."

"I'll make it work tonight," Calla replied, straightening as she held onto her necklace.

"Good, gather your things. We leave in twenty minutes."

# CHAPTER SIXTEEN

## Raven

Raven found herself guarding Aleks two days after she had stormed out of his room. Well, not technically guarding Aleks. He was in the room having lunch with Queen Lyanna. Raven kept her distance from the prince, not even saying hello in passing. It was petty; she knew it, but she didn't care. She didn't even care that her magic whimpered whenever she was far away from him and that seeing him today had made it light up with joy. Raven stared straight ahead during the entire meal, ignoring Rowan's questioning glances. Bastien and Charles guarded the door, and remained oblivious to the silent looks between her and Rowan. This was a lunch the queen didn't want anyone interrupting.

"My sister wrote to me." Queen Lyanna turned a pointed look at Aleks.

"What did my dear mother say?" Aleks closed his hand tightly over his knife. Raven tried to remain oblivious to his emotions.

"For starters, she's glad you're alive. You ran away when you were told she had promised you to the young princess of Rairene?" Queen Lyanna paused as Aleks shifted in his seat.

"She's only fifteen. If anyone should marry her, it's Joseph. Not. Me." Aleks replied.

Raven did her best to express no emotion. This was news to her. Not that it should matter. It didn't matter; she asserted.

All the windows behind the queen shattered.

The blow knocked Raven forward, hitting her head on the table.

Masked men flooded into the room.

Raven shook her head as the buzzing continued to vibrate in her ears. *What the hell?* She pulled out one of her short swords, the sound of metal on metal banishing the buzzing from her mind. Raven engaged the fighter that charged her before she could observe her surroundings. Each time she turned, another man was there, fighting her, and preventing her from assessing the battleground. Because that's what this was...a battlefield of men who formed a wall around her, keeping her from the queen.

Raven was lost in a sea of masked men.

All she could do was fight them. Fight and fight to get through their endless waves of attack. Her magic thundered in her, but she held it back. Her pulse raced as she let herself do what she did best. Fight. She pulled out one of her daggers laced with Frost, a rapid and fatal poison. She cut as many men as she could with that blade. Once Frost entered the bloodstream, it would cause an explosive chain reaction in the veins, making all of them burst.

Her vision became clouded with red as her magic sought to be used. Raven contained it, pushing it down as she blindly fought anyone in front of her. She didn't give any of them a chance to get through her defenses.

She raised her dagger to strike the next assailant, their blade coming up to block hers.

Raven's eyes widened when she came face to face with Aleks.

Her blade was less than an inch away from his cheek.

He was grim as he moved his blade away and went back to fighting. Both of them were now trapped on one side of the small army, while Rowan, Bastien, and Charles formed a defensive barrier around the queen.

A blade pierced Raven's defenses, and she grunted against the pain, refusing to give in. She ignored it, pulling out more daggers, each one with a deadly poison. Distantly, she heard Aleks whisper an enchantment into his sword. A flash of light encircled his hands before quickly flowing to his sword, enabling it to cut through anything...and anyone.

Raven sped up, thankful for the training she had. Where these men were coming from seemed to be endless, and they needed help. The five of them wouldn't last much longer.

Raven slammed the heel of her foot into an attacker's head and used the opening to sprint for the door.

She threw open the door. "The queen's under attack!"

A blade found a home in her back.

Raven turned around and jumped into the fray, going blind with rage. She let her mind go, her body taking over as it used all of her years of training. More guards came to help, she was certain, but she didn't notice. At the end, all she remembered was standing over a pile of bodies, covered in blood.

Darkness swamped her mind.

Raven woke up when the pain in her back became an unbearable fire. Instantly, she looked for her jars. She scrambled around her bed, trying to make sense of the blurry glass objects before her. She took two of each at once, sighing as she lay on her stomach.

"Sleep well?"

Raven jumped at Rowan's voice.

"How long have I been asleep? I could eat a horse," Raven groaned. She turned her head sideways to look at him.

"Two days."

"The queen?" Raven scrunched her nose. She would not be happy Raven had missed two days of protection.

"Fine." Rowan sat down next to her. "Though I don't think they were after her."

Raven lifted one eye open to see Rowan's hands fidgeting in his lap.

"Explain, I was there. It sure as hell seemed like they were going after her. They weren't going after Prince Aleksander, were they?"

"It was you, Raven."

"Please don't make me laugh. I think it'll hurt." Raven winced. "It's not possible. Sure we got separated, but that was to keep me and Prince Aleksander from getting to you...you know...better the odds?" Raven claimed, scrambling to remember what had truly happened.

"Actually," Rowan paused, "they only separated you. Let me finish." Rowan stopped her from speaking. "Aleks was on my side of the table.

They immediately moved to separate you. Aleks fought his way through to be beside you."

Raven stared at him. The first thing she remembered was that Rowan was right about where Aleks had been. The second thing she *knew* to be true was that Aleks didn't care about her and would never be so reckless with his own life.

"So you think that a group of people, or a person, is so bent on killing me they staged a fake assassination attempt on the queen?" Raven laughed, clutching at one of her injuries. "I don't have those kinds of enemies...I think."

"You're certain there wasn't a mole with your mistress?"

"I would have been told," Raven muttered. "My name...it means something to others. It would be invaluable if they knew my assassin's name and my real name."

"Raven, are you certain—"

"I would have been told. If not by my mistress, then one of my friends."

Susan opened the door, relief on her face.

"We'll discuss this later." Rowan got up from Raven's side. "I'll see you at training. Queen Lyanna has been...unpleasant...with you missing time because of your injury." He sighed.

# CHAPTER SEVENTEEN

## CALLA

The boat ride to shore was out of a horror novel to Calla. She waited for the giant sea monster to come out of the ocean's depths and swallow them whole. Fog curled thickly off the surface, playing with their minuscule boat. She sat directly in the middle of her seat, hunched over, not daring to look or go near the side. Chip remained silent, staring over her shoulder as they left the ship behind. He barely made a sound as the oars hit the water.

He swore no one, but the captain knew they were gone.

"We're certain this is the best route?" Calla whispered, though she was certain the entire kingdom could hear her.

"They close the docking in the afternoon. We're sneaking you in between ships. Luckily, the city of Aslar doesn't post a lot of guards at night. They assume that they'll notice a large ship, such as ours, moving. Queen Lyanna hates paying for more than she thinks is necessary, so there have been a lot of cuts with the guards. They're not happy about it, so they're only going to work within the definition of their jobs. Right now, only large ships aren't allowed into port, and we're not a large ship, so they're not going to care. For all they know, we're returning late from fishing." Chip smiled. At least...she thought he smiled. She couldn't tell in the dark.

Once they got to an empty post in the harbor, Chip jumped out of the boat, climbed the ladder, and tied the boat to the dock. Grabbing Calla's hand, he hoisted her up.

"Thank you, Christopher, for taking care of me. You went above your duties."

"You're welcome," Chip squeaked. "You know where to find your contact tomorrow?"

Calla nodded.

"Here." Chip handed her a small coin bag. "That'll be enough to get you a night at the inn over there." He motioned to the only building with candles still burning. "They're friendly folks. They'll help you with anything you need."

Calla hugged him quickly. She kept her magic in check as it squirmed to read Chip's history. He stood awkwardly before hugging her.

"Stay safe, stay away from Lord Edouard. If you see him before you see your contact, do not come out."

"Aye aye, captain." Calla laughed half-heartedly. She kissed his cheek and walked up the dock to the pier, heaving her trunk with her.

Calla gazed up at the inn's name, The Rose and Thorn. Nothing could have been more fitting. Inside the stone and wood building, she discovered an older woman sitting behind a rickety wooden counter, writing in an extremely old book. The smell of leather and ink washed over Calla as she took it in. The Innkeeper smiled and put her glasses on.

"Welcome to The Rose and Thorn. What can I do ya for?"

"One room for the night, please." Calla could see enough by the candlelight.

Dust coated everything in a thin layer, making her fingers twitch.

By the time the Innkeeper came in, Calla had cleaned off the counter space and a couple of chairs. The woman snorted, before motioning for Calla to follow.

Her room was in the same condition as downstairs, dimly lit and covered in dust. Her bed, if it could be called that, was nestled below a small grimy window. The only other furniture was a nightstand and a small hand mirror.

"Thank you," Calla mumbled as the Innkeeper left. She did her best not to shiver at the sight before her.

She did not sleep well. Calla blamed the bed and its lack of a real mattress. The only other time she had been so nervous was when Lady Tremaine had taken her from her family. Restless, Calla got up and got ready to find her contact. She hadn't been told what he looked like, only that he was showing up as her father. Was she supposed to guess which old man on the dock was her father?

Calla put on a plain blue dress with long sleeves and tied an apron around her waist. If her scrying was correct, and it always was, this was the right outfit for someone who was a maid in Evrotia. She tied a dull kerchief over her hair, knowing it would be useless in taming her tight brown curls. Lacing up her boots, Calla left her room before the sun could rise.

While the sun may not have been up, the same could not be said for the workers in the harbor. Everyone bustled around, giving her pause. At least she could easily navigate unseen in the chaos. Looking out to the sea, she saw Chip's ship coming into port, all the crew on deck. Navigating her way over to the docks was no easy feat, as everyone seemed to go out of their way to block her or push her trunk. She was used to not being seen, preferred it actually, but this was ridiculous. By the time she got to the docks, the ship had laid anchor and was about to disembark. Calla's heart raced. Edouard *could not* see her.

Looking at the crowd, she didn't recognize anyone.

An old man walked into the center, took out his timepiece, glared at the ship, and then crossed his arms.

"Father." Calla stumbled over to him, excitement getting the better of her. It had been over a year since she had seen her mentor, Lord Conrad.

His brown eyes softened for a moment as he faced her. Worry flashed in his eyes as he glanced between her and the ship. "Everything alright, Belle?" He asked as she hugged him.

"I'll explain, but we need to get away from the ship before the passengers get off."

Lord Conrad didn't waste a second as he grabbed her trunk and shuffled her off to a plain, single horse-drawn cart.

Calla explained her adventures at sea while Lord Conrad drove them through Aslar, taking them to the lower level. The street turned from stone to dirt to something Calla most definitely did not want to identify. The house he was in was almost worse than the inn. Inside, however, she saw he was still a creature of habit, living in luxury.

"Why not live in one of the cleaner parts of Aslar?"

"Well, I would be pretty conspicuous up there for a spy and an enchanter." He gave her his you're-smarter-than-that-question stare.

"Of course." Calla walked around, waiting for him to say something. "What's my true assignment? Lady Tremaine gave me about three." Calla listed them for him.

"Raven's assignment has become precarious in recent days. She needs a new set of ears to listen for her, someone who will be trusted implicitly upon sight. That, my protégé, is you."

"Why don't they trust Raven?"

Raven never had that issue before.

"She's a Royal Guard, and no one trusts them. Since she's also a woman, it was harder for her to gain the queen's trust. She had to do things for the queen that took away any trust the servants had in her."

"What made her role more precarious?"

"Look for yourself. Given your skills, you'll be able to see it even better than I." Lord Conrad removed a piece of fabric from his coat and handed it to her.

"It's covered in blood." Calla cradled it, pulling softly on a string of her power. "*Revelare mihi de te hominem quarare.*"

The blood poured its story into Calla's eyes. Raven stood behind a woman, whom Calla assumed was the queen. A man sat across from them, his arms crossed. Right after he slammed down his silverware, the windows shattered. Calla flinched as Raven hit her head. The more the blood revealed to her, the more Calla's heart raced. Raven had gone ballistic in that room before collapsing to the ground. The man with white hair caught her. He held something against her side, the cloth napkin. It was staunching the blood coming out of Raven.

Calla dropped the napkin.

"That's Raven's blood."

"It is." Lord Conrad threw the napkin into the fireplace.

"Is she okay? Does she need a healer?"

"She's fine—"

"Does Lady Tremaine know?"

"No. Nor will she. She might pull Raven, or worse, blow her cover for the sake of saving whatever this assignment is."

"You don't know?" Calla couldn't believe it. He was Lady Tremaine's second in command at Aumont.

"No," he grumbled. "They have not given me that information. I'm not even sure Raven is aware of why she's here outside of finding those advisors. But that's beside the point. You're here and have a new job at the palace as a maid. You start today." Lord Conrad bustled around his home and gathered some items, stuffing them in a sack before hustling Calla out the door.

"Where will I stay?"

"At the palace. They at least provide housing for their servants, but not much else. I'm afraid the meals are going to be less than desirable." He grimaced.

Calla gazed up at the imposing metal gate. It towered over her, much like the one at Aumont had when she'd first arrived and been a foot shorter. The palace was chaotic. Maids, butlers, and others bustled past each other.

"Your papers." The guard yelled in her ear.

Calla jumped as she handed them over, waiting for him to let her through.

"You can pass."

"Uh...which way?" Calla hunched her shoulders, waiting for him to yell at her horrible Evrotian.

"To the left. It says 'servants' entrance', go through there and you'll find where everyone meets for their assignments."

"Thank you." Calla briskly walked away.

Once she found the entrance, she walked in and froze. Rows of heads turned to look at her, wondering who was late. All of them sat in rows in a narrow wooden room void of any decoration. A large woman walked up to her, long nails tapping the parchment in her hand. She dominated Calla, looking her up and down, her expression unimpressed. Calla looked down at the rough stone floor beneath her. It was just like her first days in Aumont, when all of the other older enchanters had deemed her beneath them.

"You'll do." She walked away. "New girl, come get your assignment."

"Give the girl a day to settle in, Mistress," a waif of a girl commented.

"I would, Danita, but Susan is ill, so unless you want to take over for her, and not go work with the healers to become Healer Danita, then I suggest you stop commenting." Mistress barked at Danita. "You can take her there, though."

Danita walked over to Calla, a frown on her face.

"Make sure you show her to her room first. Thank you for volunteering." Mistress laughed as she handed out assignments to the others.

"I'm sorry that you—"

"I don't care. So long as I don't have to take over for Susan. Come on, newbie." Danita led Calla through the palace, showing her to her room. It was a lot better than the inn. She was only given long enough to set her trunk down before Danita dragged her out. She said little except to point out the important things Calla would need to know later. Calla's head spun as they stopped.

"Here we are. Good luck with her. I've heard she's awful."

"What am I supposed to do?"

"Take care of her for now. She was hurt, and the queen is pissed off that she's not around right now. So we would appreciate anything you can do to speed up her recovery," Danita joked.

She left before Calla could inquire further.

Calla knocked, and upon hearing a faint groan, entered. Her heart raced at facing the person no one else wanted to help. Calla walked in, bracing for the worst. Her magic coiled up inside, waiting to respond to any threat.

# CHAPTER EIGHTEEN

## RAVEN

Raven called from her bed at the knock, furrowing her brow. Susan didn't knock.

The pain in her back crept in and she longed for her medication. Gods, how she wanted them. She would need to replenish her supply soon. The headaches she had been getting were not fun.

"I'm sorry. Susan isn't well. They have assigned me to fill in today."

Raven's head spun at the voice.

"Calla?"

Calla closed the door, smiling before running over and hugging Raven.

"Ouch."

"Sorry, what can I do?" Calla's hands fluttered in front of her.

"Hug me again. I can't believe I'm seeing you right now." Raven held her close, picturing them home instead of in Evrotia.

"Did you get here okay?" Raven pulled away far enough to look at her friend. The dark circles under her eyes spoke of sleepless nights. Her hair hadn't been brushed in days, though she had attempted to tame the coils with a cloth headband. Something had gone awry on that ship. Her gold-flecked brown eyes did little to assuage Raven of any fears. Calla muttered an acknowledgment under her breath.

Something had happened.

"The real question is, are you okay? Lord Conrad gave me a napkin covered in your blood to scry."

"I will always be in awe of how he operates." Raven sighed. "It's not as bad as it looked. Thankfully, the prince jumped in to help."

"He did jump in. He risked his life for you."

It was Raven's turn to mumble incoherently and ignore the twinge of heartache in her magic.

Calla remained silent, giving Raven her I'm-going-wait-here-if-it-takes-all-day-stare. Raven stared at the delicately woven blanket under her hands. Calla would understand that she needed time. Calla kissed Raven's forehead and moved to Raven's exposed wound. She had taken care of Raven more times than Raven could count. Raven waited for Calla to mention the recent injuries, tensing each time she came across a new one. But Calla remained silent.

"Calla, before you left, was anything...compromised? My name...did my name get made public? Did the king—" Raven stopped talking.

She'd been so adamant when confronted by Rowan and Aleks, but now she wasn't sure of anything.

"Nothing has been compromised. I promise." Calla finished bandaging her wound and put a fresh tunic on her. "Why do you ask?"

"This wasn't the first time I survived a directed attack. Each time they've become more pointed. You saw...you know...but, no one is aware that I'm here. I've never been here before. The closest I've come is Trudel."

"We'll solve it. Together. Like we always do," Calla reassured her.

She pulled out Raven's kit, grabbed a small jar of serum, and began spreading it onto Raven's back.

Raven sighed in relief.

"I haven't been able to use that. They don't have it here, and I knew there would be questions if anyone saw or smelled it."

"Well then, it's a good thing I'm here," Calla murmured.

"I'm so glad to see you." Raven closed her eyes, falling asleep on her stomach to the gentle massage of her friend.

For the first time in months, Raven was at ease.

# CHAPTER NINETEEN

## CALLA

Calla eased onto her bed, wincing at the thin mattress and lack of general comfort. All she had in her room was a bed and a small dresser. Nothing else. She and the maids shared a bathtub, and they all got their meals in the servants' dining hall.

A knock on her door froze Calla in place. Her hand was currently holding a bag of potions. She had been about to siphon off some of her power, but she quelled her singing magic and stuffed the bag under her bed. No maid could keep that information a secret.

Danita smiled as Calla opened the door and walked in.

"Can I help you?"

"I see you survived her." Danita assessed Calla, sitting on her bed.

"Survived her?" Calla closed the door, one hand resting on her necklace.

"Guard Raven. I'm impressed that she didn't make you cry."

"Does she usually?" Calla questioned. What in the Gods had Raven done?

"No...but the rumors about her are not kind," Danita said. "I was wondering if you would find them true."

"I've only met her one time. How would I be able to confirm them?" Calla leaned against a wall, hiding her shaking hands. Had she already blown everything?

"Well, does she have razor-sharp teeth? Or nails sharper than a knife?"

Calla burst out laughing.

"See, you can confirm some rumors aren't true."

"People don't actually think that of the guard, do they? They make her sound like a monster."

"They think she is one. So they make her out to be one." Danita's eyes darkened. Genuine anger lit up the depth of her dark brown eyes, and Calla didn't need her magic to see that it stemmed from grief.

"What happened? Why does everyone fear her?" Calla whispered. Raven, what did you do?

"There hasn't been a female Royal Guard in years. Queen Lyanna usually ends up killing them after a month. That she's lasted this long...she must be truly heartless—"

"Do you think that of the men?" Calla challenged, her anger rising for her friend.

"They didn't kill our friend."

Ah. There it was. The reason everyone viewed her as heartless. Calla shuddered. There was no coming back from that. Lady Tremaine must have deemed the queen's trust more vital than the servants.

"Who was it?"

"The chef, Louis. He was a good man. He and Guard Raven were friends too...yet she still killed him."

"I'm sorry for your loss," Calla spoke through tear-soaked vocal cords, refusing to show any as her heart broke for Raven's sacrifice. "I'm sorry that I can't confirm Guard Raven as a monster."

"I didn't believe any of it, anyway. It's not possible." Danita smiled. "Have a good night, Calla."

"You too, Danita." Calla led Danita to her door.

"Oh, if you ask the laundress nicely, she'll give you some extra towels to line your bed with."

Calla bowed her head in thanks.

Over the next few days, Calla got used to being a maid. Susan returned the following day, and Calla's headmistress gave her a staggering list of normal daily tasks to accomplish. Which she did in record time. Calla's obsessive need to clean came in handy and gave her time to think about how to help Raven. They needed to find out why someone wanted Raven dead. She didn't think it was because of the chef. Maybe Jaq would have an idea. Reaching out would be risky, but Raven was family, and she would do anything for her. It's what they had always done.

# CHAPTER TWENTY

## RAVEN

Rowan had stopped by a couple of times, along with Charles and Bastien, while she rested. Aleks had tried. She had kicked him out. So what if he saved her life? She was still mad. They finally cleared Raven to train and go on active duty again, much to the queen's delight. No one dared ask how Raven had made such a quick recovery. As it was, she was lucky no one noticed the slight smell. It surprised her that the healers hadn't insisted on seeing her wound. She suspected that even if she hadn't recovered; they were on orders to clear her either way.

Raven bounced on her feet, all of her pent-up energy overflowing. Despite the serum, her injury still hurt, and she had run out of medication, which meant Rowan was currently beating her.

The worst part, though, was the headaches had started up, and kept getting stronger. Raven blinked against the pressure building up in her skull. Rowan knocked her to the ground, smiling as he helped her up.

"Don't get too smug." Raven smiled. He had improved a lot.

"Why don't you go take a shower and get some rest before the start of the day?" Rowan suggested.

Raven didn't turn him down. She needed a reason for them to not be seen together. To protect him.

Raven hoped the shower would help with the blinding spots in her vision. When the pain didn't ease, she paced around her room. She had to get Louis's stash. She needed to focus and think past the pain. Calla needed her to be at her best. Raven's hands shook more with each minute that passed. She could make it through this shift, and then she would get more.

With that decision made, Raven went to find Rowan with a new goal in mind.

The two had to go on patrols that night. An unexpected development. Queen Lyanna had been relentless in stepping up patrols after the attack. If Raven was going to make it through the night, she needed that medication.

Wherever it was.

All she knew was that they were in the kitchen, a kitchen that should be empty in the middle of the night. Before she met up with Rowan, Raven stripped down to her black training clothes. As she removed the breastplate, she sighed, her mind calming. With the pauldrons and vambraces gone, so were her tense muscles. By the time she removed her greaves, she was Snow White.

Grabbing a few daggers and lock picks, Raven climbed out of her window and hung off the craggy castle side. Scaling down, she pushed through the headache between her eyes as she slowly got down to the ground three stories below. Once she was on solid footing, getting to the kitchen unseen was a lot easier. If she had been given an assignment here, it would have been easy to get in and out unseen. No wonder those other men could get in and try to kill her.

All you needed to be was an amateur assassin, and you could sneak in.

A fire still burned in the kitchen, giving Raven enough light. She moved quickly and quietly, trying to think of that fateful day. She had barely been conscious enough to keep her eyes open, let alone watch him go to his supply. Rowan had probably watched, but he would never tell her. She was not about to ask her partner and only friend to find out the answer. She had her uncrossable lines, and that was one of them. Louis had gone to the back, but not far enough away that he was out of sight from her.

Raven moved to the middle wooden cabinet, her fingers tapping around on the top shelf. Moving aside a spice rack, Raven felt behind it, pausing as she listened.

Something was rolling in the jars.

Clever spot, Raven thought as she took the spice rack down and looked for the correct ones.

They weren't hard to miss.

Raven pulled out eight glass bottles full of her medications. Each one of them glowed faintly with magic. The enchanter was so weak, it could only be seen by her now because of how many were in the jar.

"Fuck."

Raven grabbed a jar and flung it against the wall.

He had given her drugs laced with enchantments.

She had asked him, and he had said no. Yet he had given them to her, anyway. No wonder she couldn't stop taking them. No wonder she felt so much better with them in her system, messing not only with her physically, but magically as well.

Raven squeezed her eyes tightly, hitting her fist against the cabinet, its coarse grain grazing her skin.

Her magic cooed at her, trying to offer comfort. What was she going to do? Raven dropped to the cold stone floor and buried her head in her hands. If she stopped taking them...the withdrawals would be...intense. She wouldn't be able to work for days, and she would lose her position.

If she kept taking them...Raven froze...she would feel better. She could hide it. That's what she would do, continue to take them, knowing that the longer she was on them...the worse the withdrawals would be. But she couldn't lose her position. She couldn't disappoint Lady Tremaine and their oath. I swear, by the blood in my veins, and the bones of my ancestors, to protect the kingdom and the crown, or may the gods strike me down. Raven repeated it as she clutched the glass bottle in her hand. She would do it.

She would knowingly take the enchanted drugs...for just a little longer.

She would be fine.

Her magic would be fine.

Raven spotted more enchanted drugs in the cabinet. She grabbed all of them, hoping to figure out what else Louis had been up to.

Raven raced to her room, getting to the door right as Rowan walked up, raising his eyebrows at her outfit.

"I wanted to stretch my muscles, get back to my roots," Raven remarked, trying not to squirm under his observant brown eyes.

"Sure." Rowan looked at her. "Ready to go?"

"One minute and I'll be out." Raven darted into her room. She took one of each pill and hid the rest under her bed.

Raven paused in front of her armor. She had to put it on. She couldn't walk around the palace without it. The serum on her back pulled tight when she tried to get it on.

"Uh, Rowan, will you help me with my armor?" She stuck her head out of the door.

Sighing, Rowan followed her, grumbling about women always needing to change outfits. She stuck her tongue out at him. As they left with Raven fully armored again, she came face to face with Aleks.

"Aleks, do you need something?" Rowan smiled.

"I was wondering if I could talk to Raven?" Prince Aleksander looked at her with wide, hope-filled, ice-blue eyes. Eyes that pulled her in and made her want to say yes, over and over.

"Nope." Raven brushed past both of them.

"Still mad at him?" Rowan commented a few minutes later.

"Whatever made you think that?" She smirked.

"Whatever or whoever he did, I'm sure it's his fault. He feels bad about it. I don't think I've ever seen him try to talk to a woman who was mad at him."

"He didn't...do much...I'm more mad at myself."

"Okay." Rowan shrugged.

Their patrol went smoothly, and as they walked, Raven only talked about her brief excursion earlier, telling Rowan about the lapses she found. She didn't tell him everything, though. She didn't tell him about the tunnel that went underground, or the hidden door under a bridge that had rusted with age. Raven only told him about the unimportant lapses, the ones she knew wouldn't come back to bite her.

Raven collapsed on her bed, her muscles melting as she closed her eyes. She was only going to get about four hours of sleep before she had to start her normal daily duty with the boys. The wound on her back spiked, making her groan. She rolled over gingerly, reaching under her bed for the bottles.

"What..." Raven flipped off her bed and tossed the mattress, trying to locate them.

"Looking for something?" The rattle of pills pissed her off more than the fact that he was in her room.

"Give them to me."

"Not until you talk to me."

"You made yourself clear about us, Prince Charming. There's nothing more to talk about." Raven turned to face where she thought he was.

He had to be in her chair. There was nowhere else.

"No, you made your assumptions, and jumped to conclusions, and out of my bed before I could say anything."

"Is that all that matters to you? That I was sleeping with you? I thought we were becoming friends, which is why I was opening up to you. Just like how I talk to Rowan. But apparently, all you wanted to do was mess around, so that answered my question." Raven folded her arms, waiting for her eyes to adjust. She would fight him for those pills if she had to.

"No. You were treating me like I was someone special to you. Friends don't talk about that stuff," Aleks asserted, coming out of the shadows.

He had been against her wall, hiding in his black suit.

Raven laughed. "What do you and your friends discuss then? That's what my friends talk about. What else is there when you're a group of assassins? You can't talk about the latest gossip at the palace or the drama splashed over the mirror. No, you talk about the weird shit you've seen, the horrible things you've done, and anything you're allowed to discuss about current assignments. And if someone is following you, you get their perspective about it. See if you're crazy, or if you should take it seriously. That's what friends talk about."

"Well, that's not...something I've ever been allowed to discuss...even with my closest friends." Aleks leaned against the wall, his eyes downcast.

"Well, that sounds like a shitty life." Raven crossed her arms, re-evaluating the prince before her. One who was alone and could never voice his concerns with another person. One who was trying to open up to her now.

"What can I do to—"

"Get me to sleep with you again?" Raven spoke.

"No." Aleks crossed the room, stopping inches away from her. "To be friends again." He slipped into his native language and whispered, "I miss you."

Though his words meant more to her than she could express, Raven had learned her lesson. The door to her heart that had swung open for him was firmly locked now. She would not unlock it for some heartfelt words.

She uncrossed her arms, and sat down, trying to get space from him and process what he'd said. "Help me figure out what is so important about those stolen map pieces, and why someone is trying to kill me."

"That's a lot to—"

"No, it's not. You're here to spy on someone as well. Why else would you have those clothes? Why would you still be here when the ball you came for happened two weeks ago? You're looking for something as well, and I'm merely suggesting we work together."

"Raven, you don't understand what—"

"I do. I'm willing to do the same in this arrangement."

Aleks nodded slowly, handing the medication to her.

"It's a good thing you're not an enchanter," he commented. "They're enchanted. Barely, but enough to make a difference."

"Then it's a good thing I'm not an enchanter," Raven whispered. Her magic tore at her like an unruly dough that was begging to touch him, to enchant, to do anything. But she kept it caged. She had to. She had no clue what would happen now that her magic was tainted.

# CHAPTER TWENTY-ONE

## CALLA

Calla was bored. The day-to-day tasks of being a maid had worn her down. It was a wonderful distraction from the constant hum of her magic. However, she wasn't sure how Lady Tremaine expected her to help Raven when she couldn't use her magic to scry. At least not without being very cautious. She and Raven couldn't even meet or sit down and talk together. It would be too suspicious. What was worse, though, was that even though she was better than the other maids, the head housekeeper, Mrs. Rosmunda, didn't even approve of her cleaning. She said it was too clean. How could something be too clean?

"Calla."

She jumped as Mrs. Rosmunda called her over. "Yes, ma'am?"

"You like to clean. I have a task for you." Mrs. Rosmunda held out a piece of paper to her. "A prince is living in this part of the palace. You are to clean his suite of rooms, take care of him, bring him meals, everything.

Am I understood?" She looked down her nose at Calla through spectacles that could use a bit of cleaning themselves.

"Everything?"

"Yes. You can even sleep with him if you like, though from what I've heard, he's a bit of a beast. May not be too suitable for your meek disposition."

Calla blushed.

That was not what she had meant. She hadn't slept with anyone. Why would they want to sleep with her? Calla took the paper and walked away quickly, head down. She gathered the bare essentials and a tray for breakfast. If he was a prince, surely his room was already pretty clean? The other maids were good enough to make sure of that.

She ambled to the wing of rooms, double-checking the map. How was this correct? She had gone up five flights of stairs and found herself in a very forgotten part of the palace. No one was up there. Why would a prince be put here?

Calla gazed out at the empty halls and rooms stretching before her. The entire wing was deserted. Dust and cobwebs covered everything. Even the carpet beneath her feet had a thin layer of dust. She could see where other maids had walked, or run, based on the distance between their steps. No one walked away from the suite of rooms before her.

Calla frowned. What kind of prince was this?

She knocked on the large wooden door and waited. She waited for five minutes before knocking again. When there was no answer, she opened the door, shrugging. He had probably left. It was late enough in the morning.

The stench punched her in the face.

It was a mixture of body odor, rotting food, and dust. Calla raised a hand over her mouth, holding back the contents of her stomach. The room was dark, forcing her to take a few seconds to let her eyes adjust. When they did, she wished they hadn't.

Plates of food were piled up on what she assumed was a dining table. The couch had been flipped over, along with some other tables and chairs. Everything was...simply put, disgusting. How anyone lived in these conditions...

"You can set the food down where you please and then leave."

Calla jumped at the deep, raspy voice, gravelly from misuse.

She turned to the bed, and there lay the prince. The cloth strips wrapped around his chest had turned brown. His head was bandaged as well, though at least those wrappings were in better condition.

"Your majesty—"

"I said to leave." He threw a pillow towards her.

"Your majesty, I've been told that I need to clean this room and take care of you." Calla set the tray down on a surface that looked stable enough.

The prince moved his large body. She hadn't been able to see just how large he was until he had removed the blankets and stood up.

She craned her neck, her hands clasped before her as he stumbled over to her. His footsteps shook the floor. His matted blond hair stuck to his forehead as he got further into the light. The bandage on his face was much worse than she had thought. So was the one wrapped around his chest. Blackened blood coated his chest and half of his face along with what she could only assume to be some type of infected puss.

"I said...GET. OUT." He said as he stood less than a foot away from her, his body taking up her entire view.

Calla no longer had to wonder why the footsteps outside his room ran away as hers chased them.

By the time she got outside the suite, she had calmed down. She smoothed down her apron and fixed her hair. She would not be deterred by him. She did not give up on an assignment just because some prince felt it was okay to be a beast.

Calla walked to his room, her shoulders squared the following morning. She had spent the previous day gathering supplies.

Calla didn't bother knocking this time.

When she walked in, she was ready for the smell. She had several sacks, rags, mops, scented candles, and supplies ready.

"Good morning, Prince Adam." Calla had learned his name.

"Piss off." His accent was thick as he spoke in Evrotian.

She gently set the tray down on what she hoped was a clean section of the table. Calla strutted over and ripped the blankets off of him. She did her best not to flinch at his growl. Not even Ella, she thought, would have been so brazen.

"You...you are going to bathe and take those disgusting bandages off. Then you're going to put on clean clothes, if there are any up here." She looked around, dismayed by the explosion before her. One couch had been tossed on its side. Both tables and nightstands had plates, glasses, and serving platters stacked on top of each other.

"Who are you to command a prince? You're nothing but a poor commoner." Prince Adam's dark eyes burned with fury as he looked upon her.

"I, your majesty...I am..." Calla froze, her bravado gone. Who was she to challenge him? She was only a merchant's daughter, nothing special. "I may be a commoner, but at least I can tell when something's infected, and at least I know how to smell and bathe myself. Something you have forgotten about. So if you want to have a chance at not being a beast, or better yet, not dying of infection, then I suggest you listen to this lowly commoner and take a bath."

Prince Adam moved. Slowly. Calla tilted her head as she watched him.

"I haven't moved since yesterday."

She walked away, picking up dishes as she went.

Prince Adam went to the washroom, slamming the door. Calla walked around, making sure she didn't miss any stray bits of food or dishes, dumping all of them into a trash sack. She then moved to his clothes, all of them stiff and dusty.

Glass shattered in the washroom, followed by a string of curses that had a blush reaching her ears. She darted for the washroom and found the prince on the floor, half of his bandages off, the rest stuck to his skin. A pair of old scissors rested next to his hand. A glass had fallen on the floor by his bare feet. He locked his gaze on the floor, only glancing up at her once.

Calla walked in and swept the glass away before she sat down beside him and reached for the scissors. Prince Adam snatched them away.

"Give me the scissors, your majesty. Let me help you."

"I vowed I would let no one see how hideous I've become."

"Wow...that is..." Calla shook her head. "So stupid." She kept her eyes down. "Plus, you're in luck. As the daughter of an unsuccessful merchant, I've been a nobody my entire life."

She took the scissors from him and began to slowly cut the cloth away from him. Even with her delicate hands, she couldn't remove all the bandages that had dried to his scars. Her magic lit up inside her at the touch of his skin. She shook it away, pulling it in.

"Now can you see why I don't let anyone see me?" he asked as he undressed and climbed into the steaming hot bath.

"Not really." Calla got up and left, ignoring the heat in her cheeks and the tingling magic in the tips of her fingers.

While he bathed, she cleaned. Coughing as dust got into her lungs, she moved around the suite of rooms. As she worked, her mind unfocused on her assignment with Raven and instead turned to the simple motions of cleaning. Calla longed for her mage room at Aumont. All of her books were at her disposal there, and she could freely use her magic. It was too bad Raven had lost her memory. If she hadn't, Calla could have read her and tried to see what might have caused everything. Her mind wandered, searching for new ways to help Raven. She didn't notice Prince Adam until he walked up and grabbed the cloth out of her hand.

Calla yelped, looking up. "Prince Adam, I'm sorry, I was—"

"Busy thinking about something important. Come, I need you to clean my wounds and re-wrap them," he ordered, walking to a chair as he pushed back his wavy blond hair.

Calla followed, grabbing some alcohol and bandages.

"So...what happened?" Calla questioned to distract him as she soaked the cloth with alcohol. Prince Adam began to tell her about the wolves. "This is going to hurt." Calla hesitated as his muscles tensed right before she placed the cloth on his exposed wound.

He roared at her as pure alcohol touched his flesh. "Stupid woman, what are you doing?" He leaped away from her, twisting around to keep the injury from her.

"I'm cleaning your wound. Soap and water aren't enough. Especially considering how poorly you've already taken care of your wounds. So, this is going to hurt, and it's probably going to hurt a lot. But you're going to deal with it if you ever want to look pretty again, and you're going to have to stay still." Calla rushed her words as he stared at her. She stared back, her heart and magic fluttering at her audacity. What had gotten into her?

Prince Adam slowly lowered himself onto his chair, careful of his wounds. Calla grabbed a new cloth, shook out her hands, and poured more over his skin. He groaned, clenching his fists around the arms of the chair, but he stayed still. He didn't yell or growl at her. It took her thirty minutes to thoroughly clean and bandage his wounds to an acceptable state.

His face was the hardest.

Their heads were so close, his mesmerizing eyes so close, Calla found it hard to concentrate on what she was doing. In the early morning light, she realized his eyes weren't dark, but hazel and flecked with emerald green. He seemed to see right through her, diving into the core of who she was. She was certain, more than once, that he had figured out who she truly was by looking at her. He could see her, therefore, he could see who she was...a liar...a spy...an enchanter. Calla quelled her magic, holding on tightly. Not a single ounce could shine through, especially not in her eyes, as it so often did.

"All done," Calla rasped, stepping away from him. "Now, I need to change all the bedding. It's disgusting."

Prince Adam smiled slightly, standing to get dressed. He stood taller now, straighter. Calla had always been aware of how short she was compared to her sisters, but compared to Prince Adam, who seemed to be a giant, she felt as though she were an ant.

Calla felt the prince's eyes on her as she continued to clean. She wondered what he thought. Would he have allowed anyone to speak to him that way in Vicuria? Probably not. Especially not a servant.

Calla cleaned everything in his set of rooms. She had tried to clean the surrounding rooms, but the headmistress had said no when she'd asked. However, she didn't let it stop her from cleaning the closest room nearby and discovering a chess set in pristine condition.

"Do you play?" She carried it into his suite and glanced over at him in his enormous bed, trying to read. She noticed he kept glancing towards the windows every couple of pages, his body slowly slumping the longer he looked at it.

"It's probably the only thing I'm good at." He laughed, his deep voice vibrating over her magic. "Do you?"

Calla grinned. She played all the time against Jaq. They currently had a board running with tallies on it. They were tied 50-50. Whoever got to 100 first would buy the other dinner. "I play a little."

"Care for a match?"

Calla hesitated. It was the first time he had spoken more than a few words to her.

"I promise not to yell this time."

"I really should work..." Calla looked around the large, spotless room.

"You've cleaned this place so many times the dust hasn't dared come out of hiding."

Calla chewed her lower lip, playing with her necklace. Her desire to do her job battled with her need to have something fun to do.

"Okay, but only one." She got everything set as Prince Adam worked on getting out of bed. His side wound, she noted, still pained him as he winced.

They sat across from each other, looking at the board. Calla moved her white pawn forward, beginning the game. They played for over thirty minutes, each one deliberate in their moves. Calla kept her eyes focused on the game, barely chancing any glances at the prince lest he distract her. As it was, whenever she glanced up, she met his studious eyes.

She didn't know what to make of it. Was he observing her to figure out who she was? Or was it something else? Calla had gotten used to people looking at her hair, touching it, feeling its difference to their own. But that didn't mean she liked it. Hated it.

"The other day..." Prince Adam moved a piece. "You said you were a nobody—"

"I am. I'm a poor commoner, remember?" She didn't dare look at him.

Prince Adam winced. "Why does that make you nobody?"

"I've always been ignored, or thought of as lesser than," Calla flinched away from the memories of her first year in Aumont. Of the awful enchanter who had gone out of her way to make Calla appear inferior. It had taken Raven to speak up for something to happen. It hadn't mattered that Calla had proven herself, repeatedly, at nine, to be a better enchanter. The others hadn't been able to accept her.

"In my kingdom, your intelligence matters, not your station in life. One of the smartest men I know is a servant. You should never feel inferior for being smarter—"

"Yet that man is still a servant?" Calla moved one of her pieces.

"Uh yes...I don't think it occurred to anyone to have him be something else."

"Maybe it should."

Prince Adam moved a piece. Check.

Calla couldn't correct him that it was her magic that made everyone try to make her smaller. She let him think it was her station in life. In some instances, he was correct.

Calla looked at the board, moving her king out of harm's way by putting Prince Adam's king in check.

"One day, maybe it will."

They neared the end of the game, and Calla won with her queen and knight remaining beside the king.

Prince Adam smiled at the loss. "I haven't lost a match in months. Well played, Calla."

She got up, hiding a smile. Calla cleared the board away before setting it up again. "Rematch?"

Prince Adam turned the board so that he was white, and she was black. "Of course."

"I didn't win because I got to go first." She chuckled.

"We can't take any chances. We'll have to see," Prince Adam said as he moved his pawn.

# CHAPTER TWENTY-TWO

## RAVEN

Raven walked down the halls, her midday nightmare haunting her. Reality and fiction blurred. All she had wanted was a nap. A nice, calming nap. But the nightmare had come along, anyway. It was the medication. She was sure of it, almost positive. The nightmares had only begun after her injury, and those cursed enchanted drugs…those wonderful drugs that made her so much…better. So much sharper, so much more paranoid. The hairs on her neck stood up constantly. She was going to strain a muscle with all her backward glances.

Calla had somehow found a mirror that she could communicate through. It had been risky scrying Raven. She had no way of knowing if Raven was alone, or even awake. Someone could have been in there and seen it glowing, and then both of them would have been killed. But Calla had insisted that the meeting was important. So Raven was out of bed, though it's not like she could sleep, anyway.

The shadows moving were her first and only clue as they morphed along the wall.

They were good. So very good to have avoided her notice. To wait until she was alone.

Raven tried to get to her swords but had to cross her arms to block the sword swinging down at her. Two of them pressed her, forcing her to back up against the wall. Her pulse raced as she moved to get her blades again and was blocked...again. A curl fell in her eyes, blocking her for a moment that she couldn't spare.

They moved with a fluid grace that she hadn't seen in the other attempts on her life. They worked together as well, keeping out of each other's way as they darted for Raven. They were a unit, and she was possibly outmatched. She panted, her magic and heart pulsing as sweat dripped down her face and back. It was the first confirmation that someone was indeed after her, and now they didn't care if she knew it or not. Probably because she wouldn't survive them. They may not have trained at Aumont, but someone had ensured they were good enough to challenge her.

As she blocked their kicks and punches, another attacker wrapped his arm around her neck and squeezed.

She gasped for air, her heart pounding as her vision blurred.

She released the hold she had on another attacker and locked her hands around the attacker's forearm. Before the air was gone, her vision blurring, she slammed her foot onto his, twisting around and kneeing him in the groin, then the stomach. Before this one could do more, she roundhouse kicked him in the head.

Now she had time to pull out her swords.

There were only three others, a number she knew she could handle. Their faces were covered, but she could sense their smiles. They looked between themselves, so confident that they had won. Each palmed knives, a slight advantage.

Raven removed any advantage of the time they would have and engaged them before they could think more about how to defeat her...an assassin addicted to enchantments, an assassin whose name was one to be feared, not mocked by these men. If only they knew who they were going against, Raven thought. She smirked. They would probably piss themselves. As it was, they realized too late that they were the ones who were outmatched.

Raven disarmed each one, her short swords cutting through their defenses.

She was death and felt jubilation race through her veins with each cut she delivered.

It was over sooner than she wished. The rush that came with each little slice or nick on her skin, a lot of nicks on her skin, she realized, was beginning to fade.

Raven's breathing became shallow and rapid.

Sweat dripped down her back.

Raven stumbled as the hallway tilted before her.

She tripped over one of the bodies. What was left of it, anyway.

"Raven?"

She twisted around faster than expected, her feet tangled up beneath her, giving out.

Aleks caught her before she could fall on the dead man.

The poison in her worked fast.

Raven could barely put thoughts...they didn't want to string...they were...floating above her...out of reach...

"Raven!"

Calla...Calla was...Raven blinked. She stared up at Aleks and his perfect white hair. She tried to touch one of his braids, but her hand remained limp at her side.

"Raven, what happened?"

She pulled her thoughts together. What had happened? What was going on? What would...

"Wraith..." Raven fluttered her eyes. She had to tell them.

"What did she say?" Aleks sounded scared. Had she not spoken? Had she not been clear?

"We have to go. Now," Calla ordered.

Raven felt the weight of her body trying to pull her down as she was lifted and taken somewhere. Her magic rose to attack the threat within her. It wanted to sing a song of battles and blood. But it couldn't. She couldn't let it do that. She couldn't lose control. Raven attempted to knead it into a loaf, a loose loaf but at least one that would hold its form and not break free.

"Wraith!" Raven burst the word out. Had they heard her? She couldn't remember if she had told them.

She turned inward, pulling her magic. She couldn't lose control. If she did, her power would explode in a burst of raw magic and kill not only her, but Aleks and Calla. So she changed her focus and kneaded in her magic. It had begun to unravel again. Wraith was making her control tenuous.

At some point, Raven was aware enough to realize she was on her bed.

"You need to remove her clothing and try to keep her still. It's only speeding up the poison." Calla sounded so far away.

Raven stirred, trying to tell Calla where her kit was. Cold air kissed her skin as they ripped her tunic off. Sweat coated her, running down her body in rivers that flooded her floor. They needed to get the antidote in her.

"Raven...Raven..."

*Did Aleks realize he was speaking in Trudelian?* Raven thought.

"You need to stay still. That maid, who's very bossy, says you need to stay still."

A hand, Aleks's hand, ran over her forehead.

"Aleks..." Raven needed to see him. If she saw him, she could maintain control. She would do it...for him. For Calla. But her lids were too heavy, demanding to stay closed.

She conceded to them this once.

She hated not getting to see his face. Though, wasn't she mad at him? Why was she in bed with him? What was wrong with her?

Who was in bed with her?

"Wraith." Raven had to tell them. She had to make sure they knew...who knew? Who were they? Raven ripped at her magic as it fought the confines she had shaped it into. It wanted to sing through her and demolish the poison. But it couldn't. She couldn't let it go. People, important people, would die. Who would die?

"What's going on with her?" Aleks demanded, continuing to speak in Trudelian. Too bad Calla didn't understand that language, Raven chuckled.

Raven tried to breathe, shaking as the air in her lungs disappeared.

Distantly, Raven heard Calla speaking, explaining to Aleks what was happening, or what she was going to do. Something cold and slimy brushed over Raven's stomach, quickly followed by liquid that blinded her with pain.

Gentle hands opened Raven's lips. Something poured down her throat, forcing Raven to swallow the disgusting contents that tasted like grass and mold.

"I need to warn you, it's going to get worse before it gets better."

"How the hell could it get—"

Raven didn't hear whatever else Aleks said as her body seized.

Her back arched off the bed.

Fire licked up her entire body.

Raven shivered, curling up against something warm. As the shaking continued, Raven maintained a stranglehold on her magic. It could not flare. Not now.

"What the fuck is going on?"

Raven could almost open her eyes at the sound of Rowan's voice. Aleks spoke in Trudelian again. She faded out of the conversation. Her heart slowed. Her breathing was shallow.

Raven seized again. She wanted to scream. Her muscles certainly were. Her blankets wrapped tighter around her.

"I have to inform the queen. This could be an attempt to weaken our defenses," Rowan said.

Why did he have to do that? Raven should stop him. She would be fine. She needed to get through this. He would see.

"The hell it is. Someone's been trying to kill Raven for months. They've only become more emboldened and not made it look like an attack on the queen," Aleks asserted.

Exactly, Raven thought. Sweat ran over her face again. She shook in her blankets, her body preparing for another seizure.

"I know Aleks, but she needs to be informed, and I would prefer it be in the line of protecting our queen."

Raven seized again, passing out.

She screamed, the fire burning her alive. She ran through the halls, trying to put it out, to get away. No matter how fast she ran, it caught up to her and enveloped her. Stumbling, she looked around, trying to find an escape. Why did she always end up here? She knew how it would end, the fire would win, and she would die. Sweat trickled down her as the flames grew hotter, came closer, and licked her cheek. They converged on her, and Raven...she screamed and screamed, and screamed.

Raven woke up slowly. She didn't even want to try moving. All she did was lay there and attempt to remember what happened.

"How can we tell it's working?" Aleks whispered.

Raven felt his gentle, calloused hand holding hers.

"She should be better by now. Or at least conscious. It must have been a stronger dose than she's ever had before, or something is interfering." Calla mumbled.

Such as the pesky pills she'd been taking.

"Before? She's been poisoned before?" Aleks' hand tightened its hold.

"Only to make sure the antidote worked," Calla replied. "In her line of work, she had to take precautions."

"You would have told her if someone knew who she was, right?"

"Of course. I'm certain she's not compromised. I would know."

"Then why is someone trying to kill her?"

Raven knew she had to speak. One of them was going to say something they shouldn't. Most likely Calla.

"Maybe it's because we're messing around," Raven mumbled in broken Rairenian. "Or did." Raven kept her eyes closed, not willing to admit how hard it was to breathe, let alone talk. Alek's cool hand touched her forehead.

"Raven, what happened?" Calla asked, her hand lightly holding Raven's other hand.

"Let me rest..." Raven slowly opened her eyes, realizing for the first time the gravity of the situation. Calla was in the room. She couldn't be there. Calla was blowing her cover. She couldn't. "What are you doing?" Raven tried to sit up, her arms melting below her. Calla could be killed.

"You almost died. I had to help. He wouldn't have known what to do," Calla defended, speaking in Rairenian.

"I love you, but you need to leave before you're seen here by more people. Prince Charming can take care of me," Raven commanded, giving Calla's hand a tight squeeze in thanks..

# CHAPTER TWENTY-THREE

## Calla

Prince Adam was staring out the windows again, looking at the towering, snow-covered mountains. They had finished up their afternoon game of chess. He had beaten her this time and was refusing a rematch. Claimed he needed to keep his ego boost while he could. Calla only shook her head and smiled. She wasn't about to tell him she was too distracted by Raven. Her smile dimmed when she noticed his gaze.

"May I ask a personal question?"

Calla continued cleaning the fireplace behind him, trying to take her mind off of finding Raven's attacker.

"Well, you've seen me naked, so I don't think we can get any more personal than that." Prince Adam laughed.

Calla's cheeks flushed.

"You can ask," he reassured her.

"Let's get that bandage cleaned while I ask. Want to sit by the window? I'll go grab what I need."

Prince Adam turned towards the window, arching a brow. By the time Calla came over with the supplies, his tunic was off, along with the bandages on his chest and face.

Calla paused, stunned into silence by him. She looked him up and down, taking all of it in. She couldn't believe she got to touch him. A prince. He sat in the sunlight, his tan skin warming in the heat. She focused on cleaning the wound and not letting her eyes wander. Which was a feat.

"Calla?"

She looked up, surprised at how close he was to her. Her heart pounded. She waited for him to hear it. To laugh at the servant girl's rapid heartbeat from his closeness.

"You were going to ask me a personal question?"

"Right." She blushed, focusing on his wound. "Why are you in this part of the palace?"

"When I first arrived, I was in terrible shape. My men...men who helped raise me, and trained me, had been slaughtered by a pack of wolves, and I was barely alive. I was informed that Queen Lyanna was there when my horse arrived with me slung over her back. She ordered me to be hidden from her daughter. She saw what I looked like. Saw how revolting I had become." Prince Adam paused, heaving a sigh. "I agreed with her. I didn't want the princess to see me, either. To see the...disfigurement...I'm meant to marry her daughter, and looking the way I do...I wanted to die or recover in solitude," Prince Adam said, not once looking at her.

Calla stared at his chest, unable to meet his eyes. He was beautiful. Painfully beautiful. Both of his cheeks dimpled when he smiled. His jaw was powerful, and his smile...it did this thing to her heart where it stuttered each time she saw it. But it was his emerald eyes that pulled her in with their depth of soul. From far away they were dark green, but the closer you got, the more variation in colors you saw. How anyone could think some scars would make him anything less...she shook her head.

"Have I upset you?"

"No, I'm not upset." Calla moved so that she could adjust the bandages around his left eye and forehead. "I don't think you look as bad as you think."

It was torture to be so close to him, her magic tingling each time she got close to him.

"Can't you try to imagine what it's like to walk into a room and everyone finds you abhorrent? That all the fears you had about only being accepted because of your looks and your riches are true? Can you understand how terrifying that thought is?" He looked into her eyes, daring her to maintain eye contact.

Calla frowned. "I don't have to imagine that." She walked away. She didn't want him to see the reality in her eyes. The pain that she knew no one found her beautiful, and she would never be accepted into any courts.

Calla did her best to hide the shaking. Her magic swirled in her veins, whispering love to her. She felt it trickle to her fingertips, waiting to be used to create something that would heal. She always created her best potions when she was in pain. Calla had thought asking Prince Adam that question would distract her from Raven. It hadn't. It had only held everything at bay. She had been so stupid to ask Raven to meet. If she hadn't...Raven may not have been attacked.

Calla got to her room and flopped on her bed. She had cleaned and cleaned, trying to think of different ways to sort out who was going after Raven. But she needed to sleep and maybe get some food. Food would be good. She couldn't remember the last time she had eaten. Calla pulled out some bread she had hidden in a pocket and gnawed on it, deciding she would reach out to Jaq and see if there was anything in Rairene he could find.

Calla grabbed her enchanted ink and scribbled a quick message that would only reveal itself to him. With that done, she pulled out a piece of clothing that was drenched in blood. She'd been able to cut it off one of Raven's attackers. It had weighed heavily in her pocket all day, begging to be read. Her magic had tried multiple times, whimpering to be used. Calla eyed the blood of the man who had tried to kill her friend...her sister. She steadied her breathing, ensured her door was bolted, crossed her legs, and held the cloth between both hands.

Calla hardly had to tune into her body to find the mass of light in her core. It was always nestled below the surface, a constant river flowing around her. She pulled gently, muttering a spell of revealing.

*"Revelare mihi de te hominem quarere."*

If she had wanted the man's entire history, she could have seen it in his blood. But she only desired one moment in time, the last couple of hours before he met the wrong end of Raven's blades. Calla analyzed all of it, not letting the image of Raven collapsing into Prince Aleksander upset her. She had seen many of Raven's fights. Studied them with her, always looking for areas of improvement. Raven was a force of strength and skill, even after getting sliced by a knife laced with Wraith...another thing for Calla to worry about. How anyone had gotten their hands on it, let alone in another kingdom...Calla sighed. Most enchanters ended up killing themselves in the process of making poisons. They would make it too strong and die from the effects it had when mixed with their magic, or they would flare out to overcome with emotion.

Calla pulled a little more magic, aware of how much her magic convulsed around her hands. It had been so long and her magic was flexing its muscles.

Calla went past the ambush, walking through his memories as though they were her own, and she saw everything.

Calla dropped the cloth, frowning at the blood.

Blood never lied.

It was the only sure way to see the truth. She picked it up again and pulled on the blood's story. Then again. A guard...a palace guard, had let the men in. They hadn't snuck in, nor did they kill the guard for the access. They simply knocked and were granted passage.

Maybe Raven was making more waves in her side investigation than she thought. Or there was another reason they had yet to find. She didn't think Raven's investigation into stolen items was important enough to yield this type of response. Especially since Raven mentioned being attacked at least one other time before the robberies.

Calla frowned when her mirror lightly glowed.

# CHAPTER TWENTY-FOUR

## RAVEN

Raven's head throbbed. She knew her head couldn't weigh so much that it felt immovable, but her body disagreed. The light outside blinded her. It was morning. At least she knew that. The sun was coming in, but it hurt too much to see anything else. She rolled onto her back, nothing but a sheet over her. Which was odd. She always slept snuggled under layers of blankets.

Raven closed her eyes, recounting what she remembered.

She had been in a fight. She had won. Barely. She'd been poisoned. By her freaking poison. Her magic ran through that poison. How they had pulled that off...she was going to need some of their blood to read it.

Calla had been there. Her beautiful Calla had almost blown everything to help her. She supposed she owed Aleks. Raven groaned internally. Aleks...how had he gotten to her so fast? She had made sure she wasn't followed. Right? Had she forgotten to take the medication that helped her focus?

No. She would have noticed...would have felt her mind become...lesser.

Raven tried to open her eyes, groaning as the light seared them. That damn poison. Why did it have to be that one? The antidote was a bitch to deal with it. She would need another full day to recover. A day she knew Queen Lyanna would not be inclined to give her. Especially since all she had as evidence of needing to recover from a fight she had survived was a few scratches. She couldn't tell her about the poison, why she had an antidote. But someone had gotten their hands on it. She may as well scream 'I'm Snow White' at the top of her lungs.

Which gave her pause.

If she had died...it would have looked as though Snow White had done it. Which meant...whoever was hunting her didn't know who she was. So then they were after her for a different reason. She needed to sort that out, fast.

Raven turned on her side. Aleks was there, sleeping in her chair. Not her bed. Her comfy fluffy chair...just like the friend he was...well, that he was working on becoming. Raven gazed at him. His white hair still fascinated her, though it shouldn't have. Ellas was the same shade. His had grown well past his shoulders now, the braids still in perfect formation. Both of them, it seemed, needed a haircut. His tunic was slightly open, revealing his muscular chest. He was relaxed, and she was in awe. She couldn't remember the last time she had been relaxed enough to not notice the other person in the room was awake.

Raven looked at his face. He wasn't as relaxed as she thought, upon seeing him awake and locking onto his ice-blue eyes. They held so much confusion and concern in their depths, emotions she did not want to acknowledge. Refused to see.

She remained quiet, keeping her eyes on him. She wasn't even sure if she could talk as her screams from the last day seemed to still coat her throat.

"Thank you," she rasped a few minutes later, finding her courage. She couldn't lift her head without seeing black spots.

Aleks nodded. "What happened to you?" He was quiet and reserved.

Raven had a feeling it had nothing to do with what happened yesterday.

"They ambushed me—"

"Not yesterday," Aleks interjected.

"Not yesterday...then...what?"

"We're...friends...and friends share things?" He looked at her. Only her. His eyes didn't wander.

Raven nodded slowly, carefully, wondering what she was agreeing to.

Aleks continued, "I trained. You saw it. I trained how to be a spy, how to be an assassin. My mother has an interesting approach to how her children are raised. But...I never...I don't have scars like that. It's why you never let me see you in the sunlight, right? Because I would see more than the scars on your stomach. But the ones on your back. Some that are so old you almost can't see them, and the others that are newer, fresher. The acid burns from poisons. The rope burns...around your wrists...around your..." Aleks fought through the words, "around your neck..."

Raven watched him struggle with his control as his magic convulsed in a faint blue glow around his hands for a moment. Just a moment. But it happened. He had almost lost control.

"You certainly had some time on your hands." Raven looked down at her wrists. She hadn't thought about that particular memory for a long time. Nor would she now. "I may have had...hard teachers. Ones who pushed a little harder. Scar me...for pleasure, or to learn a lesson, but it made me into one of the best killers there is. One of the more feared assassins—"

"But at what cost, Raven? If these people know who you are—"

"They don't."

"How can you be so certain?"

Aleks ran a hand through his hair. She wanted to run her hands through it. Wanted to hold him close. Get him to stop asking these questions. Painful questions. Questions that brought up too many memories. Memories of her and Ella struggling to survive. Working together to survive in a world both were made for.

"Trust me when I say that they aren't coming after me because of who I am as an assassin."

"I thought we were friends."

"And that means that sometimes you trust your friend," Raven said. She couldn't tell him her code name. Never.

# CHAPTER TWENTY-FIVE

## CALLA

Calla burst into prince Adam's room and found it empty. He was always reading or sleeping. She searched the entire suite. Nothing. Calla ventured into the connecting suite of rooms, and though they needed to be cleaned, she didn't find him. She would clean once she had located him.

Calla looked out the window and discovered Prince Adam outside on the balcony for the first time since she had taken care of him. The worn stone balcony faced the towering snow-capped mountains in the distance. Though they were far away, the mountains seemed to loom over the entire kingdom with their height.

"I was wondering where you had gotten to." Calla walked outside, holding clean bandages. They would hide the shaking in her hands. Hide the panic that had set in.

"Sorry, I couldn't resist it anymore." Prince Adam's smile barely quivered on his lips as he sat down on the chair she brought over to him.

"Why do you have to resist at all?"

"I didn't want to think about my home. I'll miss it too much if I do." His accent thickened as he spoke. Snow still covered the mountains, gray clouds swirling around them in a beautiful dance. It would be impossible to cross them for months.

"Can't you go visit?" Calla asked, silently kicking herself for the suggestion.

"No...I can't."

Calla stifled her sigh of relief.

"Why not?"

"I disgraced my father by not finding someone to marry after he ended my previous engagement. So he chose for me and told me I wasn't allowed to return until I had gotten married."

"What happened to the other engagement?" Calla sat down to get a better look at his wounds. They were finally healing nicely.

"She was caught—" Prince Adam paused, locking eyes with her. "They caught her doing something unbecoming of her station. Because of that, my father ended the engagement."

"Did you want it to end?"

"At first...absolutely," Prince Adam confessed. "I was furious, a family curse. I was there visiting, you see, when it happened. So when I was told what she had done, her entire palace knew how I felt." Adam's lips twitched in a small frown. "But once I calmed down, I realized I didn't want it to end. She was the only one worth marrying. She was already the most beautiful girl I had ever seen, only matched by her wit. There's been no one else like her."

"Tell me about your kingdom," Calla requested. She didn't want to hear more about him being with anyone else. She leaned forward, resting her chin on her hands and looking at him.

He looked better in the sunlight. His shoulder-length dirty blond hair was healthy and washed, she was happy to see. His hazel eyes, though full of longing, held a light she had only seen when he played chess. He sat up straighter as well, no longer pained by his injuries.

"It's beautiful. Full of grassy hills and forests that stretch forever. The mountains surround us, giving us an incredible valley full of resources. There's a five-hundred-foot waterfall falling off a cliff behind the palace. It empties into a river that rushes through my city, Oskad. The other villages and towns are much the same. They all have well-established guards and a dedicated army. It's why we're a formidable force and ally, and we have the best archers."

"What about the government?"

"Well, that's my father."

"Everything he commands is done?"

"Of course, why wouldn't it be? That's how it is here, in Rairene, and Trudel."

"I'm aware." Calla turned away from him, looking at the mountains he loved.

"What would you do instead?" Prince Adam questioned.

Calla turned farther away, hiding the blush on her cheeks.

"Oh no, you don't get to look away. You're incredibly smart Calla, please, share your thoughts. I'm curious." Prince Adam gently pulled on her arm to face him.

"I would keep the monarchy. But I would also assemble a counsel, where there's one person from each village to represent them. They get to vote, and have a say in what happens in their kingdom. That way, the people are also heard."

"And if the king doesn't like the way the people have voted?" Prince Adam dug deeper into her idea.

"Then he could overrule them. But he would do it with full knowledge that the council didn't support him. I've always believed that the people of a kingdom could have power if they only knew how to grasp it. One where children aren't growing up on the streets starving because their parents can't afford food, or they die from easily curable illnesses. One where enchanters don't have to fear for their lives if they don't fall in line with their ruler."

"That's a beautiful dream, Calla. But a dream. You'd get no one to agree to that." Prince Adam stood up and looked towards the mountains again.

"You could be the first when you become king."

Prince Adam chuckled softly. "If I did that, the noblemen in my kingdom would form a coup and overthrow me."

Prince Adam moved inside, leaving Calla sitting on her chair, with nothing but a dream for a better future for all, not just the few.

# CHAPTER TWENTY-SIX

## RAVEN

She stalked the halls with Rowan. He refused, and absolutely would not allow her to go anywhere without him. Overbearing partner, Raven growled internally. It was a wonder she could see to her digestive needs without him following her there. Queen Lyanna hadn't been pleased that Raven had missed one day.

Raven remained still, hands balled tightly as she knelt before the queen and the rest of the court.

"Raven, thank you for finally gracing us with your presence and reporting to fulfill your duties as my Royal Guard," Queen Lyanna looked down her nose at Raven. "I grow tired of these attacks on you. You've missed more days due to injuries than the rest of my guards combined. I have never had to worry about one of my other guards being competent enough to do their job."

Raven tightened her fists, keeping her eyes downcast.

"Your skills are not worth the trouble you have given me."

"Yes—"

"I. Am. Not. Finished." Each word was clipped as the queen interrupted her. "Should you find yourself injured again and need to take a day…" Queen Lyanna paused. "You will not need to bother with wearing the uniform of a Royal Guard ever again. You might as well get on a ship and go back to your kingdom before I can find you."

Raven waited a minute longer to see if she was done. When nothing else was said, Raven stood up and found her way up the stairs to stand behind the queen and beside Rowan. She straightened her shoulders and stared out amongst the courtiers and commoners.

Before court could begin, a scream carried down from the hallway outside. It was raw and filled with terror. Two city guards barreled in, a man clutched between them. The man was covered in dirt and wore tattered clothing. He struggled against the guards, his feet skidding against the stones. Raven withdrew her swords and angled herself closer to the queen, the others following suit.

"What is the meaning of this interruption?" Queen Lyanna demanded. She sat taller, her muscles tensed.

"Enchanter!" a woman standing to the side screamed.

"Stop where you are," Raven commanded. If they got any closer, the enchanter could kill her if he lost control. Not that it should have mattered, but Raven would not fail because of this evil queen.

The guards stopped, shoving the man to his knees. They crossed their swords over the back of his neck, pinning him.

"Let me go," he said in Vicurian. "Please, I was only passing through. I did not mean any offense."

"How dark is the mark?" Queen Lyanna demanded.

One guard shifted to pull back the man's tunic. "It's pretty light."

"Who turned him in?" Rowan asked.

"An innkeeper, their daughter saw the mark when he was eating dinner."

The queen continued to ask questions while the man shook, pleading to be set free. The crowd murmured around them, all of them craning their necks to see an enchanter. A woman dressed in black, her gray hair tightly pulled back, approached slowly from the back of the throne room. Raven shifted at her approach, monitoring her every move. She moved swiftly before anyone would notice her. Before the enchanter could hear her step behind him. His power had begun to come undone, released by his panic. It lightly swirled around his hands. He wasn't powerful at all. Even if he lost control, Raven imagined he would do minor damage. The man looked up from the floor, finally facing the person who held his life in her hands.

"Please...I was only passing through," he sobbed.

The guards lifted him to his feet, gripping him under his arms.

The woman was almost directly behind him.

Raven's eyes widened when she saw what the woman carried in her hands. Thick black shackles made of stone. Enchanters shackles. Raven swallowed as the woman, the enchanter, got closer to the man. For she had to be an enchanter. It was the only way the enchanter's shackles worked. They had to be imbued with the intention of blocking magic. Cutting off the enchanter from their core...their soul...their life.

Raven had been forced to wear them once. Lady Tremaine had placed her in them only once. For one minute. At the age of twelve. It had been the longest minute of her life. She had been half of herself, empty without the pulse of her power thrumming through her veins. She had begged for the shackles to be removed. To be released from them. Once shackles are placed, they can only be removed either by the enchanter who places them or by one who is stronger.

Her magic quaked at the woman's approach.

The shackles were open.

The man wept as the queen told him about her laws. Told him about how enchanters were not to be trusted.

All while her enchanter reached him.

She held both shackles open in each hand and swiftly clasped them around the man.

Where there had been light and magic wrapping up around his arms was now extinguished. He looked at his hands, at the thick black shackles, and fell to the ground.

But the guards did not let him stay there for long.

"Take him to the gallows. Let him serve as a reminder to those who think enchanters are welcome here, and as a warning to those who do not turn them over," Queen Lyanna commanded.

The guards dragged him away. He no longer screamed. He just stared...into nothing as they left the throne room.

Raven barely kept herself contained as she and Rowan went on their patrols of the palace. He had remained quiet, a constant presence at her side, reassuring her with the anger that radiated off of him. They were near Prince Adam's rooms, a place in the palace no one cared to venture.

Only Calla. Which was the sole reason Raven now insisted they patrol the abandoned wing.

To keep her Belle safe.

Lord Cenric stood in their path as they rounded a corner in a very deserted part of the palace.

Rowan lightly gripped Raven's arm as he approached.

"Lord Cenric, what can we do for you?" Rowan glanced around the dim hall, ensuring no one was lying in wait.

"I need to speak with Guard Raven."

Rowan opened his mouth, stopping when Raven lightly stepped out of his grip.

"Is there somewhere private?" she asked.

Lord Cenric opened a door, revealing a room covered in dust and white linen sheets protecting long-forgotten furniture. The smell of dust and memories of a bygone time swirled in the air, making her sneeze.

"Will this suffice?"

Raven nodded. "I'll be a few minutes, Rowan."

Rowan walked into the room, and did a sweep to make sure she was safe, and only then, once he was satisfied, did he leave the room and stand outside.

"Someone's protective," Lord Cenric muttered.

"Have you told anyone that you asked me to look into those missing items?" Raven was blunt. She had to be. She had to figure out why someone wanted her dead.

"No. I wouldn't jeopardize myself even more than I already have."

Raven laughed. "From what I'm told, you're very good at looking after your best interests. Especially since you won't tell me exactly what I'm trying to find."

"My past is of little consequence in this—"

"Is it?" Raven raised a brow. "You're very ambitious. If I solve these thefts, what do you get out of it? What glory, what ranking would you get once you tell the queen that we have caught a thief?"

"I would probably be dead," Lord Cenric confessed. He ran his hands through his thick brown hair. "These items that are missing...they aren't nostalgia the nobility cherish."

"I assumed that, but what are they? So far, they sound like scraps of paper."

"King Stewart knew his queen was up to something before he died. She had manipulated him before when they were younger. So he took precautions should anything happen to him or his daughter."

"Why not divorce her if he knew she was planning something?"

"He did not think he could leave her again without inciting a bitter war with Trudel."

"So he took precautions for him and his daughter. What does that have to do with the thefts?"

"Rumor has it he left his seven advisors as guardians over his daughter. They would rule until his daughter was of age. They would also guide and help raise her to be ready to take the throne from a secret location hidden away from Queen Lyanna. It's thought that he gave a letter to each advisor to prove this and that he gave a map to one of the Royal Guards of where the princess was hidden away."

"So what happened then? Those seven advisors are not here." Raven waited for him to mention betraying his father.

"The advisors fled. The king was killed...and they fled. I do not know if they're alive or dead. The only one I am certain of is my father, who stayed, as his king commanded him, and died because of it."

A flicker of genuine grief crossed Lord Cenric's eyes.

"The letters vanished, and the map...the royal guard who had it...he disappeared. So many died that day. No one knows if he survived and got the princess out of the palace, or if she died as well."

"But if the guard with the map disappeared, then what am I hunting?" Raven leaned forward, trying to piece it together.

"Until these thefts started happening, I didn't believe the other rumors that had been spreading silently over the years...King Stewart had a second map, split it up, and gave pieces of it to different ranking members of his court. Some servants, even. All to keep his daughter safe."

"And that's what's being stolen. Someone's trying to find the map and put it together. Why? Do they think the princess is alive? I find it hard to believe that the queen wouldn't spend enormous efforts to make sure she was dead." Raven ran her hands through her hair. She had unbraided it during their talk, needing to fidget with something. Something other than stabbing Lord Cenric for dragging her into this game, or scrying Lady Tremaine to yell at her. She was already playing more than she liked.

"I find it hard to believe as well. But you can see why I can't go to the queen about this. She would have my heart for this, see it as treason."

"I understand." Raven stood up and walked towards the door.

"What are you going to do with this information?" Lord Cenric looked at her, realizing for the first time that maybe, just maybe, he shouldn't have divulged so much information to the guard.

"I'm unsure. First, we need to find the thief." Raven left, knowing she had spoken the truth.

She didn't know what she was going to do with that information. There was a map leading to a princess. A princess whose name no one dared speak. A princess who Raven hoped could unite this kingdom and save it. She would gladly serve that princess, anyone really, over Queen Lyanna. And Raven knew that there were powerful people out there who would do whatever it took to either keep someone from finding her or to finally bring her home.

Raven bit her lower lip as she and Rowan continued their rounds.

"What did he want?" Rowan questioned once they were far enough away, and even more cut off from the palace.

"What would it mean to you if King Stewart's daughter was alive?" Raven posed the question carefully. She knew she couldn't fully tell him. Couldn't compromise him like that. He had his morals and was loyal to the crown. Far more than the queen deserved.

"Uh." Rowan's steps faltered, telling Raven all she needed. "She and I were friends. I wouldn't mind having my friend back," Rowan spoke cautiously.

"Then I hope you'll understand why I say nothing else."

Rowan nodded, slowly trying to absorb the glimmer of hope Raven had given him. She hoped it wasn't too much.

# CHAPTER TWENTY-SEVEN

## CALLA

"So, when you're not babysitting a spoiled prince, what do you do?" Prince Adam sat back from their current game of chess.

They were at a standstill, and Calla had been trying to figure out her next move for several minutes.

She turned her gaze up slowly. She always did so slowly, preparing to look at him. To view those brown eyes and lie. She'd never had a problem with it before, though if she were honest, she'd also never had to lie so much and to so many people before. And it was getting hard.

The answer to his question rose to mind quickly. I scry and read objects at night, hidden away in my closet of a room. I siphon off my magic before I can't control it anymore. I try to find Guard Raven's heritage, and why she's being hunted and by whom, all while also trying to help her spy on the queen and court. But Calla couldn't say any of that.

"I read. Think of new chess moves to beat you with." Calla smiled.

"What about your family?" he questioned.

"What about my family?" Her hand stilled on her neck, her fidgeting forgotten. She hadn't had to fabricate something about them yet.

"Don't they try to steal you away? Have you regaled them with stories about the court?" Prince Adam smiled softly.

"Oh," Calla flinched. "I don't have a family—"

"You mentioned your father is a merchant?" He furrowed his brow.

Calla hid her surprise. She had told him that weeks ago when he was upset and barely listening.

"He is..." Calla trailed off, thinking of her lie. "He lives in the city with my two younger sisters. I see them sometimes."

That was the truth she lived. At least she felt better telling him that. She didn't let herself dwell on the unknown. She did not know where her father was, or her two little sisters. They could be dead for all she knew. So she didn't linger on the image of them alone, in the cold, dying. So she told herself, every day, that her father was living with her little sisters, living their life. She would see them sometimes when she could break away. But the truth...that she hadn't seen them since she was eight...

"You'll have to bring me some time. I'd love to meet them."

The sincerity in his voice almost cracked her. "Okay," Calla mumbled, her fingers tapping on her legs, turning to the chessboard.

"Why do you do that?" Prince Adam motioned towards her hand. Calla raised her eyebrows in question. "The tapping."

"Oh...it's a habit I developed when I'm thinking. The tapping helps keep me focused. Keeps me from letting my mind wander too far." She smiled, moving her rook. It had started like that, keeping her focused. Eventually, it was something she did when her hands wished to be working on an enchantment instead of completing a meaningless task.

"What's wrong with letting your mind wander?" Prince Adam moved his knight out of harm's way.

"Nothing I guess...I think sometimes, if I were to let my mind wander, it might never come back from the world it's imagining."

"A world where everyone has a say, and no one goes hungry." Prince Adam grinned.

"Something like that." Calla blushed that he remembered.

"I see nothing wrong with letting your mind have those dreams." Prince Adam moved his queen.

Checkmate. He was smug, getting up and walking to the balcony. A storm was rolling in, the dark gray clouds painting the world in hues of blue.

"Especially when it helps me win," he added, looking at her.

Calla stuck her tongue at him before turning to the board, wondering how he had done it. Her hair was more frazzled that day as she ran her hands through it, pushing it down. She narrowed her eyes, fixating on the board and not on him. Not on the way he looked at her, as though he was figuring out who she was. She had given him a lot of half-truths, and she wondered if he saw through them. Did he see her for who she was, or who she told him she was? She hoped he saw her for her, despite the lies she spoke.

# CHAPTER TWENTY-EIGHT

## RAVEN

Raven didn't dare give Rowan any more of the information Lord Cenric had divulged to her. He had also told her how to locate one of those advisors. Why he hadn't reached out himself, Raven didn't know. She also knew she would not tell Rowan that she was writing a letter to said advisor. Because Rowan...he would have to go to Queen Lyanna, and she had seen the glimmer of hope in his eyes. She had already compromised him enough with that single question. At least she was looking for what Lady Tremaine wanted, and thus the crown. Maybe they wanted to overthrow the queen? If Raven found those advisors before anyone else even knew to look, then they could dethrone Queen Lyanna.

Raven wondered about the Queen of Trudel and what she would do in response to aid her sister. Though she already knew she was ruthless and cunning. Cunning enough to send her son to spy on her sister. Use Queen Lyanna's favorite nephew against her. Someone she wouldn't bat an eye at for asking questions, giving advice, or staying longer than expected. Was he even engaged to Princess Celeste? She wasn't sure what to believe. What kind of family was this? She didn't want to know, but she wanted to get some answers.

Raven wandered down the halls, her steps silent. Her short swords strapped to her back, ready for anything. It surprised Raven that Rowan hadn't tracked her down already and yelled at her for walking alone. The queen couldn't care less about her safety. Her only comment today had been that she was pleased to see Raven was still alive. Raven could have sworn she detected the slightest sound of sadness in the queen's voice, that she hadn't died.

Raven shook the thought away as she approached Aleks door.

She didn't knock. Never had before.

As soon as she walked in, she wished she had.

Raven froze. "Aleks—"

Prince Aleksander was in his bed, naked, a maid beneath him.

She tried to avert her eyes. Desperately wanted to stop seeing him with someone else. But despite what her heart wanted, her body refused. It was happening all over again.

He was going to leave her next.

Tell her he didn't love her.

It had all been lies. Lies. All of it.

No.

Raven shook herself. This wasn't Jason.

This was Aleks.

They were friends. *Friends.*

So why was her magic leaping to protect her?

"Raven!" Aleks jumped out of bed.

As soon as his icy blue eyes consumed with shame looked at her, Raven remembered how to move.

So she left.

She turned on her toes and got out of that room, shutting the door behind her. Raven kept walking. Didn't stop when a blurry-eyed nobleman opened his door to see who was yelling in the middle of the night.

He paused, open-mouthed at the murder in Raven's eyes.

She moved past him, not looking at anyone. She walked out of the palace, wrapped a spare cloak around her shoulders, covered her face, and went into Aslar.

She went to the harbor and the fighting ring she knew would still be there. She didn't notice anything, and no one dared approach her. Ice ran through her veins, turning her cold. Her magic roared through her, clawing at her insides to be used. But Raven controlled it, kept it tucked in as she turned into Snow White.

The Stage Master smirked at her, his grin almost bigger than the gold piling up in his eyes.

"Why would I let you fight?" he questioned. The audience had yet to notice her. Yet to notice the delay in fighting as they dragged one man out of the arena, a line of blood followed him.

The fighter in the ring was a giant man with muscles thicker than her leg, and probably a good foot taller. She hadn't even seen him fight.

"Because I'll make you a bunch of coin," Raven snarled, her magic flaring in her eyes. Why was he stalling? He would let her in. Raven almost always won and was a guaranteed coin maker. Especially in a place where no one knew who she was, and what she could do. The Stage Master conceded, letting her enter.

The bouncer's jaw dropped.

Raven kept her cloak on but unsheathed her daggers. She couldn't remove her cloak or she would reveal herself as a royal guard with most of her armor still on.

For a split second, she saw Rowan. But shook it away. She would ignore him. She couldn't unleash her magic, not like she had last time, but she had to get the sludge out of her body. It crawled over her, its muddy texture rolling through her veins and over her bones. She wanted it eradicated, this feeling of shame and embarrassment. Of sadness. Broken trust. The sludge of her emotions was taking over, and she had to release it.

Last time, Ella had been there. They had gone into the forest, a glass bottle of clear liquid in hand, and unleashed all of her pain into that poison. Not now.

Raven smiled.

She observed her opponent and let her rational mind go.

For the first time since she had arrived in Evrotia, she didn't hold herself back from the fight.

It didn't matter that Rowan was seeing her fight at this level. That she had held back to not scare him, Charles, or Bastien. Who cared if he was frightened now? He would probably leave her one day as well. They always did.

She knew that after ten seconds of fighting, everyone who had bet against her was dying to change their decision. She didn't use any of her weapons. Didn't need them. Plus, she enjoyed the challenge of fighting someone this large without them. Enjoyed seeing the smile that had once been so large on his face slowly falter, and then disappear.

Raven toyed with him, letting him think he was winning, and then she would attack with the one dagger she had kept hidden.

They fought for over five minutes, the man tiring, while Raven bounced on her feet.

The fighter lunged for her, his last-ditch effort to defeat her. His last moment of breathing.

Because Raven killed him.

She snapped his neck as though it were nothing.

The crowd went ballistic. They chanted Raven's name, The Noble Lady, over and over.

Yet the sludge remained. It dug into the fractures of her heart, and all she wanted to do was reach inside and remove the black chunk of her heart that was left. She was a heartless bitch, and this emotion...she wanted nothing to do with it.

She left the ring and found Rowan waiting for her. She didn't think he would stay after what she had done. How she had killed that fighter. The Stage Master was furious. At least until he saw how much she had brought to him. He stopped his yelling then.

Raven didn't stop where Rowan stood. She continued on towards the palace. At least the fight had been enough to take the edge off. Enough for her to be mad at herself. She and Prince Charming were friends. That's what they had agreed to. Had discussed. Friendship. So then, why did it hurt so much?

"Are you alright?"

They were almost at the palace, the rest of Aslar asleep. Only the guards were awake, walking around the grounds.

"I will be." It was all she could utter. All she would say. She ignored Rowan's other questions. She sank farther into Snow White and refused to rise out of her for him.

# CHAPTER TWENTY-NINE

## CALLA

Calla lost herself in the chess match. Prince Adam had cornered her, and the way out was not a move she wanted to make. She would have to sacrifice her queen.

The door slammed open.

Prince Adam jumped up, drawing out a knife. Before she knew what had happened, Prince Adam had positioned himself between her and whoever had entered the room.

His shoulders tensed, his legs defensive, coiled to pounce.

Princess Arianna strode into his room, barely glancing at his dagger.

"Well, the reports were right. You have improved."

Prince Adam relaxed slowly, putting the dagger away as he followed her every move like a prey being stalked.

"Princess Arianna, it's a pleasure to meet you at last." Prince Adam nodded.

Calla noticed his fingers twitch, his hands moving toward where the injury on his face remained. He stopped himself before he tried to cover it. There was no point.

"How can I be of service?"

Prince Arianna continued to move around the room. Even at fifteen, she already knew how to command a room. Her golden hair curled down to her waist, her dress the highest fashion in a pink concoction of swirling skirts and a decorative armored bodice.

"I thought I would come see your progress for myself." Princess Arianna strutted over to him. "After all, I want to make sure I get what I want out of this whole arrangement."

She stood before him and unwrapped the bandage covering his left eye and forehead. Calla opened her mouth to stop her. It could make the injury worse if she exposed it for too long, but she stopped. Who was she to question a princess?

Princess Arianna, however, noticed. She turned her attention to Calla through slitted green eyes and slapped her before Calla could even think to move.

"I would not ask your opinion, servant."

Calla cradled her cheek, remaining silent as her eyes watered. She held it in as the mark throbbing, turning her skin a dark red.

Princess Arianna moved to strike her again.

But her hand did not touch her this time. Calla opened her eyes to find Prince Adam standing before her, the princess's wrist caught in his hand. Princess Arianna's face turned red as she looked up at him.

"I do not condone the abuse of my servants," Prince Adam said, his voice low enough that guards could not hear.

"Well." Princess Arianna pulled her hand out of his. "She's not *your* servant, and you would do well to remember your place in my kingdom," Princess Arianna said as she turned to Prince Adam. She removed the bandage, her eyes widening.

Calla knew it was from his beauty. No one could resist his perfectly sculpted jawline, cheekbones, or lips. No one would ever be able to pull out of the gaze of those emerald eyes.

"Idiot." It was hushed as Princess Arianna's fingers gently touched the scar above his eye.

It was still healing, still pink from all the times Calla had cleaned it, making sure no infection remained. Prince Adam had been so strong when she'd had to cut it open and clean it out. She had feared he would lose his eye if she didn't.

Princess Arianna slapped Calla so hard she spun to the ground, hitting her knees on the unforgiving wood floor.

"You marred his face. His perfect face." Princess Arianna chased Calla up against a wall. "He'll have a scar because you couldn't treat him well enough."

Calla dropped into a ball.

Prince Adam moved. Princess Arianna spun and leveled a dagger at him.

"If you help her, despite how she deformed you, you will not be allowed to remain in this palace."

Prince Adam stood there looking between the dagger and Calla. Calla stared up at him. Her heart pounded, and her magic pulsed in her veins. Calla shoved it down.

"He won't help you," Princess Arianna sneered. "He knows you messed up. It's why he hasn't been able to show himself in court. It's why he won't be the wonderful king they promised me, only a consort. You ruined his life. And he knows that if our engagement ends, he will never be allowed back into his kingdom."

"I'm sorry, I only—"

Princess Arianna kicked her.

Calla repeated her apology.

Over and over.

She knew it wasn't her fault. But she wanted it to stop. Calla clutched her cheek, blood dripping between her fingers. Her magic raced through her, roaring to be used for Calla to lose control and let forth a wave of raw magic.

"Fix. Him." Princess Arianna turned away, stopping beside Prince Adam. "I'm sorry that she had to be punished. But you need to learn that the only way to get these servants to do their job is through fear, not compassion. We'll still get married, but we'll have to see how well it heals before we figure out how much of a role you'll have in my court when I'm queen."

Calla nearly vomited at the thought of her as a queen. That horrid girl, a ruler of a kingdom.

Calla kept her head covered, fearing Princess Arianna may not have left.

A hand lightly rested on Calla's arm. She swatted it away, looking up through unshed tears. She had kept them back from the princess. Something in her gut told her it would only be worse for her if Princess Arianna had seen them.

The tears fell freely into the nail slices on her face, cleaning them. Calla narrowed her eyes at him, pulling herself in tighter.

"Calla—"

"Stay away from me." She reverted to Rairenian.

"Calla, please." Prince Adam sat beside her.

"You did nothing," she spoke in Evrotian, catching herself. She kept her eyes on her hands, watching them shake.

"I know."

She lifted her head. "She slapped me, and you…" Calla choked out through gritted teeth.

"I know." It was all he seemed capable of saying.

"Why?" Calla's face burned, her body vibrating with magic.

"Calla—"

"Is that what it will be like when you marry her? She's going to walk all over you and your kingdom?"

"No…it will not be like that." Prince Adam locked eyes with her.

His hands twitched, his magic flaring dimly for half a second.

"If you can't defend one person against a fifteen-year-old, how are you going to defend a kingdom?" Calla threw out her arms.

"I'll find a way," Adam ground out. "I couldn't defend you, Calla. You're right. I have no power here."

"Why?"

"It's as she said. If this engagement ends, so does my life," Adam confessed. His magic flared in agreement.

Calla paused, her anger frozen. "I—"

"I do not approve of that behavior, or that the only way to rule is through fear. I haven't had time to see what the court here is like. I've yet to be invited because of this." Prince Adam motioned at the exposed wound on his face. He lightly touched her shoulder so that she turned to face him. "For you...for all that you've done for me...I'm sorry that happened."

"Prince Adam—"

"Adam, please," he whispered, staring into her brown eyes.

"Why?"

"Because I would like for us to be friends."

Adam stood up and held out a hand to her, waiting to pull her up. Calla grasped it, wiping away her tears and blood as she stood.

"Can you show me where the bandages are? I would like to help you with that," he said as he walked her over to the couch.

"They're in the washroom, in the cabinet," Calla said. Aleks returned a minute later with her healing kit in hand. She directed him on what to grab and how to clean her wound. His deep emerald eyes were so close she was certain he could see into her soul and reveal all of the lies she had ever told him.

# CHAPTER THIRTY

## RAVEN

Raven shoved a pill in her mouth as she walked through the palace gates into Aslar. She had finally been given a night off. All of her hard work had paid off, all the extra work had finally shown the queen that she was back. That Raven deserved a break.

The court had become her hunting ground as the queen ordered her to kill anyone who begged too much. Queen Lyanna discovered she enjoyed making her Royal Guard kill peasants in front of her. Raven had been quick the first two times, giving them a merciful killing. Until Queen Lyanna had dug her gauntleted hand into Raven's biceps. Until she had demanded Raven make the kills take longer. Be slow for wasting their queen's time by groveling before her.

Raven shuddered at today's kill.

It had been bad. The commoner...she'd barely been over the age of fourteen. Too young to be begging before the queen.

Too young to look that wise.

She had asked to make a partial payment on the taxes her parents owed. They could only scrape together so much of it. Tears had streaked her dirty face. The queen's eyes had glittered when she'd turned to Raven with her torture. The worst she'd ever had to endure, killing innocent people.

Raven's stomach threatened to rebel each time.

But she did it.

She made sure to not vomit in front of everyone. No, that came later. By herself. Even Rowan hadn't tried to push his way in. Aleks had abandoned her, as she'd expected. Everyone stayed away. She was alone. They all whispered 'Hunter', 'Murderer', when her back was to them. She didn't blame them. Said nothing. Let them fear her. It would make it easier should she ever be ordered to kill any of them.

The pill had taken effect by the time Raven got into the fighting ring. She was empty and saw everything. The stage master once again accepted her into his good graces. They all enjoyed seeing her fight. They cheered for someone who killed their people. They put Raven up against three men. All of them, she assessed, were criminals of some sort. One was a low level thief. The other two, low-level grunts for some crime lord.

Raven sized them up in a second.

She didn't want to give them a chance to look her over and see a weakness. Notice that her right arm was still weak and sore from where the queen had dug her gauntlet into her. That she couldn't move that arm as fast anymore. They would destroy her if they noticed that. So she didn't let it show. She moved quickly, disarming the two grunts first. They knew each other and would therefore take her on together. She knew taking them out was her priority. The thief was not a low-level thief. He held his own against her...for a minute. Then he was disarmed and facing a killing blow. A blow she knew she could give and not be punished for.

But Raven was tired of killing.

She was...tired.

She couldn't admit it to anyone, especially not herself.

Raven only fought one time that night, even though the crowds frantically pleaded for her to stay. To entertain them. Fuck them. She left through a hidden door and out into a deserted alleyway.

"What are you doing?" Prince Aleksander stepped out of the shadows, his cloak was as black as hers.

"Fighting, why do you care?" Raven walked past him. She couldn't stop moving. Her magic was in chaos, rising rapidly to meet her tumultuous emotions.

"You've become reckless, Raven. That thief, that low-level, common thief, who probably couldn't even pick a lock, got through *your* defenses, Raven." Prince Aleksander kept his voice low as he briskly walked beside her.

"Again, why do you care, Prince Charming?" Her throat constricted around the words, barely able to squeeze them out.

"Oh, we're back to that, are we?" He sighed. "I thought we were friends, or trying to be," he conceded.

"We are," she spoke through gritted teeth. She needed to get to her room. She poured her energy into keeping her emotions in check, keeping her magic stuffed down in the deepest, darkest places of her soul.

"Then talk to me. We're all concerned. For some reason, my aunt has decided to torture you by having you kill all of those people. Today..."

Prince Aleksander trailed off, trying to wipe the horror from his face. "We all know that must have been difficult—"

"It wasn't," Raven dismissed, hiding how her heart wept. "I'm an assassin. It's my job to kill people. Your aunt is merely utilizing my skills properly." Raven ignored the tightening in her throat. The swell of pain in her chest.

Prince Aleksander jumped in front of her and held her shoulders. His eyes searched hers, looking for any sign of life. Too bad he would not find any.

"But it's not your job to kill children," he whispered.

Raven wasn't prepared for how much those eight words would strike her. That girl was seared into all of their minds. Her brown hair darkened as the blood on the floor soaked into it. Raven had defied the queen's wishes for all deaths to be slow. She had been quick and efficient; emotionless. She had walked right past the gauntlet and down the stairs towards the girl. The poor thing didn't even realize what was about to happen until it was done. In one quick motion, Raven had cut off the girl's head as she pleaded for mercy from her queen. Raven had tensed, barely able to hold in her bile.

Raven kept her eyes locked on Aleks's. Felt the warmth of his hands on her arms.

"I'm sorry that my aunt is putting you through this." He lightly squeezed her.

Raven didn't have the capability of stopping the tears at that gentle touch. She didn't deserve that empathy or kindness. Not even from him. She deserved nothing, not after today. The grief became too much as Raven covered her face. Aleks wrapped his arms around her, tucking her under his cloak. He held her up as her legs shook. Raven gripped him, holding on tightly as she cried into his chest. He rested his head on hers, rubbing her back. Raven didn't make the tears stop. She couldn't, as years' worth of sorrow poured forth.

# CHAPTER THIRTY-ONE

## CALLA

Calla had done her best to fix Prince Adam, as the princess had ordered. Not that there was anything that needed to be fixed. She even brought out the serum she had carried with her from Rairene.

Prince Adam eyed it quizzically. "Calla, is that an enchanted potion?" He stepped away from her.

"It is—"

"I can't have that. No matter what Princess Arianna wants, I can't...I'm an—" He stopped talking, turning his back to her. He lifted his hair, revealing his dark brown enchanter's mark.

"The other day...does the queen know?" Calla didn't want to think about the other day more than she had to.

"Of course." Prince Adam spat. "She wants to control me. It's why enchanters are banished. If you let her control you, then you're free to be part of her secret spy cabal."

"That doesn't sound like freedom to me." Calla stepped towards him. "The potion won't mix with your magic. The serum... holds magic but works to speed up healing. I have used it on other enchanters without incident," Calla assured.

Prince Adam nodded, sitting before her.

They hadn't spoken about the other day. Sometimes she wondered if she imagined the entire incident. But the bruise on her cheek, and the scratches...those told her it was real. It had happened.

She still called him Prince Adam. Didn't dare say Adam...it was crossing over that line. She couldn't handle crossing that line. There were so many things she couldn't tell him. Things she wanted to, but knew, deep down, if she told him, he would turn away from her. He would hand her over to the queen. Probably wouldn't even bat an eye. She was a commoner, a servant. A lowly maid who could be beaten.

She had avoided Raven. She wouldn't be able to lie to her, and if Raven saw...she would kill the princess. Raven tolerated no one being abused. No matter who that person was. It was the one redeeming quality the servants discussed whenever Raven was mentioned. They talked in hushed tones about the day Raven stood up to some lord. How she had nearly killed him. It made the women fear her less, and worship her a little more. Though recently...Calla shook her head. Everyone knew Raven didn't have a choice, but it didn't help.

Calla finished cleaning everything for the day. Though most days now she had nothing to clean. Prince Adam had kept everything clean after her first three deep cleanings. She had wanted to do more, but he had insisted she was not too deep clean anymore.

He remained silent all day, sitting on the balcony, staring at the mountains.

The silence was killing her.

Calla straightened her shoulders and walked outside. The mountains were especially beautiful covered in snow as low-lying wispy clouds nestled in close, storm clouds reigning supreme above.

He didn't look over at her. His shoulders were tense, his hands twitching before he crossed them.

"Why don't you have any power here?" Calla sat near him, folding her hands between her knees. She gazed at him, falling into the memory of his fingers brushing against her skin as he wiped away the blood.

"I'm sorry?" His mouth opened slightly in surprise. Was he surprised that she had remembered?

"The other day." Calla visibly flinched. "You said you have no power here. Why don't you have any power?"

He turned into a statue before her, so she turned her attention away from him, sensing that he needed her to not focus on him. Calla played with her necklace, running her fingers over the petals.

"I'm a visiting prince, who is only here to wed the heir to the throne. Queen Lyanna drives a hard price for her daughter. She made it very clear to my father that her daughter would decide how much power my word carried here. That I would have none until she decided that. Should I leave this room, and re-enter court, they will invite me to meetings, and I'll see Queen Lyanna hold court. However, I am not to give my opinion unless asked."

"That must be very difficult."

"It is, especially when I cannot protect those I care about." He dared a glance at her.

Calla blushed, her eyes widening as she observed the mountains. "Prince Adam—"

"There's an unwritten law here, Calla. It forbids anyone of the noble class from having relations with someone who is not of that...class. It's punishable by death, for the person who is not of noble birth." Prince Adam captured her attention.

He switched to Vicurian, whispering to her in a language he thought she did not understand, his voice sending shivers down her spine.

"I would take your hand if I could, and hold it every day. I would take your hand and run away with you, run away from here." Prince Adam looked up at the cracking palace walls behind them, his hazel eyes dazzling her. He sat before her, his hands clasped tightly and held between his knees. "I wish I could run away with you. Looking at you, seeing you walk through the door...has my magic swirling to the surface, wanting to dance with you. I've only heard tales of magic responding like that to someone and never imagined I would find that power and emotion here. But none of this matters."

Prince Adam rubbed his hands over his face and into his hair as he blinked.

"But what I want doesn't matter. I don't want this life. I thought I did. I thought I wanted to marry the most beautiful person in the kingdom and to rule as my father has." He moved to touch her, to hold her, but stopped.

Calla thought her heart might break as he pulled away. He wouldn't give up everything for her. Why would anyone give up anything for her?

"You...changed my way of thinking. You challenged me. You...are inspiring. If I were to take your hand and run away with you...that wouldn't be a life I would want you to live. We could never stop running. I can't return home, not with how I left with my father. I won't put you in a worse position than you already are. At least here...I can try to help you stay safe. Somehow...I'll keep you safe."

It took everything in Calla not to break. Each word splintered her as she held back. She couldn't tell him who she was.

She couldn't even shed a single tear in understanding.

And that broke her.

It broke her more than leaving her family. More than being separated from her soul sisters. Pretending...lying to this man...she was disgusted with herself for not being brave enough. For not telling him. But she had more than herself to think about if she was ever going to break free of the cage that kept her.

# CHAPTER THIRTY-TWO

## Raven

*Raven ran through the palace halls, fire chasing her. She kept tripping over her damn dress, stumbling through the hallways. Yet no matter how fast she ran, the fire always caught up to her. She careened around a corner, slamming into a body. A royal guard held her still, holding her to him. She couldn't make out his face, didn't dare try. She didn't know if it was from fear or safety that she kept her eyes downcast. She wanted to keep him safe. Because she knew they would kill him for helping her. For picking her up and helping her run faster than the fire.*

Raven bolted up in bed, her arms wrapped around her. The taste of smoke rolled in her lungs. She got out of bed and drank a glass of water. Before she could get her uniform on, a knock at her door stilled her. It was early enough that no one in their right mind would be awake.

Raven stepped on feather-light feet towards her door. She picked up one of her short swords and slowly opened her door. Raven sighed when she saw Rowan.

"Let's go riding. Queen Lyanna gave our unit the day off, and I could use a pleasant ride. Horseback ride," Rowan clarified.

"You don't think we'll be attacked? Our track record isn't that great."

"We won't go near the forest…just in case."

Raven smiled. Thirty minutes later, they were riding across the open country behind the palace. The tall grass rippled silver in the wind as they raced through hills, staying to the border of the forest looming before them.

She let her horse run free as she closed her eyes and smiled as the wind danced across her exposed face. They ran for what felt like days…years…Raven didn't care, so long as it kept her away from the palace. Her black hair snapped in the wind, unbound. No one was trying to kill or hunt her at this moment. She almost gave in to the urge to drop her short swords. Gray clouds rolled in over the mountains, carrying rain in their depths. Eventually, the horses slowed as they reached the forest.

"So what did you want to talk about?" Raven looked over at her partner. Her friend, she amended. They had become friends over these months.

"I'm surprised you haven't asked about Rairene the entire time you've been here." Rowan looked at her.

"That's why you dragged us out here?" *Had he heard her conversation with Ella a few weeks ago?* She'd been careful. "I was barely privy to what was happening in my kingdom while I was there. I never thought to ask about it. Why?"

*Has Ella done something?*

"Something's happening. Something big, I can feel it." Rowan's brow furrowed, his lips pursed. He hadn't voiced this to anyone else.

"What makes you uneasy?" Raven questioned. Maybe he had heard her. Though it would only validate that she had been a guard in Rairene.

"There's a ball happening for the prince's eighteenth birthday."

"Okay?" She frowned. "Rowan, I haven't paid attention to the politics of my kingdom since arriving here. I've been too focused on the ones here to notice."

He ran a hand through his hair. "Prince David is meant to proclaim his engagement as part of the peace treaty he's signing with the Kingdom of Trudel. Though there's a rumor that an old friend, a Lady Eleanor, has returned after being away for nine years, and if he doesn't choose Princess Lena, Alek's sister...if he refuses—"

"What? A spoiled princess will cry?"

"War. He will end a twenty-year truce."

*Shit. What had Ella been tossed into?*

"A twenty-year peace treaty hinges on their marriage? Surely another one could be negotiated."

"Well, there's Aleks, but it would be a slap in the face to the Queen of Trudel to not place one of her children in line to rule."

"What happens to Aleks?"

"He's supposedly meant to marry Prince David's younger sister. Though, I think he's been resisting since he's not over there helping smooth things over with his sister."

Their horses ventured into the forest. Raven didn't stop them. There was no way someone was waiting out here, given that they hadn't followed a specific path. They continued to walk through the forest, going deeper than either of them had ever been. Light barely broke through the trees as gray clouds rolled overhead.

"If those two kingdoms go to war over a piece of paper, that means we will as well," Raven whispered. Ella had been too successful then in her mission to protect Prince David. If he was debating on ending a treaty over her...oh Ella.

"It means—" Rowan stopped short.

Both of them lost all thought as their horses came upon a small clearing in the forest. Someone had torched the ground. Nothing grew within the burned area, though the damage had been done years ago.

"What is this?" She knew what it was. She couldn't believe she was seeing one. A mass grave.

"I think this is where they burned everyone."

"Burned everyone?" Raven felt the prick of pain in the corner of her eyes. She would control herself. Her magic writhed, wanting to pour itself over the wounded earth. Raven soothed it back, took hold, and contained it.

She was an assassin.

She did not let death get the best of her.

"After the coup, when Queen Lyanna took power..." Rowan turned to face her.

"Tell me, Rowan. What happened?" She had to know. It felt related to her nightmares and the fires that haunted her there.

"When the king died, there was mass panic, and everyone grieved. No one could stop it. Not even the king's seven advisors. Those who stayed behind, those who defended the palace, tried to hold it for the princess..." Rowan trailed off. "They tried to protect her. But they couldn't. All of them were killed. Some...the ones who were high ranking, were executed in front of all of Aslar. Rounded up and hung in front of the palace. All of their bodies must have been brought here and burned. I'm surprised she didn't burn them in front of everyone."

"You saw it?" Raven couldn't believe he worked for her.

"It was eleven years ago. So I was seven. I have fragments of it. Most of it, I heard from other guards."

"Not your father?"

"He never speaks about that day. He's never spoken about any part of his time at the palace, even though he served there for twenty years. He's loyal to the king, even now."

"What makes you say that?" Raven thought about the rumored guard Lord Cenric had shared.

"He retired after she was crowned. She never forgave him for leaving her guard. It's why I can't see him. She refuses it."

"I'm sorry."

Rowan said nothing as he turned away from the burned ground. It was silent around the grave. No animal ventured near. Raven wondered if the princess was in there as well. If the guard had failed his king and had subjected himself to a life of poverty because of it.

Raven glanced at the mirror warming in her hand. She was lucky Rowan had wanted to shower before going out and into Aslar for the evening. So so lucky. Raven opened the mirror, pulling some magic. She nearly dropped it when Luca stared at her.

*Luca?* Why was he scrying her? What did he need?

*I need a favor, and you can't tell anyone. Before I ask, if you don't tell me, it could hurt Ella—*

*Isn't she supposed to protect Prince David?* Raven's heart hammered. Something was wrong.

*Lady Tremaine said the crown changed her protection detail. Ella's been told she has to kill him the night of the ball.*

Raven's heart stopped. As Luca explained all that had happened, Raven sat down, absorbing everything her sister had been going through. By the time he was done, Raven's head rested on her hand.

*I'm coming home.*

*Raven—*

She looked up from the floor and into Luca's brown eyes. *I'm coming home.*

# CHAPTER THIRTY-THREE

## CALLA

Calla and Adam pretended as though nothing had happened all of those weeks ago. She hadn't been attacked, and he hadn't told her about why he couldn't be with her. Her magic crumbled within her, diminishing into a small ball of inner light.

So, even though it gutted her, she continued to care for him. To clean his wounds. Though they were mostly healed. He didn't even need to keep them wrapped anymore. The serum had done as much as it could, and by the time it was fully healed, only a light scar would remain.

She debated asking for a new assignment. But the idea of not being able to see him anymore...not having a reason to see him...that she truly couldn't stomach. If she was reassigned and then discovered with him...they would kill her, of that she was certain. So she would continue her form of personal torture.

Calla held her necklace as she looked at the chessboard. She and Prince Adam had kept score of their wins. They were tied at thirty apiece.

"So, what's his name?"

Calla tilted her head in question.

"The name of the lovesick puppy who gave you that necklace." He pointed at the golden rose.

Calla reached behind her neck and unclasped it. She handed it over to him, watching him carefully hold it.

"No lovesick puppy is waiting for me, Prince Adam—"

"I've asked you to call—"

"Prince Adam," Calla interrupted. It was not lost on her that no other prince would allow such disobedience. "That necklace was my mothers, and is the last thing I ever received from my father."

He examined the flower. Calla knew it was heavier than it looked. Calla loved its simple beauty, a perfectly opened golden rose. Adam rubbed it between his hands, turning it over.

"You constantly twist it in your hand. I was curious," he mumbled, handing it over.

"My father always said if I ever needed him, all I had to do was squeeze tightly and he would come." Calla clasped it back around her neck, relaxing at its weight.

"I'm sure he's always with you in spirit," he replied.

Calla turned slightly away from him. "I'm sure he is, as well. He used to call me his little Belle. It means beauty in my kingdom. Boy, was he wrong there," Calla laughed, trying to quickly swipe away a tear.

"I would say he—"

Calla cut him off. "Eventually it changed to mean something else to me."

"Oh?" Adam allowed her diversion.

"Safety. With my friends, it would mean safety. That they were safe, or that I was safe. They would call me Belle to let me know I was safe."

"Why would you need reminding?" Adam looked at their game as Calla made her move.

"Because," she sat back, taking pride in getting into a check position, "this isn't a safe world."

# CHAPTER THIRTY-FOUR

## RAVEN

Raven pulled out her blades as her door opened.

"Did you hear what happened?" Susan bustled past Raven and her swords, moving around the room.

"Hear what?" Raven relaxed, sheathing her blades to drink some coffee.

"The entire palace is buzzing with some announcement from the queen later today."

"I've heard nothing, Susan, sorry." Raven was too busy packing.

"The rumor is it's about Rairene."

Raven quirked a brow. Ella had been successful at saving the prince...good. At least she could leave the royal family behind, though the urgency to go thrummed through Raven's veins. She had to leave. Calla had to leave. Tonight. She and Calla would get out tonight. Her mind settled as Susan adjusted the last piece of her armor.

"Guard Raven," a man shouted through her door.

Raven narrowed her eyes as Susan approached. The man burst in.

"Guard Raven, you are to surrender yourself and go before the queen."

Five more men filtered into her compact room.

Raven stood slowly, unable to reach for her short swords. "On what grounds?"

"You have been charged with treason against the crown and the Kingdom of Evrotia."

Raven unsheathed one blade, leveling it at the six men. Her pulse raced as she looked back and forth between the guards. "What proof do you have?"

"That is not for us to determine. Your life is at the mercy of our queen. I suggest you come quietly and wait to hear what she has to say."

"Raven—"

The guard slapped Susan.

"If you want to die, you'll hit her again. If you want to live, you'll walk out of that door." Raven's magic boiled as Susan cupped her face.

Raven couldn't have been prouder as Susan glared at the guard, though her expression quickly morphed into concern as she looked at Raven. Raven stood taller.

The guard motioned quickly towards Susan, a hand raised in a mock gesture. He didn't get the chance to hit her, his hand falling to the ground before he could blink. The man fell to his knees, clutching his wrist as blood pooled out.

"I would go see a healer," Raven commented.

The remaining five attacked her.

They didn't stand a chance.

Raven moved quickly, her blades an extension of herself as she dived into the fray. She killed three of them quickly. The other two she forced into the hallway, away from Susan. She would never let her get hurt again.

Raven cut down the other two swiftly. She looked up at the sound of thunder that approached her.

"Raven." Rowan ran down the hall.

She spun to face him, distracted enough for the guards to throw ropes and chains around her, pulling tight.

She glared at him, her magic rioting. "I didn't do anything, Rowan."

Charles and Bastien were right behind him.

"I promise. I did nothing." She would never betray her oath to her crown.

"We know." Rowan grabbed some of the rope and chains from a guard. So did Charles and Bastien. His eyes were wide, filled with fear as he gripped her restraints.

Raven looked at them, waiting for them to unbind her.

"But we still have to take you to her."

Raven moved her arms against the chains, shaking as they tightened.

"She'll kill me, Rowan. You know she will. She's hated me since the day I arrived."

"We don't."

"Shut your mouth, Guard Rowan," Charles muttered. He tightened the chains holding her, a silent reminder.

Rowan shot her a quick glance, the fear coming to the surface once more before he put on his own emotionless expression. He couldn't look sympathetic if he wanted to live as well.

They walked quietly. Raven held her head high. She had done nothing wrong. The queen couldn't possibly have anything on her. Queen Lyanna had hired her. She knew what Raven was, who she had invited into her home.

Raven's shoulders slumped when they walked into the throne room. They had summoned every member of the noble class. They all watched as she and her unit, her friends, walked towards the throne and Queen Lyanna. The queen's dark red dress seemed to bleed into the floor, a black sash draped across her armored bodice. Who had died?

Aleks stood to the right of her, a silver circlet on his head. He looked weary. What had happened? Prince Adam was even there. Calla had worked wonders on his face. He stood off to the left, his towering height noticeable, despite being behind Princess Arianna and her unit. So, everyone was truly here.

"Guard Raven, we have arrested you for espionage and treason." Queen Lyanna was downright gleeful.

"I have done nothing, my queen," Raven spoke softly, standing tall, ignoring the weight of the chains.

"You also killed three of my guards."

"One of them struck my maid." Raven shrugged. She didn't regret those deaths. Never would.

"Have you been stealing items of value from the members of my court? Items given to them by my late husband?"

Raven looked up at her.

Only her.

She didn't dare flick a glance toward Lord Cenric, the bastard. Or towards Aleks, who had shifted on his feet enough for her to notice.

"I was attempting to recover those items and return them. I did not steal them, nor did I think a petty thief was worthy of your concern. Besides, I was unsuccessful in locating a single one."

"You will let me decide what is and is not worthy of my concern!"

For the first time since arriving, Raven heard the queen yell, her voice screeching around the room.

"While you were out yesterday with Guard Rowan, my men searched your room. It was very interesting what they discovered, Raven. An enchanted mirror, potions, lots of them, and all of those valuable items you claim to have never found. If that's not damning, then I don't know what is."

Raven didn't look at Rowan. Couldn't bear it. She felt the rope slacken in his hands. He hadn't been part of the ruse to get her out of the palace. They had set her up.

Someone had planted those items.

"You have nothing to say for yourself?" One of the queen's loyal advisors stepped forward, disgust on his face.

"My words will hold little meaning right now." Raven memorized his face, his ruddy complexion that turned redder the longer Raven stared him down.

"I should kill you right now." Queen Lyanna stood up and gracefully descended to her. "But I want to learn what you know. What you've sold about me."

"I'm not a spy." Raven tensed as the queen stopped inches away from her.

There was no fear in the queen's eyes as she looked Raven over. Though she wouldn't have a reason to be, given that Raven was in chains.

Queen Lyanna leaned in close, pulling Raven towards her in an iron grip as she whispered, "it's too bad your mistress, my very dear old friend Lady Tremaine, gave you up. I know exactly who you are...*Snow White.*"

Raven collapsed as the queen released her.

She stared at the floor in disbelief. Lady Tremaine had abandoned her? What about Calla? Was she still safe? She would be safe. She had to be safe. Raven's magic roared in her ears, vying to protect her, to save her, to hide her. It would do it. It would unleash itself and take everyone in the room down with them. Raven held it back. It was getting too close to the skin, too close to revealing her. If she did...she knew she wouldn't walk out. Rowan wouldn't walk out. He would be caught up in her raw power, so would every other innocent person in the room. So Raven held it in. For them.

"Take her to the dungeon."

The ropes and chains pulled on her. But Raven didn't move.

Couldn't move.

She couldn't get up. Couldn't force herself to continue. She had been betrayed. She would die.

"Raven." Someone said her name. But she could barely hear its whisper.

She was going to die here. She would never see her friends. Ella. She had to get to Ella. Had to help her.

"Raven, get up," Rowan whispered, tugging on the chains. "Stand up. Now."

Raven found the will, Ella's face before her, giving her magic life to stand up. She would escape. She would not let herself, or her friends, be killed because of an evil queen.

Raven walked out of the room, her head held high.

Raven's eyes watered at the stench emitting from the dungeon. She'd never gone down there, with good reason.

Only death lived there.

The dungeons were in a far corner of the palace grounds, tucked away in an old stone building. It was dark, the stones cold beneath her boots. Water dripped down every wall.

Once they were in the dungeons, away from peering eyes, her friends slowly took off her chains, though they left the ropes.

"I could kill all three of you right now and make a break for it," Raven whispered.

"We're aware." Bastien squeezed her shoulder.

"So why don't you?" Charles asked at the same time as he ran a hand through his black hair.

"You're my friends."

"Plus, you saw all the guards she had trailing us here. They'll all be ready to fight you if we don't come out of here." Rowan added, squeezing her hand.

"That too," Raven muttered, squeezing his hand. However, all she had to do was unleash every single skill she had learned and she could probably break free. She might die, Raven acknowledged, and there were still people who needed her. So she would bide her time and wait.

"Though it would be glorious to see you take all of them on, Raven," Charles added, trying to crack a smile.

"It would be." Raven could not answer his smile with her own.

They walked her into a cold, wet cell. It was in the middle of the dungeon, and completely isolated. There would be no one for her to talk to. Before they removed the final ropes, they locked her hands in separate metal cuffs, each one anchored with thick chains to the middle of the cell. The chain was long enough for her to reach the bars, and no further. Only then did they remove the final ropes.

# CHAPTER THIRTY-FIVE

## RAVEN

"Did you know her?"

Raven hadn't noticed him in the dungeon. He must have run ahead and hidden in the dungeons, waiting.

Aleks looked down at her through the bars. Raven had collapsed in the middle of her cage, head cupped in her hand.

"Know who?" She spoke slowly. Aleks shook in front of her. His hair was a mess, and his eyes were bloodshot. He was dressed entirely in black, his silver circlet shining in the dim light.

"My cousin. Eleanor. Did you know her?" He was pressed up against the bars, hands gripping the cold metal.

"I don't know anyone of royal blood." Raven stood slowly, ignoring the weight of the chains.

"Liar," Aleks spat. "You knew her!"

"Aleks, I promise, I don't know who you're talking about. I only know an Ella—" Raven paused. Ella had never mentioned she was of royal blood.

Maybe she hadn't known. Her mother had died so long ago. What had happened? Why had he been crying? And why did he keep referring to her in the past? Raven's heart beat with her denial.

"You do." Aleks latched onto her hesitation. "I knew there was something weird about your question."

"What question?"

There was no way she had said something. She couldn't have. And Ella couldn't be his cousin. She would have told Raven.

"You asked about my white hair. She has white hair like me, doesn't she? Your friend, *Ella*."

"So what if she does?" Raven challenged him, standing up to be on level ground. "You said so yourself that others could have it—"

"I said that to throw you off. No one besides me, my mom, my older brother, and my grandfather have white hair."

"Why does it matter, then?" Raven muttered. Something was wrong. Aleks kept pacing, his hands fisted around his crown, knuckles white.

"Because she was alive," he roared. "She was alive...all these years. She was...there." Aleks's voice broke.

"Well, she's still there, Aleks. If you're so obsessed with her, go get her," Raven screamed, her voice echoing off the walls. What had Ella done? Hadn't she been successful? Raven's magic spiraled through her, demanding to know. Maybe this was another ruse to get her to break. Lady Tremaine had no problem throwing her to the wolves. Maybe she'd done the same thing to Ella.

She needed to know.

Aleks laughed.

To Raven's horror, his laughter dissolved into sobs.

"She's dead, Raven."

"Liar." Raven barely let the word through her teeth. But she had to. She had to say it. It couldn't be true. "You're. Lying." Raven strained against the chains, pulling them taunt. Her magic burst within her for a second before she pulled it back. Raven rolled it up and pushed her magic down as her heart fractured. It wasn't true. It was just a lie to get her to break, to see how hopeless her situation was. Ella was alive. She was alive and Raven wouldn't believe anything else.

"I'm not." Aleks paused as he looked at her.

Raven strained so hard against the chains, trying to get to him, to break free, that they cut her skin open. She knew he saw everything. Saw a face warped in grief, willing for him to be lying.

*Please be lying.*

"You're lying." Raven gulped for air. "Why are you torturing me like this?" Raven dropped to the stones, her black hair draped over her face.

"Trust me."

Raven snapped her head up, eyes slit.

"This isn't the torture my aunt will put you through."

"What happened?" Raven whispered. She needed to hear it.

"There was an assassination attempt on Prince David." Aleks began. He visibly swallowed as he stepped up to the bars separating them. "Eleanor foiled it, taking an arrow through her shoulder." He pinched the bridge of his nose, eyes squeezed shut. "It wasn't a fatal shot, but the arrow had poison on it that killed her. Prince David has gone into hiding until they can find the killers."

Raven fell to her side.

He started to leave.

"Wait."

Aleks stopped.

"Calla...please...help her. Protect her. She truly has done nothing wrong."

"I'll see what I can do." Aleks left her lying on the dirty floor.

Raven curled up as best as she could, her throat sore from the restrained tears that burned down. Her heart barely sputtered as Aleks's damning information broke her over and over again.

Ella was dead.

# CHAPTER THIRTY-SIX

## CALLA

Calla cleaned his entire suite. For the first time since being his maid, he truly was nowhere to be found. Though he had left a note. He had been summoned to court and would return shortly. So she cleaned, knowing they could play more chess if she was done with everything. Or maybe read. Reading would be good too.

The mirror in Adam's room glowed.

A forced communication?

As royalty, Adam could have one. Calla turned towards it, her jaw dropping as she saw Ella dancing with the Prince of Rairene. She looked...not good. She was panicked and tense as she danced and whispered to the prince. Something had gone wrong.

An enchanter spoke through the mirror, delivering the King of Rairene's message. The prince was in hiding until his assassins could be stopped, and his friend, Lady Eleanor of House Aumont, died from injuries sustained while protecting the prince.

Ella was dead.

Calla dropped her cleaning cloth and sprinted for her cleaning supplies. This couldn't be happening. She dug out a small mirror, a mirror she and Jaq had enchanted for emergency communication. As soon as she opened it, Jaq's face was before her in a forced message. A message she had missed. His hair was a mess, his tunic wrinkled, all grave signs. Why hadn't she kept it on her? Why had she been so focused on Adam that she couldn't do her actual job?

*It's gotten bad, Belle.* He glanced around at a noise Calla couldn't hear. *I messed up.* He pressed his hands against his eyes. *I'm not sure what to do to fix this. I've sent you some items to read, maybe you'll have better luck than me.*

He was crying. Visibly shaking. He only did that when he had exhausted all of his magic. Why had he done that? What had happened? Calla wanted to yell at him and get answers, but it was an old message. Jaq went on, saying he had found some information Calla had requested about Raven. He had figured out where she was from, why someone might hunt her, trying to kill her. Calla almost dropped the mirror in shock. It couldn't be true.

Raven was from Evrotia.

Somehow, she was from this kingdom.

Calla closed and reopened the mirror, envisioning her friend. His brown hair, blue eyes, how he lit up a room when performing an enchantment. He had never feared his magic, always embraced it. Unlike her, siphoning it away so that she wouldn't hold more than she could control.

But the scry didn't work.

Even if he hadn't been able to grab the mirror to add his magic, it should have let her find him. But her magic...it found nothing. There was no trace of him. Anywhere. Which could only mean one thing...Jaq was dead.

He was dead. Ella was dead.

Calla took a breath. Her friends were gone.

Her magic sang its sorrow, rubbing her muscles, fueling her fingers to be used. Calla made it smaller.

She sat in front of the mirror and watched Ella with the prince. Saw her approach on unsteady feet to the prince as he danced with someone else. Why was Ella unsteady? Calla took a moment to approach the mirror. Who cared if she was caught right now? She needed answers. Calla pulled on some magic and focused the mirror on Ella, analyzing what was before her. Ella was in pain. A lot. Her eyes kept darting, as though she was seeing things that weren't there. Ella had already been poisoned, and by the shaking in her arms, by more than one. What had happened while she was gone?

Ella spun, and Calla saw her back, saw some of the fresh wounds on her skin. She'd been tortured. By Lucifer. Calla's hand balled as she maintained her focus and looked over every piece of information that she could. Unfortunately, she couldn't see what happened once the message stopped. She didn't have a direct line to the source. But she would find out.

But for now...she would absorb and control herself. Calla released the mirror, sat down, pulled her knees up to her chest, and held on tightly. Tears blinded her as they fell. She kept hoping the enchanters of Rairene would have another message, something new. Ella was alive. Jaq was alive.

She pulled out her mirror again, using her magic, pulling more and more, trying to connect to him.

Calla dived deep, pulling up large amounts of her power and whispering her scrying spell, forcing the enchantment. It would work. It had to work. He couldn't be gone. Not Jaq. He was too powerful. He would have defended himself. But nothing changed. No matter how much Calla poured into the mirror, nothing came.

The mirror shattered.

Calla screamed as she dropped the mirror and pounded her hands against the floor. The floor was covered in shards. The fractured mirror sliced her palm, grounding her, and breaking her out of her spell.

Adam would be back soon. She couldn't let him see her like this. He would ask questions. Calla rallied herself, wrapped her hand, washed her face, and poked at her puffy eyes.

Adam walked in right as Calla walked out of the washroom. He looked so handsome in his official uniform. How anyone could think he wasn't perfect...Calla shook the thoughts away.

"You were gone for a while," Calla remarked. She couldn't believe how calm her voice sounded. "How was your first day at court?"

"Interesting," Adam spoke slowly. "One of the royal guards, the woman, was arrested and taken to the dungeon."

Adam hadn't been looking at Calla, so luckily he missed her freezing, faltering as she tried to ingest another blow.

Calla couldn't process it. Couldn't take in the information.

"What? What was she arrested for?" Calla attempted to remain calm. Tried to keep the tension out of her voice.

"Treason and espionage if you can believe it," Adam dismissed. His attention was solely focused on the mirror now. On Ella dancing before him.

"You don't think she did it?" Calla positioned herself so that she couldn't see Ella.

"She looked defeated but was defiant in the allegations. If she committed those crimes, she's one hell of a player."

"What do you think will happen to her?" Calla pried. She was treading on very thin ground.

"She'll probably be hung. The queen looked thrilled."

Calla dropped a cup, chipping it. "I see."

Only then did Adam turn to face her.

"What's wrong? What happened to your hand?" He lightly held her arms, turning her to look at him. His brow furrowed at the still-bleeding cut.

"A lot has happened, it seems." Calla glanced at the mirror.

"Right, you're from there. At least he's in hiding and didn't die. It's a shame about his friend."

Calla could only nod her head. Even then, she couldn't stop the tears.

Ella was dead.

Raven was in the dungeon.

Jaq was dead.

What were they going to do?

# CHAPTER THIRTY-SEVEN

## CALLA

Calla silently ripped her small, claustrophobic room apart. She had to.

Though she had lived there for several months, it wasn't until that moment, when she wanted to be alone and unheard, that she realized how small the space was. She couldn't even cry without someone potentially hearing. The last several hours with Adam had been torture, unlike anything she had experienced. And even now...she couldn't cry. She couldn't even stop to breathe. All she could do was try to locate her loose black tunic, trousers, and cloak.

So she ripped her room apart.

The clothing that she desperately needed rested at the base of her tiny closet, neatly folded and tucked out of sight. In the exact spot, she had left them upon her arrival. Calla never thought she would need them. She had laughed when Ella had given them to her. Before putting them on, she opened her door and looked around, ensuring no one was around to see or hear anything.

Assured she was alone, Calla pulled on the river of power in her center and focused on the garments in front of her.

*"Protege me ab omnibus vagi oculis."* Calla repeated it several times as she infused her power with the clothing and ordered them to hide her from all others. She pulled a little more power than was needed and ended the enchantment. Her power flashed for a moment.

No one came running.

Calla threw on the clothing and left her room.

The maids had been kind enough to gossip about Raven's arrest all day. So much so that she knew exactly where Raven was. Despite holding a renowned assassin in their dungeon, the guards in the palace didn't seem worried as Calla's enchanted clothing came upon its first test.

She rounded a corner and found herself in front of three guards on patrol. Calla stood in the open, flames burning nearby.

Not one of them glanced her way.

None of them noticed the shadow that grew on the stone as their torch got closer to her.

She shook her head. They should have noticed her shadow. But...this was the folly of Queen Lyanna's ban. None of them even knew to look for it. Calla wasted no more time sneaking around. As long as she was silent, none of the guards would even think to look for her.

Calla skidded to a halt in front of the prisoner tower. It was tucked away in a corner of the palace grounds. The tall circular building barely stood together from Calla's observation. Wooden beams and stones supported the entire tower. Calla noticed that there were multiple entrances connecting it to sections of the guard's living quarters.

She walked around the entrances, waiting for a door to be opened. The one thing she couldn't keep people from seeing was a door opening and closing of its own accord. Calla leaned against the wall and waited.

And waited.

She looked around, looking for another spot. This one was perfectly placed out of eyesight and in the shadows. No one would notice anything outside. It was what was inside the tower that concerned her. Calla threw her arms up as she paced around. If no one had come out by now, maybe no one was on the other side. She moved to the open door, pausing when the handle turned.

Calla scampered into the shadows.

One guard opened the door and walked out, and Calla walked in.

Ten guards sat at various tables before her. None of them looked up when she came in, or the door stayed open a little longer than it should have.

Calla assessed the space before her. The only thing the maids could talk about was Raven being arrested and dragged to the worst dungeon in the palace. Where that meant once she was inside the dungeon, was beyond Calla. Three of the guards stood around a table eating while the other seven played cards at a table near one of three open passageways.

Calla headed toward it when she noticed that several of them kept eyeing the one in the middle as though they were waiting for a monster to come flying out of its depths.

Only one person in the kingdom could elicit that type of response.

Calla didn't think twice about it.

She walked towards the passage and through it, making sure her feet remained silent.

It didn't take Calla long to find her sister.

Raven was in one of the farthest cells. As though distance would keep her from breaking free. Water dripped down around them as the stones withered with age. No one had been kept down here in a long time. Calla's eyes adjusted to find Raven curled up on her side, shivering against the cold, her back to Calla.

"Raven," Calla whispered as she knelt down. She pulled off her cloak's hood and ripped off a piece of her tunic, tossing it towards Raven.

"Calla?" Raven turned to her. Her face was splotchy and stained with tears as she picked up the fabric. "Tell me it's not true."

"What?" Calla sat on the floor, unbothered by the dirt and mold. "What's not true?"

"Ella...it's...it's not true...right?" Raven whispered.

Calla slumped against the bars of Raven's cell as the pain of those simple words strung together brought back everything she had been working to avoid.

"It's true.." She let the words slip past her lips like poison. Calla choked as the reality of those two words pulled her under.

"No." Raven tried to get closer, but the chains restrained her. Calla reached a hand through to her sister, grabbing her hand.

"We can't lose her, Calla. I can't...I can't lose her." Raven clutched Calla's hand hard enough that she winced.

"I know...I can't..." Calla sucked in a breath. "I can't lose any of you." Her magic sparked at her pain, rising out of her core. It cooed around her veins, trying to calm her.

Then she felt the shift.

The spiking, sickly pain of Raven's magic.

It had only happened two other times in their years of friendship. Both of their emotions were heightened enough that their magic tried to mix together. Raven's grief became Calla's, as hers would become Raven's.

An unending pit of loss opened up in Calla's magic, swamping her eyes with darkness. She wanted to fall in. She wanted to give in to her power and let it overwhelm her into a numbing oblivion. She could finally stop attempting to control it and release her power on the kingdom and all those who harmed her and her sisters. The unending well of loss promised all of this and more to her. She would no longer feel her heart being shredded into pieces at the loss of Ella. The pain of being in love with Adam while not being able to be with him...the well of a pain-free life sang to her. All she had to do was fall off the ledge...and let go...

"Calla..." Raven's voice drifted over to her from a faraway place.

"Raven...I can't...I can't bear it. I can't lose her. I can't lose you. I can't lose...I can't..." Calla buried her head in her cloak and squeezed her eyes tightly. The darkness deepened in front of her, welcoming her in. It whispered sweet thoughts of no more emotions. She would no longer have to feel *anything*. Her magic continued to flood her, expanding beyond anything she had tried to control before.

"Calla, rein it in. You're...you're glowing. Your magic is spilling out. *You* control your power. It does *not* control you." Raven's voice whispered around her. Calla squeezed Raven's hand, reminding herself that she was right there. Raven was there with her.

Raven's hand left hers.

A flood of emotions deserted her body in a mass exodus that left Calla falling onto the hard stone floor. She had come so close to falling in. So close to giving over to her emotions and unlocking the cage that held her power. Calla gasped for air as her vision returned.

"I want to grieve with you, Calla, but I can't lose you as well. You can't lose yourself to your power."

Calla rubbed her eyes, smudging the tears into her skin.

She whispered, "I just...I miss her. I've missed you. I don't want..."

"Calla, look at me," Raven commanded.

Calla looked up as she saw Raven strain against the chains, kneeling on the ground, leaning forward as far as she could go.

"I love you. Ella loved you. I am here for you. No matter what. You won't lose me like you lost your family."

Calla took a moment to gather herself. She reached through the bars and rested her hands on Raven's cheek, cupping her face. "I love you too." She wiped more tears from her eyes, clearing her vision. "We can grieve later. Right now, I need to get you out of here."

Calla pulled on her magic until it was manageable again as she shook out her fingers and rubbed her face once more. She needed to clearly see, and her tears were not doing her any favors.

"I think I can enchant the lock to open—"

Searing heat tore through Calla's hands, imprinting them with a magical burn as the enchantment in the lock gripped her. Calla did her best to keep her mouth clamped shut, containing her scream as she peeled her fingers off the lock one by one, but one slipped out. The enchantment held strong, continuing to burn her with its protection the longer her fingers stayed wrapped around it. Her hands thrummed in pain as needle pricks danced over her skin. Calla gazed in horror at her hands as the telltale signs of magic rippled across her skin.

"Calla, look at me," Raven ordered.

Calla looked up.

"You're okay. It's going to hurt for a while. I'm not sure if anyone heard anything, but you have to get out of here. Now," Raven commanded.

Calla nodded as she pulled on her hood and ran around the corner as guards got down the hallway.

She sprinted, not concerned about sound so much as not being seen.

A door was before her and Calla took it, not bothering to wonder where it led, only that it led somewhere else. She opened one of her hands; the muscles protesting as they cramped. Calla squeezed her eyes in pain, forcing her hand to grip the handle long enough to twist it open.

A barracks of sorts spread out before her. Several guards slept in their beds. None of them moved. She briskly walked past all of them toward the door. Another door. Calla glared at the handle she had to grasp and turn. She turned her head and bit a section of her cloak as she opened her hand again and gripped the knob hard enough to open it. Calla headed straight for her room, cradling her hands against her chest as fire continued to pulse in streaks down her fingers.

She didn't dare look at them.

Not yet.

She didn't want to see the damage. Her hands, all enchanter's hands, were the channel by which they used their magic. If she couldn't use her hands...she couldn't enchant. That or it would be excruciating to try anything. Calla had never injured her hands badly enough to be concerned about the pain associated with that, but she knew she would find out soon.

She hadn't realized how many doors were in the palace until each one she came upon made her pulse skyrocket with the anticipated pain each one would elicit. Everyone still slept in the servant's quarters, to her relief. The moon had crested in the night sky, giving her the precious hours she now needed to conceal her crime.

Calla got to her room and stared at her door.

One more door.

She would have to turn one more handle.

She had to turn the handle and get inside. So she did. One more time. Calla held the handle and twisted as every single muscle in her arm and hand cramped with the effort. A single candle continued to burn in her room, giving her enough light to witness the destruction of her fingers. Calla unfolded them in the light to finally view them. Streaks of red slashed across her hands like lightning strikes in the sky. The largest markings were in the palms of her hands, where she had gripped the lock. They continued to darken as time went on and the longer she left it untreated, the more identifiable it would become.

Calla looked at her chaotic room and spun around, searching for the small jar of serum she had. She had used more of it on Prince Adam's face, but the last bit should be enough for her. Calla pried the lid off, ignoring the burning as she scooped out part of the serum and rubbed it between her hands until the underside of her hands were completely covered. Calla searched for some fabric and wrapped it over the serum, allowing it to work while she tried to formulate a plan to get Raven out of the dungeon and bring both of them home.

# CHAPTER THIRTY-EIGHT

## RAVEN

Raven collapsed into her cell two days later.

Another day of torture. Another day of screaming. But she hadn't given in, hadn't given them anything. They still thought the best way to get information from her was through poison.

Her poison.

Raven could barely laugh at the idea.

*Her* weapon was being used against her. There was some mercy in that she supposed. It was her own magic twisting its way into her, not someone else's. At least she knew exactly how it would feel. They didn't.

All the pathetic guards did was watch and laugh at her.

Today's choice of poison was Fenith. A vicious poison that made her mind experience the feel of each bone breaking. At one point, she did actually think her entire body had broken.

Ella had been the one to get her through it. She had been with Raven on the day she first developed it. Ella was with her today as well. The first time was the worst. Raven had laid down in bed and taken her poison, despite Ella's warning. Ella knew it had to be done, though. If Raven wanted to use the poison as her weapon, she needed to understand it, and this was the best way. At eleven, Ella was wiser than Raven's twelve. She had gone through a lot already, lessons Raven knew better than to ask about. But Ella had been adamant it was the life she wanted.

Both of them sat on Raven's bed while the poison took over her mind. She laid there in shock as it worked its way through her body, tricking her mind into thinking each bone was breaking. Raven screamed each time, and each time, Ella had been there with a washcloth, wiping away the sweat.

There was no antidote to Fenith.

All you could do was let it work out of your system. But given too much and you would die from the pain.

Ella had cleaned up the vomit after it was done. She'd bathed her and walked her to bed to sleep. This time, all Raven had was the memory of her and Ella sitting in her room, reading and walking. Being normal. Raven retreated to that place of normalcy, her sanctuary for torture.

Raven found the strength to somehow move her head to the side in time as her stomach revolted the small amount of bread she'd been able to eat. She leaned heavily against the bars of her cell, her chains grounding her. Even now, they still chained her. It was the only smart thing they had done. If they left her unchained, she would escape.

Footsteps echoed down the hall.

The queen coming to gloat. Again. She'd visited the last two nights.

"Here."

Raven stiffened at his voice.

Slowly, painstakingly, Raven turned her head away from the wet, moldy stones to look up and find Rowan staring down at her, a shadow lurking next to him. He was in his uniform, sword out, feet defensive.

"I'm not going to attack you," she rasped. Gods, her lungs hurt.

"I know." He sheathed his sword. A glimmer of concern flashed before being replaced by steely resolve.

"What are you doing here? If the queen finds out..." Raven didn't need to finish the statement. Both of them would be punished if he was discovered. It's why she wasn't hurt that he hadn't visited.

"My father—"

"I needed to see you." The shadow took the hood off. Raven barely remembered him from all of those months ago when he had helped save her. So much had changed.

Something wet snuffled her hand. Raven glanced down at a black dog sniffing, tail wagging. Raven managed a small smile.

"It must be important if you're willing to risk your son's life." Raven mustered a growl. The dog looked up at his owner in confusion.

"It is." Rowan's father crouched down so that he was at eye level with her. "I heard about why you were thrown in here. That you had been collecting pieces of information King Stewart left behind for others to locate his advisors?"

Rowan paced behind him. "Father, please, they're rumors. Lord Cenric probably fed that information to Raven to get her in trouble."

"They're not rumors."

"How would you know that?" Raven tried to focus, shaking her head to get rid of the remnants of the poison. Her head pulsed, and it was only partly because of the Fenith.

"I was one of King Stewart's Royal Guards before he died."

"I remember being told that," Raven mumbled.

"I was also here during the coup. Queen Lyanna trusted me, thought I was her spy within her husband's guards. King Stewart made sure she and I were friends from the day she arrived, so that she would never question me or my allegiance to her."

"Father, what are you saying?" Rowan stopped pacing, leaning against the far wall, far away from both of them, his face hidden.

"I'm saying that I know where the princess is."

Rowan's arms fell to his side as he pushed off the wall and stumbled over to them. His brown eyes are full of so much longing.

"She's alive?" Rowan asked.

The relief on his face was more than Raven could bear.

"My friend is alive?"

"That day, when the fire was burning...Queen Lyanna ordered me to take the princess into the forest, kill her, and bring her heart."

Rowan snarled.

"I was still loyal to my king...my friend...who had been killed. So I grabbed the princess, still dressed in her mourning clothes, and took her to an enchanter. They used a special potion to hide her memories from her so that she wouldn't know who she was or where she came from. Only that she had been in an accident. Then I bought passage for her on a smuggler's ship—"

"You sent a seven-year-old girl out alone—" Rowan began.

"Son, let me finish," his father snapped.

Raven kept her eyes locked on his, trying to read between the lines and the poison.

"I sent her with someone I trusted to get her hidden. I told them where to take her, where to hide her. King Stewart had been adamant that should anything happen to him, and his advisors, I was to send her across the sea to a friend of his, a Duke in Rairene. The Duke of Aumont."

She closed her eyes, pressing her hand firmly against her pounding skull. Raven couldn't think clearly with the headache crushing her mind, sending blinding stars in her eyes. The cold stones were a relief as everything she had been trying to piece together for months collided.

"She's you, Raven. You're the little girl I sent away."

Raven coughed. "I'm no princess. I'm Raven, trained to be one of the most feared assassins in all of Rairene, doing the king's bidding."

"Didn't you ever wonder why you have a tattoo? Why your memories never came back?"

Raven froze, thinking of the raven tattooed on her back.

"The enchanter, his ink, was enchanted to hide your memories from you. There's a reason Feather is so attached to you. He was your dog." Rowan's father looked at the old dog, who hadn't moved his head away from Raven's hand. "You named him that because—"

"We're birds of a feather," Raven blurted. "His fur...is as dark as my...hair-" She almost said mark. She barely remembered to keep that secret to herself.

Rowan's father crinkled his brow. So he knew, but wouldn't say anything.

"You see—"

"No, I don't believe you. I'm an assassin, and that's all I am." Raven crossed her arms.

"I'm sorry that you've had to bear that. That was never supposed to happen. You grew up in a happy home. If I had known what happened—"

"I lived a good life, old man. There's nothing to be sorry about. But I'm not the princess you sent away, or are hoping for."

"You are Raven. You look like your mother. I'm surprised Queen Lyanna hasn't realized it."

Rowan, Raven noticed, had remained silent. She needed to know what he was thinking. There she was, his friend, returned from the dead. What a let down she must be. All of that hope he held at the simple thought of his princess returning, only to be wasted on her.

"Whose heart did you bring to the queen?" Rowan whispered.

His father looked at him.

"You said she ordered you to bring her a heart. There's no way you're still alive, and I'm a Royal Guard if she thought you had failed."

"I killed a deer and brought the heart to her. She wasn't going to notice the difference. I knew she wouldn't have an enchanter read it. She barely trusts them now."

"Is that why you stopped serving her? Because your king was dead?" Raven whispered.

"If she was willing to kill an innocent child..." Rowan's father choked on his words.

Raven narrowed her eyes. "There's more to it than that. What happened?"

Rowan's father flicked his eyes towards Rowan, towards the scar on his face.

"Rowan doesn't remember. He was with the princess, with you, when the coup started. One of the queen's men tried to take you...and Rowan...he got in the way. My seven-year-old son defended his friend, and was almost killed—" Rowan's father stopped talking.

"That's why you never told Rowan how he got that scar. He—"

"He was knocked out, but it would have been worse if I hadn't arrived when I did," Rowan's father whispered.

"Yet you didn't bother to share any of this with him?" Raven questioned. Rowan remained silent, staring at her as he processed what his father was telling him.

"No, I couldn't risk her finding out. It started and ended with me, and me alone."

"Until today," Rowan ground out.

"Why?" She leaned harder against the bars, blinking rapidly as her knees dug into the cell.

"Take your rightful place on the throne. Your father's advisors will raise their banners for you. The advisor's men are still loyal to King Stewart and will come to your summons." Rowan's father shook with excitement and hope.

All Raven could do was stare. He was serious.

He truly believed she was his lost princess. She wasn't sure whether to laugh at the audacity or cry at the truth.

"I need to think." It was all she could say. All she would say. Raven turned away from them, moving her hand away from Feather.

He huffed, displeased by her denial.

They moved a few moments later, their steps fading.

Raven continued to sit there, in all the filth, her filth, and stare at the wall. She began counting each stone on the wall. She'd done it already. There were exactly one thousand, three hundred, and fifty-six stones preventing her from freedom. Out there she wouldn't be Snow White, or this princess, just Raven. She would find Ella...no...she wouldn't find Ella.

Ella was dead.

Raven held in a sob. Ella was dead. She wasn't pulling a prank on them. She was gone. Calla was hopefully far, far away, and she was...she was alone. No one would come to help her.

"Are you okay?"

Raven fell over when Aleks spoke behind her.

"How do you do that?" she hissed, rubbing her head.

Aleks looked her over. She didn't bother trying to make herself look better. Didn't bother with her knotted hair, her dirt and sweat covered skin. Raven adjusted her uniform. She hadn't been allowed to change, and her armor had been removed.

"Are you okay?" he asked again.

"Do I sound okay?" her voice rasped.

"You sound like someone whose been—"

"Screaming for hours because the pain won't go away? And not in a good way?" She finished for him.

"You could answer the questions they ask you," he mumbled.

Raven wheezed a laugh. "Even if they asked me questions, I won't answer them."

And she never would. She would never cave.

Aleks snapped his head up. "They haven't tried to get you to answer any questions?"

"Not a single one. All they do is laugh."

"I heard what Rowan's father told you," Aleks whispered.

"What do you think about his claim?" Raven leaned sideways on the bars, looking him over. He was tired and wasn't getting any sleep. Probably from the guilt of her being framed for his espionage. His eyes weren't red anymore, she noted. His hair was still a mess, the braids barely staying together.

"I'm not sure what to think. Nine years ago I was told that my cousin died in a shipwreck, and two years before that I learned that my...they had killed my friend in a coup. Now apparently, all of those were lies."

"It may not be true. Do you think I look like the former queen?" Raven asked.

"I don't remember her. They removed all the portraits when my aunt became queen."

"Find me proof, Aleks."

He opened his mouth to protest.

"I need more than the ramblings of an old man who thinks my tattoo means something. I don't even care if it's that I'm not this lost princess. Show me proof. Either way. You owe me."

"What will you do if you are the lost princess?"

"Fuck if I know. But at least I'll have a better sense of where I come from, of who I am."

"I'll do my best Raven, use that iron will of yours to hold out for a bit more."

Raven only nodded. Her headache had gotten progressively worse. So it wasn't from the Fenith. It was from the drugs she hadn't taken in days. Her body was not happy, and she knew it would only get worse.

# CHAPTER THIRTY-NINE

## CALLA

Calla woke up earlier than usual. She needed to see Prince Aleksander and no one could bear witness. Climbing out of bed, Calla habitually grabbed a potion bottle filled with water and was about to siphon off her magic when she stopped. Her fingers cramped and stiffened at holding the bottle. Glancing down, she was reminded of the magical burn she bore. She did not know when she could enchant anything. Calla couldn't even enchant more serum without causing immense pain.

Calla took a slow breath. She would be okay. She could go a few days without siphoning off her power. She would be *fine*.

Donning her cloak, Calla darted through the palace before the sun could begin to kiss the night sky. She had scoped out where the prince slept a day ago, but he hadn't been there. Hopefully, at this time of day, he would be.

Her one disadvantage right now was that he would need to answer the door. Quickly. If she was caught near any of the royal family suites, she could be killed for any perceived relations. It would be imperative that Prince Aleksander let her inside.

She approached his wooden door quietly, not giving the idea any further thought. She would talk herself out of it, and she couldn't do that.

Not now.

Not when Raven needed her.

She would be brave.

Calla knocked on his door three times, careful to not be loud. Her heart hammered with each millisecond that passed and the door didn't open. The unmistakable sound of someone stumbling into furniture followed by muffled swearing came through the door right before it opened.

Prince Aleksander stood before her, blurry-eyed and yet completely awake. Barely an ounce of sleep graced his ice-blue eyes as he looked her up and down. No more than the assessing gaze she gave him. Here was the prince who her sister had fallen in love with. Raven didn't realize it, but Calla had seen the way Raven responded to him during her ambush. He was alarmingly beautiful and disarming. Prince Aleksander had never fully looked at her, and as he did now, she couldn't help but wonder what he saw, for it felt as though her entire self was laid out before him.

He pulled her roughly inside, shutting his door behind her.

"Are you mad?" His voice was thick as he walked toward his bed. Though his eyes were present and calculating, the rest of his body projected an entirely different story. His white hair and braids were tangled, and his clothing was wrinkled as though he had collapsed onto his bed without bothering to change.

"I have to get her out of there." Calla didn't bother with niceties. He had an idea of who she was, and Calla was willing to bet he wouldn't turn her over for his love of Raven.

"You have to leave," Prince Aleksander said.

"I won't. Not until I get Raven out of there."

"Raven is the one who asked for me to keep you safe. The only way to do that is if you leave. My aunt is searching for anyone else involved with Raven, and she will be told that you've helped her."

"We can't leave her in the dungeon." Calla squeezed her hands, blinking against the pain.

"I know, but I don't know how to get her out." Prince Aleksander ran a hand over his face as he slouched on his bed.

"When they transport her, we could—"

"Have you seen what they do to transport her?" Prince Aleksander walked over to her. It was like watching a tormented soul find its bearings after being listless for decades. Eventually, he found his footing, becoming his true royal self before her.

Calla shook her head.

"They drug her. She's unconscious as one guard carries her over his shoulder, and four other guards surround them. On top of that, her wrists and ankles are chained together. So even if on the off chance she isn't passed out, she can't get far on her own. As much as I hate to admit this, I wouldn't be able to get her out of that and away to safety. Neither could you. Don't even start on trying to get her out of the cell—"

"I know. I tried." Calla revealed her hands. The serum had done wonders, but there would always be the faintest of scars on her hands once the injury healed.

"Then you figured out that rescuing her is practically impossible." Prince Aleksander walked away from her, lying on his bed.

"I'm still going to try. There are things that can be done." Calla fisted her hands as she looked at him. He had closed his eyes and folded his hands on his stomach, his legs dangling off the edge. He breathed slowly, as if he was trying to calm himself.

"Then you better hurry. She can't handle much more, and my aunt has only begun," Prince Aleksander mumbled.

Calla remained calm until she got to her room.

Then she punched the pillow that was just thick enough to provide some type of support at night. Then she punched it again. And again. She gripped her hair and pulled. What was she going to do? All reasonable options were off the table. For now.

But until a reasonable option to break Raven out of the dungeon presented itself to her, she would have to think of the unreasonable...a new potion. A new potion that would tell the enchanted cell to unlock. Her intentions would have to be extremely focused, with the sole purpose being to get the door to unlock.

Calla looked at her hands. The marks had faded into pink lines that danced over her palms. But it could have been so much worse. She looked at the empty jar that had contained her serum. She couldn't make more right now. It was a long and arduous process. It was a miracle for everyone at Aumont. Calla knew she wasn't being boastful either. It had never been accomplished by another enchanter.

And it had been a complete accident.

She could try again.

Calla paced around the confines of her room, weighing her options. She had spent *days* working on dozens of enchantments. Days of no sleep and barely any food. But she had done it. Never again would she...Calla stopped pacing as the image of Drea, lying on the ground of a rickety shack with blood pooling underneath her, burst before Calla's eyes. Her failure had been her inspiration. If it hadn't been for her...no. She couldn't go down that path. Not now. Calla shook her head, the image vanishing as she continued to pace.

She didn't have days.

And she didn't have the freedom to be shut in a room where she could openly enchant. But that didn't mean she would not try.

Calla pulled out an empty bottle and held it before her. She looked inward at the river of power coursing through her veins. She pulled enough for a trial run of the potion. An enchantment of unlocking wasn't something she had tried before. Most locks weren't enchanted to stay locked, and if they were, it was very hard to break them. To undo the lock, she would have to deduce the intention given to the enchantment to stay locked, and more importantly, to defend. It was no ordinary lock on that cell. Luckily, Calla was no ordinary enchanter.

She'd created something new before.

She would do it again.

*"Obliviscere praesidium tuum, thesauros tuos resera."* Calla spoke softly, starting with a basic enchantment that would counteract an enchantment to protect something or someone special.

As she pulled on her power, it swirled around inside her skin and down to her hands, the pressure in her fingers built. Sparks pricked along her fingers, cramping her muscles.

Calla bit back against the pain, squeezing her eyes as she pressed on.

She continued to mutter the enchantment. Her power built and swirled around her hands. Spikes of pain gripped her muscles until the bottle was locked in her fingers.

She couldn't let go.

Her hands were paralyzed.

Calla's eyes widened as she tried to move her fingers. They didn't respond. What was she going to do? She'd never experienced this before.

Fire pulsed in her hands as her power begged to merge with the potion.

She had to sever the enchantment.

And it was going to hurt.

Calla spun towards her bed and laid down with her face in the pillow as she gave a final push of her power to solidify the enchantment as pure, raw, undefined power shot through her body.

Calla screamed into the mattress as softly as possible.

The fire rampaged through her as the rest of her power rippled into her body. Calla lay still, waiting for the ebb and flow of her power to settle. Eventually, the pain subsided and her breathing calmed down as she sat up. Her arms shook as she looked at them and the bottle clutched in her hands.

One by one, Calla detached her fingers from the bottle.

A pale white substance swirled within, but there was hardly any power within its depths. Her hands, however, were a different story. The power that should have transferred to the potion had instead marked her. New red streaks, like shattered glass, broke out over her palms.

Calla stared at the potion bottle, getting lost in a memory she would rather forget.

Drea...on the ground of that shack.

Helpless.

Bleeding.

Calla gazed at her broken hands.

She couldn't enchant.

Not until they were healed.

Calla shook her head and straightened her spine. She would fight through it if she had to. She had to do something to save Raven, and if it meant permanently scarring her hands...it would be worth it.

# CHAPTER FORTY

## CALLA

Prince Adam wasn't there when she arrived the next morning. He must have been allowed to observe the court proceedings for the morning. Calla had waited for word from Lord Conrad, hoping he would have something for her. Orders from Lady Tremaine about what to do. Information about the plan they had to free Raven. But nothing. There has been *nothing*. And while Calla would do as she was told, she refused to believe that nothing was the answer.

She pulled out a small mirror and grabbed some of her magic. It would hurt, but she had to try. She had to do *something* because doing nothing was driving her insane. She would need to scry someone she thought she would never reach out to.

Drea.

Calla pictured her beautiful dark curly hair, pale skin, shining green eyes, and the scar that marked her skin. Calla flinched in shame. She hadn't been talented enough then...but now...Calla's fingers sent shocks of fire down her arms for a moment and then...Drea's face lit up the mirror, her eyes wary, face puffy.

*Calla?*

The mirror went dark, their connection lost. It came back quickly.

*Hi Drea,* Calla whispered.

*Calla, why are you scrying me? You're in Evrotia, they could—*

*It's gotten bad here, Drea. Raven's in the dungeon, for treason, and I...I don't...I don't know what to do.*

*It's bad here too.* Drea looked away.

*I know about Ella.* Calla's voice hitched. She wouldn't cry right now. *That she's dead.*

*I'm sorry for your loss, Calla.* Drea kept her eyes trained on her lap.

*Can I...is Lady Tremaine somewhere? I've been trying to reach Jaq, and I...is he—* She couldn't say it. Even though she knew it was true. She couldn't say the words out loud. Not yet.

*They're both dead, Calla. Jaq died defending Ella...and my mom...Ella killed her.* Drea locked eyes with her this time.

Calla almost dropped her mirror. Ella had killed her...*Why?*

As Drea relayed the last few days' events, Calla felt herself grow numb. Everything they thought they had been doing...was a lie. Calla couldn't even comprehend all the damage they had done over the years to the Kingdom of Rairene, thinking it was for their protection.

*I'm sorry for your loss.* It was all Calla could muster in the moment as her world crumbled.

Drea nodded. *Stay where you are, Calla. I'm not sure how to get you out right now.*

Calla stared at the wall as everything whirled through her mind. Her first reaction wasn't to go into the middle of the fight she saw looming. Nor was it to run. It was to simply stay put. She was frozen with indecision, and it was not a sentiment easily worn by her. She needed to prepare for every circumstance that came across her path. But this...she had never expected being on the wrong side of a war. She had been protecting...she hadn't been protecting *anyone*.

Calla ground the palms of her hands into her closed eyes. She didn't have the answer for this in any of her books or her mind. So she did what she always did when she didn't know the answer. She went to her mentor.

If only she could find him.

She had tried several times to scry Lord Conrad, despite the pain it caused each time. And nothing. It wasn't the same as when she had tried Jaq and felt...nothing. Lord Conrad was simply put, ignoring her.

So she did the only logical thing there was to do.

Go to him instead.

Calla closed her mirror and left Prince Adam's room. Though she had only been at his residence once, she remembered the way perfectly. She walked past the guards with confidence and down into a section of Aslar she had hoped to never return.

It was a strange moment for Calla to have a raised heartbeat and hurried steps while walking past others who didn't feel the same sense of urgency as she did. No one else had to rush over cobblestones that would twist an ankle if stepped on wrong, or through muddy alleyways while worried about a friend currently being held prisoner. As the people of Aslar went about their day, as if the entire kingdom wasn't falling apart before their eyes, Calla walked with the cracks of her world crumbling around her.

She got to Lord Conrad's home in a blur, knocking quietly at his door.

And then knocking again.

And again.

But he didn't answer.

Calla stepped away and looked at her surroundings. He couldn't have moved. He was too settled there, and if there was anything her mentor loved more than luxury, it was comfort. More specifically, comfort in the known. So while he would have despised living in the worst part of Aslar, it would have become a comfort to him. She looked at the other poorly patched homes that could barely stay standing and then down towards the pub at the end of the street. If he wasn't home, she could soundly guess he would be there. She hoped.

The pub wasn't nearly as rundown as the surrounding homes. The stones they had built their walls with had withstood the aging. The wooden pillars looked newer than the rest of the entire city, and inside the pub were tables that were well crafted and could support anyone's weight without them giving it a second thought.

Calla's shoulders relaxed when she spied her mentor in a corner of the pub, hiding in the shadows while eating with the prim elegance she had come to love. Lord Conrad didn't even spare her a glance when she sat down across from him. He merely continued eating his stew and bread before using his napkin to dab his lips and then finally look up at her.

"Daughter."

"Father," Calla whispered. "Have you—"

"Which part?" he grumbled as he crossed his arms. "The part where a guard is in the dungeon for espionage? The part where Eleanor died? Or the part where she killed our mistress?"

"All of it." Calla leaned back and watched him.

He was a creature of habit, and being a creature of habit meant he didn't always react well when something changed his world. Calla had always thought it odd about him given their line of work, but even she was struggling with this shift in their perspectives. Which made her wonder how much he had been aware of their true purpose.

"Did you know?"

"I said—"

"Did you know what our oath was really about? Did you know that everything we had been...everything *I* had been told...was a lie?"

"Ah." He leaned back as well, his arms uncrossed as he held her gaze.

He had. He had known, and he had never told her. Never told any of them they were not serving the interests of Rairene. Calla fisted her hands as the small piece of her heart that had held onto hope that he had been duped as well died.

"What are you going to do now?" Calla couldn't stop the revulsion from crossing her face for a split second. She was fully aware of who her mentor was, and since he had known the whole time, she could no longer trust anything he suggested. She wasn't even sure she could trust what he had taught her. Who knew how much he had withheld from her in fear of causing her to flare out? Or worse, to keep her from succeeding and becoming a better, more powerful enchanter than him?

"I'm going to leave, and I suggest you do the same."

"What about Snow?"

"What about her?" Lord Conrad stood up and looked down at her.

"She needs us. She would do anything to get us."

"She did this to herself—"

"She didn't." Calla stood up and faced down the man who had helped raise her. Who had taught her everything she knew about using her power and not letting it overpower her. He looked smaller now. Though she was never physically taller than him, he shrunk before her eyes.

"She's on her own, like the rest of us." He left before Calla could respond.

She sat down in the booth, her eyes following him as he tottered away. She had always known...deep down...that if she had ever gotten into trouble, he would never risk himself for her. Why had she expected him to do anything for Raven? Calla twisted her hands as her magic whispered coos of comfort. She could almost feel it wrapping around her in a hug, or petting her cheek. She pulled on her magic until it was once again a small creek flowing within her. Calla pressed her hands to her face. She had to do something. Anything. If it was the other way around, Raven would have already figured something out. She wouldn't have cared if Calla was unconscious as they transported her. She would have attacked either way and gotten her out.

But Calla wasn't Raven.

She couldn't do that. She was an enchanter who was stuck as a maid in a kingdom that hated enchanters. She'd seen the warnings. Another enchanter had been caught and hung recently. Calla rubbed her wrists as she thought about the black shackles that had been on the enchanter's arms. Enchanter's shackles...she shuddered.

Calla left the pub and walked to the palace as her mind churned. She would think of something.

# CHAPTER FORTY-ONE

## RAVEN

"What am I going to do, El?" Raven turned her head away from the moldy stone walls to stare at Ella. She stood above her. Raven's training clothes were torn and blood had dried on her. Yet Ella still stood beside her. Her white hair fell in perfect loose waves down to her waist. Her blue eyes, sharp and assessing.

"I'm not sure what you can do." Ella tilted her head as she looked closer at Raven.

"I need your help, El. I'm too deep right now."

"I know." Ella reached over and brushed a piece of hair out of Raven's eyes.

"I want to go home. I want to be home with you, Mira, and Calla. I miss all of you. I wish I had never come here."

"We want you to come home as well." Ella moved closer, laying down, so that they were next to each other.

"I miss you." Tears rolled down Raven's cheeks.

"I'm sorry that I couldn't say goodbye," Ella whispered.

"What do you mean? You're here with me now." Raven tried to sit up. Something held her down.

"You know the answer, Raven." Ella remained lying next to her, their faces inches apart. Her blue eyes were so kind, so full of life. Nothing like Raven's dark and stormy ones.

"Ella, please...don't go. Don't go." Raven felt more tears well up in her soul, in her magic's core. "Please don't leave me."

"I love you so much, Snowy." Ella stood up and took Raven's face in her hands.

"I love you too," Raven spoke through her constricted throat. Her eyes clouded over, Ella blurring before her.

"Stay strong Raven. Don't let them break you."

"I won't." Raven sniffled.

"I'm sorry that I can't fight beside you."

"Because you're dead," Raven choked out.

"Because I'm dead." Ella's eyes filled with tenderness as she looked at her friend, her sister. Ella was right in front of her now, her face inches away.

"You are stronger than them. You are stronger than this. We went through worse. You can do it again. You have to do it again. Make them pay. Make them suffer."

"For you," Raven gasped, something sharp piercing through her mind.

"And for you," Ella whispered. "Blood in my veins."

"Bones of my ancestors."

Ella was gone.

Not a whisper of her was left. Raven knew none of it had been real. Ella was dead. Her friend was dead, and she...she had to survive. Somehow, she would do it.

Raven screamed in pain.

Something hot stabbed her again. Burned her flesh. The calm world she had created disappeared in a snap, disorienting Raven. The room was the same, but Ella was gone, and her torturer was still there, a heated rod in his hand.

Queen Lyanna stood on the other side of the room, grinning. She had started attending their 'little sessions', as she liked to call them.

That was when the guards had really started being cruel.

How much more could she take? Her heart was already broken. Lady Tremaine had handed her over. What was the point?

Calla.

Calla was the point. She would protect Calla. Then she would escape, and she would kill Lady Tremaine and the queen if she could. Someone had to pay the price for Ella's death.

Sweat drenched her as her magic became a writhing mass that she could barely contain.

"Bring her to her cell. We've done enough for today," Queen Lyanna commanded. She waltzed over to Raven. "I will break you, Snow White. You will give me what I want," she whispered, the guards too far away to hear.

"You haven't asked me anything," Raven muttered.

"Oh, I know. I'm just tenderizing you first. I want to make sure you're pliant when I ask."

"I'll never tell you anything," Raven whispered, turning away from her as her vision blackened with each shallow breath.

Raven slumped against her cell, barely able to sit upright. Her eyes fought hard to stay open, her muscles throbbing. Raven didn't think that had to do with the heated rod, though. She'd got nauseous and shaky the day before. Her entire body ached, and her headache had never vanished. It had been a long time since she had taken either medication, and her body was not enjoying their absence. She was going into withdrawal. After six months of constantly being on them, her body was out of it.

Raven curled up on her side, shaking with chills.

"Raven?"

She couldn't respond, unable to form a sound.

"Raven?" Aleks spoke louder this time.

It must be important. She should answer him. But the shaking wouldn't stop.

"Raven, answer me, please."

"Aleks," she croaked out his name. That was all. The screams had finally caught up to her.

"What happened?"

"Mire," she muttered, her back to him. "They dosed me with Mire. It's a hallucinogen. I saw...I saw *her*." Raven swallowed. "She was right there. In front of me. Talking to me and then she was gone. Gone. I could have sworn it was real. That she was real. That I had imagined her death. Why couldn't it have been imagined?" Sobs wracked her as she curled in on herself more.

"I'm sorry."

"Everything hurts," she whispered.

"Does that happen with that poison?"

He pressed closer to her, somehow resting his hand on her shoulder. Her magic went into shock at being touched by him again. Raven folded it in.

"No...my entire body hurts. My bones ache, and my muscles are exploding. I can't even—"

Raven vomited.

"Shit."

"What can I do?" His hand rested firmly on her back.

"I'm going into withdrawal," Raven rasped.

Aleks remained silent.

Raven threw up again. But he kept his hand on her.

"Distract me," she pleaded.

"I've been searching the palace for any sign of your heritage. Unfortunately, this palace is massive, and almost all of it is in use. Even the West Wing that my aunt had closed off is being used by Prince Adam."

"Why was it closed off?" Raven shuffled closer to him.

Absent-mindedly, he rubbed her back. Raven closed her eyes, relaxing at his touch. Her magic sparked again.

"My aunt closed it shortly after the coup. She said it was damaged and needed to be redone. Except, I've seen nothing done to it. Until Prince Adam was there, no one had stepped foot in those hallways for ten years."

"It sounds like she might hide something there," Raven murmured. Exhaustion pulled at her.

"Possibly, but whatever it is, I doubt it's there now if Prince Adam is there."

"I don't—" Raven stopped, her body convulsing. A chill raced through her, sweat breaking out of her forehead. "The night he arrived..it was complete chaos. I don't think the queen had time to move anything."

"I'll try it," Aleks whispered. His hand moved away from her.

"Prince Charming...stay with me? For a little longer...please."

Aleks sat down, rubbing circles on her back as she heaved again.

The vomiting stopped in time for the guards to drag Raven out of her cell and take her to what she now called her torture suite. She wasn't sure when Aleks had left, only that he had. She knew he couldn't be caught, especially not down there. He would never know how much it meant to her to have his hand on her, rubbing her. How reassuring it had been to not be alone.

Raven wondered how much poison they were going to give her today. If they would ask her questions, or laugh as they watched. They seemed to enjoy that...her suffering. If she truly was this lost princess, they would be the first to go. She'd memorized all of their faces, the sound of their voices, the way they moved, everything. If they ever left her unlocked for one second, they would all be dead.

She would see to that.

And she would enjoy it. Oh, how she would enjoy getting to end the lives of the men who relished her pain.

The heavy, uneven steps of the head guard echoed down to her. His limp had gotten progressively worse over the times he'd come for her. The other guards, all four of them, reeked of alcohol and sweat. Each time she looked at them, she memorized something new. This time it was how they stood close together, as though they shared a secret.

Raven hated this next part.

She always tried to hold her breath, but it was useless as they shoved an herb under her nose, knocking her unconscious. Each time, she hoped it wouldn't work. Hoped she could use that time to break free. But each time she woke up strapped to the wooden table, her arms above her head, chained to the ground beneath her. Her legs were chained as well.

One day, she told herself.

The metal chains were a new feature of her suite. Rusted and caked with blood, yet not hers. Then she found out their true purpose. Someone cranked a lever, and the chains moved, pulling her arms a little tighter.

"What should I ask you?" A woman with gray hair piled on top of her head and violet eyes gleaming in the shadows stepped into Raven's view, her red lips smirking. "That's always the question, really. What to ask? What will benefit me or the queen? What will cause you pain to answer? Those are the best questions, the ones that cause you pain."

Raven blinked. She'd seen her before. Once...in the throne room...with shackles for an enchanter. Her heart quickened as she looked at her hands, expecting to find the black stone shackles in her hands. Her thick body seemed to disappear in the shadows, her clothing swirling around her in wisps. Raven blinked again, trying to regain her focus. She could do this.

She could control her magic and remain hidden. She would withstand her. Whoever she was.

"How about what kingdom you hail from? That's an easy one."

Raven narrowed her eyes, keeping her mouth shut.

"No?" A smile spread over the woman's face. "Pet, be a dear, move that lever half a space."

The chains pulled ever so gently on Raven's wrists.

"I'll never tell you anything," Raven spat.

"I believe you." Her torturer placed a cloth over Raven's face.

Water poured over her face. She convulsed on the table, unable to breathe as the water continued to pour over her. Raven's magic shook in anger, strengthening itself to defend her. She pulled it back. If she revealed herself now, she was either dead or they would place her in the enchanter's shackles. A fate worse than death.

Raven gasped as they ripped the cloth off her face. She sucked in air, trying to control her breathing, control her magic. It was spiraling now, chomping to be free. With each breath, she stuffed it down farther, making sure it was contained. Raven didn't take her eyes off of the woman.

"Morgan." The woman spun towards the voice.

Raven would have shuddered if she could have.

"Ask her why she was searching for my late husband's advisors." Queen Lyanna stepped out of the shadows, her compact frame towering over Raven.

Raven silently snarled.

The queen flicked her eyes to someone, and the lever moved.

Morgan came over and pressed a piece of metal to Raven's skin. Her body was so cold that the hot metal instantly shocked her, forcing Raven's body to jump. The pain of the heat against her frozen skin was more than she could bear.

"Tell her why you were searching for the late king's advisors," Morgan cooed, brushing a hand over Raven's cheek.

Raven locked eyes with her soulless purple ones, challenging her. Morgan shrugged before covering Raven's face again.

They took turns, Morgan and the queen. Sometimes it was water, other times the burning metal. They always pulled her body a little tighter until Raven screamed.

Eventually, her only relief from screaming came when her throat could no longer make any noise at all.

Raven waited for her bones to pop, for everything to give up. But it didn't. Her body held on. Her mind, however, could not.

Raven would not answer their questions, but to do that, she had to create a place where they didn't even exist.

She was in her room, lying in bed. Jason had left her. She had been crying, trying to hide her shame. But never from Ella, never Calla, or Mira. They were beside her, protecting her. They didn't even say a word. They never needed to. They were there for her, and they always would be. Ella kept running her hands through Raven's short hair, twirling it around and around. Calla was deep in a book, looking up an enchantment. Mira was going through Raven's clothes, looking for an acceptable dress for her to wear. According to Mira, they were going out to have some fun. Normal fun, she clarified.

Out of everyone in their group, Mira was the only one to have had a life before coming to Aumont. She never spoke about it, but the way she carried herself, dressed herself, Raven knew she was from some noble house. Mira said something that had Ella and Calla laughing. Raven had missed it, smiling at her instead. Mira walked over, her flaming red hair a halo around her. She knelt down and cupped Raven's face.

"Men are pointless, Raven."

"I know," she whispered, though she wasn't sure how much she believed it.

Raven was ripped from her room as she struggled to breathe. The moment fractured.

Water continued to pour over her. The cloth was suctioned to her mouth. Raven wondered if they wouldn't remove it in time. The sensation of drowning...Raven had to keep reminding herself that she wasn't actually drowning. She would get through this. Had to get through this. She had survived worse. She needed to survive so that she could rip the beating heart right out of the queen's body.

Hours later, Raven couldn't speak. Her lungs burned with an attempt. Her head fell to the side. After a day of questions, she could no longer stay conscious enough to even try escaping.

They dumped her in her cell. She didn't bother to try standing, let alone try to fight, as one guard sat on her until they chained her to the floor.

It was worse this time. The pain.

At least when she'd been poisoned, it wore off. Gradually it would fade into a whisper of a memory in her muscles and bones. But this...actual torture, actual pain, this would last for days, not hours. Her muscles were a mound of nothing.

Raven curled in on herself, trying to find relief.

"Raven."

She couldn't even move to acknowledge him.

"Raven?"

She muttered something, hoping it was loud enough for him to hear.

"I'm here." Aleks reached through the bars and lightly rested his hand on her.

She flinched. She'd never done that before. Flinched in pain. She tried to apologize, to tell him it wasn't him.

"Aleks." Raven got his name to slip out.

"I'm here." He lightly rubbed her back.

"I'm tired." Raven tried to ignore the defeat in her voice. She was fading and there was nothing she could do. All she had to hold on to was the image of using the queen's gauntlet to relieve her of her black heart.

# CHAPTER FORTY-TWO

## CALLA

"Calla?"

Calla stared out the window in Prince Adam's room as she cleaned. She held the drapes in her hands, rubbing the thick embroidered fabric between her calloused fingers. Her hands had finally healed enough that she could move them with only mild shocks of pain. That or she had acclimated to the little pricks of pain. She couldn't tell anymore. She had barely made it to the prince's room. Sleep had eluded her for the last few nights.

"Calla?"

"Hmmm?" She continued to look out the window. What was she going to do? She hadn't been able to get the potion to work. There wasn't a way to get Raven out of the dungeon. She was useless. Worthless. As a friend. As an enchanter. She had failed her friend. Grief threatened to loom over her in a tidal wave of emotions that—

"Calla." Strong hands gripped her biceps and turned her away from the window.

She stared into Prince Adam's warm brown eyes, drowning in their depths. At least here, in his room, she had a modicum of normalcy before returning to her nightmare.

"What's wrong?" He looked her over again with a kindness she didn't deserve.

"Nothing." She blinked slowly, trying to keep her eyes open. She could hardly tell him that she had been up every night trying to create a new potion to break her sister out of the dungeon.

"Over these last few months, I've learned that you are clever, intelligent, caring, and more courageous than you know, but I never would have listed a liar among those other qualities."

Calla stepped backwards at the assertion. He didn't know how correct he was.

"I'm just...I haven't been getting a lot of sleep." She averted her gaze. She couldn't look at him or everything would tumble out of her.

"I think there's more to it than that." He sat down in front of her on the plush rug, waiting for her to join him. She did so slowly. His thick blond hair settled loosely around his face, down to his shoulders. He looked healthy and full of life.

Calla twisted her hands together, wincing at the pain. She had to tell him something. Anything that would be good enough and yet not be seen as a lie.

"I recently found out that a close friend of mine in Rairene died," she whispered. It was the closest truth she could muster. Her chest tightened as her lungs tried to breathe through the sorrow pulling her down. Calla hid her face in her hands.

"Why didn't you tell me sooner?" Adam spoke softly as he scooted closer to her. His leg pressed against her knees. "I'm so sorry."

Calla took a shuddering breath before losing all rational thought and wrapping her arms around him. They had never been so close before. But right then, she needed a friend and as she sat on the ground with him, she found no shame in letting herself cry before her friend.

Calla buried her head in her hands as she let all the tears that had been building up over losing Jaq and Ella tumble forth. Her magic was a soft hum as she kept it contained, not once rising to protect her. It knew she was safe.

Eventually, Adam picked her up as though she weighed nothing, and sat down with her on the couch facing the mountains. She curled herself against him, finding solace in being so small in stature for the first time in her life. He stroked her hair, whispering to her in Vicurian. Adam told her such wonderful things. He told her she was beautiful, strong, smart, loyal, and dozens of other words she had never identified with herself. He saw all of it. But he couldn't share it with her in a language he thought she knew. Because they could never be. Even now, in his room, if someone walked in unannounced, they would kill her.

But Calla didn't care.

She had lost so much. She would not lose this moment with him, where for the first time since she was eight, she felt safe. At some point, Adam got up and finished cleaning the drapes while she watched from the confines of the quilted blanket he had wrapped her in. By the time she left his rooms, the sun had begun to set and streaked the sky in hues of pinks and purples.

Calla collapsed on her bed. She had forgotten how exhausting emotions were. And she was spent. But she had to keep trying her new potion. She had to keep going. She could do this.

Calla looked at the small dresser filled with ruined enchanted bottles. Each one swirled with her power. Power that was useless. She had a gift for potions and rarely had to hide it. But right now...she felt eight years old as she stumbled to learn her enchantments. Not that this was one anyone knew. It was rarely done. Calla had done some research after she had created her serum on how new enchantments were developed. There was very little information to glean from the texts in Aumont's library. Either no one had attempted a new enchantment in hundreds of years, or the library was out of date. Calla had a sneaking suspicion it was somewhere in the middle. What she had learned, though, was that anyone who attempted to create a new enchantment had spent months to years carefully crafting their enchantments. They had to make sure the enchantment was intended correctly and that there wouldn't be any adverse side effects.

Calla didn't have months or years.

She didn't even have weeks.

She had days.

Maybe less.

Raven had been held captive for over a week now and the palace was buzzing with rumors of her impending death. Queen Lyanna had circulated that Raven was the reason all the commoners had been killed in the throne room. There was, of course, no mention that the queen had been the one to order their deaths.

The entire palace and all of Aslar were primed for her death.

Calla sat up and grabbed another empty bottle. She closed her eyes and focused on the feel of the glass in her hands. The strikes in her fingers caused pricks of pain in her hands. The bottle rolled in her hands, perfectly balanced. Taking a steady breath, Calla focused on the river of power she held. Gleefully, it rose to her summons, twisting and spiraling around.

Deep breath.

Calla breathed with her magic, getting it to focus on her rhythm and intentions.

*"Dimittis quod tenes intus,"* Calla whispered the new enchantment. She'd changed her focus from one of protection to one of release. Calla had realized early in the process that this enchantment would be different. Most objects could be enchanted. But an object that was already enchanted to defend and protect...that was a different level of enchantment and if she couldn't touch the bars, she would have to create something else that could.

Calla repeated the enchantment over and over until the pressure building in her hands was too much. She sealed it, hiding the flash of power under her pillow. Calla clamped down on her teeth as shocks of pain flickered up her arms.

Opening her eyes, she looked at that potion.

Milky liquid floated in the bottle.

Close. She was so close. But not yet.

Calla groaned as she lay down. She had been *so close*. She could feel it. It was almost right.

*Calla got to the shack first, though it more resembled a rundown single-family cabin. It resembled her home...Calla realized. That didn't matter. Drea was in trouble.*

*Lady Tremaine had been frantic.*

*When they had figured out where Drea was, she had sent Calla. Calla still didn't understand why. She was no expert healer.*

*She was only fourteen.*

*But she had come...because Drea had always been kind.*

*Calla shoved the door open on rusted hinges, falling into the room. There had been a struggle. Chairs were broken, and the table, well what had been a table, was now broken in multiple places. But none of that was important.*

*The body before her had yet to move.*

*Drea lay on the rotting wooden floorboards, with barely a breath left inside her. Calla jumped over and pulled on Drea's body. She had been lying on her stomach, a pool of blood slowly growing around her left leg. Calla gripped her satchel filled with enchantments. But this was Drea.*

*She couldn't take any.*

*Calla brushed Drea's sweaty, curly brown hair out of her face. Her eyes were closed and a fresh scar from an enchanter's loss of control stood out in stark contrast to Drea's sickly pale skin.*

*"Drea...what happened..." Calla whispered.*

*Drea opened her green eyes slowly, staring at Calla. She did nothing else as Calla took in the damage. She turned to the source of Drea's bleeding. A blade wound deep in her thigh. Calla ripped away Drea's skirts until she could assess and clean it.*

*"Leave me, Calla."*

*"No. You will survive."*

*"There's nothing you can do to help me," Drea spoke softly, as though the very movement of her lips was too much.*

*"I have been ordered to save you."*

*"I could become addicted," Drea whispered, her voice gaining strength.*

*Calla closed her eyes. She would not cry, she would save her.*

*"I've been ordered to do everything I can."*

*"Please...Calla."*

*"I'll do what I can."*

*Drea closed her eyes in relief as Calla poured water over the wound and cleaned it. It was deep. Too deep. Only magic would be able to fully save her leg. Calla chewed the inside of her cheek as she worked and dressed the wound. She packed it with clean dressings and applied pressure. It was all she knew to do without enlisting her potions.*

*Drea's hand gripped Calla's arm hard enough to bruise.*

*Calla looked over, meeting her eyes.*

*"I would rather die now than become addicted to any potion. Do you hear me, Calla? Please." Drea didn't let go until Calla nodded her head. She hoped the others would get here with enough time to help. Drea laid her head down and closed her eyes while Calla did all that she could to save an enchanter.*

# CHAPTER FORTY-THREE

## CALLA

Calla had tried to enchant three more times that morning, with nothing to show for it besides dark circles under her eyes. Pounding footsteps reached her from down the hall. Calla frowned as she walked to her door and cracked it open.

Palace guards were going into the servants' rooms.

Her magic rose to face the threat.

She quietly closed her door, rushed to her drawer of potion bottles, and found a cleaning bucket in her washroom. She opened all of them with shaking hands and poured the contents into the water. The potions mixed together, blending into a black liquid. Calla took the empty bottles and divided them up as she placed them around her room.

The guards came in without knocking.

"May I help you?" Calla asked as the two of them began searching her room.

"We're searching all the servants' rooms," one guard replied as he shoved past her.

"For what?" Calla barely got out of their way as they tossed her room.

"None of your concern. What are these bottles for?" The guard held up some bottles she'd emptied.

"Tonics and healing medicines. I got an illness." Calla crossed her arms.

The queen didn't know. How could she? She was searching all of the servants' rooms. Of course she didn't know, Calla reassured herself. She didn't want to think about being imprisoned or possibly tortured. Of course, her sisters had done their best to train her, to prepare her for a day when she might need to resist being tortured...she never thought that day might be so close.

Calla clutched her necklace, hiding the shaking in her hands.

The guards left without another question, having demolished her room in the space of three minutes. Calla left her room in the shambles it had become as she put on her uniform, ignoring the way the muscles in her legs turned to jelly as she thought about the guards searching her room. Her fingers played with her curly hair, trying to tame it as she walked down to the dining hall. All the servants and palace staff muttered amongst each other, passing rumors around.

"Calla, are you all set for the ball?" Betsy asked as she sat across from her in the dining hall.

"The ball?" She looked up in a daze from her porridge.

"The servant's ball that the queen is hosting. It's an annual tradition. I'm glad she didn't decide to cancel it with all that's been happening," Betsy murmured.

"Oh uh, I don't think so."

"You have to go, Calla." Susan sat next to her.

Over the weeks, the three of them had formed a friendship of sorts, Calla liked to think. Especially over the last few days. No one thought any of them were involved with Raven, but all three of them had interacted with her, and the other servants had distanced themselves. They would probably distance themselves more after this morning.

"I'm not much of a dancer." Calla lied. In truth, she loved to dance. It was one of the few times her brain didn't have to think and she could let her body move.

"Please come," Betsy pleaded.

"I'll try," Calla acquiesced.

She left shortly afterwards, hoping to get a few more attempts done while Adam was at court. The queen had demanded his presence almost every day now. But not today. She had canceled court. Calla frowned.

"I thought you would be happy that you're not left up here by yourself," Prince Adam joked.

"Isn't it odd?" She tilted her head.

"You're really disappointed I won't be gone." Prince Adam smiled, though his shoulders slumped.

"It's not that. I enjoy spending the day with you. I just...I'm still processing my friend's death, and the time alone is helpful." Calla grasped for reasons.

"Ahhh." Prince Adam walked over to her. "I was thinking about that and I wanted to offer you something. If you have anything that your friend gave you, I could read it and show you...if you'd like? Let you relive the memory."

Calla's jaw dropped. "You can do that? Share readings?" She'd always felt that she could do that, but Lord Conrad had never taught her. He wouldn't even show her, and she'd been too afraid to try with any of her friends. What if she had hurt them? At least now she knew she had to do more research on what enchanters could do. Lord Conrad certainly hadn't taught her everything.

"Yes. Here." Prince Adam picked up the queen from the chessboard. He wrapped Calla's hand around it and then his around hers.

She ignored the fluttering in her stomach from a simple touch.

Calla felt him pull his magic, the shocks flying over her. It ran over her in giddy joy, forcing her to pull her stream of power into a tiny puddle before he could realize she had power too. Calla tried to focus on the chess piece in her hand, and not on how Prince Adam smelled of fresh rain and books, or that he was so close to her again. She really tried to not focus on the fact that his warm, calloused hand wrapped around hers. Then, she was lost in the image before her.

They were playing chess. Prince Adam had said something to make her laugh. Her hair was perfect, her eyes bright. Calla looked at herself as they played. She glowed in the chess piece's memory. What an interesting thing for it to remember. Calla looked at herself again. Had she been letting out too much magic? Was that why she was glowing? She needed to get better control of herself and siphon off more magic. Calla looked at Adam, though he wasn't as well defined as she was in the chess piece's memory.

Prince Adam released her hand.

Calla was dimmer the second his touch left hers.

"How can anyone find enchanters distrustful? Or banish them? What you showed me..." Calla bit her lip.

"I'm hoping I can change that. Enchanters used to be welcome here."

"I don't think Princess Arianna will split from her mother's decisions."

"Maybe not, but I can try. Every other kingdom has welcomed enchanters. Some...not so well." Adam winced. "But if we were to go to war, we would be easily defeated, unless we can bring enchanters back."

Prince Adam got up and walked out to the balcony. She watched him go, wondering what bothered him. His face had more color in it now and he was eating better. He was always on that balcony, absorbing the fresh spring air. His hazel eyes glowed each time she saw him. He was so happy being in court, being a part of something. Being with other people. He would barely notice when she was gone.

Because Calla was leaving. She had to. As soon as she figured out how to free Raven, she would be gone and Prince Adam wouldn't have to worry about her.

He came in a minute later, shaking his hands. They glowed enough for her to notice. Why was he having trouble controlling his magic?

"If you have anything of your friends that you want me to read, I'm here for you."

"Thank you," Calla whispered. She fought to get the words out.

"Are you going to the servant's ball tomorrow?" He switched topics.

"I'm not sure. Probably not. I don't have a proper dress." Calla shrugged, smiling at him.

"It would mean a lot to me if you showed up. It's my first formal appearance since all of this," Prince Adam motioned at his face. The scar had healed into a thin pink line. "It would make me less nervous if you were there."

"Really?" She tilted her head, looking for the lie.

"Really, plus you can introduce me to the servants whose good sides I need to be on."

"You'll really need to work on that. Some of them still haven't forgiven you for how you treated them those first few weeks." Calla smiled as he winced.

"Even more reason for you to be there."

"I still have nothing to wear."

"Are you sure?" Prince Adam got up and walked over to his wardrobe, pulling out a dress made for a princess, not a servant girl.

Calla paced around her room, ignoring the ballgown Prince Adam had given to her yesterday. She stood tall as she walked, rolling the empty potion bottle. She would do it. Tonight was the night. She could feel it in her magic. It was ready. Her hands were ready. The scarring had healed as much as it could. It was now or never.

Calla whispered softly to her power, pulling on it gently, coaxing a stream to flow down to her fingers. It was giddy to do as she bid, surging forward. Calla calmed it again. Her power had built up too much over the last few days, and if she didn't do something with it soon, she might burst.

She mumbled her enchantment through her teeth, focusing all of her intentions on the idea of safety. She didn't know why it had taken her so long to figure out the enchantment guarding Raven. It wanted to keep her safe. The reaction it had was that of protection and guarding. If it had been one simply to keep someone out, all it needed to do was remain locked. No, that enchantment had struck her. It had wanted her to remember it would bite when provoked. So Calla enchanted the potion to be soothing and reassuring. It would calm the lock and put it into a slumber.

*"omnia tuta sunt, nihil solliciti."* Calla focused on the bottle, smiling as her power spun within her. Sparks of joy danced along her arms as her power built with each layer of enchanting until she could contain it no more. With one last whisper, Calla sealed her power into the potion, watching as it flashed, turning the clear liquid into a calm violet that spun with power.

Calla looked at it, grinning.

She had done it.

She was certain.

It would work. She could get Raven out. She needed a bit more help from Prince—

"Calla, let's go!" Betsy called from outside her door.

Calla fumbled the bottle, catching it before it broke. She put it under her pillow and opened the door.

"Where are we going?" She peeked her head out.

"To the servant's ball. Didn't you get a dress?" Betsy stepped in farther.

"No, I forgot about it. I've been busy making sure Prince Adam is healed."

"I wish I had worked for him. You have to wear it, Calla. It'll be rude to not wear it with him in attendance."

"Do you think he'll show up? The other servants are saying they never—"

"If he gave you this, he'll be there." Betsy touched the dress, rubbing it between her fingers.

"Do you think Prince Aleksander will be there?" Calla whispered. That was her moment to talk to him. If he was there.

Betsy smiled at Calla. "Are you trying to get more than one prince to fall in love with you?"

Calla sputtered. "I'm not...he's not. Prince Adam is not in love with me. It's forbidden." Calla folded her arms.

Betsy smiled at her as she took the gown off its hanger and carried it over to Calla.

"Only one way to find out. Let's get this on you and get to the ball. And yes, Prince Aleksander tends to come to these events. He's always gotten along well with the palace staff."

"Okay, good. That's good," Calla muttered.

# CHAPTER FORTY-FOUR

## RAVEN

Raven lay in her cell. She hadn't given them anything. She never would. They knew it too. She'd been abandoned. Calla hadn't been able to get her out. She hoped, prayed, Calla was far away. As far away as possible. If they had caught her...Raven would do everything in her power to set her free. Her magic flared in response to the thought. She would find a way. For Calla. Her innocent Belle, who knew nothing of the genuine horrors of their world. If she was captured...Raven shuddered.

Aleks hadn't stopped by yet.

Raven hadn't realized how dependent she was on seeing him once the guards discarded her like yesterday's filth. How much she needed his contact. Her magic whimpered at the loneliness. At least when he was there, she knew she wasn't as alone.

Raven didn't let herself fall into the black pit that had become her core. Didn't stumble down and down. She wanted to let it swallow her up.

Aleks skidded to a halt in front of her cell. Raven shivered, curling in tighter. Her sweat had dried, and she didn't want to know what she looked like now. She stank of body odor, blood, and fear.

"I have it. I have your proof."

Raven didn't turn toward him. She couldn't. She didn't want to see the look on his face.

"What's the answer?" Raven whispered in Trudelian, bracing herself.

Aleks responded in his native language in case anyone listened in, "Rowan's father was right. You're the lost princess...my friend..." Aleks trailed off. "I'm getting you out there right now."

"How do you know?" She turned to look at him. He was dressed in attire fit for a ball, wearing a beautiful suit with silver embroidery and a black circlet on top of his white hair.

"This is all you need." Aleks let the portrait gripped in his hand unfurl in the dim candlelight.

It was a simple portrait. A happy one. King Stewart was so handsome, his brown hair perfect, his bright green eyes sparkling with laughter. The little girl was grinning from ear to ear. Her curly black hair was messy enough that Raven knew she had been playing shortly before the portrait was painted. She sat on the king's lap, no older than three. But it was the queen that drew her eye. She was Raven's twin. The queen's black hair curled loosely to her waist, her own blue eyes gazed at the little girl with so much love, Raven could hardly breathe.

She had been loved.

She'd had a family...and they had been happy.

Raven stood up on solid feet for the first time in two weeks.

"What am I going to do, Aleks? She's going to hang me tomorrow."

"No, she's not," Aleks spoke through gritted teeth.

"Aleks, she's won. There's no getting out of this. You can't touch the lock, it'll hurt you. There isn't time to assemble an army to come rescue me. No one is going to save me."

"You're going to let her win? Rowan's father must have a plan. We can't let her get away with what she did to us-you."

"Us?" Raven looked him up and down, assessing. "How did she hurt you? You're her favorite nephew."

"We were friends growing up, you and I. And Rowan. She stole that from us."

Raven stepped back. He was hiding something from her. Something bigger to make him this upset. She needed more time, and she was out of it.

"Did Calla get away?" Raven asked, hoping the answer was yes, but secretly needing it to be no. Needing her to still be in the palace.

Aleks froze.

"I think so. I haven't been able to find her." Aleks kept his eyes down.

"Oh." Raven didn't relax. "I'm glad she got away."

Raven tried to not let the sinking pit of black swallow her. She tried...

She was alone. Calla wasn't trying to get her free. She had no one. Ella was gone. Ella was dead. Raven repeated, reminded herself. Calla was the one who was gone. Maybe it was a good thing she was going to die tomorrow. At least that way, she would have Ella with her again.

Raven pressed her hand into her eyes. She would not cry. Not after everything that had happened.

"Raven—"

"Is that even my name?" she choked out.

Raven rocked back and forth on her feet, holding her knees close to her chest.

"It is if you want it to be," Aleks whispered.

"What was my name?" Raven tilted her head to look at him. He was pressed against the bars, as close as he could get to her.

"Astrid."

"Astrid." Raven tried the name out on her tongue. She didn't know what she thought about it. All she knew was that she was tired and wanted to sleep. Possibly, if the gods were kind, they would let her die in the cell.

"What can I do?"

"Nothing. Do nothing. I want to sleep." Raven laid down on her side. She didn't make any noise when Aleks slipped his cloak through the bars and dropped it so that it landed on her. She didn't move an inch when he left.

Only once he was gone did she arrange the cloak to cover her, keeping her warm and breathing in his scent. The only good thing left in her world and he had walked out...and she had let him.

# CHAPTER FORTY-FIVE

## Calla

Calla gave herself a last glance in the small mirror before heading out for the ball. Betsy had perfectly laced up the back of the gown. Her unruly hair was pulled halfway up with two delicate combs that somehow held it from her face while the rest cascaded down to cover the wolf tattoo over her mark. Her rose necklace glinted in the candlelight. By the time they were done, the ball had started, and Betsy hurried them along, grinning from ear to ear.

Calla bit her lip at having to leave her potion behind, but Betsy was adamant they go, and wouldn't give her time alone to grab it.

"You look like a princess, and the rest of the servants need to see it." She beamed.

Calla turned scarlet as they practically ran down the empty hall.

She had barely gotten to come to this part of the palace. So when the double wooden doors opened before them, Calla lost her breath as she took in the throne room. The arched stone columns and vaulted ceiling disappeared in the darkness as the moon shined in through the stained glass windows. The floor was filled with dancing servants, and even some members of the nobility were already present.

When Calla stopped staring at her surroundings, she found everyone had stopped to stare at her. Her golden gown sparkled in the candlelight, its voluminous layers swirling as she stopped at the entrance. The golden hue of the gown contrasted perfectly with her dark skin, a sun goddess incarnate. Calla flicked her eyes to the floor. What she wore cost more than anyone of her station should be able to afford.

"Well, you've come a long way."

Calla looked up at the familiar voice and smiled. Chip stood before her, smiling, a hand stretched toward her.

"Care to dance?"

She nodded her head as she gripped his hand, trying to hide how much they shook. "What are you doing here?"

"My mother works here. I think she might be one of your head mistresses." He winced.

As they danced, everyone went to their own partners, and the conversation quickly resumed. Calla tuned all of it out, looking around the room for Prince Aleksander.

"Not used to dancing?" He chuckled.

"Not used to everyone staring." Calla frowned. Where was he? Betsy had been sure he would show up.

"Calla, look at me," Chip whispered. "Breathe, focus." He breathed in and out, Calla following. "Now, who are you looking for?"

She gave him a quizzical glance.

"I may not be a courtier, but I can tell when someone is distracted while in my arms. Trust me, they usually aren't." He smiled.

Calla fumbled for words. "I...I'm sorry, Chip. You're right, I am distracted. I need to tell someone something, and they're not here."

"May I help you?" He asked, leaning closer. "Would it have anything to do with why I smuggled you here all of those weeks ago?"

"Maybe, I really don't want to get you into trouble—"

"I'll cut in." The voice struck Calla sharply across the cheek as she was transported to the ship that had carried her to Evrotia as she turned to face Lord Edouard.

Calla stiffened in Chip's arms, trying to not shrink against his side.

"If it pleases the lady," Chip muttered. He released one hand, and Calla felt as though she'd been tossed into the raging sea without a boat to save her.

She looked up to see the twisted grin spread across his square-jawed face, knowing that she couldn't refuse him, even here, at the servant's ball. Calla's magic twisted in her, revolted by his presence, begging to be used.

A glimpse of white hair pulled Calla's attention away. "Actually, I have to go talk to the Prince." Surely he wouldn't keep her from someone of royal blood.

"I wasn't asking for permission," Lord Edouard sneered. He shoved Chip hard enough that he stumbled backwards, releasing Calla.

Calla turned and walked away, trying to find Prince Aleksander.

He had been *right there*.

Prince Aleksander was right in front of the throne.

A hand grabbed her wrist and pulled.

"Let me go." Calla tried to rip herself free of him, but he only brought her closer to him.

"You're going to dance with me and then you're going to leave with me. No one says no to me, especially not a peasant maid," he whispered, twisting her wrist.

"I'm not going anywhere with you," Calla seethed. She could do this. She could stand up to him. She didn't want to be hit, not again, though that was the least of her concerns as Prince Aleksander disappeared from sight again.

"Let. Me. Go."

"Not a—"

"I believe she said to let her go."

"And who do you think you are?" Lord Edouard spun them around.

Prince Adam's fist connected with Lord Edouard's face, throwing him to the ground.

Calla fell with him, tangled in her gown.

Calla rubbed her temple as she waited for the room to stop spinning. Adam helped her up quickly, pulling her away from Lord Edouard. Pulling her closer to him. Her cheeks warmed at his rapid heartbeat beneath her hand. Several maids, Danita and Betsy included, moved to her side. Betsy frowned as she looked at Calla.

"I'm fine...I'll be fine," Calla whispered. She patted Betsy's shoulder as she walked away to follow Prince Adam onto the dance floor.

"Thank you," she whispered to Prince Adam.

Prince Adam brought them smoothly into the waltz, his hand gently holding her. "Who was that?" His voice dropped an octave.

"No one," she mumbled. She gripped his hand tightly, taking strength from him. She hadn't been able to stand up for herself...again.

"Calla, you're shaking. What did he say to you?"

"It's not important."

"We can talk about it tomorrow. For now, let's dance." Prince Adam stood taller as they moved across the throne room. "You look beautiful," he whispered in Vicurian.

He looked stunning. Too stunning for words. He was dressed in formal attire, a blue suit with a sash covered in medals. His medals, she realized. His blond hair was pulled back, revealing his perfect face, scar and all. Calla was oblivious to everything else. Even Prince Aleksander faded from her mind. It was only her and Adam.

Her Adam.

Calla threw out any traitorous thoughts and tried to enjoy the moment with him. The feel of his hand holding hers, swirling her around the floor. This was their life. They would always be dancing, the world fading away from them. Calla looked into his eyes and drowned. She never wanted to leave. At least...not him. He would forget her soon enough.

But right now, she didn't think about any of those things. She was dancing with a prince. A prince who looked at her as if she were his entire world as well. Calla smiled at him, beaming as they circled around and around.

"Come now, Prince Adam, you can't dance with her all night." Prince Aleksandar stepped up next to them, stopping their moment.

Prince Adam glared up at the other prince, and for a split second, Calla thought he would punch Prince Aleksandar as well. Prince Aleksander leaned over and whispered in Prince Adam's ear.

"What did you say?" Calla whispered as Prince Aleksander stepped in and Prince Adam walked away.

"I told him that if he didn't want anyone to get the wrong impression, he should let someone else dance with you." Prince Aleksander swirled her around. "You're as much trouble as Raven."

"How is she?" Calla whispered.

"Alive. The better question is, why are you here? You're supposed to have left." Prince Aleksander's blue eyes flashed in panic.

"I told you I'm not leaving until I can get Raven out."

"And I told you that's practically impossible—"

"*Practically* impossible, and I figured out how to get her out. I need some horses and I can get her out tonight."

"What is it?" Prince Aleksander gripped her hand.

She hid her wince of pain as he leaned in close.

"I—" Calla stopped. She couldn't tell him. He would turn her over. She was an enchanter...and they weren't allowed. She couldn't risk that he had the same biases as his aunt. "I can't tell you."

"You can't...why?"

"Please...just...get me the horses and I'll get her out. I'll get her safely away."

"I'll get them," Prince Aleksander said softly as the dance ended. He stepped away from her, delicately kissing her hand.

Calla turned away from him, ready to get the potion and pack her things. She would do it. She would get Raven out, and they would be free. Prince Adam stepped up to her, holding out his hand once more. One more dance. One more moment with him, and then she would never see his hazel eyes again. She smiled at him as he led her onto the floor.

The doors slammed open, a resounding echo silencing the room.

Guards marched in, the servants paralyzed.

"No." It was barely a whisper. But she was sure Adam heard. She clutched his hand.

Lord Edouard walked up beside her. "You won't get away with embarrassing me."

Queen Lyanna and Princess Arianna strode in, guards behind them.

A sharp pain pierced her side.

Calla gasped, eyes wide as she looked at Lord Edouard and the blood covered dagger in his hand.

"Adam—" She twisted to look at him, her hand covered in blood. Her magic rolled in protest. Calla pulled the river of power in, making sure it was contained.

"Calla?" Prince Adam's eyes went wide when he saw the blood. "Guards arrest that man. He attacked my servant." Prince Adam ordered as he drew his sword and pointed it at Lord Edouard. "If you don't, I'll handle him myself."

"Darling, we're here to arrest your servant," Princess Arianna crowed. She motioned for him to come to her side.

Prince Adam gripped Calla's hand tighter, worry crossing his eyes for a moment as he looked between the two. "You must be mistaken. My servant couldn't have committed any crime. She's not capable."

If only he knew, Calla thought. She had indeed committed several in the last few hours alone.

"I'm afraid she's been conspiring with the former Royal Guard. For that, we have charged her with treason." Princess Arianna smirked.

Adam's hand went limp as every muscle in his body slumped.

Calla stood frozen. Either from the pain or the shock, she wasn't sure which. If she moved, she would collapse. She had never been in this position, and she wasn't sure how to think her way out of it past the blinding pain as blood continued to run over her fingers. She wasn't Raven or Ella who could have talked, or at least fought, themselves out of this in their sleep. She couldn't even enchant without experiencing pain.

Before Calla could respond, or form any time of protest, two guards flanked her, shackling her wrists. Calla yelped at the flare of pain in her side.

"I didn't do anything." Calla ground out. They had nothing to tie her to Raven. "I only helped her get ready once when her maid was ill."

"Liar. They sent you to work with her in a coup," Princess Arianna snapped. She walked across the ten feet of separation and gripped Adam's bicep. "Adam, they sent her to kill you. It's why she worked so hard to become your maid. She was only trying to get near you." Princess Arianna didn't break eye contact with Calla the entire time.

"She's lying." Calla tried to shake out of the guard's grip, but it was too strong. She had to get him to believe her. It was truly all a lie. "Please, Adam—"

Princess Arianna slapped her.

"How dare you be so informal with my fiancé."

He didn't look at her. Calla pulled harder, ignoring the fire on her side, the power building within. She needed him to look at her. He would look at her and see it was all a lie.

"It's all lies," Calla whispered.

Adam stepped away. It was only a few inches, but it may as well have been miles. Calla's magic wept as it tried to repair her heart. Tried to keep the fractured organ beating. He was the only person who could defend her. And he did *nothing*.

"Take her to the dungeons," Queen Lyanna commanded, her crown glinting red in the firelight.

"Adam, please!" Her voice cracked. Her last chance. Somehow, he could get her out of this.

"She can rot there while her friend hangs for their crime." Princess Arianna said.

"Please, I did nothing," Calla pleaded, resisting the guards. But they were stronger than her, and she had never learned how to fight.

Her magic spiraled, demanding to be used. If she would let it go, she could take all of them out. Calla tapped down on it. Not now.

She would hurt Adam.

As much as she wanted to let go, to give in to the anger, the grief, the pain...she couldn't. She would hurt so many others. Too many others.

Calla knew that...deep down, she knew that if she let go...it would be devastating, and she wasn't ready to die.

Calla glanced to the side, saw Chip and his mom, their faces empty as they watched her get dragged out of the throne room. But she didn't go quietly. She may have committed treason by simply existing, but she had not done what they had claimed.

She had not conspired with Raven to kill Adam.

"I didn't do this. I didn't—"

Blackness descended on Calla as she was knocked out.

# CHAPTER FORTY-SIX

## RAVEN

Raven turned over and looked at the ceiling of her cell. She blinked slowly as her eyes pleaded with heavy lids to close and go to sleep. But what was the point of sleep when she was going to die in the morning? Her fingers shook as she pulled Alek's cloak tighter around her, relaxing as his scent of snow and trees coated her senses. Her magic whimpered, wishing it was his arms wrapped around her instead. She should have told him how much she cared for him. How she could no longer imagine going a day without seeing him. How her heart skidded and fluttered whenever he smiled at her, and how despite how frustrating he could be, she still knew...deep down...that she was safe with him.

Raven closed her eyes for a moment, the wet tears sliding over her blood and dust covered skin. But, eventually, morning came. She wished it could have waited a little longer.

She prepared herself for the guards' arrival. She got the cloak securely around her shoulders, clasped in place. It would lend her the strength she would need just to move. Her legs hadn't stopped pulsing or cramping, and her arms were limp by her side. She doubted she could even disarm a young page. But if given the chance, she would take it.

So she prepared herself for the weight of having to walk to her death, weak and alone. At least she would get to see Aleks...one last time.

She would only look at him in the daylight, with no shadows between them.

Their footsteps reached her first, the heavy boots echoing off the damp stones.

They funneled into her cell, creating an impenetrable wall. They wrapped more chains around her, binding her arms close before unchaining her from the floor. It didn't matter how much weight they added, standing would have been a feat in itself for her.

Raven moved her feet one at a time, dragging them across the rough stones slowly. It wasn't that she wanted to prolong her life anymore, but rather that she needed the time to pull her power to her. While there was no way out for her, she could at least make a last stand and take out the one person who mattered; the queen.

She could do that.

She would see Aleks, and then lose all control over her vast well of power. Calla may not know her strength, but Raven was well aware of the black mark at the base of her neck, and finally relinquishing that control would be glorious.

Of course she would die as well, but she was already heading toward it.

Might as well make a difference with her death.

As they trudged through the guards' tower, and into the first court-yard, Raven noticed one thing: the palace was quiet.

The large stone courtyard was void of all noise. As they continued their pace, silence was all that greeted her. Raven tried to not think about it as she continued to pull on her magic, shaping it into the largest possible mass of dough that she could control...for now. She had to make sure she didn't start to reveal evidence of what she truly was. If she displayed any form of power beforehand, they would most likely knock her out. So as her power built and built from her deep well, she contained it in a tight spiraling dough that continued to grow in her core. It expanded and fluctuated inside her as she braided it, trilling at finally being used.

She only paid attention to where they were until the guards beside her settled heavy hands on her shoulders, stopping her. Raven's power roared in her ears, a cacophony of endless buzzing that threatened to overwhelm her. Her hands shook as she quieted her magic and hid it from anyone looking at her.

Because people were looking at her.

She gaped at the main courtyard full of noblemen and palace staff. All of them mingled together. None of them dared speak. Raven spotted the guards stationed at the perimeter, bows drawn as they faced the crown, waiting. Queen Lyanna should have known that her staff would never fight back, not over the Royal Guard they all despised. But for their lost princess? Raven's eyes widened. Had Queen Lyanna figured out who she was?

She would never know.

The guards shoved her again towards the haphazardly built gallows. It was near the back entrance, the towering mountains and forest a beautiful backdrop for where she would be killed. The sun had crested the mountain tops, lighting up the sky in hues of red.

Raven had to walk through all of these people she had protected. All of her people. Her kingdom. However, based on the hate filling their eyes, all of them were happy to see her die. The Queen had done a wonderful job at ensuring the will of the people would be turned against her. She was The Hunter, and the person who had killed so many of their citizens.

Raven's fingers itched to run through her hair, to do something, anything but be idle, and detangling the hair that had grown well past her shoulders, and was covered in dirt, sweat, and blood, seemed to be the most mundane and best option. But all she could do as they walked forward was stare straight ahead, her face as calm as possible.

She would show no emotion.

She would not give Queen Lyanna the satisfaction.

She'd degraded herself in front of her enough already. Raven squared her shoulders the closer they got to the gallows. Her magic sputtered as she took in the five wooden steps leading to what had to be the most unstable platform. Raven's heart thundered in her chest and her power slipped from her grip for a moment. She reined it in before it could manifest externally.

Raven froze before the first step. It wasn't because her power had filled every crevice of her body, or that she couldn't get it to quiet down as it grew giddy. It was simply that she didn't want to take that step.

She couldn't do it. Couldn't move. Couldn't think past the thought that she didn't want to die. She wanted to fight, to scream, to *live*, and if she went up those five small steps, all of that would end.

At least she would get one last look at Aleks.

She hadn't looked to where she knew Queen Lyanna, Princess Arianna, and other highly ranked members of the royal court would be sitting. She hadn't wanted to lay eyes on the woman who had destroyed her kingdom. If Raven had seen her before getting to the top of the gallows, she would have lost control right then. So she hadn't looked at the stage opposite her.

Her magic sent powerful shocks all over as she continued to pull. She was powerful, but she hadn't realized how much there was to dredge up. She zeroed all of her focus in on keeping it contained, not alerting anyone to her power, and getting to see Aleks.

She would look only at him, and she would be okay.

The guards shifted behind her, shoving her forward.

Raven's hands hit the rough wood first, splinters cutting her fingers. She pushed off to stand up, finding strength as the chains tried to let gravity keep her down.

Raven took shaky, deliberate steps until she got to the top.

She blinked tired eyes as she turned and looked once more at the crowd that had already condemned her. But they were her people, and even though they didn't know that, she would face them.

She would face her people, face the queen, and face Aleks.

Raven scanned the crowd quickly, shame clogging her throat as she gazed upon them. Betsy and Susan stood next to a guard, their faces full of fear. They wouldn't be afraid for much longer.

Her eyes shot around the stage across from her, seeking Aleks.

He wasn't there.

Raven's heart shuddered. Her magic stopped growing and collapsed as it hit her.

*He wasn't there.*

She couldn't see him one last time.

Her breathing shortened as she gasped for air as her single shred of solace dropped out from under her.

Maybe he was in the crowd, somewhere no one would bother him. But she didn't see him anywhere. There was no white hair to guide her to his dazzling blue eyes.

The rough rope slipped over her head and tightened as she searched for him.

Raven swallowed as the rope scratched her neck.

She would not break.

Not over a man.

Never again.

The chains were removed, save the ones binding her hands.

Raven swallowed the fear that further shortened her breath as her chest rose quickly.

"I have charged you with espionage and treason and found you guilty." Queen Lyanna's voice rang out over the crowd. Some of them even flinched at the sound of her high-pitched tone. "For your crimes, you will die, witnessed by the people you have betrayed."

Queen Lyanna stood up to give the words to hang her. Raven watched her move around the stage. She had somehow outdone herself in honor of Raven's death, wearing a vivid red gown that was closely fitted around her bodice with decorative black armor that twirled around her chest, and skirts that draped around her, giving her a taller appearance. The seven pointed crown, Raven's crown, rested on her blond curls, glinting in the early morning light.

Before she could give the guards the signal, a man next to Princess Arianna stood up. He was dressed in black, and had his shoulder-length blond hair pulled part way back, revealing a handsome face, marred only by a faint scar that was healing well. He towered over the queen.

"Queen Lyanna, shouldn't the traitor get to have some last words?" Prince Adam asked loud enough that Raven could hear.

If looks could have killed, Prince Adam would have died five times over with the gaze Queen Lyanna leveled at him.

"The traitor may have a final word." Queen Lyanna permitted through gritted teeth.

Raven stared in shock.

"Unless you would rather remain silent in your guilt?" she challenged.

Raven's magic had built up, fueled her with confidence as she took a small step forward, as far as the rope would allow.

"My name..." Raven's voice cut off as it rasped out over vocal chords that had only known the pain of screaming. She swallowed as she stepped back enough to let herself talk more freely. "My name is Princess Astrid of Evrotia. I am King Stewart's daughter and heir to the throne!" Somehow she could vocalize loudly, though she needn't have bothered. It was already quieter than a graveyard.

"Liar," Queen Lyanna hissed. "They killed her."

"I am the rightful heir, and you have built *your* throne on treason—"

"Kill her!"

"—and corruption. I will not—"

Raven stopped as the noose tightened.

Her magic rose to the surface as the guard pulled on the lever that would drop the floor out from under her.

She kept her eyes focused on the queen that screamed for her death as Raven raised her hands and fell.

And then continued to fall.

Raven's feet slammed into the stones beneath her, the rope falling beside her. She looked up and found a dagger still vibrating in the wood above her.

A horse barreled through the back entrance a foot away, a black cloaked rider on top.

Raven stifled her magic as it convulsed around her fingers. She couldn't lose control now. The queen would live, and from her current angle, everyone who was innocent would die. Chaos erupted around the platform as the guards tried to aim at the horse while not hurting the bystanders. All of the nobility had scattered at the horse's entrance, and the palace staff, they had stayed in their places. For a moment, Raven thought they had been too frightened to move, but one quick glance at their determination showed her they had chosen to stay. Because the guards couldn't get a shot in. The palace staff, her people, were giving her a way out. The guards would have to kill them to get to her.

Raven ran for the man on the horse, not caring about who they were. He held out a hand to her and helped her up. Arrows flew by as she lifted her shackled arms up and over his head to hold on. Her magic jolted, singing in her veins to the point of explosion. Raven barely had time to register the smell of snow and trees as the horse broke into a gallop and raced through the silently waking streets of Aslar and towards the mountains beyond.

Not a word was spoken as Raven and Aleks continued to ride through the royal forest and beyond. They didn't stop for over an hour, getting as much distance as possible between the palace and Queen Lyanna.

A small, hidden lake opened up before them amongst the towering oak trees.

Only then did they finally come to a stop.

Raven got off the horse and watched him gracefully dismount. He removed his cloak, revealing his striking white hair.

"You betrayed your aunt." She didn't know why, but that was all she could think of. The only thing she could say as nerves suddenly took over.

Aleks shrugged. "She doesn't deserve her crown." He moved around to the other side of his horse, putting space between them.

Raven watched him as he whistled. Another one answering.

The sudden realization that she was alive and had been saved by the man she was falling for rocked through her, nearly knocking her to the ground. She had been so close.

Two more horses walked out of the forest, carrying supplies...and Rowan.

Rowan was on the horse.

"What are you doing here?"

"As flattered as I am that you thought I could pull all of this off on my own, I needed some help. We knew as soon as the queen found out who you were that Rowan's life and his father's would be forfeited. So he came along."

"You couldn't have known I would do that." Raven asserted at his brazen gamble.

"I had a feeling that if Prince Adam gave you the chance to speak that you would," Aleks replied. "It's a good thing he was willing to help me with my favor."

"You've risked his life."

Aleks waved a dismissive hand.

"Your father?" Raven asked, turning to Rowan. Sadness rested in his eyes as anger straightened his shoulders.

"He left on a ship two days ago."

"Good. I'm glad he got away." Raven looked around the forest, needing some place, anyplace to look at emotions that threatened to overwhelm her. They had risked everything for her. They had done all of this for her. She trusted very few people to take care of her. Shame washed through her that they hadn't been on that list. At least until today.

Her power fluttered up and around inside her. She had pulled on so much in her lead up to dying that it was quickly demanding her focus. Raven soothed it as she twisted her hands. The chains of her shackles clicked together. She looked down at them, rubbing her hands together.

"What do we do next?" Rowan asked. He walked over to examine the shackles on her wrists.

"Raven couldn't complete her assignment here. But I can still complete mine," Aleks said, his voice soft. His eyes dimmed as he got closer to her.

She wanted to rush into his arms...feel them wrap around her for the first time in weeks. Feel safe in his embrace now that this is truly over. She was free of the queen. Mostly, she wanted to whisper in his ear how thankful she was to him for being there after the tortures. For being her anchor in the storm. A small smile pulled on her lips as he stopped before her.

"What was your assignment?" Rowan crossed his arms.

"To find the lost princess of Evrotia," he whispered.

Raven's eyes widened.

He had never told her that.

"And bring her home with me."


To be continued.

# EPILOGUE

## DREA

Drea needed a moment to herself.

A moment to process.

To think.

To breathe.

So she went to the last place anyone would look for her; her mother's office. The darkness that permeated the space was a welcoming embrace. Pain shot down her leg so swiftly she could hardly breathe through it. She tightened her grip on her cane until her knuckles turned white and her wrist ached with the added weight. She hobbled over to her mother's large wooden desk and collapsed into the plush black chair. The cane lay on the floor by her feet, forgotten as she massaged her leg muscles. The cramping wasn't unusual. It happened all the time. Sometimes it was sudden and fierce, other times it was a slow ache that built up whenever she did too much in one day.

Drea leaned back and closed her eyes, letting her magic settle.

Her mother was dead.

The words washed over her for the hundredth time, nevertheless; they seemed unreal. Ella had killed her. Ella had run her father's sword right through her. Drea's mind was blank, her heart unfeeling. Though she had witnessed it, she couldn't process it. Everything was empty, a void yawning before her, waiting to swallow her up.

Her magic sprung up, fighting for her. She would *not* go away without fighting.

She kept her eyes closed. Had it just been a few hours ago that their entire world had gone upside down? It felt like days.

Drea sighed. What were they going to do?

The large mirror behind her mother's desk glowed.

Drea cracked open an eye, coming back to herself as she pulled on a sliver of power, and touched the mirror.

*Elizabeth, what happened? Lena's going on a rampage and—* Queen Laila froze in the mirror.

Drea had only seen the queen once since they had come to Rairene. Prior, she had seen her almost every day growing up in Queen Laila's palace in the mountains of Trudel. Her white hair was perfectly placed, despite the early morning hour, and the only sign that not all was as it seemed was the old shawl wrapped tightly around the queen's shoulders.

*Drizella.* Queen Laila's ice-blue eyes looked around the area behind Drea. *Where's your mother? I need to speak with her.*

*She's dead.* Drea choked back unexpected tears.

Her throat constricted around them, denying their meaning. She looked up at the Queen of Trudel, straightening her spine. She had always been mildly terrified of the queen of her home. Those sentiments had not changed with age, Drea found as the queen observed her. Whatever thoughts Queen Laila had had died on her lips, her delicate fingers twisted the shawl tighter around her.

*Who?*

*My step sister Ella—*

*I see.* Queen Laila sighed. *I instructed Elizabeth to kill that girl nine years ago. She disobeyed a direct order. I have to admit that I was in shock when Lena told me she was alive.*

Drea kept herself from blinking at the queen's statement. Somehow, she maintained her composure. Her mother had disobeyed her closest friend and queen? Why? Why keep Ella alive?

*Foolish.* Queen Laila found a way to look down her nose at Drea. *You're not foolish. Tell me you have that girl in chains.*

Drea took a small breath. *I've been informed that she died while protecting Prince David, who is now in hiding until they can find those who want him dead.*

*Informed? By whom?* Queen Laila's voice reached a new low as she frowned.

This conversation was not going how the queen had planned.

*Prince David's Champion, Lord Henry. He informed me that Ella died of her wounds.* Drea paused, debating on asking her question. *Should I move forward with dissolving the house and sending anyone who wishes to you?*

She held her breath, hoping, praying to the gods for it to be this easy. Let it end this easily.

*No. We've come too far to let your mother's failures ruin everything.* Queen Laila paced in the mirror. *I'm sending Lena to Aumont. She'll act as my interim ambassador and oversee everything with you and Anastasia.*

Drea opened her mouth to protest. That was the *last* thing she needed to deal with. Lena and Anastasia got along extremely well, especially these last three years. Drea and Lena...she shuddered.

*Drizella, do you swear you remain loyal to me and the Kingdom of Trudel? And that any disobedience will be seen as treason and punishable by death?* Queen Laila examined her.

*I do,* Drea whispered. Her magic writhed against the order. She did not want to yield. She wanted nothing to do with her and the game she and her mother had played for over twenty years.

*Good, because your mother's failures are now yours and Anastasia's to bear.*

Drea remained sitting before the mirror long after it went dark.

Ella felt nothing.

She opened her eyes to look up at the blue cloudless sky above, trying to remain calm. David had instructed her to remain calm. So she would. It was all she knew. David had said...he hovered over her, his mouth silently moving, his warm brown eyes comforting.

At first, the edges of her vision blurred before swamping her mind with darkness.

*She was in the attic.*

No. She couldn't be here. Not again.

*She'd behaved. She had done nothing. Why was she back here? A shadow prowled behind her, laughing. Lucifer. The leopard stalked around, making her twist around, her feet tangling up as she fell to the ground.*

*Ella curled in on herself, his laughter covering her in whip lashings. Fenith consumed her and played with her.*

Ella screamed into the hallucination, fighting back. Though she sensed her eyes were open, the poison didn't let her see the real world.

*Chains dug into her wrists, keeping her still, pinning her arms to her body. Lucifer's nails dragged across her cheek before gripping her chin, forcing her to face him. She squeezed her eyes tight, blocking out the whip she knew was coming for her.*

*It never did.*

*Ella cracked open one eye, daring to hope. The fire burned around her. Sweat poured down her back, but Lucifer was gone. As the fire in the attic licked closer to her, Ella had nowhere to go. It was her worst nightmare. She had always feared Lady Tremaine would let the fire go beyond dripping burning wax on her neck or touching her with candles. Now she had. Tears trickled down Ella's cheeks as she fell to her knees, covering her face as the fire burned everything...including her.*

Ella opened her eyes as the heat faded. She didn't dare look down to assess the damage done to her body. She noticed, though, that the attic had been replaced by her bedroom in Aumont. A shiver ran down her spine, her only warning that danger lurked in the places her candlelight could not reach.

*Lady Tremaine stood over her. The woman who had ripped her away from a life of splendor and molded her into a weapon, granting her the life of her greatest desire, looked down her nose at Ella with disdain.*

*"You've disappointed me, Ella," she said as her gaze swept over her.*

*"I haven't done anything, I promise. I did as you asked. I swear. I upheld my oath. I've done nothing," Ella whispered. Inside, Ella knew she had no reason to fear her. She was no longer a child who cowered in fear of disappointing Lady Tremaine.*

*So she didn't.*

*Yet, when invisible hands grabbed Ella and threw her to the bed, flipping her onto her stomach and holding her tightly, she couldn't stop the whimper from escaping her lips. Lady Tremaine let the whip in her hand unfurl to the floor before letting it sing a song Ella knew so well against her back.*

*Over and over.*

*But she didn't beg. Didn't plead for it to stop. She wouldn't give Lady Tremaine the satisfaction of hearing the panic in her voice. She was alone in body, but not in spirit. Ella gritted her teeth as the hallucination rocked through her, willing it to end. She would get through this. She had to for them.*

*Raven, Calla, and Mira needed her.*

*She needed them.*

*But she didn't need them to save herself. She didn't need anyone. Ella pulled against the hands holding her down, fighting the bonds. Using every ounce of strength she had left, she ripped herself free.*

The first thing Ella noticed was her beating heart and the sweat dripping down her body. Then, it was the light of the sun pouring in through the curtains, and the sound of waves crashing along the shore just outside her glass window.

David had done it. He had gotten them to Oakwell.

She jumped when her door creaked, pain flashing on her side and shoulder. She blinked against the pain as she watched David come bearing a tray of food.

He paused when he saw she was awake. "How are you feeling?"

"What happened?" Ella croaked. Her voice scratched over her lungs as though she had been screaming for days.

"You fell out of the saddle when the poisons became too much for your body. I carried you into your parent's room. I wasn't sure where else you would want to be..." He tailed off, shifting on his feet, the tray still in his hands. "Tea?" David held out a steaming mug to her. "I know you're not a fan, but it'll help with your sore throat."

She took it gingerly, sniffing for anything outside of the normal smells.

"It's just herbal tea. I promise there's nothing else in it." David set down the tray of food.

"How long was I...out?"

"Two days—"

"Two days?" Ella tensed, gripping the cup of tea until the warmth burned her hands. Two days had passed?

Ella pulled back the thick blanket covering her and swung her legs out. She stood up and fell face-first toward the wooden floor.

David caught her, grabbing the tea before it could spill over her. Her body sighed against him as David slowly lowered her back to the bed.

"It's going to take you a few more days to fully recover. You might hallucinate more. I'm just glad you're awake."

"Hallucinate more? Did I say anything?" Ella blanched at the thought of saying something embarrassing, or worse, something revealing.

"It was mostly unintelligible," David mumbled, not meeting her gaze.

Ella narrowed her eyes at the lie. He had heard something. Had she threatened to kill him? Had she divulged something dark? David left the room before she could ask, claiming he needed to check on something in the kitchen.

A few minutes went by and Ella tested her legs again. She got out of bed slowly, adjusting to the pain burning in her shoulder that competed with the injury on her side. She dug through a dusty trunk at the foot of the bed and withdrew the comfiest piece of clothing she could find before heading towards the bathtub David had been kind enough to prepare for her.

His actions spoke a language of love and kindness she didn't deserve. Yet his golden brown eyes spoke the language of distrust as he looked at her.

By the time she got out of the tub, it was midday and her stomach would no longer be denied. She padded down the three flights of wooden stairs, memory guiding her. How had David carried her up three flights of stairs?

She turned back towards the direction of the kitchen, navigating past the shadows that leaped out at her. *They were not real.* They were residuals of the poisons. She took a breath and charged forward into the darkness.

She reached the kitchen and scavage for food in their packs as her stomach growled. Pulling out some bread and dried meat, she headed toward the living room, searching for David.

Nothing.

The large room was empty. Silent...and peaceful. She dropped onto the sagging couch and closed her eyes. What were they going to do? This was not the plan. They were about ten plans adjacent to the original plan. Ella ground her palms into her eyes, rubbing them until the stars burst in the darkness.

She opened them just in time to see the wave of shadows cover her in a swath of darkness. Ella scrambled further up on the couch, looking for any source of light. All she saw was the shadows encasing her, convulsing around her.

She whimpered, and the shadows jumped down her throat.

Frozen slime slid within her, freezing her to the couch. She was exposed. She would die. No one would help her. She couldn't even help herself.

"El—"

Whispers floated around her as sharp knives grabbed her arms, pressing into her.

"Ella," they yelled, echoing around her skull.

She collapsed against the cough, warmth flooding her. Fire pulsed along her, purging the ice from her body. Murmurs flitted into her ear, begging her to open her eyes. To stay with him. Who was he?

"Ella, please come back to me," David whispered.

His hands rubbed her arms, bringing warmth back to her body. Had his hand just been on her cheek? Or was that also a hallucination?

Her vision blurred back into focus, with David sitting beside her, his warm brown eyes wide.

"Thank you...I tried to find you earlier," Ella mumbled.

David mustered a small smile. "I was in my room."

"Apparently, my lovely cocktail of poisons is still active." Ella rubbed her head as she sat up straighter. She was inches away from him. Inches from lips that had once kissed her, cherished her. Now, they were a flat, assessing line.

"At least this one was shorter, so they're wearing off," David said as he stood up.

"Shorter? How long were the others?"

"Long enough." David walked around the couch, rubbing his eyes.

Ella grabbed Jaq's satchel, needing a distraction. There was so much in it. How was she supposed to know what any of it meant? Ella pulled out each item, wondering what Jaq's intentions were for choosing each one. On top sat a dagger that she had never seen in his possession before. The metal glinted in the early light, its handle shaped into the body of a raven. Why would he put something most likely intended for Raven in here? Ella turned it over, looking at the engraving on the blade. It was written in Evrotian and translated into 'cold death'.

She looked it over again. "What am I supposed to do?" A map to another kingdom was hidden inside the blade sheath.

"Can I help?" David asked.

"Yes, please." Ella leaned back against the couch. "I don't know what he was thinking while packing all of this...and I'm not an enchanter, so I don't know…I don't know…" Ella hyperventilated as she pulled out item after item from the bag. "I don't know."

"Ella, it's okay," David said. He crouched down in front of her. "He thought he would be here to help you."

"Well, he's not. He's not here, and I can't read this. He died. He died making sure I had this. It had to be for something."

"We'll figure it out together," David replied. He tilted Ella's chin up to pull her eyes away from the bag and to look at him. "We'll sort it out, item by item. Can I see it?"

Ella handed the dagger over. "I don't know what good it will do. It's meant for Snow White."

"Why do you say that?" David turned the blade over in his hands.

"Cold Death is what happens after her mark takes her golden apple poison," Ella explained. She did not elaborate on the raven handle. If David and Raven had ever crossed paths, she wasn't about to expose her name.

"And you know Snow White? We've been trying to pin her down for years."

"She's my closest friend and if you ever…" Ella swallowed her threat. "I don't know how it related to finding The Huntsman. He left us over a year ago. I would rather rip out his heart than ask for his help," Ella grumbled, folding her arms.

"Is it that easy for you to kill people?"

"I'm trained to kill, David. So yes, it's that easy. Just like it would be easy for you, given the way you fight. But that doesn't mean I enjoy it," Ella said, glaring at him as she sunk into the couch.

David flicked her eyes away, concentrating on the dagger in his hands. "Is it okay if I read the dagger?" He looked to her for confirmation.

Ella nodded her head, watching as he stilled. The blade glowed as David's power writhed around it, tasting it. David frowned, his brows creasing the longer he read it.

David's magic withdrew. "I didn't see all of it. I wasn't sure what was happening. Would you be okay joining me and seeing it?" David held out his hand to her.

"You can do that?" Ella had never seen another enchanter ever share a reading.

"Of course, all enchanters can." David lightly grabbed her hand, his magic racing over her fingers. She could have sworn his magic was happy as it zipped over her.

Ella held in her smile at the magic's glee.

David guided her hand to the hilt of the blade and wrapped his fingers over hers. "I need you to focus with me. Try to keep your focus on what you see and what you're observing. We can't get distracted."

Ella nodded as David closed his eyes and dove back into the blade, taking her with him. Cool metal washed over her, covering her body from head to toe. She kept her eyes shut as an image came into focus around her. It was Jaq's mage room, only he was younger and smiling.

*"I need you to hold on to this."*

*Ella looked at the mirror behind Jaq and saw who was speaking. She'd almost forgotten how handsome he was. However, the Jason she knew looked completely different. His usually joyful green eyes were dim with sorrow, his wide smile gone. This was not the Jason she knew.*

Ella dropped the dagger.

She rocked on the couch, adjusting her shoulders.

David looked sideways at her.

"I wasn't expecting to see…him." It was Jason. The Huntsman. This was his dagger.

Ella picked it up again, sure in her grip as David's hand wrapped around hers and they once again fell into the cool metal.

*"Why do you need me to hold on to this? Who's it for?" Jaq eyed the blade wearily.*

*"It's for Raven. If she ever needs to find me. If she's ever in danger. This will help her."*

*"You're leaving?" Jaq's jaw dropped.*

*"I am—"*

*"Is Raven—"*

*"No, she's staying here. She won't want to see me, and I hope you never need to give this to her. But if anything ever goes wrong. If it all turns to shit, please Jaq, promise me you'll give this to her. Only to her."*

*"I promise." Jaq gripped the dagger, watching the Huntsman walk away.*

David dove deeper into the blade's memory. It had been so long that some memories had begun to fade away. Their images appeared as shredded ribbons around them.

When they stopped, it was just Jason looking at the blade.

*"Raven, my love." He paused. "I know you must hate me. I haven't broken your heart yet, but I know you'll never…"*

*Jason's image faded in and out.*

*"If you ever need me, I'll be there for you...please understand. I did this for—"*

*He was cut off again.*

Ella frowned.

*"I'm going to Holodal to call in a favor. After that I hope to—"*

She wanted to scream at the degraded memory. David's hand tightened around hers, trying to pull as much of the memory as he could.

*"I love you, Raven. Never forget that."*

David released Ella's hand, the dagger dimming.

"Does any of that mean anything to you?" he asked.

Ella sat in shock, absorbing everything Jason had said. "It does...it means going to Holodal is everyone's goal. Whoever he ran into there might know where he was going. We should leave in the morning."

"No," David spoke confidently. "Not until you're healed, at least until the poisons are out of your body."

"David—"

"Ella, you almost died out there. I know you're not aware of that, but it was bad. I won't travel until you're in a better place to do so."

She frowned, turning away from him. She knew he was right, but the urge in her legs to run to the horses and make haste for Holodal was overwhelming. Her eyes caught onto an object she had tossed next to the satchel. She pulled on the chain, a necklace coming free from the pile. The large crescent moon pendant stared back at her, its large sapphire dazzling her eyes.

"When did he have time to get this? Why bring it?"

"It's enchanted," David said as he reached for it.

He was knocked backward, flying five feet across the room. David's brown eyes widened as he got up off the floor.

"Are you sure you're not trying to kill me?" It was a grim joke.

"No!" Ella looked between him and the necklace. "David, I promise—"

"When I reached for it, what were you thinking?"

"I thought that I didn't want you to...oh..." she hadn't wanted him to take it from her. "How did he...I've never heard of an enchantment working like that."

"Ella...how much do you know about how enchantments work?"

"Not a lot." Ella motioned at all the items in front of them before raising her eyebrows at David.

"You understand the basics though, given that you've helped Snow White and your friend Jaq," David said. "So then you know that all of our magic is fueled by emotions and intentions. Jaq looked at you with love, which means if he enchanted that gem specifically for you and poured all of his magic into it intending to protect you, then it will be incredibly strong." David held out his hand, waiting for Ella to willingly place the necklace in his palm.

"That night...he said he couldn't defend himself, remember?"

Ella nodded. "It was ridiculous. Lady Tremaine would never have made him drain himself like that."

"I don't think she did." David turned the necklace over. "How dark was his mark?"

"Dark brown, almost light black."

David's eyebrows rose.

"Why?" Ella shifted in her seat as she bit her lip.

"I think he spent what time he had left pouring his magic, his love, into this necklace for you—"

"He would never endanger himself like that." Ella's hand covered her heart as if the weight of her hand might steady her suddenly beating heart. He couldn't have done that. Not for her.

"When an enchanter dies...you know what happens." David paused as they both remembered the attack in the courtroom and the enchanter who had lost control of her power. "You saw all she could do was direct her blast directly at us. But Jaq not only drained his power, he also loved you so much that he could control his blast. He kept it from hurting you and instead shattered everything else within the room. I've never been in such awe of another enchanter before. That amount of control...I've never heard of anything like it."

"What's your point?" She wanted this conversation to end. She needed to get away from the memories of relaxing in the one comfy chair in Jaq's mage room, talking while he worked. Blood flashed before her and she wasn't sure if it was a hallucination or just a horrible memory she would rather forget.

"My point is that he did all that he could to protect you." David handed the necklace back to her, the weight of its meaning sinking through her.

Ella didn't say a word as she clasped it around her neck and left.

# GLOSSARY

## Enchanters Potions

- Force - red potion - gives enhanced strength
- Velocity - yellow potion - enhance speed
- Insomnia - purple potion - awake for prolonged periods
- Spotlight - green potion - intense focus
- Vivifica - blue potion - reduces physical or mental pain
- Fray - black potion - enhances combat skills
- Solacium - white potion - heals wounds and illness
- Callidus - grey potion - stealth, ability to slip past enchanted mirrors

## Snow White's Poisons

- Mire - induces hallucinations
- Fenith - the sensation of bones breaking
- Frost - induces hypothermia
- Blaze - induces high fever
- Malice - cold sweats with hallucinations
- Wraith - mindless paralysis
- Golden Apple - instant death that turns you pale

## Enchanters Mark Power Ranking (Most to Least)

Midnight

Obsidian

Onyx

Black

Dark Brown

Chestnut

Medium

Light

Tan

Pale

# REVIEWS MATTER

Did you enjoy The Poisoned Crown?
Want a free way to support an Indie Author?
Leave a Review about The Poisoned Crown!
Reviews help with social proof and gets the book
promoted more on Amazon.

Go to Amazon and look up The Poisoned Crown to
leave your review!

# THANK YOU

## To Those Who Support Me

This book wouldn't be possible without all of my various families. There's a perception that writing is a solitary business, but I've found that the only way to be successful is to lean on the people who are always cheering you on and doing what they can to help you. To my fiance TJ, thank you so much for being my rock in the storm, my biggest fan, and best alarm system for when I'm pushing myself too far.

There's a reason this book is dedicated to my found british family Marie, Tammy, Harpy, Todd, and Alex. We've been in each others lives for over ten years and are the true meaning of 'found family'. As we all formed our bonds around our small rectangle table in our tiny group kitchen with four fridges and dedicated cabinets, I felt as though I belonged somewhere for the first time. I didn't have to fit in and be someone who I wasn't. I could be me. I no longer had to morph myself to 'fit in'. These friendships are what I wanted for my characters and it wouldn't be the same without you inspiring it.

To my parents who both have supported me throughout all of my wild dreams and really supported me in my decision to self-publish. Your love and encouragement has meant the world to me. Getting to share my publishing moments with each of you has been some of my biggest highlights throughout this process.

For my adoptive sisters Lauren and Ashley and bonus mom Elsa. Who would have guessed that working for a credit union and bonding over The Bachelor would have led to three relationships that I hold close to my heart. It's my biggest honor to be called your sister and daughter. The three of you have supported me so much throughout this process whether it's bringing my first book on cruises to be left for others to read, reading my early draft, or completing the book when you don't like to read. Each of these make my day and bring me so much joy.

Thanks so much to my League of Ladies. Arpi, Brittney, and Puneet, the three of you were my sounding board for more social media, cover input, advice, etc. than I could possibly name. Our friendship means more than the three of you could know. It's not often that I find a group of ladies that I have cliqued with so easily and who have accepted me into their group so quickly. I am so thankful for all of the late-night conversations we've had where I'm waffling back and forth over font, colors, etc., and have each of you talk me through it and make the best decision. I love you all so much!

To my Alpha Readers Jessica and Brittney. Both of you gave me such amazing insight after reading The Poisoned Crown before anyone else. Thank you for all of your work on this. I know it's a lot of work to be an alpha reader and your comments and hard work helped me out so much. To my Beta Readers Lauren, Gary, Kati, Natasha, and Trina each of you caught typos, double spaces, and gave me comments that helped the final version of this book.

A huge shoutout to my best friend Natalie who has always been my mental break, and Disney partner in crime! Our trips to Disneyland are always a wonderful reprieve for me from work life and writing life. My writing group ladies are the reason I chose to make the jump into self-publishing. If it hadn't been for our writer's retreat in 2023 and all of your encouragement, I wouldn't be here today. Christina our weekly writing sessions, and your support have been more impactful than you could know. Who would have guessed that being in the same new hire group in work would lead to such a wonderful friendship?  A hug shoutout to my parent-in-laws Mary and Gary. Both of you have wowed me with the amount of support you've given to me, whether it's simply asking about how the book is doing, how I'm doing, or coming up with different ideas to promote the book, all of it has meant the world to me. Love you!

I have to thank the three people who have been incredibly instrumental and helpful in getting this book created. Beth Gilbert designed this beautiful cover, she can be found on Instagram @bethgilbert_art. Her work is beautiful and amazing and she's one of the sweetest artists to work with. And my beta reader/editor August Head. Your edits, remarks, and comments always impress me and push me to think about my characters and make sure the story is on track to match what I want. To my editor Fiona, your insight and brainstorming helped me work out the final kinks of the beginning and end of this book. It was good before, but because of your input it became great! Thank you so much for your guidance and brainstorming wisdom!

Finally, I can't end this without thanking my friends and supporters on social media to help me run my promotional campaign! Thank you to the hosts at MTMC – thereaderandthechef, storytime.withb, sarahslittleobession, paperfury, enchantments_of_books_and_tea, jxssreads, & readingwithnour.

Thank you so much to the hosts at BOMM – Michelle, Elise, Mia, Maria, Jenny, Ana, Ashley, Loesha, Ruby, Chloe, Maria, Jenniger, Carsen, Kata, Cara, Saphra, Amanda, Emily, Jessica, Tara, Ariesy, Ashley, Eirini, Amber, Clare, Joy, Arana, Jamie, Jericha, Makenzie, Alyssa, Anna, Noelle, Sara, Dominique, Heidi, Cathryn, Anastasia, Amber, Amna, Heidi, Amanda, Sarah, Susan, Amy, Amanda Stelle & Brittney Barin.

# ABOUT ME

Kelsey grew up in a beautiful seaside town where adventures were just a few minutes outside her doorstep. Her hot chocolate addiction keeps her fueled when she writes, along with the sound of rain and cold weather. She loves to create worlds about Dragons, Assassins, and Magic, just not all at once. Though she will admit that sounds like the beginning of an awesome story! When she's not writing or working she can be found hiking, waterfall chasing, and traveling, or bingeing the next great show like Bridgerton or The Great British Bake Off.

## CONNECT WITH ME!

www.ingramcontent.com/pod-product-compliance
Lightning Source LLC
Chambersburg PA
CBHW060606300726

48975CB00005B/1465